BLOOD *IN THE BEDROOM*

"Yes!" hissed Angela menacingly as she advanced toward Celeste, brandishing the knife. "I'm going to kill you, you bitch! But before I do I'm going to mark you up good. Do you think I'll let you take my husband from me without a fight? If you want him, Celeste, you better fight—because I'm willing to die for what I want!"

Angela slashed at her husband's mistress.

"Whore!" Celeste spat as Angela moved in for the kill.

Scott watched the two women, not believing his eyes.

Celeste caught Angela's wrist as the knife flashed close to her eyes and held her attacker off. But with black hair flying Angela bore down, banging Celeste's head against the leg of a chair and scoring her cheek with long sharp nails.

Scott started across the room, but before he could put an end to the combat Angela sliced a long oozing trail of blood between Celeste's breasts and down over her stomach. She shrieked like a madwoman, and Angela's eyes glowed with bloodlust.

Don't miss the first two volumes of the tempestuous saga of Angela Carlyle by Michele DuBarry:

INTO PASSION'S DAWN	(LEISURE 902)
ACROSS CAPTIVE SEAS	(LEISURE 932)

The Loves of
Angela Carlyle Vol. 3

TOWARD LOVE'S HORIZON

Michele DuBarry

LEISURE BOOKS NEW YORK CITY

For B.E., cushla machree;
and everyone else who believes in
love at first sight.

A LEISURE BOOK

Published by

Nordon Publications, Inc.
Two Park Avenue
New York, N.Y. 10016

Printed in the United States

PROLOGUE

Reality's Dark Dream

The Caribbean

1810

My grief on the sea,
        How the waves of it roll!
For they heave between me
        and the love of my soul!

—Anonymous

The Caribbean stretched forever beneath the hot blue vault of the sky. It was breathtakingly beautiful but merciless and deadly. And against the sheer-spun haze in the north, like an enormous black velvet curtain, hung an advancing line of thunderstorms.

A deluge of lovely turquoise water inundated the tiny raft. It receded momentarily, only to be repeated again—and again and again. Angela choked and gasped as the salt water burned into her eyes, nostrils, and throat.

It had to be a nightmare. If it was reality it could not be borne.

"Please, make it a dream," she pleaded. "Let me wake up now!"

But it wasn't a dream. It was all too real.

Angela raised her stinging eyes to the awful sight as it spread, stretching out on the horizon, curving round to embrace them with the kiss of death. Another huge wave washed over and she held her breath, feeling the rope that bound her to the spindly mast tauten and hold her safe.

It was her lifeline, for after four days at sea with hardly any food or water, she was as weak as a newborn kitten. Seasickness, exposure, and shock had drained her strength. Shock, at what had happened to her four nights ago in the Bahamas. Shock, at what she had been forced to do.

Gaston Laporte and his beautiful evil protégé, Jules, were dead. Angela Harrington had killed them with her own hands. But she didn't regret it and knew she never would. It was what went before that haunted her—what she had done to protect her children.

If only she had known in the beginning why the pirate had attacked and sunk the *Dark Lady*. Why he had been so elated to find himself holding Scott Harrington's wife and two children hostage. But she hadn't known, until that last night on the island, that her husband was the man who had horribly crippled and scarred Laporte.

She had resisted long and hard the veiled threats, then the demands. But when Laporte had her maid Molly raped to death by his whole crew, right before Angela's horrified eyes, she realized that he meant what he said.

When he told her what he proposed for her children, her blood ran cold. Robert was only three and Lorna six, but what mother, with children of any age, wouldn't sacrifice herself instead? So Angela gave in and became Laporte's mistress. And though he brutalized her till she thought she must surely go insane, not one complaint crossed her lips till that night—the night he shared her with Jules.

Both of them were filthy, roaring drunk when Jules made his mistake. He inadvertently let slip that Angela had not bought her children's lives with her exquisite body—just postponed the inevitable.

It was over now—over! And she had saved not only the children but herself, with the help of a friend. For without Ezra there would be no raft and if not for Angela he would have been flogged to death in Jamaica. They had exchanged favors, she buying him and then setting him free; Ezra building the raft and saving them from Laporte's cohorts. And now their lives were forfeit again, for they both knew they would never survive the storm.

"It's the wrong time of year for a hurricane," Ezra assured her, but her pale, glittering eyes held only disbelief. "It must be some squalls preceding colder weather."

"Just remember your promise, Ezra."

He nodded slowly, sick at the thought of saving the children at the cost of her life. But he had vowed that he would do everything within his power to see the children safely to their father in Australia.

With shaking fingers Angela withdrew from her soaking bodice papers carefully wrapped in oilskin. It was her reason for leaving the safety of England and dragging the children halfway around the world—to save the man she loved. For the Duke of Brightling had been convicted of a crime and transported to Botany Bay for fourteen years on the testimony of a bribed witness. It had taken her several agonizing years to discover the treachery but now she held the key to Scott's freedom.

Ezra took the pardon from her reluctantly and placed it securely in his pocket. It seemed of small consequence but he knew Angela too well. She was finally giving up in the face of overwhelming adversity. A lesser woman would have given up long ago, but Angela was strong. She had weathered more in her short lifetime than a dozen men could be expected to face, and though she never emerged totally unscathed at least she was alive.

The rain was as cold as ice and it hissed as it struck the warm waters, stinging and lashing everything in its path. Lightning sizzled with blinding white light and the wind blew into a tempest. The waves were gray mountains now, capped with white.

It was then that the raft began breaking up.

The *Silver Bear* sailed into the wind, her captain at the helm. He was huge and unmoving, impervious to the elements buffeting his ship, and only when the call came from the crow's nest did he look up.

It was perilous work rescuing survivors in a heavy sea but he gave it not a second thought—that was the kind of man he was. And when he saw that there were children he went for them himself.

The woman was unconscious but between the captain and the Negro they dragged her aboard too. She streamed water like a mermaid all the way to his cabin, black hair plastered over her sunburned face, twined round her neck and arms and waist like seaweed. She set his bunk awash in a high tide as the man knelt beside her pushing the hair out of her face with strangely gentle fingers.

The captain lit the oil lamps dispelling the cramped gloom and as the light fell full on her face she opened her eyes. He took a shocked step back as her sorrow-haunted, aquamarine eyes focused, then dilated as they fastened on his face. She half rose on one elbow, her other hand, as fragile as a shell, pressed against her throbbing bosom.

He was at her side in an instant, thoughtlessly shoving

her companion aside, an amazed smile dawning through his close-cropped silver beard. Her fingers trembled as they reached out and his arm slid beneath her shoulders supporting her and drawing her close. Head falling back against the crook of his arm, she stared as in a daze, her fingertips tracing the large downward curving mustache that quirked beneath his hawklike nose.

"Duchess! My sweet little girl!"

With an all too audible indrawn breath Angela looked deep into those unforgettable pewter-gray eyes. The words never reached her lips. For his mouth, firm and gentle and warm, pressed against her cold lips taking her breath away.

She was flying through insubstantial space as sheer and ethereal as a wisp of mist. He was warm. Why had she thought it must be cold? His thick hair slid between her fingers—it seemed like only yesterday.

But they had hung him in London on a winter day five long years ago.

Then Angela knew for a certainty that she was dead.

PART ONE

A Pirate's Revenge

Cayo Hueso

1810

Those fiends upon a shaking fen
  Fixed me, in dark tempestuous night.
    —George Crabbe

one

Angela was not dead. She lay sleeping beneath yards of mosquito netting in a small but lovely green and white room. A mocking bird chattered on the windowsill as dawn's virgin light spilled across the sea slowly gilding the small island.

She was so tired. Her eyelids fluttered like dying butterflies as she tried to open them. The mocking bird scolded her shrilly and flew away. She had absolutely no idea where she was.

Through the window was the glint of the ocean, wavering through shadowy palm fronds, and a ship rode at anchor in the harbor. There was no storm. What had it all been—a dream within a dream?

The door opened slowly and he stood there filling the doorway with such a tender look for her. The silence spoke loudly and eloquently of feelings never to be forgotten, alive and quivering invisibly between them.

Angela was the one that shattered the silence. "Jack? My God, this can't be real!"

He went straight to her and took her hand, bending from his great height to press a kiss on her fingers. He was a little older, his hair all silver now, but the humor and compassion were still the same. Jack Newton—the infamous highwayman, Gentleman Jack—could never change. In England he lived on in legend, and here—wherever here was—he was very, very real.

Sitting beside her on the bed Jack hugged Angela to him stroking her soft, dusky curls; the prickle of his whiskers against her cheek too familiar to resist. This was no ghost, that she knew. He was as solid as a granite boulder and as gentle as a mother with an only child. She was safe!

Jack released her with a grin, and none too soon, for a moment later a voluptuous, aristocratic looking blond woman entered the room with a tray in her hands. She smiled with genuine pleasure to see Angela awake at last with the color returning to her cheeks. She had nursed her for a week through a dreadful fever and now there was relief in her soft brown eyes.

The last time Angela had seen her was at the trial—Amy, Jack's wife—the love of his life, he had called her.

"Welcome to Cayo Hueso, and our home," Amy said, setting the tray down on a table beside the bed. "I hope you will be our guest for as long as you possibly can."

Angela stared at her, bemused. Such a gracious welcome for her, Jack's former lover, when she must be the most unwelcome of visitors. She would never have been able to accept so easily the reverse situation, welcoming one of Scott's women, and heaven only knew there had been enough of them.

"Thank you," Angela said guardedly. "I'm so grateful you took us in."

But if Amy sensed the undercurrent or her unease she smoothed right over it deftly changing the subject. "Your children are most charming! You should see them. Right now they are in the kitchen pulling taffy and are sticky from head to toe."

"I hope they haven't been underfoot."

"Nonsense! I love children. I wouldn't mind a few more myself. . . ."

"Good lord, woman!" said Jack going to stand beside her and slipping his arm around her waist. "Isn't six enough?"

Just watching them together Angela could see the great and enduring love they shared. It was as if her affair with Jack had never existed, even though it must have been excruciatingly painful when Amy had found out—even worse than discovering her husband's true profession. For Jack had abducted Angela and held her for ransom, and then fell in love with his intended victim. Their affair had ended abruptly with his capture, but burst like fireworks over London when the scandalmongers caught the scent. Every detail had been dragged into the light of day and examined eagerly beneath the magnifying glass of rumor and innuendo, embellished beyond all recognition. The same thing had happened to her again two years ago in the same city when false gossip credited her with four simultaneous affairs, including one with the Prince of Wales!

"Drink your tea," Amy coaxed, "and I will leave you two to get acquainted again and fill in all those missing years." She left them then, confidently and considerately, closing the door behind her.

Jack dragged a chair close to Angela's bed and poured her a cup of steaming tea, and all the while she was unable to keep the amazement from her face. Jack—alive! He had saved her from the sea.

"Angela, Angela, I never thought I would see you again. Do you think it's some part of a master plan? Our lives crossed so briefly and you fought so valiantly for mine when you could have turned your back on all the unpleasantness. Now we meet again, in the middle of the ocean, half a world away from home! This time it was my turn to help you—and your children. They are wonderful! So you did marry your Scott after all."

"Yes," she said with a dreamy, faraway smile. "Oh, Jack, I'm so glad you are alive. It wasn't easy after I thought you were executed. . . ."

"But then Scott came back and swept you off your feet!"

"Literally!" Angela laughed, her aqua eyes sparkling as they hadn't for over a month. "He put a pistol to my head and snatched me from right under Keith's nose at the altar. Oh how I hated him then! I fought him all the way to Scotland. But I don't want to talk about myself anymore. Tell me everything, Jack, simply everything!"

"Well, where shall I start?" he wondered out loud.

"Right after the trial," Angela replied, settling back against the plump pillows and sipping her tea.

"All right. I gave the hangman the slip by getting transported instead."

"New South Wales?"

"Yes, the same as Scott. The only difference is that I never made it there. We were shipwrecked off the coast of Africa in the worst storm I have ever seen in my life. I was sure I was dead but somehow managed to make it to shore along with three other convicts.

"A damned inhospitable place! One of my companions died within the week of injuries and another just disappeared a month later. We finally found our way to a village and shipped out on a slaver bound for the West Indies. I signed on for two years but jumped ship in Kingston.

"Then I heard there was a lucrative business going on in Cayo Hueso so I saved all my money and came here. Within three years I had enough for a ship and a year later I sent for Amy. I made more money last year than I did in five as a highwayman."

"You're not a—a pirate!" Her stricken expression made him laugh.

"No! The snobs of my profession call themselves salvagers but what I really am is a wrecker."

"But don't they lure unsuspecting ships onto the rocks. . . ."

"I'm afraid many have," Jack said with a sad shake of his leonine head, "which is why wrecking has a bad reputation. But I decided to give up my life of crime. Promised Amy. Besides, the strategic location of this island makes that unnecessary.

"There are treacherous reefs everywhere and the channels are not marked, so if a captain's charts are not accurate or there's a storm the inevitable happens.

When the ship is aground then the race is on! The first one to reach the vessel in distress is proclaimed Wrecking Master."

"What does that mean?" Angela inquired with a little frown between her brows.

"That he gets to salvage the cargo and gets a large percentage of the take."

"Jack, it sounds dangerous. Have you ever been hurt?"

"No, Duchess, I'm very careful and if you know what you are doing that lessens the risk. Why ships from the four corners of the world pass offshore! They carry wine and liquor, mahogany and timber, silks and silver—then it's auctioned off in Havana."

"And you get rich!" Angela laughed. "Jack, you will never change. Your business is legal but rather shady, and you love the excitement!"

"I'll have to admit to it," he said, lowering his voice to a conspiratorial whisper. "If you promise not to tell I'll let you in on a little secret of mine. I'm addicted to excitement! I'm afraid I never did get over my days as Gentleman Jack!"

They reminisced the day away and Jack put her completely at ease making her almost believe that the past was only a bad dream. But Angela told him nothing about Laporte; she didn't ever want to utter that fiend's name. That shameful secret would go with her to her grave.

She was sick of being sick. Another whole week had passed and the fever was completely gone but Angela felt as sick as she had on the raft.

"You poor thing," cooed Amy wiping Angela's face with a damp cloth. "Why didn't you tell me?"

"Tell you what?" she asked snatching the cloth away crossly and pressing it tightly against her mouth as another wave of nausea started.

With an understanding look Amy got the basin again and helped her sit up. When it was over she fell back limply, her face white.

"I feel wretched!" Angela moaned rocking back and forth on the bed. Her stomach was in a tight knot and she couldn't keep anything down.

"I'll take care of that. I have a concoction that will settle your stomach like magic. I don't think I could have managed any of my pregnancies without it."

Angela's shocked eyes flew open. "But—but I'm not. It's impossible!"

A frown creased Amy's brow. "But, I was so sure—you have all the symptoms. But after all you should know. . . ."

"No! No! No!" her voice rose to a shattering crescendo. "I can't be! I won't let myself be!"

But Amy was right and even as she uttered her protest she knew it was true. She was pregnant. Laporte's final revenge! And Angela writhed in misery before the cold hard facts.

She started crying, loud agonizing sobs. She was carrying the seed of a monster, a reminder that would haunt her the rest of her life. The things he had done to her she could hide, but not this last humiliation. He had ruined everything! How could she go to Scott now, heavy with a pirate's child, a bastard? He would never understand.

"Leave me alone!" she screamed at Amy, furious because she was the one that revealed her condition. "Get out!"

Amy left in a panic at the raving madwoman Angela had turned into, running for Ezra. He would know what to do. They were close and she had a feeling he knew all her secrets. Where was he?

Staggering from the bed Angela made her way to the window holding onto the furniture. She leaned out the window swaying. The gravel path was far below. Hadn't she done this once before in terrified desperation? She knew nothing only that there was an unclean creature, a deformed little parasite growing inside her sucking away her strength and life. She must be rid of it at any cost!

Her legs were dead weight but slowly she managed to

get one knee on the windowsill. Her arms trembled, hardly able to bear her slight weight. Now. She had to do it now, before the thing infected her with its presence, before she felt it move.

She had just accomplished the monumental task of getting the other knee up when the door behind her crashed open. Not even bothering to look Angela threw herself forward, for an instant falling free. There was a smothered scream and then she was caught by the waist, hanging outside the window before Ezra dragged her back in.

"Let me go! I have to—don't you see?" she screamed in a frenzy kicking at Ezra. But her feeble struggles were ineffectual.

He threw her on the bed holding her down, visibly shaken. Amy stood in the doorway whitefaced with her hand over her mouth. Angela was screaming like a banshee, her mouth open wide and her head thrown back as if in a convulsion.

"Stop it!" ordered Ezra shaking her, not quite sure what was happening or what to do with a hysterical woman. He put his hand over her mouth muffling the sounds but snatched it away again when her face turned purple. "Stop, you will make yourself sick. What's wrong? Shut up, damn it!"

"She is with child," Amy said in Ezra's ear. "When I mentioned it she started carrying on."

"Oh no. No!" A look of impotent rage gave way to one of anxiety.

"Mrs. Newton, do you have something to make her sleep? I think that's the only thing we can do right now—later maybe I can talk to her."

"Yes, I'll get it right away." She ran smack into Jack on the stairs.

"What is going on?"

"Come to the kitchen with me, Ezra is with her."

Once in the kitchen Amy closed the door and with shaking hands unlocked the cupboard where the medicine was kept. Selecting a small brown bottle she measured a spoonful into a glass of water, then on second thought added another.

"Well?" Jack prompted.

"It seems your friend is going to have a baby and didn't know until I said something. She threw herself out the window."

"Did you send for the doctor?" Jack sprang up off the chair.

"She is not hurt. Ezra caught hold of her as she was falling. I shudder to think of what would have happened if he had reached her a second later."

"Pregnant. I wonder who the father is—not her husband that's for sure. He's in New South Wales." Jack's eyebrows drew together in a heavy frown. "Angela has been in the Bahamas for the past two months, and before that Jamaica."

"I'll leave you to your speculations. I had better get this upstairs before poor Ezra's eardrums are shattered."

With Ezra holding Angela down Amy managed to get about half of the medication down her, the rest spilled onto the pillows. A few minutes later the screams gave way to hoarse cries and her eyes closed. When at last Angela fell asleep she still made small whimpering sounds and Ezra turned distressed amber eyes on Amy.

"Thank you," he said. "Please, don't condemn her for what she tried to do. If you knew what had happened—but I say too much."

"Was she raped?" inquired Amy and his eyes didn't waver as he made no reply.

"You can go if you want. I'll stay here with her till she wakes." He turned his attention back to Angela.

"It will be a long time."

"It doesn't matter. She needs me. I will stay."

"You love her very much, don't you, Ezra?"

"She saved my life," he replied simply.

And he was still there when she woke from dark swirling dreams that threatened to suffocate her. She couldn't remember exactly what they were only that she felt as lost and alone as an abandoned child. Everything was fuzzy, even the small night light cast a fractured glow and Ezra's face was distorted as if Angela was seeing through invisible rippling heat waves.

"Here, my lady, drink this. It will make you feel better."

After she drank she did feel better. The tightly clenched knot in her stomach relaxed and she lay there trying to remember.

"Ezra," her voice was rough from screaming, "you have to help me—you will, won't you?"

"You know I will!"

"There is a baby, Laporte's, and I have to get rid of it. If I don't I will die!"

"Shh—be still," he soothed. "Think about it tomorrow. Get your strength back and we will find a solution to your problem."

"I'm not supposed to have any more children. The doctor in Scotland told me that. Oh, what was his name?" Angela frowned searching her memory. "I can't think straight. But he said another child would kill me. I wouldn't care if it were Scott's. I wanted the one I lost, but not this one—not his!"

There was anguished understanding in Ezra's eyes as he spoke to her. "I know how you must hate the child because of its father and what he did, but part of it is you too. You can't hate what is your own flesh and blood!"

"Yes—yes! I hate it and myself. How could I have let this happen?"

"It just did. There's no sense to anything that happens in people's lives. But what is important is you! You must never, never try and harm yourself again. There is Robert and Lorna to think of, Scott waiting for you in Australia. You are too important in their lives to let a little setback like this spoil your life. Please," Ezra pleaded vehemently, "think it through. You will see that I am right."

She just lay there shaking her head, large eyes eclipsing her face. "I can't have his baby. I can't, and I won't!"

Eyes followed her everywhere: brown eyes, gray eyes,

anxious amber eyes. She wasn't to be left alone for a minute for fear of what she might do to herself. Only after she promised not to jump out the window again did Ezra give up his nightly vigil of dozing lightly in a chair beside her bed. Now at least her nights were private.

Regaining her strength Angela drank down Amy's concoction every day and it worked, warding off the morning sickness. She had never had it with any of the other children and it only reinforced the thought that the child was defective.

Angela sat in the garden beneath the flamboyantly blooming poinciana tree. Its foliage made feathery patterns on the grass and when the fitful breeze blew, red flowers showered down. The sweet fragrance of orange blossoms drifted in the air, supplanted only by the salty tang of the ocean.

The house was small but lovely, the finest on the island, where most people opted for tumbledown shacks. A ship's carpenter had constructed it out of the choicest mahogany salvaged from an ill-fated ship. It was entirely fitted together with wooden pegs in the Bahamian style with deep double porches. Coral vines clung tenaciously to the delicately carved grills around the porches. On the roof was the captain's walk where someone was constantly on watch for the wrecks that their livelihood depended on.

It gleamed white in the blazing sun and Angela caught a glimmer from the telescope lens reflecting the light. Jack was up there on the roof carefully scanning the ocean. There had been no wrecks since she had arrived but there soon would be. Summer brought daily thunderstorms often violent in nature and the winds were unpredictable. Then there was always the chance of a hurricane.

Amy often worried about that eventuality. She had never been through one and from what she had heard she didn't want to. She told Angela frightening stories of the ocean washing across the entire island taking everything and everyone with it, of winds that could pick up a ship and deposit it on dry land. There would be no safety in Cayo Hueso if a hurricane struck.

Cayo Hueso, Bone Island, the Spanish called it because of the piles of Indian bones they had found bleaching in the tropical sun. Americans called it Key West; a tiny dot in the Atlantic sandwiched between the Gulf of Mexico and the Caribbean. The Gulf Stream bathed the shores in clear warm water then headed out to open sea. Only four miles long and less than two miles wide it was populated by Bahamians, Cubans, Negros, and a smattering of Americans and Englishmen.

The ocean was just a stone's throw away, ever changing in mood and disposition. Angela could see part of it shining between the orchid trees covered with pale purple blooms. The garden was wildly unkempt but that only added to its charm. No well-ordered English garden in the tropics! The plants grew so fast in the warm climate that it would take a dozen gardeners to keep up with it. As it was there was only one besides Amy, who loved to putter around in it.

Now she knelt transplanting some low lacy ferns beside a bordered path. Amy looked up quickly as Angela got up and walked around the side of the house. She hurried after her, stripping off her gloves.

"Are you going for a walk?" she called gaily. "May I come with you?"

"I would like to be alone," Angela explained. "Just for a while. You understand, don't you? I want to walk along the beach and think without having to make conversation and with no one watching me." She laughed at Amy's woebegone expression. "I won't throw myself in the ocean if that's what you are worrying about! I promise to come back in one piece. Does that satisfy you?"

"Well," Amy hedged. Jack would have a fit if anything happened to Angela and she was supposed to be taking care of her now. "It's only that we are all concerned about your safety."

"You think I'm a lunatic!"

"You did give us quite a scare, but no—not a lunatic. You were upset, overwrought. I can understand. It must have been a nightmare to have—"

"To have what? Just what did Ezra tell you?"

"Why, nothing. I guessed. No woman could hate her own unborn child so much unless—"

"Unless what? You seem to be unable to complete your sentences. Do I upset you that much?"

"Unless it was forced on you," she finished in a rush, nervously tucking a strand of golden hair into the coil at the back of her neck.

Angela started laughing, harsh bitter sounds. "You think I was raped! Well I wasn't. I did it willingly. That was one of Laporte's stipulations and I did it. I did everything he told me to." Her mouth was turned down as if she was going to cry and a hot flush appeared high on her cheeks. "Don't you know a slut when you see one? I'm nothing but a whore disguised as a lady and this," she placed a hand on her belly, "is the bastard of a pirate!"

She wheeled and ran along the path toward the ocean leaving Amy stunned in the garden. Kicking angrily at the sand she sent it spurting before her in a pale golden spray. "Why me?" she asked clenching her fists, needing a target to direct her blows at. But she knew the answer and rail as she might against the course her life was taking she was once again powerless to stop it.

Bending down Angela removed her shoes and left them beneath a palm tree. The sand was hot beneath her feet, too hot to stand in one place so she started walking briskly toward the water and the cool, wet sand. Aimlessly she strolled along the beach, heedless of the foaming waves wetting the hem of her skirt. It was good to forget momentarily.

Voiding her mind of the continual problems that plagued her Angela concentrated on nothing more than feeling. She was alive and healthy, rich and beautiful, that should count for something. The soft wet sand felt delicious and made sucking noises as she walked kicking spurts of salt water before her. The sun was hot, melting into her with a comforting warmth, dancing on the surf.

"Angela!" Jack's voice came rolling toward her over the soothing ocean sounds.

She turned, shading her eyes from the sun and stood waiting. So Amy had run to him with her angry words ringing in her ears. Had she expected any less? In the back of her mind she had known this would happen and that he would come.

The foam swirled over his boots and he stood looking down at Angela with a scowl on his face. Then he threw back his head and loosed loud laughter into the blue-vaulted sky.

"Duchess, you are priceless! Shock Amy speechless and escape from under her nose as cool as a cucumber. I don't know whether to spank you or—"

"Or what?" Angela asked with a smile trembling on her lips.

"Never mind! You always get your way, don't you?"

The smile disappeared and a shadow of grief flitted across her face. "Not always, not nearly enough. I meant what I said. I'm sorry if I upset Amy but I was cross."

"But not any more," Jack observed, "only sad. You never had that quality, those sorrowful eyes, when I knew you before. How can any man be immune to you now?"

He took her hand, so soft and small, lost in his callused hand. "Come, little girl," Jack said indulgently. "We will walk and talk, and you can tell me the things that have changed you."

"I can't—"

"You have been hurt deeply, yet you blame yourself for what others have done. Sometimes a wound seems healed on the surface but still festers unseen, so it must be lanced and cleaned to heal properly."

Angela tilted her head, glancing sideways at him as they walked. He was so positive, taking command of every situation. He had that particular quality that made her feel as if she had known him forever—that he cared immensely what happened to her. And there was still a spark between them—in spite of Scott—in spite of Amy.

They strolled down the beach in silence watching the pelicans swoop down into the ocean to capture fish in their expanding pouches below their beaks. They were ungainly, almost clumsy looking birds but somehow they managed to fly and they dove cleanly into the water emerging with their prizes.

Jack drew her after him, up the beach away from the fishing boats to a more secluded spot hedged about with palm trees and sea grape bushes. He sat down with his back against the long smooth trunk of a tree, his legs stretched out in front of him. Angela sat with her chin on her knees, arms around her legs and buried her bare feet in the warm sand. She didn't look at him, gazing instead at the blue hypnotically moving sea.

"Talk to me, Duchess—tell me what happened to turn you into such an unhappy woman. Tell me about Gaston Laporte. . . ."

"No!" She hid her face against her knees cringing from the hated name.

His hand touched her bent head, big fingers moving in the dark silk of her hair. "I love you, Angela—still. I told you once I would never forget you and though I tried I couldn't. No matter what you have done I'll understand. Love forgives everything!"

"You love Amy."

"Yes, Amy is the love of my life. Without her I would be like a ship without a rudder. But where is it written that a man can only love one woman at a time? You and she are as different as day and night, yet could we continue to exist without either?"

Jack was removing the pins from her hair, caressing the back of her neck lightly with the tips of his fingers. She wanted to remain indifferent, stubbornly resisting his efforts to make her relax. But the touch and his masculine scent made her tremble with a melting sweetness of remembered yesterdays.

Raising her head Angela looked into the calm determined eyes and he smiled, his gaze like light kisses brushing her face. Jack searched the twin aquamarine pools, plumbing the depths of her soul. Then putting a finger beneath her willful chin he tipped her face up and covered her slightly parted lips with his.

His kiss was infinitely tender, searching yet demanding nothing, giving everything. The familiar pressure of his mouth, the soft prickle of his beard and mustache were making her swoon with pleasure, in some subtle way more intimate than total possession.

"Sweet," he panted in her ear. "Your kisses are sweeter than honey and I know only too well what they can do to me!"

"Oh, Jack!" She felt lethargic, completely in his power, desperately wanted him never to stop. But no! "We can never be lovers again."

"I know," he whispered aware of the forbidden danger of their closeness. "The time for that is long past. We have different lives, different loves. Things have changed and we can never go back."

"There will always be the past. No one can take our memories away."

What was she doing clasped in Jack's arms speaking of love when it was Scott she loved? Yet she couldn't think of this as a betrayal. There was something indefinable—a feeling between them, an attraction that was obvious.

He released Angela at last but kept her hand clasped in his, as if their touching kept open the lines of communication between them. Slowly, with a gentle firmness Jack drew her story from her, making her relive the pain and horror of the past months.

She told it as if it had happened to someone else, not her, and he worried over the cold unemotional way she spoke. At one point he almost told her to stop, touched to the quick by the suffering she had gone through. No wonder she was unhappy and couldn't bear the thought of having this child.

When Angela finished she sat silently staring straight ahead, not looking at him, and her hand was cold in his. To think that she had been driven to kill them with her own delicate hands, like a trapped animal goaded beyond endurance, protecting itself and its offspring.

"My poor abused little girl," murmured Jack pulling her stiff body into the circle of his arms.

He rocked her like a child and spoke healing words that she couldn't remember afterwards. Had she even heard the words over her sudden outpouring of tears or just derived comfort from their tone? But as they walked slowly back home, the afternoon spent, there was a peacefulness that descended like a balm upon her and she knew he had been right.

two

Fishermen scattered as the powerful black gelding pounded over the beach sending sand and water splashing in every direction. They were used to her—the mad English duchess who galloped about the island at breakneck speed dressed in a pair of loose white trousers and a white blouse. It was a wonder she didn't fall off and kill herself but she seemed a part of the animal and clung like a second skin to his back.

She rode astride like a man, unable to find a single sidesaddle on the whole island, and her hair, as black as a summer storm, streamed behind her like a hurricane. The locals were proud of her, it was almost like being visited by royalty. In all of these southern waters only Key West could boast of having a resident duchess. Why, sometimes she even deigned to bestow a smile on them but often as not she passed them by without a glance, a faraway look on her face.

Today she left behind a silvery stream of laughter and they stared after her long after she had disappeared.

Hundreds of birds streaked upward into the sky, a fleeing white cloud, and Angela slowed her mount and finally stopped. She was breathing as fast as her horse, Neptune, exhilarated by her wild ride. Her clothes clung damply to her perspiring body and she lifted her hair off her neck. It was so hot and still, hardly a leaf or blade of grass stirred. But there was a promise of relief sitting over the ocean.

Huge thunderheads piled up on the horizon darkening the sky. She could see the storm forming, black angry clouds boiling as if in a cauldron. It grew and moved with a life of its own, surging ever higher into the sky. Distant tongues of fire flashed through the mass, proclaiming its awesome power.

Angela sat motionless caught up in the drama of the birth of a storm. The birds circled warily and then glided back down to the salt ponds where they nested every year. She often came to watch the great variety of birds: herons, cranes, cormorants, ducks, and once a pink billowing froth of flamingos. But today there was electricity in the air and the birds were ignored.

Her greatest pleasure was riding, and once she had gotten used to riding astride vowed never to use a ridiculous sidesaddle again. But there was a method to her madness and each day after a morning of galloping she went home and bathed, then she lay down, waiting and praying for the hot shooting pain in her belly that would free her from self-exile.

Jack had given Angela back her self-respect but no one could make her want this baby. Amy had protested at first when she had bought the horse but Jack had silenced her with just a look. Then he went and found her a saddle and the wonderfully unrestrictive trousers. He hadn't said so, but Angela knew he approved of what she was doing. Ever since their long revealing afternoon on the beach he never reproached her for her actions.

It was just a matter of time before the baby would be jolted free, losing its tenacious grip on her life—of that Angela was sure. The thought of another seven months in Key West was unbearable. Not that she didn't enjoy the Newtons' company, but it was time to move on. She had things to do and goals to pursue and there was always the shadowy retreating figure of Scott just beyond her reach.

How long she sat there motionless she didn't know. A

rapidly moving group of thunderstorms spawned by the Gulf Stream turned the eastern sky black. Sheets of solid rain maneuvered, advancing like an army into battle. Angela could see the line of demarcation as if it had been drawn with a ruler; on one side a torrential downpour lashed the sea into a gray fury, next to it blue rolling waves sparkled with sunlight.

Neptune tossed his head, stirring restively as a blast of cold air accompanied by a loud clap of thunder encompassed them. Angela kept a firm hand on him mesmerized by the savage rampage that unleashed a primitive response deep inside her. She could only think of that other storm in the Highlands that had snatched the shredded flag from her grasp like a living entity. The dreadful, stained piece of tattered silk that she had discovered beneath the peaked roof of the round tower at Seafield Castle.

No modern person, no matter how superstitious, could possibly believe in a curse. But at times Angela felt a very real fear of the Bratach Sith. Why even the legend was laughable—a flag given to Clan Campbell aeons ago by a fairy, to be flown in times of disaster or war to bring victory to the clan. Now really—a fairy! But her ancestors had obviously at one time believed in the legend and the curse. Good lord! The curse. Pregnant with Laporte's child she could actually believe that some indescribable malediction was conspiring against her and Scott.

What horrendous events had occurred since Scott flew the Fairy Flag to win a war—the very real war that he and Angela had fought since the first day they met. And he had won. She gave in and married him; she broke down completely and loved him with all her heart and soul.

And then, when everything in the world went wrong and life wasn't worth living another day, Angela had taken matters into her own hands and shredded the flag to pieces. It didn't matter that whoever touched the Bratach Sith was doomed to be showered with evils for the rest of their lives; she had to be rid of it once and for all. Ever since then things had gone from bad to worse and it was so easy to blame her desperate straits on an ancient curse rather than on herself. But almost everything that had happened had been outside Angela's sphere of influence. So she fluctuated wildly between belief and disbelief, and right now she believed. Both she and Scott had touched the Bratach Sith and they were apart.

A jagged bolt of lightning plunged into the sea, ending her daydream, flashing silver-white, so brilliant that for a time she couldn't see. When her eyes once more became accustomed to the encroaching dimness she cried out in surprise.

In the midst of the commotion stood a huge unwavering rainbow. Never in her life had Angela seen such a brilliant vault of colors seeming to span the whole breadth of the ocean. The magnificence was breathtaking, vivid colors arching into the heavens. The bright splendor dazzled her eyes and at that moment she wished she was more artistically inclined, for to capture that sight on canvas would be a coup beyond compare.

As quickly as it had appeared the curve of colors dissolved into mist. A spattering of raindrops preceded the storm, and Angela saw the grey curtain move swiftly toward her. She laughed and wheeled the horse. She would race the storm and see who was fleeter, Neptune the god of the sea or Aeolus the ruler of the winds.

A gust of raging wind almost blew her off her mount and she urged him on. With a quick glance behind she saw the rain gaining on her and a minute later huge stinging drops lashed down on her. She was soaked to the skin in an instant, thunder ringing in her ears. She laughed out loud. It was wonderful—nature's wild assault!

The whole sky was falling and she was drowning in the tempest, bending low over Neptune's neck as flashes of lightning sizzled around her. On a flat island like this the electric charges were attracted to the highest objects and Angela on her horse was a moving target. But she wasn't afraid, feeling really alive for the first time in months.

As she raced past a huge old banyan tree a firebolt

from heaven rent the air and the crash of thunder was like cannons booming in her ears. The whole world coruscated a blinding white and the tree glowed, then exploded into a million burning pieces. Every hair on Angela's body stood on end and blazing chunks of the tree showered down on her.

Neptune reared in sheer panic and streaked away almost as fast as the lightning. She couldn't control the crazed animal and held on for dear life as the landscape whirled by in a blur. She saw the gale uproot a tree and a bush blew right in front of them.

Her breath came hard and fast, her heart pounding like a drum against her ribs. Angela's legs ached from clasping Neptune's back and her arms strained to control him. But in spite of the danger or perhaps because of it, she was fiercely invigorated, her wild laughter louder than the thunder.

Neptune was tiring, slowing down, heading by instinct to the shed that served as his stable not far from Jack's house. He stopped, quivering all over just outside and Angela slipped from his back just as Jack threw open the door. She led him into the shed.

"You were magnificent!" Jack grasped her by the waist his hands circling it easily. "I watched you through the telescope. I have never seen anyone ride like that. You should have been a highwayman!"

The wind rattled the shed, threatening to tear off the tin roof and the rain sounded like a barrage of shot. Jack's eyes darkened to slate-gray as they glanced over her, clothes and hair plastered to her body. She looked like a mermaid dredged up from the bottom of the sea, streaming with water, her breasts heaving beneath the now transparent blouse.

He was soaked too, leaving nothing to the imagination, and Angela knew what he wanted, why he had been waiting and she wanted it too.

They came together like the sea and the storm, his mouth devouring hers with kisses so violent she felt like the tree that had exploded when touched by lightning. She surged against him in a frenzy, hanging with her arms around his neck because her legs gave way.

There was no storm, no Amy; only Angela and Jack falling onto the pile of fresh sweet-smelling hay in the corner, an elemental passion unleashed within them.

The buttons ripped from her blouse and Jack's lips moved on her bare breasts scorching her nipples. His hands tugged at the white trousers that clung maddeningly to her like a second skin. So shaken was Angela that she could only cling to his shoulders, gasping beneath the unexpected eruption of desire that possessed them both.

Jack tensed and his head lifted with a frown furrowing his brow. It was still raining but the worst was over. Angela's hands were teasing him beyond endurance but then he heard the sound again.

"What was that?" asked Angela, not really caring, only wanting his full attention again.

Distant shouts penetrated the shed and he surged to his feet rearranging his clothes and shaking his great silvery head as if to clear it of his momentary madness. Then she heard it, the words ringing out clearly.

"A wreck on the reef! A wreck on the reef!"

"Sorry, Duchess," was all he said as he ran from the shed.

Angela looked after him in confusion. She tingled all over and felt like screaming with frustration. Was he sorry he had almost made love to her or sorry because he had left without completing it?

There were sounds of horns—no the huge conch shells they blew into to attract everyone's attention.

"Damn!" She jumped to her feet clutching the blouse over her bosom. "I'm not going to miss out on all the excitement!"

Running as fast as she could Angela rounded the shed and cut through the garden. Everyone was on the beach or headed for it and she was no exception. Reaching Jack's boat as he and Ezra launched it into the surf she plunged in after them and heaved herself aboard.

"What the—get out, Angela!" Jack shouted over the commotion. "A wreck is no place for a woman!"

"I'm going," she stated determinedly. "Or are you going to waste time talking me out of it? Hurry! Almost everyone has a head start on you!"

As he bent to the oars he swore but ended up laughing. "If you're going to be in the thick of it would you please do something with your shirt! My men won't have their minds on wrecking—and that's for sure!"

Angela gave him a sidelong glance that Ezra couldn't help but notice. The whole exchange and her state of dishabille could mean only one thing. He wondered if they had been dressing or undressing.

"You could have left me with some buttons!" she said tartly, tying the blouse beneath her breasts. It wasn't much better so she shook her hair forward over her shoulders to cover what the material could not. Jack started to protest her words but she cut him off. "Don't be a prude—Ezra knows. I can tell by the look in his eyes. Don't worry, he can keep his mouth shut."

With two such powerful men propelling the boat through the water with all their might they reached Jack's ship in record time. She scrambled nimbly up the rope ladder and stood carefully on the slippery deck. Everything was in readiness and as soon as they were aboard the ship plunged through the sea.

The ship was fast and sleek, more than a match for the rowboats and smaller vessels. Soon they were outdistanced, and Angela stood clinging to the railing in the steady rain scanning the ocean for the wrecked ship.

Then she saw it, sitting lopsided buffeted by the wind and sea but immovably fixed on a hidden reef. Only someone that knew these waters would have known the danger there. To Angela it looked as safe and deep as the rest of the ocean.

Jack had reached the wreck first riding several hundred yards away lest his ship too succumb. A triumphant cheer went up and the men lowered all boats ready and eager for the grueling work ahead. Jack was Wrecking Master!

"Oh no!" said Jack as Angela eyed one of the boats. "You stay here. If my guess is right they are caught on the edge of that reef. Below is a deep trench and the ship could break up or go down at any minute."

"But—"

"No! There will be passengers to rescue. Make yourself useful and see that they are comfortable. Put them anywhere but in my cabin."

With that he left and Ezra came to stand beside her. "Aren't you going?" she asked petulantly.

"No, I don't know what to do and would only be in the way. So would you." His amber eyes were full of questions. "Why?"

She turned away concentrating on the action below. She had given no thought to the consequences of her actions with Jack.

"If I knew myself, do you think I would tell you?"

"That's right, my lady, put me in my place!"

"I'm sorry, Ezra," she said genuinely repentant. "I wish I knew myself. Sometimes things just happen."

"Don't I know! I'm not trying to pry. I'm just concerned about you. I don't think you should get in over your head."

"I haven't!"

The boats reached the disabled craft and she saw the sailors swarm onto it. While most of them went into the bowels of the ship looking for cargo several were assigned to help get the passengers into the boats. Not all captains were so scrupulous; some were interested in money first then survivors.

The smell of cooking food came from the galley. The men would work straight through the day and night, as long as the ship was accessible, only taking time out to gulp down a hasty meal and a ration of rum. They were big, hearty men suited to the hard life of wrecking. Physical fortitude and grit were prerequisites as they toiled for sometimes twenty-four hours in storms and other adverse conditions.

The boats were returning, and Angela and Ezra learned that the ship was Spanish. Among the survivors were several women and children who weren't quite sure what to make of Angela in her outlandish garb and eyed her as if she was a female pirate out to do them mischief. Once they were settled in the cabins she went back to the deck, this time with Jack's spyglass in hand.

Looking through the instrument was almost like being on the stranded ship and she watched, fascinated. Jack directed the activities mostly from the deck sometimes going below. The seamen worked fast with no wasted movements. They had done this dozens, sometimes hundreds of times before, knowing the dangers involved but ignoring them.

Piles of crates, baskets, chests, and boxes were stacked on the tilted deck, each awaiting a short trip over the side, into the boats, and onto the *Silver Bear*. The clutter gradually grew on Jack's ship and Angela had to be careful where she walked. It would be later when the Spanish ship was devoid of cargo that there would be time to organize the spoils.

She saw Jack and the Spanish captain arguing vehemently over a group of massive, handsomely carved wooden chests, each one carefully padlocked. Finally throwing up his hands in defeat the Spanish captain gave in to whatever they were fighting over and sat down dejectedly on one of the chests.

They worked on as the rain gave way to a light drizzle and then stopped completely. The clouds moved westward and as the sun slipped toward the horizon it lit up the storm blood-red and edged it with gold. The whole sky flamed, shading from red to orange to delicate pink and in the distance silver streaks of lightning still flashed.

What a day of nature's beauty and destruction! Angela would never be able to forget the sights she had seen. The first star appeared in the darker blue patch of sky in the east and she gave a stifled scream as the Spanish ship shifted, tilting alarmingly. Boxes, crates, and men flew in every direction, wreckers reaching out and clinging to masts, railings, whatever was fastened down.

One man was crushed beneath an avalanche of crates and some boxes broke through the railing at the stern splashing into the sea. When the ship settled everyone was back to work again as if nothing had happened. She saw Jack bending over the motionless form of the man that was injured and gave a sigh of relief. He was safe for the moment. The day was flying and darkness was taking over. Soon there would be only lantern light making work much more dangerous.

Much later, after Angela had eaten dinner in Jack's cabin with Ezra, they were back at the railing watching the tiny spots of light dancing like fireflies over the sea in the interminable trips back and forth. It was no longer possible to see individuals, only a golden glow came from the slanted deck. There was no moon and the stars were so low they scraped the sea, a multitude of twinkling white dots merging into a gauzy swath across the ebony sky.

Angela was exhausted but still she couldn't tear herself away. How many opportunities would she have to see such sights? Jane was in England carefully ensconced in the country having babies with Owen. And here in Key West on a tropical sea, the deck of a ship rolling beneath her feet, was Angela, the antithesis of English womanhood, tearing around with an ex-highway man turned wrecker and a freed slave.

She shook back her now dry hair raking her fingers through it. The men were too busy to give her a second glance though their first had been scrutinizing enough. She had caught a glimpse of herself in a tiny mirror in Jack's cabin and almost couldn't believe that the wild-eyed, tousle-haired gypsy was she. No wonder the women had been frightened of her.

"Duchess!" Jack stood behind her, lines of exhaustion etched into his rugged face. "I'd like to see you in my cabin. Ezra, would you mind getting me some food? I'm famished!" There was a strange exuberant quality to his voice in spite of his fatigue.

The dark wooden chests, six of them, that she had seen Jack and the Spanish captain arguing over were stacked in his cabin taking over most of the floor space. Jack, bare to the waist, wearing only tight fitting breeches and high boots sank onto the only chair and smiled broadly. Angela poured him a generous brandy and handed it to him. He tossed it off in one gulp and settled back in the chair.

"Open that chest, Angela," he directed pointing to the one in a far corner.

Puzzled, she obeyed, struggling with the heavy lid, noticing the broken padlock. "Oh—oh—oh!" She was on her knees in front of it stunned by the riches revealed.

Jewels of every description filled it, pearls, rubies, diamonds, sapphires, all in a jumble, sparkling and gleaming in spite of the dim light. Without being able to stop herself Angela plunged her hands into the shining mass and let the cool stones trickle luxuriantly through her fingers. It was a king's ransom—a pirate's treasure!

"Open that one, Duchess!"

Lifting another lid she stepped back, this time without words. Stacks of rough brick-shaped gold bars glowed dully right up to the top of the chest.

"Gold bullion," Jack explained, "bound for Spain from South America. Five chests of gold!"

"It—it must be worth millions of pounds!"

"Yes, and two of those chests are mine!"

"Jack—Jack—you have finally made your fortune!"

"Yes, but I don't know if it is worth what I had to give up for it—what we almost had today."

"Of course it is!" she exclaimed laughing and throwing her arms around his neck.

For a moment he held her tightly, his face lost against the soft spill of her breasts. Then there came a sharp knock on the door and they hastily separated as Ezra brought in Jack's dinner. His amber eyes bulged with shock at the revealed riches.

"Quite a haul, hey, Ezra? Not bad for a night's work!"

"Hell, I might become a wrecker myself!" Ezra backed out the door his eyes glued to the treasure until it vanished from sight.

"Angela," Jack pulled something from his pocket

holding it in his clenched hand so she couldn't see it, "turn around."

He lifted the hair off the back of her neck and fastened something around it. She felt something hard and cold dangling between her breasts and instinctively touched it. It was rough, irregularly shaped, a huge uncut emerald all the more spectacular in its natural state. It glowed from within with green fire like something alive—hacked from the heart of a steaming Brazilian jungle.

"You should give it to Amy," she protested, fingering the stone, not wanting to part with it in spite of her words.

"No, she wouldn't wear it. I have pearls for Amy. But the emerald was made for you. Beneath your ladylike veneer you are an untamed little barbarian. Don't you feel as if it's part of you, my fierce little Duchess?"

"Yes—oh yes!"

"When you wear it, think of me and know that if you ever need me I will be there. Even if oceans separate us, our love and friendship exist deep inside each of us. When you are sad or troubled, just touch it and I will be with you comforting you, loving you, soothing away the hurt."

She turned, her glowing aqua eyes brimming with tears like diamonds. "Oh, Jack. You always say and do the right thing at the right time."

"Not always, little girl," he sighed. "If I did, I would be a saint and that I'm not. You better than anyone else know that. But I feel you will need my help when I can't be there and if the emerald endowed with love can work its magic that's all either of us can ask."

The sitting room opened onto the porch with wide French doors and a balmy breeze blew through it. The furniture was Sheraton upholstered in pale pink, green, and white, and lent to the cool unruffled serenity, a reflection of Amy's own qualities.

They sat drinking tea out of delicate bone china cups

from France, and Robert stuffed a whole scone into his mouth only to be elbowed by Lorna. Amy laughed touching the perfectly matched pearls around her neck that glowed a creamy-pink. Jack was in Havana auctioning off the cargo and tending to business affairs.

The wreck had been the most profitable in Key West history and word spread like wildfire throughout the islands about Jack Newton's good fortune. It brought prosperity to the key and the locals superstitiously whispered that their duchess had brought the luck. Hadn't she been aboard the *Silver Bear* when the treasure was discovered? It was all her doing.

Amy shot an uneasy glance at Angela. She had been unusually subdued since Jack's departure, though she still went on her morning rides of which Amy heartily disapproved. She could just see her nine months gone galloping all over the island with everyone gaping at her. She had tried to become Angela's friend but they didn't really communicate, and Amy had no idea of what went on in her mind. That was Jack's department and she was sure he knew everything about the eccentric duchess, but he never discussed it with her.

It was so hot that Angela felt wilted already. The only relief came at night when the breezes cooled things down and she took to riding earlier in the morning to take advantage of the day before it started sizzling. The fishermen were just putting out at dawn when she went galloping by with a determined look on her face.

So far nothing had happened and she began to despair. If the storm, pounding ride, and all the activity on the day of the wreck hadn't made her miscarry she began to think nothing would. She was depressed especially since Jack had left and she couldn't talk to him. Sometimes she took out the emerald and looked at it but never wore it around Amy. They had curbed their sensual attraction very effectively since what had almost happened during the storm.

Angela went stiff all of a sudden, the teacup slipping from her nervous fingers and shattering on the floor. It was moving! The nasty little worm was gnawing at her insides! The flutter came again and she knew exactly what it was—Laporte's baby taking over her life and body, making itself known.

"Quickly, Lorna—fetch my smelling salts!" Amy was at her side looking down at Angela's white face and the closed trembling eyelids. "Angela, are you all right? Are you in pain?"

Amy's voice was far away. The only reality was the movement of the child in her belly, unwanted and unloved, forced upon her by a sadistic, revenge-filled pirate. He was truly avenging himself now, not even his death could stop his vengeance.

Amy waved the smelling salts under Angela's nose and with a burst of revived rage she struck it from Amy's hand and jumped to her feet. "Leave me alone!" she screamed bursting into tears. "Just leave me alone!" Wheeling, Angela ran half-blinded, stumbling up the stairs and into her room.

"I'm a shrew," she sobbed collapsing on the bed. "An ill-tempered bitch!"

She lay there for a long time until all her tears were spent and she felt dry and brittle inside. But all the crying in the world wouldn't change the situation. She was caught in woman's age-old trap.

Swearing Angela flounced off the bed and stripped off her clothes. Examining herself in front of the mirror she saw hardly any change, only slightly fuller breasts. Her belly was as flat as ever, but she usually didn't start showing till the fourth month.

Cruelly she dug her fingernails into the flesh of her abdomen as if she could reach and crush the separate being that was slowly turning her life into chaos. It was no use, it would take more than willing it dead to get rid of the bastard. She was desperate and she knew now what she had to do.

The decision made, Angela pulled on her trousers and a blouse rolling up the long sleeves. It was too hot to wear anything and she would have preferred it that way. Giggling, she found herself startled that she could still find any humor in the world, but the thought of the way everyone's eyes would pop out of their heads if she emulated Lady Godiva was amusing. The fishermen would be sure to make a tangled mess out of their nets and lines.

She saddled Neptune herself and galloped toward the salt pools. The sun was high, meltingly hot, and even breathing was an effort. After all her months in the tropics it was turning Angela's exposed skin a soft golden brown and her eyes were even more startling against the tan. She looked more like a gypsy than a great lady and at the moment felt like one too.

Angela sat gazing out at the turquoise sparkle of the ocean, so bright it hurt her eyes. She was soaked to the skin already but it didn't matter, it was cooler that way. What was it they said—only mad dogs and Englishmen go out in the noonday sun? She wasn't in India but she might as well be, and it was getting hotter by the minute.

There would be a thunderstorm today. Huge, wonderfully fantastic clouds were piling up on the horizon as they did almost every afternoon, though none had struck with the force of the first storm of the season. That should cool things down a bit and add more rainwater to the storage tanks scattered across the island. For although there were a few sweet-water wells they wouldn't provide enough for this sun-dazzled island.

A sea gull circled, screeching, awakening her from a pleasant dream to scorching reality. Turning her horse she set off at an easy pace, in no rush. The island was small and she would be there before she knew it. Angela wondered if she had the nerve to follow it through to completion.

"Yes," she told herself, "there is no alternative."

The tiny hut was a patchwork made up of odd pieces of wood, tin, and tar paper. As Angela dismounted she speculated as to how it had survived the storm. A sort of porch was connected to the front, of woven palm leaves shakily propped up on two poles. It seemed deserted.

She tied Neptune to a tree and walked toward the hut. The shade of the makeshift porch was reviving but still she hesitated. Angela couldn't even remember how she had heard of this place but everyone on the island knew of the Old Lady, as they called her. She was a last resort but sooner or later everyone made her acquaintance and Angela was no exception.

The rickety door on leather hinges was open and she had to duck her head to enter. It was almost dark inside, bright cracks of sunlight penetrating where mismatched pieces of the walls failed to meet. She sensed a movement and as her eyes became accustomed to the dimness found herself being scrutinized by the oldest, most shriveled little Negro she had ever seen.

She looked like a monkey with bright piercing eyes and arms like gnarled sticks. Dressed all in black she was a shadow hunched over a table in the corner of the hut. Her eyes moved, sharp and alive, the only things about her that had any vitality, and her gaze swept over Angela's unconventional garb.

"I know you," she said her voice as dry as autumn leaves crunching underfoot. "You are the duchess that rides like the devil. What is pursuing you? Or is it something within you that drives you?"

Angela took a step backward letting out a deeply held breath.

"Don't be afraid."

"I'm not."

"No, I wouldn't think you would be. You leave dead men in your wake like a hurricane on a rampage. You should not tamper with legends and curses—they are more powerful than you think. They can change fate."

"I know."

Did the old woman know everything about her? It was impossible—yet she was hearing it with her own ears. They said she had the power and Angela was beginning to believe it. After all hadn't she seen things with her own eyes that defied understanding?

"You have come here for a purpose. To rid youself of the child of an evil one. But you should have learned long ago that some things cannot be changed."

"You mean you won't help me?" A cat brushed against Angela's legs and she jumped.

The woman didn't answer, going about the work she had been at before Angela's coming. She was crushing dried things in a crudely made pestle and mortar. Herbs and strange looking plants hung in bunches from the tin roof and there was an assortment of earthenware bottles lined up on shelves.

"I will pay you." Angela took two gold coins from her pocket and laid them on the table. They shone brightly in a shaft of light.

The Old Lady still hesitated. "The one inside you will bring love and peace wherever she goes. She is destined for great things. Do I dare interfere?"

How could she know it was a girl? How dare she try and dissuade her! "It is a monster and I will be rid of it!" Angela laid four more coins beside the others. They made a tempting pile.

"You will need a powerful potion if it is to work against what is foreordained. Such a draught could kill you."

"I don't care! Give it to me and be done with it. I'm determined to do it and won't be stopped. If you don't help me I will find another way!"

"Why not wait till she is born and get rid of her. Give her away—then there will be no danger."

"No!" Angela took the rest of the coins from her pocket and flung them on the table. Several fell to the hard-packed earthen floor. "Whatever happens to me or it, you won't be blamed. I take full responsibility for the consequences. Let it be on my head!"

"So be it," replied the Old Lady ignoring the money. "It will take several days to concoct the right mixture. Return to me at midnight by the dark of the moon. It will be ready."

The sun was hot but Angela was shivering with cold as she mounted Neptune and rode away. Why did she tell her all those things? What was the use when the child would never be born? Great love and peace indeed! The offspring of such a father could only spread hate. The Old Lady had just wanted more gold; she had given in readily enough when Angela's pocket was empty. Yet she had known certain things. Could what she said about the baby have been true?

"Impossible!" she concluded urging her horse faster.

It was dark as black velvet, the only relief millions of stars dashed against the sky. An apparition in white rode a black horse slowly through the night. Angela had crept stealthily from the house hours after everyone else was asleep. She had made no sound as she went through the garden and saddled Neptune. Even he had been quiet as if joining in the conspiracy with her and now he picked his way carefully over the island to the deserted section where the Old Lady made her home. They went more by instinct than any sense of direction for it was impossible to make out any landmarks in the pitch-black darkness.

Light flickered from the cracks in the walls spilling out the open doorway. It was a relief to be there and out of the enveloping night. Angela walked into the tiny room and the Old Lady didn't even look up. She was pouring a nauseous looking liquid into a small bottle. When the last drop was poured she sealed it with a cork stopper.

In the guttering lamplight she looked ghastly, all lines, angles, and hollows and Angela knew why they called her witch and feared her magic. She handed the brown bottle to Angela and it was still warm.

"Go to the beach and bathe three times in the ocean. Then drink the potion. It must be done tonight before sunrise."

"Will it work?"

The gnomelike creature began chanting in a strange heathensounding language. Her eyes were closed and she rocked back and forth. Then she stopped, coming back from wherever she had gone in her mind.

"You are tempting the fates. I do not know if it can be done. I have told you the risks. The rest is up to you." She pointed to the door. "Go!"

With the bottle clenched tightly in one hand she left and the chanting followed her out the door. Without thinking, without even knowing where she was going Angela set out. Wherever she went she would reach the ocean so it didn't matter.

The sound of the surf was in her ears. Neptune had gone back to his shed so Angela unsaddled him and left, walking toward the beach. Sand crunched beneath her boots, a strangely comforting sound.

Removing her clothes she placed the bottle on the neatly folded pile and started toward the ocean. Foam swirled around her ankles as soft as down. She clutched the emerald in her hand and it soothed her. There was nothing to worry about. Soon this would be nothing but an unpleasant memory and the secret would be safely buried within her forever. Scott would never know of her degradation.

The water was tepid, warmer than the air but she plunged in, swimming for a few yards before going out again. Three times and then Angela was fumbling for her clothes, pulling them on with difficulty over her wet skin.

Sitting on the sand she uncorked the bottle and sniffed, wrinkling her nose. She felt very cool since the swim. Taking a deep breath she put the bottle to her lips and drank it down in a few big gulps.

Immediately fire burst through her veins and the stars began spinning wildly overhead. She had to get back to her room and staggered to her feet only to fall full length on the soft yielding sand. A horrible pain stabbed through her belly and she rolled onto her side curling into a tight ball, moaning through clenched teeth.

It was as bad as having a baby after carrying it for a full nine months. But this one would not survive. She couldn't get up, couldn't even crawl and she writhed in agony calling for Amy. The house was not far away. Could she hear her cries for help? Would she come and take her back to her small green and white room where she could at least lie on the bed?

Angela could hardly breathe. Sand gritted between her teeth as she rolled onto her back gasping for air. The stars hung low touching her with their white-hot brilliance, torturing her beyond endurance. When would it end? It must be over soon!

There was loud pounding on the door, frantic voices calling her name. "Mrs. Newton, Mrs. Newton! Come quick! The duchess is dying on the beach!"

Amy rolled over. It had to be a dream, but her eyes opened and a servant was knocking on her bedroom door.

It usually took a good hour for her to come fully awake each morning but not today. Shoving her feet into a pair of slippers she hastily tied the robe around her waist and stumbled from the room. She ran into Ezra in the hall.

"What is it?"

"I don't know," he replied running down the stairs two at a time with Amy streaking after him.

A group of dirty, bewhiskered fishermen smelling of rum and fish were on the porch and they led the way to the beach.

Angela lay as white and motionless as a marble statue on the golden sand. Amy fell to her hands and knees beside her. There was sand in her hair and on one side of her face but she seemed untouched. There was a great green chunk of stone suspended on a thin chain lying on her unmoving bosom.

Ezra pressed his ear against her chest while the baffled fishermen looked on. She couldn't be dead—not their duchess! There wasn't a mark on her and she was as beautiful as an angel. Besides who would dare lay a finger on her?

"Is she alive?" Amy laid a tentative hand on her cool brow.

"I don't know." Ezra's face was several shades lighter as he turned to her. "Let's get her home."

"There is no doctor," Amy reminded him. "He's on board the *Silver Bear.*"

The group of fishermen parted in awe before the tiny imposing figure in a tattered black dress. Her sharp black eyes took in everything and everyone in a glance, missing nothing.

"It's the Old Lady," whispered the fishermen in awe. She rarely ventured to this part of the island, preferring to keep close to her hut. People always went to her.

"Get away!" she commanded with queenlike dignity. Kneeling beside the small prone figure her knobby hands lifted Angela's wrist feeling for the beat of life.

"She lives. Take her into the house and I will see if I can save her before the spark goes out."

Ezra lifted Angela in his powerful arms. She was a light burden but his heart felt as heavy as a millstone. If anyone could save her the Old Lady could.

The odd almost funereal procession was headed by Ezra, then Amy and the Old Lady, with the fishermen trailing behind. The short walk took forever.

When Angela was laid in her own bed, the Old Lady ordered them all out of the room. Amy hesitated, torn between hope and despair, but Ezra propelled her toward the door and she went. They heard the key click in the lock, heard the low chanting sounds.

The woman piled blankets on Angela, then forced a liquid she had brought with her between the slack lips. She should have been dead by now but something had protected her. Reaching beneath the covers she withdrew the green stone. It was warm and glowing. Yes—it was endowed with a great power far beyond her own magic. The power of love was grand beyond compare.

Placing the stone on Angela's lips the Old Lady sang and chanted, moving around the bed. The potion had worked against the mother instead of the baby as if a shield protected the tiny being. She had warned the duchess of going contrary to what was meant to be. But she would live and the child too.

When Angela opened her eyes she saw the wizened face of the Old Lady bending over her. The last thing she remembered was lying on the beach with stars whizzing over her head. So it was over at last. Thank goodness!

She closed her eyes again but was shaken violently by

the woman. "Open your eyes! Yes, that's right." She raised Angela's hand and closed it around the stone. "You know what that is?"

"Yes," Angela whispered wishing she would go away so she could sleep.

"The child is still in you." Angela winced but she continued, "You almost died. The next time you surely will. Swear on everything that stone means to you that you will never make another attempt to rid yourself of this baby!"

"No!"

"Yes! You will swear and when the child is born—if you still do not want her—bring her to me. I will take her." The black eyes shone strongly, willing a response. "Do you understand what I am saying?" Angela nodded. "Then swear!"

"I promise," relented Angela, tears of weak despair slipping down into her outflung hair.

three

Laughter from the garden drifted into the sitting room where Amy sat embroidering the tiny clothes she had kept a secret from Angela. It was good to hear her laughing with the children and then she heard Jack's booming voice. But of course, Jack had always had a way with women.

There was no cause for concern about a renewed romance between them because Angela was now in her ninth month and heavy with child. Her recovery after the attempted abortion that almost took her life had been nothing short of amazing. By the time the Old Lady had emerged from her room Angela was safely past the crisis. Amy never found out what had transpired behind the locked door and didn't dare ask. She was just immensely thankful that by the time Jack returned from Havana their guest was back to normal. She was also thankful that there were no more attempts to abort the child.

Angela still remained adamant about not wanting the baby but had decided to wait it out. She couldn't do any less after the dreadful warning and the promise she had made to the Old Lady. She had brought her back from death's door and for that Angela was grateful. There had been no contact between them since she had left reminding her that she would take the baby if Angela didn't want it.

Every time Angela thought about it she had to laugh. What a fitting beginning for the offspring of a pirate—to be raised by a witch and spend her childhood in a tumbledown hovel. In her mind she saw a small replica of Laporte, but in tattered skirts and bare feet, wreaking havoc on the Key.

As Angela entered the sitting room Amy hurriedly slipped the baby clothes into her work basket and pretended to examine a torn ruffle on one of Lorna's dresses.

"I'm going to have it today," Angela said as calmly as if she was announcing dinner. What a relief it would be to have her body to herself again, to be rid of the kicking squirming thing that inhabited her.

"When did the pains start?"

"They haven't. But I know it will be today."

Amy didn't argue with her. She knew a woman could instinctively tell when the time was right.

"Lord, I'd love to go horseback riding!"

Amy laughed, she had gone riding up to about a month ago. But by now nothing Angela did shocked her or the islanders. They were used to her self-willed ways and were disappointed when she didn't act eccentric.

Amy got to her feet. "I will get things ready."

Angela went out to the porch and leaned against the railing half sitting on it. She could hear the children playing with Jack. It was almost beyond belief that it was December. Flowers bloomed, birds sang, and the breeze off the ocean was warm. It was more like an English summer. She would have to get used to strange climates because where she was going the seasons were upside down. She wondered how long they would remain in Australia after she and Scott were reunited again.

With a deep sigh she wished they were all sitting by a cozy fire in Seafield Castle with a blizzard howling outside. She had been ecstatically happy there—for a shorter period of time than she cared to remember. It seemed as if she had been unhappy the major part of the last eight years, with only a few brief respites.

A pain gripped her and Angela waited silently for it to pass. It was unusually strong for the first one. When it was over she started upstairs, but another pain caught her halfway up and she sat down on a step panting from the exertion. Sweat broke out on her forehead and there was a sudden gush of water soaking her skirt.

This baby was waiting for no one and was anxious to make an appearance! She made it to the open door of her room and saw Amy turning down the bed. She must have gasped because Amy turned, taking in the situation with a glance. She helped Angela into a nightgown and into bed, then called for the servants.

Always before it had taken long grueling hours, days of hard labor to produce her precious children. But less than four hours later as the winter sun plunged into the sea, the baby was born. Amy received the wet, slippery girl into her hands and it cried lustily for a minute then slipped its tiny thumb into a puckered mouth and was quiet.

When the baby was clean and wrapped in a blanket she brought it over to the bed but Angela thrust her hand out. "No! I don't want to see it or hold it! Get her out of my sight!"

"But—but—" stammered Amy. She had hoped that Angela would relent in her harsh attitude once the baby was a reality. "You are her mother. How will she survive if you don't feed her?"

"I don't know and don't care!" she screamed angrily. "Weight it down with stones and throw it into the ocean—give it to the witch—keep it yourself! I don't give a damn what you do with the little monster. Just keep it out of my sight!"

Amy took the baby out of the room. Jack was standing in the hall. "Did you hear?"

"Yes," he said inspecting the small bundle critically. "It is so tiny. Is it all right?"

"Perfect. Now all we have to do is get her mother to accept her. Poor little girl," she crooned, rocking her in her arms.

Angela was tired but felt fine. The doctor had been wrong, this had been the easiest birth yet, and the shortest. She opened her eyes as Jack came into the room, walking quietly in case she was sleeping.

He hid a smile at the sudden stubborn tilt of her chin and the determined set of her mouth. She was expecting an argument about the child but he disappointed her.

"I'm glad you're all right, little one." He sat on the edge of the bed smiling down at her. His gray eyes were sympathetic. "I worry about you, Angela. You are so headstrong and soon you will be sailing off again for parts unknown. You will be careful?"

"Yes," she sighed, her eyes half hidden by her lowered lashes. "What else could happen?"

"With you—anything! You make a very poor houseguest." That brought a smile to her face. "Poor Amy—you have scared her out of her wits several times and she has always been the calm type."

"She will be glad when I go. Your lives will be uncomplicated again."

"Yes, but some complications add spice to life. I will miss you, and the children." He brushed a quick kiss against her forehead. "But we won't talk of partings yet. You are tired. Sleep."

Amy dipped a clean twist of cloth into a bowl of warm milk and inserted it into the baby's open, birdlike mouth. She sucked greedily and then waited patiently as Amy repeated the process. It was as if the child knew the extraordinary efforts Amy was using to keep her alive.

She fed her every few hours, hoping that the baby was getting enough to eat. She rarely cried and at first Amy thought she might be weakly but she was vigorous enough. Her wide blue eyes drank in the small world around her with intense interest.

It had been two days and Angela still refused to see the baby. Amy had coaxed her, tried to reason with her and at last resorted to shouting at her, all to no avail. And she was off gallivanting all over the island on her black horse, declaring she had never felt better and wanted to regain her figure.

Jack had scoured the island to find a nursing mother

to wet-nurse the baby but couldn't. There was one pregnant woman but she wasn't due for another month, and Amy wondered if she could keep the child alive that long.

She was exhausted by her vigil with the baby, unable to comprehend how any mother could reject her own flesh and blood no matter who the father was. The motion between the bowl and the mouth was repeated mechanically. Angela was dooming the child to death. Heaven knew she had tried her best already, even before its birth.

Jack entered the room, his face set in grim lines. "I did it, talked to her but she won't give in." He eased himself into a chair and watched his wife with the infant in her arms. She was growing attached to it already he could tell. For that matter so was he. "She won't even see her for just a minute."

"I'm going to keep her!" Amy said vehemently, daring Jack to contradict her. "Somehow I am going to keep her alive until Mrs. Fitzpatrick has her baby."

"Here," said Jack reaching out his arms, "let me feed our new daughter. You're the one that is likely to die of exhaustion before this is over. Go lie down and get some sleep."

Amy didn't argue with him. A smile lit up her face at his usual loving concern and she put the baby in his arms. Jack began feeding her, imitating Amy but clumsily. She stood there watching them. Against his immense bulk the baby looked tinier than ever. She dropped a kiss on his whiskered cheek and one on the incredibly soft skin of the infant's forehead and went to bed.

Jack was one in a million! How many other men would have put up with such a situation, and patiently at that? As she drifted off to sleep Amy heard the quiet sounds of the baby sucking on the cloth and Jack talking softly to her, urging her to eat. It was music to her ears.

When Angela got back from her ride the house was oddly quiet. Ezra was giving the children their lessons in the library and the door to Jack and Amy's room was closed. She knew the baby was in there, she had heard it crying last night and now hurried by.

It was better not to think about it; let time erase the memory. She felt wonderfully free and young since the birth, full of vitality. The only reminder of the child was the milk swelling in her breasts. But she bound them tightly with a strip of cloth and hoped it would dry up soon. It was very inconvenient, but that too would pass.

The ride had cleared her head of all the hurtful angry words that she had flung at Jack. She had known that eventually Amy would talk him into confronting her. But nothing either of them said, or could say, made her want to see the baby. She didn't feel like its mother and the fact that she had abandoned it didn't bother her at all. Let Amy and Jack raise her, she would have a good life with them—much better than if she was brought up by a mother that hated the sight of her.

The only problem was that Lorna was absolutely entranced by her baby sister. How could she ever understand why they must leave her behind when they set out on their search again? She would try and explain it to her daughter and if she still didn't understand would just have to leave it at that. There was only so much a seven-year-old could absorb no matter how smart.

It would be good to be at sea again on a quest that was spanning years. The interminable delays only made her anxious to be gone soon. Angela had decided to buy a ship and inquiries were already being made in Havana by the agents Jack had commissioned. Any day now they would receive word that a ship was available. Just the thought set her heart leaping with excitement.

The thought of Scott's mouth on hers of lying in his bed and joining with a wild frenzy made Angela dizzy. It was three years since his transportation and no man had pleasured her since. True, there had been a few blissfully forgetful moments in Jack's arms but that had led to a dead end. Their love affair was over once and for all. The times with Keith and Laporte were better obliterated.

But how could she force herself to forget the two men that she had killed? The Old Lady was right—Angela was a disaster to men. Thurston Vaughn, Owen's brother, the richest most powerful man in Britain, had committed suicide because he couldn't have her, and because he had lost everything to her: estates, money, even his title on the turn of a card. He had calmly and efficiently slit his wrists in his gold-plated tub and bled to death in style, sipping brandy.

Then Keith. She closed her eyes with a spasm of pain. Keith Montgomery, Jane's brother; her friend and protector and knight in shining armor; her golden lover, her husband. But what a price he had paid to make Angela his wife—conspiring with Captain Latham to have Scott arrested and transported, deceiving the whole world into believing Scott had died of cholera aboard the *Columbine* on his way to Australia so she would be free to marry him. And marry him she did, only to regret it immediately, for no man could ever replace Scott.

What a murderous rage she had felt when she found out the truth! The hoax, her own bigamy, the agony Keith had subjected Scott to, not to mention herself and the children. Beyond stopping herself Angela had challenged Keith to a duel and shot him in cold blood. He hadn't even made a pretense of defending himself—wouldn't raise a pistol against her, the woman he loved. He had deliberately forced her hand, knowing he could never live without her, knowing she would leave him for Scott.

Why not think on more pleasant things? Going to her jewelry box Angela quickly found the golden locket and opened it, gazing lovingly at Scott's image smiling up at her with a rakish charm. His eyes were warm and brown, and the golden specks dancing in them seemed alive with love for her. Every well-remembered line of his face beguiled her: the firm jaw and cleft chin; the sensual lips that could cause such havoc when pressed to hers; the straight classical nose; the wavy bronze hair that she loved to run her fingers through. If only he was here right now to make her dreams a wonderful, shattering reality!

But he wasn't, and when her eyes shifted to the other side of the locket and saw the miniature of the *Dark Lady,* Angela was instantly depressed again. The ship was now a wreck at the bottom of the ocean. It had all been Laporte's doing, that and so much else.

With a click Angela snapped shut the small heart and lay down on the bed grasping it tightly in her hand. She was tired. Perhaps she had been overdoing it so soon after the baby's birth. As she drifted toward sleep she vowed to remove the painting of the *Dark Lady* and have it replaced with a miniature of Robert and Lorna. Bad memories could be destroyed. Only the good would be allowed to remain.

A baby was crying. The crying stopped abruptly and Angela struggled into a sitting position. She had been lying on her stomach and the front of her nightgown was wet with milk. Her breasts were swollen to the bursting point and even the delicate cloth clinging to them made them hurt unbearably.

Taking off the nightgown Angela poured tepid water into a basin and washed the stickiness from her throbbing bosom. She moaned as the damp cloth touched her fevered flesh. Her pain was Laporte's doing, her torment of flesh and spirit, his fault. The grimacing smile rose before her eyes and his harsh choking laughter filled her ears. "No, go away!" she cried closing her eyes, putting her hands over her ears. Would she never be rid of his memory, his ghost? Would he haunt her all her living days?

Rage and despair welled up in her and Angela felt like striking out at him—but how? He was dead yet his memory taunted her. His child slept in a room just down the hall.

Pulling on a clean nightgown she found herself gliding silently toward Jack and Amy's room. The door was partly open and as her fingertips found the tangible reality of carved wood it swung inward, soundlessly on well-oiled hinges.

The two shapes on the bed slept the sleep of exhaustion unaware of the invasion of their privacy. Amy's golden head rested on Jack's shoulder and she stirred, moving closer to the solid comfort of his body. Though even in sleep her ears were tuned to the needs of the infant not far away, Angela's movements were as silent as a shadow flitting across the floor.

The cradle was lit by a spill of moonbeams like a beacon drawing Angela on. She looked into the recesses of the cradle and the silent baby looked back at her, its wide round eyes disconcertingly serene. With a swift movement Angela drew the blanket over the baby's face. She couldn't stand to see the creature but she could still discern its movement beneath the blanket. If only it would be still!

She picked it up and it curled warmly against her shoulder as if it belonged there. With a jerk Angela pulled the soft bundle from her body and held it in both hands in front of her. That was better. The other more intimate contact had been too disturbing.

The baby squirmed, encased in the blanket, and Angela wondered if it would smother beneath the folds. To be rid of this reminder of Laporte's degradation would be the ultimate relief.

Amy stirred and she slipped silently from the room, down the stairs on cat-quiet feet with a dark purpose forming in the back of her mind. The swift, merciless sea was the solution to her problem. The Gulf Stream was notorious for seldom giving up its dead. Once the deed was done they could all wonder to no avail what had become of the child.

The sand was soft and warm beneath Angela's bare feet and she laughed at the specter following her. How fitting that a pirate's daughter should return to the sea. She could follow in her father's footsteps—and he was dead!

The rolling moonlit waves rushed forward swirling around her ankles, wetting the bottom of her nightgown. A bird cried shrilly in the shadows and the baby still moved in her outstretched hands. It was so small and warm, emitting no sound as if resigned to whatever fate had in store for her.

She should have removed the nightgown. It clung and made her stumble as it wrapped tenaciously around her legs. Even though the infant couldn't have weighed more than seven pounds the strain of carrying it in such an unnatural position pulled at Angela's arms. Slowly she lowered the burden until the water lapped at the trailing blanket.

Laporte's harsh laughter was still in her ears as the child began to cry.

Amy's heart bumped painfully against her ribs as she stared open-mouthed at the empty cradle. As if to reinforce the baby's absence she touched the cool embroidered sheets she had spent so many happy hours working on.

"Jack." The whisper didn't even make him stir. "Jack!" He sat bolt upright at her half-strangled scream.

She shook like an autumn leaf in the wind, her trembling lips moving soundlessly now that she had his attention. Amy pointed wordlessly to the vacant cradle, thinking the worst, knowing something dreadful had happened.

Jack swore softly as he came to stand by her side. He slipped his arm about her waist and she buried her head against his shoulder, saying pathetically, "She's gone and I wanted her. Angela hated her, couldn't even stand the sight of her own baby. What do you think she has done to her?"

"Calm down, Amy. Let's find out what has happened before you go to pieces."

With one accord they rushed to Angela's room only to find it empty, and Amy was sure she would never see the baby again. The whole household was aroused and a frantic and fruitless search of the house and grounds ensued.

"We must search the island," Ezra declared, visibly upset. After all he, more than anyone, knew the depths of Angela's hatred for Laporte and the child he had forced upon her. "She has to be somewhere and it shouldn't take that long to find her. Maybe she went to see the Old Lady."

"But Neptune is still in the shed. . . ." began Amy.

"Well dammit she has to be somewhere! She can't just have disappeared off the face of the earth!" Jack turned to Ezra. "Get some men together and go to the Old Lady's. Spread out and search that section of the island thoroughly. I'll take the other half of the key."

In the brightening light of dawn everyone scattered, each in a different direction and each with his own fears as to what he would find. Amy remained behind with the children, impotent to help, wishing she could have at least accompanied Jack. But he would search more efficiently without her along.

Dawn split the sky with golden rays driving black thunderheads before it. The storm skirted the key and headed out to sea leaving behind a clear azure sky lightening with yellow and amethyst waves. The sea reflected the heavens and was reflected back by the strange rolling clouds until each was indistinguishable from the other. The curved horizon melted softly beneath the warming rays of the sun.

Daybreak always brought a comforting reaffirmation to Angela, and this morning she felt a rebirth of her old spirit and a compassion that had been dormant for some time. The tiny rosebud mouth closed around her nipple and tugged gently, spreading a feeling of tranquility and acceptance through her whole body. With a slight smile playing at the corners of her mouth she touched the plump pink and white dimpled fist kneading her breast.

At the last moment she had been unable to go through with it. That awful moment when Scott had plunged her beneath the waves had flashed before her with such electrifying brilliance she had frozen where she was. How long she stood there with the waves lapping around her knees she couldn't remember. But her feet led her back up the beach and in the bright moonlight she had undressed the baby and examined it minutely for any defect.

She was perfect with her guileless blue eyes and a surprisingly thick thatch of hair the color of cornsilk. Her sturdy little limbs had flailed protestingly until unable to resist the inevitable, Angela had begun suckling the hungry baby.

There was nothing about the infant that reminded her of Laporte, in fact there was such a striking resemblance to her own mother that Angela had been dumbfounded. The eyes, the hair, the tiny features, usually indistinguishable in such a new creation, were a mirror image of Clarissa. That, more than anything else, had decided Angela.

"Poor little girl," Angela crooned rocking her gently, watching the eyes close. "Everyone wanted you but me—your own mother! I'm afraid we must make the best of it now, you and I. But you will help me, won't you? And I will try and love you, try to make up for everything that went before."

Good lord, she thought removing the sleeping child from her breast and covering herself, how would she ever explain her existence to Scott? Then Angela's chin lifted defiantly and her eyes glared out to sea. Whatever the future held, she would worry about it then and there. There was no use causing herself anxiety now over some problem that might never occur.

The beach began stirring with life and the eagle-eyed fishermen spotted her sitting against a palm tree with a tiny bundle in her arms. They approached cautiously but only a few eyebrows were raised at the fact that she was only wearing a nightgown. If the duchess preferred a morning walk in her nightgown who were they to say it was strange? Perhaps it was the style now in faraway London where the chemise dresses left little to the imagination.

Carlos, a short lithe Cuban, reached her first and he smiled broadly, his sun-darkened face splitting into a hundred wrinkles. He sank down on the hot sand to her level, just a few feet away and the others soon joined him. There was silence in the thronged circle of sea-roughened men but their eyes held a faraway delight reminiscent of better times and other lands.

With a dimpled smile of pride Angela showed them the sleeping fairy-child that nestled so naturally against her. The sun glinted on the fair hair and the wistful fishermen gazed in wonder, unable to tear their eyes away. They were complete opposites, this lady of the darkness and her child of the dawning. But the fishermen knew they belonged together as surely as day follows night.

Ezra found her on the beach, a queen holding court before the stunned silent homage of her dazzled subjects.

PART TWO

Forgotten Yesterdays

New South Wales

1811-1812

Divorce me, untie, or break that knot again;
Take me to you, imprison me, for I,
Except you enthrall me, never shall be free,
Nor ever chaste except you ravish me.

—John Donne

four

After the endless vistas of countless oceans the huge headlands guarding the entrance to Port Jackson seemed about to tumble in on the *Cygnet*. The deep channel of dancing blue water cut a mile wide swath of grandeur between the headlands to their final destination, Sydney Cove. They were all assembled on the deck—Ezra, Lorna, and Robert, and Clare was clasped tightly in Angela's arms. She was a year old, her curls as pale as freshly churned butter shining yellow-gold in the bright sunlight. With unperturbed acceptance she observed the alien shore with her quiet all-encompassing gaze. Ezra took her from Angela keeping a sharp eye on the two mischief makers, as he called them.

The inlet swallowed them up and Angela leaned on the railing straining for a glimpse of civilization. The sharp, pungent scent of eucalyptus trees vied with the familiar smell of the sea. And on the horizon, blurred with strange gray-green vegetation, she made out a jumble of buildings carved from a wilderness.

How different it must have looked to other eyes when the First Fleet arrived in 1788. Landfall had actually been Botany Bay six miles to the south, but the glowing report of Captain Cook was not realized. Instead they found a port wide open to the sea with no protection for the ships. The fresh water had been too scanty for their needs and the swamps, sand dunes, scrub, and low-lying land were definitely inhospitable.

After a brief exploration, Captain Arthur Phillips had moved the colony to its present site at Sydney Cove. There they had water, stone, and timber with which to hack for themselves a niche in a world that had rejected them as the flotsam of society. It had been a struggle against all odds.

In spite of the desolation and feeling of utter isolation there was a harsh, exotic beauty to the land. Angela, who had seen so many strange places, caught her breath at the wooded coast, the inlets and bays that poked deep blue fingers into the primeval land and the peninsulas jutting boldly into the port. Fine sandy beaches spread like white blankets at the foot of the cliffs and promontories, and the surf crashed as they passed.

Then they glided into Sydney Cove and her eyes were full of the meandering, ramshackle town held in a close embrace by the arms of the bay. It was a rough unbeautiful place, houses hastily thrown together for shelter and nothing more. But as Angela's eyes swept the shore she picked out a handful of simple gracious dwellings holding their own with the squalor of the rest of the colony.

It's a penal colony, she reminded herself, made up mostly of convicts. But it didn't matter what the place looked like because Scott was there! The culmination of all her dreams lay somewhere on this largely unexplored continent so far from home.

She touched Ezra's arm and he turned his gaze from the new land to her shining eyes. Without a word between them he knew exactly what she was feeling, the exaltation and overwhelming joy of a journey accomplished, a search almost at its end. He smiled, sharing the moment with the intimacy of long acquaintance and the full knowledge of all the odds overcome to bring her plans to fruition.

"It won't be long now," he said noting her determined, undaunted air. "When you sweep into New

South Wales like a gale no barriers will be able to stand. I predict your husband will be found within a fortnight."

"What, are you a gypsy fortuneteller too?" she laughed. "As long as I find him safe and unharmed I don't care if it takes another year."

Angela's hand tightened on his arm and they both looked back at Sydney. There was a nervous flutter in her stomach. Almost a year after her decision to keep Clare there was still a nagging doubt in the back of her mind. All the incidents from her past that she would rather keep secret from Scott would now have to be aired—and soon!

She had gone over imagined conversations a thousand different times and ways in her mind and still didn't know how she could tell him. What to say, when to say it. Her speculations always ended in a jumble, with Scott angry and hurt and somehow enraged with her.

It wasn't that she hadn't accepted Clare; she had. In fact guiltily she showered her youngest daughter with extra affection trying to make up for the hatred she had felt at first and all those attempts to get rid of the baby before and after her birth. And the child was a delight in every way, growing more like her namesake, Angela's mother, with each passing day.

So, that was her only reservation about their meeting, the hurt that would have to be breached before they could get on with their lives and their loving. The very thought of Scott's lovemaking made her knees so weak that Angela leaned on Ezra for support and she silently scolded herself for letting her daydreaming interfere with the more important matters at hand.

The first place Angela went when she stepped on dry ground was up the hill to Government House. It was a white, crumbling, two-story residence that had seen better days. The setting though was tranquil, with lovely gardens and a grand view of Sydney Cove.

Governor Lachlan Macquarie's secretary was flustered by her appearance and after seating her he rushed off like a nervous old maid to inquire if the governor could see her. Angela smiled to herself and confidently smoothed her white muslin dress embroidered in red. The gold locket rested against the swell of her breasts containing the miniature of Scott that might prove invaluable in her search. And in her reticule was the pardon, slightly worse for wear, but still the most important thing she had brought on her journey. With it she held the key to Scott's freedom.

She was glad the governor was in residence for he frequently toured the countryside with a nabob's camp equipage that cost over £551 and had earned him a stern reproof from Whitehall. But when in Sydney he was a hard-working man that kept regular office hours and liked to make himself available to the people.

In just the few hours she had been in New South Wales Angela had picked up an amazing amount of information all of which she took with a grain of salt. Cut off from the world the colony was gossip starved and any juicy tidbit of information was thoroughly masticated and digested before being passed on. So any fresh tales from England were as welcome as a ship full of gold and any new ears to pour their stories into would keep the ladies of the town in ecstasy for weeks.

The secretary hurried back and with much bowing and scraping escorted Angela into the governor's office. The man rose from behind his desk and his eyes were coldly assessing. He obviously hadn't expected anyone like Angela to be a duchess but he kept the surprise from his face, wondering what she was doing in New South Wales and what she wanted of him. A land grant no doubt, that's what most people passed through his office for.

Some malicious gossip he had heard about the Duchess of Brightling buzzed in the back of his mind but Governor Macquarie dismissed it with a smile at the woman sitting before his desk. A woman as beautiful as she was could be excused a few faux pas.

"Now, Your Grace, what can I do for you?"

"I am looking for my husband, Governor Macquarie," explained Angela drawing the papers out of her reticule. "He was transported at the end of 1807."

Governor Macquarie's veneer cracked with surprise and she almost laughed at the incredulous look on his face. But a moment later his distinguished military bearing was back in place and he asked, "Do you mean to tell me that your husband, a duke, is a convict here in New South Wales?"

Angela nodded and handed him the papers. "This should explain partly what happened during that miscarriage of justice that was called a trial. He was convicted of murder by witnesses whom we later found out had been bribed. Considering the fact that they perjured themselves the judge granted my husband a full pardon and has wiped the blot from our name."

The governor read the pardon quickly, the only sound in the room the crackling paper and birds singing in the gardens outside. When he looked up Angela said simply, "Now all I have to do is find him. Can you help me do that?"

Her wide aquamarine eyes with that indefinable air of past sorrows melted his reserve. He couldn't help but admire her and the fact that she had made such a voyage dragging herself and her children halfway around the world. She could have sent agents to do the job.

"Lady Harrington," he replied getting to his feet. "I will do everything within my power to help you."

He looked through the files himself searching for the name Scott Harrington. Over an hour later he shook his head dejectedly and Angela's heart sank. It was going to be harder than she had expected at first but she should have anticipated that. After all nothing had been going right for the past four years—why should it be easy now?

"There is no record of him, but don't lose hope. Your husband must have arrived in 1808 and Governor Bligh was in charge here then. Things were very disorganized—what with all the graft and corruption among the officers. You must have heard of the Rum Corps? A thoroughly bad business culminating in Governor Bligh's arrest.

"Records could easily have been lost; in fact a lot of Bligh's personal things disappeared without a trace. Sometimes too, no records at all were sent on the convict ships. There was no way of knowing a convict's name or the sentence the courts had handed down. It was left to the discretion of the governor as to how long each man or woman would serve."

"Then there is a chance that he arrived and is here—somewhere. . . ." she choked on the last word, her worst fears looming before her.

When Keith had tricked her into believing Scott dead he had used a plausible enough story since many of the convicts died en route to the penal colony. What if the sham had been true after all unknown to Keith and Scott really had died on board the ship, never reaching this land? Frantically Angela pushed aside the thought. She couldn't go to pieces in front of Governor Macquarie. Her search couldn't end so abruptly.

"Please, Lady Harrington, don't distress yourself. If your husband is here I assure you we will find him. Perhaps he assumed another name," he suggested soothingly. "Without records many convicts did that hoping to spare their families' names."

Governor Macquarie went to the door and called his secretary. "Have tea sent in. And send for Captain Macdonald. I want him here within the hour!"

The governor further allayed Angela's fears over an excellent tea which she choked down for his benefit. He told her about the colony and some of its history and his plans for future growth. Already since his arrival in 1809 the colony was vastly improved.

He had broken the power of the Rum Corps, the officers of which had drawn their army pay while engaging in their own business ventures. They had been granted huge parcels of land and used their time farming and lining their own pockets, seemingly safe under cover of the vast distance from home and England's preoccupation with the French war.

From their position of authority they monopolized trade setting prices and robbing the government, prisoners, and small holders. Rum was the means of exchange, for with it they could acquire anything: convict labor, land grants, houses, luxuries from home. Rum was used like money, and though it was illicit they were so powerful who could stop them?

So they broke every rule of their service and every law of the land, making themselves rich in the process. When Governor Macquarie arrived he brought his own regiment with him, the Seventy-third Highlanders, and had the 102nd Regiment of the Line alias the Rum Corps recalled to England.

Now under his benevolent dictatorship the colony flourished. Licensed public houses in Sydney were reduced from seventy-five to twenty. He widened the streets and forbade the erection of temporary buildings. New buildings went up: a granary, barracks for one thousand soldiers, a market near Cockle Bay—and there were grand plans for a future hospital and church. The Parramatta Road was repaired and the stumps removed, and he advocated morality by encouraging marriage and pardoning convict women who found respectable husbands.

"There will be no problem finding your husband, Lady Harrington. After all we are a small colony. Our perimeters are limited to the area approximately fifty miles around Sydney. After that the bush and the Blue Mountains take over and no white man has made it past there. So you see, with some time and patience he is sure to be found."

Angela smiled, relieved by his optimistic outlook but he hadn't told her about the outpost settlements. Let her start with Sydney, Parramatta, and the Hawkesbury areas first. Then she could search Brisbane, Newcastle, Norfolk Island, and Van Diemen's Land where the most vicious scum of all were sent.

"I'm going to assign Captain Macdonald the task of helping you find your husband. He knows the area and many of the settlers from here to the mountains. Then you will need to find a place to stay and servants. I'll assign you as many convicts as you need and Macdonald can see to all the details. Yes, he's your man to get things done."

"Governor Macquarie," Angela said bemusing him momentarily with her most dazzling smile. "I'm forever in your debt. I can't thank you enough for your help. . . ." A knock on the door interrupted her, and the governor barked an order to enter.

Captain Macdonald hesitated, stifling a yawn with one hand on the doorknob. He had been in this godforsaken place for two full years now and cursed the impulse that had made him join the Seventy-third Highlanders. But who would have thought at that time that the regiment would be posted to Sydney?

Sick to death of the monotonous rounds in London, the endless partying, gambling, and debaucheries he had joined the regiment for a diversion. Besides, all his riotous living in London hadn't been able to blot out the terrible void of his lost love. No other woman had even come close to filling that gap.

He had gone from one extreme to the other; from excesses in London to burying himself in his moldering old castle in Scotland for months at a time. The fact that the woman he loved was married to another man who treated her badly didn't help matters any.

Now he was the one moldering away in New South Wales, a scruffy dumping ground for felons. But lately his interest had been picking up in the things around him. He had received a land grant on the Hawkesbury River and was fascinated by the speculations of what lay beyond the Blue Mountains. Men were predicting land of untold fertility and he was itching to be part of an expedition.

Imagine being the first white man to cross the mountains and see what no one but the aborigines had laid eyes on before. It had been tried several times before but no way could be found past the barrier of the mountains. But he had a new theory that they should follow the ridges instead of the valleys, and had proposed it to the governor. His blood coursed faster—maybe the summons was good news. Could an expedition have been formed?

Captain Macdonald burst into the room with boyish enthusiasm, his sun-bleached sandy hair falling across his forehead. The woman in the chair glanced up at him and he paled visibly beneath his dark tan, petrified into speechlessness.

"Clyde!" Angela cried rising gracefully and rushing at him. Somehow both of her hands were in his and her warm smile was melting away the shock that froze him. "Clyde Macdonald! Of all the people to meet at the end of the world! I'm so glad to see you again, although our parting was rather—abrupt!"

There was a mischievous gleam in her eyes reminding them both of their last meeting and his ignoble departure. Being booted in the seat of his pants down a long flight of stone stairs by her husband was definitely not an impression he had relished leaving her with. But considering the towering rage Lord Harrington had been in, the faster his exit, the better.

He filled his eyes with her, sure the mirage would waver and vanish. But this was no illusion and she squeezed his hands and he couldn't help but respond to her silvery laughter. He smiled in bewilderment and lines crinkled at the corners of his boyish green eyes.

"Angela! Angela! I never thought I would see you again. And to meet you here of all places—why here?"

The governor cleared his throat and brought the young officer back to reality. He had completely forgotten the summons, where he was, and the fact that Macquarie was in the background watching the whole scene. Dropping Angela's hands Clyde saluted smartly and the governor hid his smile.

Things were becoming quite interesting, Macquarie thought, and all in the matter of a few hours. The fact that they were acquainted was astounding and to break the awkward silence he said, "Obviously introductions are unnecessary."

"You must forgive us, Governor, but Clyde and I are old friends," explained Angela taking a seat again. "We were neighbors in Scotland. Why our castles were separated only by a small stretch of water and some mountains, which in the Highlands is like living on each other's doorsteps."

Clyde listened with a perplexed frown as Governor Macquarie explained his assignment. It was all as clear as mud with only the sketchiest of explanations. "If Lady Harrington wishes she can fill in more of the details but I will leave that to her discretion."

Lachlan Macquarie fixed him with a stern look. "Of course, everything said here today is in the strictest confidence, Captain Macdonald, and does not bear repeating. I will expect a full report from you once a fortnight as to your progress."

As Angela left the office on Clyde's arm she was cheered immensely. To find a friend when she had expected none and to have acquired the full cooperation of the governor made her sure her quest would end soon and successfully. On the carriage ride back to the *Cygnet* she filled in the details of her life during the five-year interval since she and Clyde had last met. Not all the details by any means, but just enough so that the puzzled look left his eyes.

As the sun shone down on them in the open carriage she marveled that he had grown from an average looking boy into a handsome man. Perhaps it was the sun-darkened face and the red and white uniform with the dully glinting gold braid, or could it be his confident military bearing? Well neither one of them was the same as they had been but one thing was the same; he couldn't hide the open admiration in his eyes or the fact that he was still wildly infatuated with her.

Within a week Angela was settled in a small but charming red brick house overlooking Cockle Bay. It was on the outskirts of town away from all the noise, squalor, and hustle and bustle. The bush pressed in very close to them and she liked that. It was more like living in the country and she caught occasional glimpses of exotic birds—parakeets and cockatoos—flashing brightly against the dull gray-green of the gum trees.

The house had only one floor with three bedrooms, a dining room, a sitting room, and a lean-to kitchen. But there was a stable out back large enough for four horses and the green hill they occupied was laid out like a well-ordered English garden. The rent was outrageous but then the price of everything here was wildly inflated.

Clyde had been instrumental in finding the house and the two horses that now resided in the stable. He insisted she use his carriage until one could be found for her and after all his activities of getting her situated he spent his evenings tirelessly seeking out convicts wherever they were and searching their faces. Lachlan Macquarie had been right, he was efficent and to Angela indispensable. She was relying on him more and more with each passing day.

It had rained, just enough to wet down the streets so that the dust didn't take to the air covering everything. Now it was very hot and the sun beat down mercilessly on the lush garden of English flowers that seemed so incongruously out of place in such an exotic land.

Angela stood beneath a wattle tree heavily weighed down with golden blooms, taking advantage of its shade. For the past three mornings at exactly ten o'clock the same bedraggled procession had made its way up the hill and into her garden, for as of today no proper servants had been found. She wrinkled her nose in disgust as Clyde herded a group of smelly, filthy convict women through the gate.

Would she never find even two suitable servants? She had the pick of all the unemployed convicts in the colony but couldn't bring herself to choose one of those sluttish, evil-looking creatures to entrust with the care of the house to say nothing of the children. With a soft sigh she watched as Clyde lined them up for her inspection.

They all looked alike: their hair lank and greasy the color of mud, their bodies covered indecently with rags, the dirt so ingrained into their skin that it was gray. Only their shapes and eyes were different and the eyes were those of dangerous caged beasts filled with hate or sly boldness.

Angela tried to hold her breath against the foul odor as she walked slowly down the straggling line. She didn't get too close for they were alive with lice and after the first day she knew why Clyde had insisted on bringing them no farther than the garden.

She was almost at the end of the line, utterly depressed, thinking of Scott in the same condition. What if she had passed him by without recognizing him? It was quite possible when humans were reduced to a degrading sameness. Had he been shackled to one of those repulsive chain gangs she had seen being driven like cattle through the city? Surely she would know if she passed that close to him—her heart would signal her, he would call out her name or she would recognize those golden-brown eyes that haunted her dreams.

The two grotesque scarecrows at the very end of the line clung together as closely as Siamese twins with their heads bowed staring at the grass. They were much younger than the others.

"Your name?" inquired Angela of the taller of the two.

"Kate Murray, milady," she said with a thick brogue and a little bob of a curtsy that made the girl she was clinging to dip too. She looked up with wide gray eyes filled with despair and a certain resignation.

"How old are you, Kate?" asked Angela, her interest sparked by a dim flicker of impudence in her eyes.

"Nineteen, milady, and my sister Maggie is seventeen," she said with a quick glance at the smaller girl she held onto.

"Can you cook and sew? Have you ever looked after children?"

"Oh, yes! I'm the oldest and there are thirteen little ones in me family. Both of us can cook and sew, plant potatoes, shear sheep, spin wool, weave. . . ."

"How long is your sentence?"

"Seven years—for the both of us, milady."

"And the crime?"

"Why for the crime of being Irish!"

"Don't be impertinent!" snapped Clyde slapping his riding whip threateningly against a shiny black boot.

" 'Tis the truth, sir!" she looked appealingly at

Angela. "I swear on all the holy saints, milady. Me Da was hidin' guns in the loft and the soldiers came and burned down the house. They shot me Da in the field and carted us all off." Tears traced grimy rivers down her cheeks. "We were all separated except Maggie and me and us not knowin' what's become of the rest!

"Seven years, the judge said, though we told himself we didn't know our Da had the guns."

Maggie was crying now too, silently with just the shaking of her thin body as proof of her distress. They looked like two abandoned kittens clinging together for safety in the midst of a storm. Somehow Angela knew Kate was telling the truth and her heart went out to them. How many more tragedies would send innocents like Kate and Maggie to their doom?

"I'll take these two," she told Clyde. "But how will I ever get them clean?"

"I suppose they are probably the best you will find, Angela. But don't be taken in by their story. Every convict here is innocent—according to their version." He gave her a wry smile. "Can you manage them while I get the rest of these sluts back?"

"Of course I can, Clyde," Angela laughed. "You don't know me very well—I can handle anything!"

He gave her a piercing look. "Someday you just might come up against a situation that you won't be able to handle!" But she kept laughing and waved him off, turning her attention back to the two Murrays baking in the sun.

"You, my girls, are going to have a bath." Kate smiled at her nodding in agreement. "Ezra!" she called walking toward the house. "Ezra!"

He came through the back door ducking so he wouldn't bump his head. "Look what I have found," she said turning toward the girls just in time to see Kate cross herself several times as she stared in horror at Ezra. "Two servants fresh from Ireland. . . ."

"I'd hardly say fresh," commented Ezra as he got a little closer and caught a whiff of them.

"You didn't smell like a rose yourself when I found

you,'' she admonished with mock severity, behind which lurked a smile.

Ezra brought a big tin tub out into the garden and strung ropes between several trees from which he hung blankets to provide a secluded outdoor bathroom for the girls to bathe. They watched him with fear, for neither of them had ever seen a Negro before. When his amber eyes glanced their way Kate's lips moved as if she was praying for deliverance under her breath.

Under Angela's watchful gaze they bathed and washed their hair with strong lye soap. She made them repeat the process several times, rinsing their hair with strong disinfectant while Ezra burned their clothes. When they were finally clean and she was properly satisfied the vermin were gone she stood back and surveyed her handiwork.

They were both utterly transformed and Angela noted with surprise what wonders could be accomplished with soap and water. Kate's hair was a fiery red and her short nose was generously peppered with golden freckles—not a pretty girl by any stretch of the imagination, but once she gained a little weight men wouldn't find her unattractive. Maggie had brown hair and enormous brown eyes that eclipsed her pointed little face. So far she hadn't spoken one word even when Angela questioned her.

''She doesn't talk,'' Kate informed her, ''not a word from her lips since. . . .'' Her sentence dangled in the hot summer air.

''Since what?''

''Since the jail,'' Kate answered almost too quickly. ''Terrible it was!''

Angela had a feeling she wasn't being told the whole truth about Maggie's muteness, but wasn't even a convict entitled to privacy? So instead of prying she spent part of the afternoon showing them what their duties would be. And when they met the children Maggie showed a spark of interest as Clare crawled over to her and hauled herself erect on her skirts. With a shy, fearful glance at her new mistress Maggie tentatively touched a golden curl on the baby's head and when Angela nodded she bent and scooped her up burying her face against Clare's soft shoulder.

Clare smelled delightfully of powder and milk and Maggie breathed in the familiar baby scent with a remembered longing. Clare laughed and tugged at her thick hair and when the small Irish girl raised her head there was almost a smile on her lips. Angela's youngest had made another conquest as she was wont to do with speedy ease, and tears of joy trembled on the brink of overflow in Maggie's big brown eyes.

With the household in order after the Murrays settled into the daily routine Angela, Clyde, and Ezra began a systematic search of the town. Block by block they scoured the homes, warehouses, stores, lumberyards, and brickworks for Scott. They questioned the people employing convicts and scanned a thousand different faces.

The felons of the colony fell into many different categories. They were clerks, overseers, servants, and gardeners. They built roads and houses and ran farms, ranches and businesses for absentee landowners. Tracking down one anonymous man was like looking for a needle in a haystack. So during the daylight hours they continued their quest and Angela spent the early mornings and evenings with the children. Respectable people didn't venture outdoors at night but locked themselves into their houses behind heavy bolted doors. The crooked dusty streets weren't safe at night with so many ex-murderers, thieves, and felons lurking everywhere. Only on very special occasions did the privileged venture forth at night and then it was en masse for there was safety in numbers.

But as the days went by Angela discovered that Sydney wasn't as grim as first glance would have it. There was gaiety and color to be found also. In just the short time since Governor Macquarie's arrival he had improved things immensely. Elegant houses of brick and stone were replacing the mud and daub houses originally thrown up. Hyde Park had been laid out containing a racecourse, but it bore no resemblance to its London namesake. There ladies and gentlemen could walk or ride, picnic or listen to the band that played till dusk.

Dinner and card parties abounded, always ending before sundown which came with a swift finality like a candle being blown out in a dark room. And on fine days there were excursions to Watson's Bay or boating on the harbor with the ladies dressed in out-of-date finery and the soldiers colorful in their uniforms. On the whole it was very provincial but Sydney was fast growing up, considering the colony was only twenty-three years old.

The warm summer evening of December 31, 1811 was one of the few exceptions to the rule of staying home at night. Angela had received a coveted invitation to the dinner party and ball at Government House not long after her arrival in Sydney. It was unthinkable that she not attend because everyone was clamoring for a look at the duchess even though she had met many of them in her daily travels through the town. Besides she was sure to meet many influential landowners who employed hundreds of convicts from as far away as the Hawkesbury and the Cow Pasture's District. One of them might be instrumental in helping her find her lost husband.

Kate helped her dress and when she was finished, turning in front of the mirror for a final inspection all the girl could say was, "Milady! Oh, milady!"

Angela smiled at her bedazzled expression thanked her for helping, then she swept from the room to kiss the children goodnight, leaving a flash of elegance behind her the likes of which the house had never seen before. Clyde was waiting in the sitting room resplendent in his dress uniform stiff with gold braid. His usual, carefully guarded expression dissolved into complete adoration for a moment before the blind came down again.

"You look lovely, Angela," he murmured. "I will be the escort of the most beautiful woman in the colony tonight. Will you save me at least one dance?"

"Of course I will, Clyde." She tossed her glossy black curls adding to the artful disarray that was caught up on top of her head with a green ribbon and allowed to cascade to her shoulders. The palest apricot silk of her dress matched the healthy blush on her cheeks and the emerald green satin ribbons twined around her slim waist brought out the green sparks in her eyes.

Clyde could hardly keep his eyes away from the much revealed bosom that curved enticingly above her décolletage, and the huge dully gleaming emerald nestled in the soft cleft drew his attention like a magnet. Could any jewel have a more perfect setting? So instead he concentrated on the assured smile on her lips and breathed a sigh of momentary relief as he draped a lace shawl over her shoulders and the exciting expanse of bare skin was partly concealed from view.

He was burning for her and as he handed Angela into his carriage Clyde wondered how he would manage to get through the evening without making advances. She's married, he reminded himself a thousand times as they drove through the fragrant evening, but he was sweating beneath the heavy uniform and his breath was as short as a nervous schoolboy in the presence of a beloved goddess.

Under cover of darkness Government House took on an aura of beauty that was dispelled in the harsh daylight. As they waited in the line of carriages Angela noted the sweet scent of orange blossoms. The columns supporting the veranda were twined with vines and beneath the wide overhang were decorations of orange tree branches and many different colorful flowers interspersed with lamps. The rich foliage gave the entrance to the house the desired festive atmosphere.

A huge saffron moon rose over the cove gilding a wavering pathway on the waters. Angela leaned back against the seat and smiled to herself, turning her head to one side. She would never get used to an upside down man in the moon.

Clyde took her gloved hand in his. "Look," he said

with a slight nod of his head. "The first evening star." It was huge and brilliant against the blue-black softness of a cloudless sky.

With his head bent close to hers in the concealing night he whispered in her ear, "You are like that star, Angela—distant and dazzling. When the others appear they are insignificant. Only you outshine the moon, the night." Her fingers curled warmly against his and she sighed so softly he wondered if it was only the gentle breeze.

A moment later she sat stiffly upright looking wildly about her, searching for she knew not what in the night. Angela's heart fluttered like a caged bird beating with frantic wings against her ribs. Her breath came in short gasps and Clyde could feel the tension suffuse her whole body.

"What is it?" he asked alarmed. "Do you feel faint?"

Faint! She felt wonderfully, radiantly alive, all her senses perceptively alert to the scene around her. She surged to her feet scanning the shadowy forms of the people inhabiting the other vehicles patiently awaiting their turn to alight. What was the matter with her? Angela didn't know herself, only that something was about to unfold before her eyes. It was like waiting in a dim theater for the play to begin.

"Are you all right, Angela?"

She sat down and tried to calm herself but that strange exhilaration wouldn't be stilled. The eyes she turned to Clyde caught the light glowing like big cat's eyes. He could feel the trembling of her body beside him and even though the reaction had come immediately after his veiled allusion to his feelings for her, he knew her reaction came not from himself but from an outside source.

He too looked around but saw nothing out of the ordinary. Could it be that she was high strung and nervous about her first ball in Sydney? Clyde dismissed that as soon as it popped into his mind. Not this woman who had remained unflustered in the company of princes and kings. Her actions made him uneasy and he was only too glad when they descended from the carriage and swept in through the front door.

The business of formal greetings and introductions seemed to settle Angela down a bit but Clyde noticed the way her aquamarine eyes flitted restlessly from one face to another. She smiled and chatted easily but he had the feeling she was only half there, caught up in an emotional happening even she didn't quite understand.

The fifty-foot-long reception room was elegantly decked with huge vases of exotic flowers, flickering candles, and a press of local gentry eagerly craning their necks for a glimpse of Angela. The flush of her cheeks was pronounced and her eyes sparkled as if with a fever. The emerald felt hot and heavy, glowing against her flesh and Angela snapped open her fan to try and cool the still air.

All the time she couldn't help thinking that Scott was near. But that was impossible! What would a convict be doing at the governor's ball? It was a flight of fantasy to even imagine it. But hadn't she always had an overactive imagination? Scott had chided her about it often enough. Still she couldn't help hoping, couldn't keep her eyes still or her heart hushed.

Then Angela's attention riveted on a group across the room. One woman laughed gaily, surrounded by a crowd of eager suitors. She was tall and Junoesque with heavy auburn hair. She wore a pale sea-green dress and her hazel eyes met Angela's spanning the distance.

Never in her life had Angela felt such an intense hatred of any woman at first sight! The air fairly crackled between the two and Angela felt ice enter into her veins. They stared at each other in a silent duel and she sensed that the woman felt the same antipathy she did.

It was all so odd and over in a split second as dinner was announced and Clyde escorted Angela into the dining room.

The rest of the night passed in a haze of laughter, music, and dancing. Angela's dance card was full and she whirled on the polished floor until she was dizzy. She drank too much champagne and Clyde took her for a cooling walk in the garden. He kissed her once, passionately but briefly and it was as if it had happened to someone else, not her.

five

She wore a dress of daffodil-yellow muslin embroidered in green and it reminded her of a far-off golden day spent by a lake in early spring. A secret smile curved Angela's lips. She had dreamed about that unforgettable time last night—perhaps that was why she chose the dress.

The children bounced into her room all set for the outing she had promised them. They chattered excitedly all at the same time looking forward eagerly to the picnic they had planned. She kissed Lorna and Clare and rumpled Robert's brown hair for at the grown up age of five he tried to squirm out of any embrace. But that would change, she mused, if he was anything like his father.

"Are we all ready?" Angela teased, looking around the room thoughtfully as if she had forgotten something.

"Yes!" exclaimed Lorna and Robert at the same time and Clare repeated it after them.

"She's learning to talk, Mama," observed Lorna wisely as if she herself was the mother of a prodigy.

"And about time too!" said Angela scooping up the toddler.

"Ezra has the carriage all ready," Robert told them hopping restlessly about the room. "And I helped Maggie pack the hamper."

"I wanted to do it," shouted Lorna. "What's in it?"

"I'm not telling," laughed Robert secretively. "You were too busy trying to get Clare to say 'Papa.'"

"Papa, Papa," gurgled Clare quite content now that she was in Angela's arms.

"She said it!" Robert hooted with glee. "She wouldn't say it for Lorna but she said it for me!" He ran from the room with Lorna streaking after him.

"Mama, Mama!" Clare laid her head against Angela's breast and breathed in the wonderful wildflower scent that meant her mother. Her little hands stroked Angela's hair as she nestled contentedly.

"Yes, little one," sighed Angela, her carefree mood broken, "at least you have a mother, my poor fatherless Clare! But what a one you chose."

On her way out she stopped at the kitchen and greeted Kate and Maggie. The girls were a wonderful find and flourished under a little attention and good food. Once Angela gave orders she didn't have to think about them again. The efficient Murrays were hard workers and knew how to get things done.

Kate was visibly excited as she removed a big apron and smoothed her new dark-blue dress. She was going along to watch the children. If only Maggie could go too—but that would be asking too much. This way she could tell her sister all about the day when she returned. If their situations had been reversed she would never find out what happened because, as everyone knew, Maggie never spoke. So Kate hefted the weighty hamper and headed for the door.

"And what delicious culinary delights did you make for our picnic?" Angela asked not expecting an answer. "You are a wonder in the kitchen, Maggie. Why at this rate I'll be so fat and matronly by the time I find my husband that he will never recognize me!"

A shy smile lit up her pointed face at the compliment and the ludicrous mental picture of a corpulent Lady Harrington. Why she was like a fairy princess that had rescued them from misery and degradation. Maggie Murray would have gladly laid down her life for the duchess.

It was a perfect day for a picnic. The sky was full of little white cotton-puffs of clouds that provided some shade but promised no rain. The spell of blistering weather had broken and a cooling breeze swept in from the cove like a warm spring day. The *Cygnet* bobbed gently at anchor and other smaller craft went about their daily business.

The windmills, used for grinding corn, were silhouetted against the brilliant blue sky and beyond them was the mysterious bush and the hazy unreality of the Blue Mountains. Today they were purple-shadowed, a smudge on the horizon and Angela thought of Clyde and his enthusiastic imaginings about what lay on the other side. Somehow she had a feeling that Clyde would stay in this strange new land that was slowly winning him away from the tame civilization of the place they called home. There was no doubt that there was something rugged and exciting about Australia.

After the vista of the bush, the mountains, and the sea Hyde Park was tame by comparison. Ezra spread two big rugs beneath a shady tree not far from a pond with blue water lilies. A kookaburra laughed at them from the trees as they fell upon the picnic lunch with ravenous appetites and devoured the meal. Replete with his favorite apple tart Robert scattered the few remaining crumbs for the birds. He and Lorna ran off to play beneath the watchful eyes of Kate.

Angela leaned back against the tree with Clare's sleepy head on her lap watching as Lorna launched a very battered toy boat on the pond. "I still remember the day he gave Lorna that boat," she said to Ezra. "He was so sure she was a boy and brought a boat. Little did I know then that boats and lead soldiers would suit her.

"Sometimes, Ezra, I get such feelings about things—almost as if I know something important is going to happen. I felt like that last night as we were arriving at Government House. I was so sure I would find Scott last night, but I didn't."

"Maybe you're wishing it to happen so intensely. . ."

"No. There was an incident at the ball—if you could

call it that. There was a woman and we looked at each other and I hated her the instant I saw her."

"Who was it?"

"I don't know," she puzzled staring off into nothingness. "We were never introduced and never spoke, but it was so strange. How could I hate someone I have never met, and how could she hate me?"

"I hated Annee Wallace on sight," Ezra said.

"But that was different. She had just bought you. There's no comparison in situations. I'll have to ask Clyde if he knows her."

"Clyde is in love with you."

"I know," Angela sighed with a frown. "He has been since the day I met him on the Isle of Skye. But what can I do? I certainly don't encourage him."

"Men just have to look at you to fall in love at first sight."

"I'm afraid I talked too much when I was sick and you know far too much about me, Ezra. I hope the rest of my life goes at a slightly less frantic pace."

"Yes, you could use a rest from adventures."

"Umm," agreed Angela dreamily, "a long lovely rest—after I find Scott. We never did have a honeymoon. I don't care where we go as long as we are together. But I'm dreaming again. Where is that man? Everyone in the colony knows of my arrival. You would think he was hiding from me."

Ezra was silent for a few minutes and then he said, "A man would have to be a fool to do that. Have you thought that he might be in Van Diemen's Land?"

She nodded slowly but although she had considered that Scott might be there she didn't want to believe it. They said it was a living hell where only the incorrigibles, the most hardened and desperate criminals were sent. Convicts that committed new crimes in New South Wales were transported again—to that island. Angela had thought the ragged, subhuman chain gangs pitiful, but being sent to Van Diemen's Land was a fate worse than death. Men begged to be hanged rather than be sent there.

The forced labor was brutal and if they didn't die from that then there was slow starvation, floggings, disease—they died like flies on that wretched island. Angela could not quite bring herself to imagine Scott there, for to do that was like condemning him to death in her mind and her mind could not accept that—yet. Not until Sydney and Parramatta and the Hawkesbury had been searched with a fine-toothed comb, not until every convict in every outpost settlement was examined by her personally.

Laying the sleeping Clare carefully on the rug Angela got to her feet. All the lazy contentedness had gone out of the day and a fear that had weighed on her came back anew. She remembered with painful clarity the agony that had accompanied Keith's announcement of Scott's death. No! No! she screamed inside her whole being, it can't be. There would be no reason then to go on.

She started walking, she couldn't stay still now with so many fears preying on her mind. Ezra gave a curt order to Kate and went after Angela, catching up with her easily although she was walking very fast.

"My lady!" He grabbed her arm, much upset by the abstracted look of her. "I'm sorry. I shouldn't have said that. If I could take it back and then cut out my tongue so that the words had never been uttered I would! He's not in Van Diemen's Land, he's here, somewhere! Maybe you will run into him around the next corner. . . ."

"And maybe I will not!" Angela's eyes were sorrow-haunted. "You are right, Ezra. If he was here he would know I'm looking for him. Somehow, some way, Scott would get word to me. You have faced the reality that he isn't in this colony—now so must I." Her voice sounded dead and she pulled free of his grasp running from him in desperation.

Ezra caught up with her again. He couldn't let her out of his sight for fear of what she might do. He had seen her like this before and in spite of her protests or anger he couldn't let her rush about the streets of Sydney alone.

"Go away, Ezra. Leave me alone." People were looking at them curiously, at a huge Negro accosting a very upset and obviously well-to-do lady. Even in Sydney such goings-on wouldn't be condoned for much longer. So Ezra fell back and let Angela continue blindly out of the park and down the street. But he followed her at a safe distance and it wouldn't have mattered if he was only one step behind her for she wouldn't have noticed.

It was hotter now and Ezra had been following her for the better part of an hour at a quick walk. Dust from the street trailed behind her like foaming waves and still she kept going. They were in a business district of stores and a few scattered houses. Sawdust from the lumber mill filled the air.

Angela stopped for just a moment to catch her breath. Her heart beat madly and she felt faint from the sun beating down on her unprotected head. She had left her wide-brimmed straw hat on the rugs in Hyde Park and her face was pink from exertion and the sun. Then she didn't feel faint at all for a sudden revitalizing spark surged through her and she found her eyes riveted on a heavy wagon halfway down the street.

It was being loaded in the midday sun by two convicts in trousers with bare chests and heads. She watched them go into the store and come out with sacks and boxes and thought it looked like hot work. A handsome stallion was tied to the back of the wagon and quite a few men were openly admiring the fine piece of horseflesh.

The street was crowded with women shopping, convict servants, and various vehicles. Several horsemen trotted down the road. There was nothing extraordinary about the scene but Angela was breathing even faster and for all the world she couldn't tear her eyes away from it. It was the same strange sensation she had realized last night before the ball.

A tall, lean man emerged from the store and stood in the shadow of the overhanging roof watching the loading of the wagon. Now she couldn't breathe at all!

He wore a white shirt open to the waist and black trousers tucked into dusty boots. He moved to help steady a tottering box and the sun glinted on his bronze hair. He turned, issuing an order and his profile burned into her memory like a hot brand.

Ezra had been about to approach Angela again since she was still for so long just staring down the street, but his mouth fell open in amazement as she streaked down the road. Her hands held her dress free of her feet and he caught the slim flash of her ankles as she became a blurred motion.

She ran at full tilt into a man and he caught her shoulders, spinning around to save them both a fall. Then, much to Ezra's surprise, instead of releasing Angela he clutched her to him as if he was a drowning man holding onto a ship's timber to save himself from a furious ocean.

Their lips met in a fiery paroxysm and his tongue engaged hers in an intimate duel. Lightning entered into Angela coursing through her veins with all the fury of a Caribbean thunderstorm. Her hands were beneath his shirt feeling the suddenly tense muscles of his back, running frantically up and down, pressing him closer.

And he was like a great solid oak, caught too in their storm of passion and shaken to his very roots. Sanity fled and feeling took over. There was no dusty street, no blazing sun, no curious ring of onlookers growing larger by the second. The only sound that reached their ears was the rushing wind of their own desire.

The crowd was huge now and Ezra was part of it, shoving his way to the front. Shopkeepers had abandoned their stores and joined the amazed ranks. They all stood with their eyes popping out of their heads like a catch of glassy-eyed fish.

The kiss went on forever with no sign of ending and whispering broke out. Someone recognized Angela as the Duchess of Brightling and the rumor spread like fire through dry bush. They were practically raping each other on the street and Ezra had to do something to bring them back to their senses.

"Scott Harrington!" The name ripped through their reunion like a blast of winter snow, for Ezra had no doubt who the man was.

Scott raised his head and angry golden fire leaped in flames from his brown eyes scorching everyone in sight. He looked up at the huge negro man who had called his name and who looked back at him with recognition in his amber eyes even though they had never met. Angela lay against his chest shaking, as limp as a wet dishrag.

The next thing she knew she was sitting in front of Scott on the magnificent stallion looking down at the upturned faces of a sea of people. There were numerous conflicting emotions reflected on every face: jealousy, envy, lust, curiosity, shock, and several people were smiling with nostalgic expressions.

He wheeled the horse around and the mass of tightly packed people fell back and parted. The wind fanned her face as the horse broke into a trot and her loosened hair blew back caressing Scott's sun-browned face. One arm was tight around her waist and with the other he easily controlled his mount. The pressure of his hard thighs was intoxicating and she leaned her head back on his broad shoulder so she could again see his profile.

The ascent from the depths of despair to the verge of rapture had been a wild, dizzying journey and Angela was not sure she wasn't dreaming. If she was she never wanted to wake up as she was swept off by her own husband like an ancient war lord carrying off a battle prize.

"Scott! Scott!" she whispered not caring if the whole world dissolved in flames at that exact moment because nothing could touch their happiness.

"Angel," he murmured huskily, the hard line of his mouth relaxing into a curve of triumph.

Her heart soared with love and pride that he was her husband and they were together once again. Soon they would be reunited in every way and that was just as it should be. Too many wasted years lay between them to make up for and she ached with a terrible longing to know at last the total fulfillment of their love.

Somehow the ride was at an end and she was too

dazed with happiness to question how he had found the way to her house. He dismounted and held his arms out to her and Angela fell into them eagerly with exuberant laughter and he joined her. They laughed crazily as Scott carried her to the house and a startled Maggie appeared in the doorway with large frightened eyes.

"It's all right, Maggie," she cried over his shoulder, unable to stop laughing. And then they were alone in her bedroom with a solid door between them and the world. Then it was as it had been before, everything shut out of their lives but their all-consuming need of each other.

There were no words said between them for their lips were too busy exploring and rediscovering the delights of kissing. With a frantic impatience Scott all but ripped the dress from Angela, all the while holding her close against his pounding heart. He laid her on the bed and it took only seconds for him to remove his own clothes and join her.

Shudders coursed through her at just the look in his eyes as they blazed a smoldering trail over her body, taking in every detail. Her eyes turned as dark and unfathomable as a tropical sea at night and this time she held her arms out to him writhing with pleasure as the weight of his body descended upon her.

Scott kissed the dimples in the hollows beneath her cheekbones, her closed eyelids and her temples, then traced a trail to her delicate ears and nibbled at the pink lobes. He fingered the scar on her shoulder and then let his hand cup the firm fullness of her breast. She couldn't help gasping at the contact—it had been so long!

The slightest brush of his lips or movement of his fingers set her trembling on the brink of bliss. When she returned his caresses with a boldness designed to drive him wild he tore her hands away from his shuddering flesh.

"Don't, love," he groaned, "or it will be over before we start."

Demanding lips captured each rosy nipple in turn,

torturing her with exquisite delight until they blossomed hard and quivering in his mouth. Angela was gasping for breath, her head lashing back and forth on the slim column of her neck, tangling them both in a web of long black hair. Her fingernails dug into the corded muscles of Scott's biceps as he leaned over her teasing her beyond endurance.

She could stand it no longer and neither could he and their bodies melded together with a frenzy not to be denied. The tumultuous motion carried Angela past thinking, like a swift mountain river sweeping her helplessly along in its current. There was thunder in her ears like the pounding of a great waterfall not far off and the torrent carried her closer and closer to the edge of ecstasy. The final thrust plunged her over in a wild fall of icy water, hot sun, and froth-pounded rocks below.

"Mr. Mosely! Mr. Mosely!" Celeste Carew looked around the dim store that smelled of pickles, leather, and dust, tapping her foot impatiently. "Damn! Where is that man?"

Peter Mosely hunched lower behind a highly heaped counter in the corner of his store and hoped she would go away. He was a small toadlike man with a shiny pate fringed with gray hair and a paunch that hung over his belt. Small wire-rimmed glasses perched on the end of his long thin nose, the only feature about him that was not round.

"Mr. Mosely, where are you?"

She really sounded angry now and he cringed at the thought of an encounter with her. Mrs. Carew was a redhead with a furious temper when crossed and he didn't want to be the one to break the bad news to her. He had seen everything of course since it had taken place right in front of his store. At the time he had been as fascinated by the shenanigans as everyone else, but not now. Now that shrew was standing in his store shouting for his attention and he wished he hadn't witnessed anything.

"Mr. Mosely! Come out from behind that counter! It's no use hiding. I saw the light glinting off your glasses. What are you doing skulking back there—are you deaf?"

"No, no, Mrs. Carew," he stammered, most upset by her discovery. "I . . . I was just—I had dozed off—"

Haughty hazel eyes snapped down at him as he sidled from behind the counter, for she was a whole head taller than he was. "Now, suppose you tell me where my overseer is."

"Your overseer?" Sweat stood out on his bald head.

"Yes, you dolt! He is only the man that has been my overseer for four years now. Are you going senile?" Her voice was contemptuous. "Stretch your memory to this morning. Where is Scott Harris?"

"I . . . I . . . I don't know."

"You don't know!" Celeste slammed her parasol down on the counter making him jump with the sound. "My wagon is out in front of your store fully loaded with the horses waiting patiently. But it seems that my overseer, his horse, and two of my convicts have vanished into thin air. What's going on around here?"

Narrowed black eyes stared at her through the thick glasses. Everyone knew she was carrying on a flagrant affair with that overseer of hers. The man was as wild as a hawk and dangerous looking to boot. No, he wouldn't want to inform on him. Rumor had it that he had been transported for murder and Peter Mosely could believe it when he looked at the dark piratical face and those hard flashing eyes. Scott Harris was not a man to cross.

He had almost passed out when he had seen Mr. Harris by the wagon kissing the most exquisitely beautiful woman he had ever seen in his life. Peter Mosely could still feel that kiss right through him—and so had everyone else from the looks on their faces. They had practically fornicated in the street right in front of his store until a big Negro called out to him. But he had called him by another name.

Then the overseer swept her off like a knight rescuing his princess—except she was a duchess, they said—the one that was searching for her husband, Scott Harrington! Yes, that was the name the Negro had called him, not a far cry from Harris now that he thought of it. So Harris was really Harrington and that made him the Duke of Brightling and her husband. The more he discovered the less he felt like telling Mrs. Carew.

For all that he was a convict Scott Harris—Harrington, Peter Mosely corrected himself—was a much respected part of the colony. Everyone knew what had happened on that ill-fated ship he had come over on, Captain Carew's ship. Cholera broke out only weeks after embarkation and swept convict and crew alike being no respecter of station. With most of the crew dead and half the felons gone Captain Carew had been frantic. An urgent appeal went below for anyone who knew anything about sailing a ship.

What luck! Scott Harrington had owned a ship, he knew everything from unfurling the sails to navigation. He and the captain almost singlehandedly sailed the *Columbine* to Sydney. He arrived a conquering hero, though a convict, and was immediately assigned to Captain Carew for the length of his sentence. Then the captain succumbed to the loathsome disease himself and died in agony, but at least in his own bed, attended by his faithful overseer.

Now Scott Harrington ruled supreme at Mrs. Carew's vast estate on the Hawkesbury River. Thornhill was the prize of the district and year by year her overseer made the profits soar. He had the devil's own luck, they said, and secretly Peter Mosely thought he might very well be the fallen Lucifer. But he didn't envy him Mrs. Carew for a lover, the woman could tear you apart with her eyes. No, he wouldn't be in Scott Harrington's shoes for all the tea in China when it came time for explanations.

"What are you looking at?" shouted Celeste Carew boiling over at the stupid, vacant eyes focused fuzzily on her face. "Where is Scott Harris? He was supposed to meet me two hours ago! You must know where he is!"

Mr. Mosely just shook his head and shrugged his round shoulders inexpressively. No, he wouldn't cross that devil and reap his wrath and that of Mrs. Carew. He wasn't foolish enough to go mixing in other people's business. That would be like mixing fire and gunpowder and he would be the one blown sky-high.

They lay together exhausted in the darkened room. Three times they had made love with all the intensity of two colliding hurricanes. Angela's head was on his shoulder tilted so that she could look at his face. Her breasts pressed against his side and one of her slim thighs rested over his. She wasn't quite sure if Scott was sleeping or not but he lay very still with his eyes closed, breathing evenly.

Joy radiated from her like light from the sun and she was satiated and wonderfully drowsy. But still she wouldn't let herself drift off—not yet. She was too engrossed in studying him unawares. Scott was the same but different. The sun had worked its magic turning his skin dark brown, lightening his brown hair to a tarnished bronze. There were new lines on his face, around his eyes, and creasing his forehead. Marks of pain and suffering and their long separation.

His eyes were the same golden-brown but more secretive now. Several times he had looked at her coldly, harshly even during the heat of their lovemaking. His body was even more magnificent than she remembered and Angela couldn't keep her hands still. She smoothed her fingers across the mat of curly hair on his chest and felt his skin tense beneath her touch. Yes, he was the same but different and he wasn't asleep, only pretending so that now that the fire was banked they wouldn't have to talk.

"Scott," she whispered, leaning closer, kissing his ear. "I love you—now, more than ever! Our reunion was everything I thought it would be and more!"

His eyes flickered open slowly and he looked at her very strangely for a long time as if memorizing her features. Scott's lips curved into a bitter smile and she squirmed in his embrace.

"Darling, is something wrong?" She smoothed the

hair back from his forehead, a tiny worry starting in her mind.

"Bitch!" He said the word with a ferocity that stunned her and turned pinning her to the bed and kissing her so brutally he knocked the breath from her. He hurt her purposely and she struggled against the sudden change that was starting.

When he finally raised his mouth from her bruised lips she could only stare at him in complete confusion, with wide bewildered eyes.

He laughed at her harshly, a sardonic expression twisting his face. "But such a sweet, beautiful little bitch! You can drive a man wild. I think you were born a whore!"

She gasped in utter surprise and bafflement. No love words now, only a bitter torrent of abuse. He rose from the bed and began pulling on his clothes. Different—but what had brought about the sudden change? Or was it a sudden change—had it happened gradually over the four years they had been separated? He was looking at her as if he hated her.

"Scott?" Her voice quavered and she got up reaching for a robe. She belted it around herself and faced him warily. The wonder of the day lay at her feet shattered into a thousand pieces. "Why are you talking to me like that?"

"Here, Angel." He took a coin from his pocket and threw it at her feet. The gold glinted dully in the shuttered room. "You were worth every penny!"

"Stop it!" Angela kicked the money and it rolled beneath the bed. "Stop being so cruel, stop playing games with me!"

"It's no game, love. I always pay for services rendered."

Every time he spoke she jerked like he was stabbing her with a knife and fury began spilling from her blazing eyes. Hot spots of red mounted on her cheeks and she was so angry that her lips moved but no sound escaped them.

Scott produced another coin holding it up for her to

see. "Shall we do it again? I always did enjoy raping you."

Angela crossed the room and struck the money out of his hand but he caught her wrists before she could claw at his eyes.

"Why are you doing this? Tell me why you are destroying everything that has happened here today."

"You know, Angel. I had the papers sent to you in London."

"What papers?"

"Do you mean to say you didn't receive them? This gets better and better!"

"What papers?"

"Why the suit I brought against you for a divorce."

"Divorce!" she screamed struggling in his grasp, aqua eyes incredulous in a now white face. "You are divorcing me, but why?"

"Your reputation has preceded you, Your Grace!" Scott threw her onto the bed and she crouched there like a cat ready to spring. Sitting on the chair he stretched his long legs out before him regarding her with hard, disparaging eyes. "We may be sixteen thousand miles from London but rumors fly here on the wings of birds.

"You are a disgrace, an unfit wife and mother! Did you think I would never find out about your escapades? How as soon as I left you were gallivanting all over the city and sleeping with half the lords?"

She made a tiny squeak of protest and collapsed limply on the bed. Scott couldn't be saying such things to her, not after this afternoon, not after everything they meant to each other. She was frozen to the rumpled covers in an impotent rage as Scott continued on a rampage with words.

"It was bad enough your being the mistress of the Duke of Remington and his brother at the same time, but did you have to keep the younger one as your paramour? Was it necessary to play one against the other until they dueled? You lying treacherous shrew! You even wagered yourself in a game of cards to win your favorite lover a title and wealth. And all the time you were married to me, dragging my name through the mud in a way I never did even at the height of my trial!

"Oh, but the best is yet to come. Not content with two lovers you added a few more to your bed—the stalwart Keith Montgomery and the Prince of Wales. Could four fulfill your insatiable lust, or were there others that no one knew about? Then, you committed the ultimate offense by marrying Montgomery! Not only are you a four-timing slut but a bigamist!"

"It's not true," Angela said in a very subdued voice. "To think that you would believe rumors, lies. You know how people gossip. You know how one little incident is blown up into a thousand indicretions by the scandalmongers of London. Anyone not as corrupt and decadent as they are, they want to smear with dirt—bring them down to their own level, which is the gutter!"

"You deny it then?" Scott shouted jumping to his feet and towering over her. "None of it is true—not one thing?"

"Well—"

"Well nothing! I don't want any lying explanations. I'm sick of deceit and sick of you! The Queen of Hearts, the prince called you, but he should have called you the Queen of Whores!"

She was crying, big silent tears slipping down chalk-white cheeks and he looked at her in disgust and crossed to the table. He dumped the contents of her jewelry box onto the bed beside her and picked out the diamond bracelet.

"Spare me the dramatics," he sneered holding the sparkling jewels before her nose like an accusation. "Exactly as described by the . . . . scandalmongers. Six heart-shaped diamonds. Who gave it to you?"

"The . . . . the Prince of Wales."

"And why would he have that bracelet specially made for a woman who was just a casual acquaintance?"

"He admired me." Angela's voice wasn't above a whisper.

"Admired you! That's a good one! A man doesn't

give away a fortune in jewels unless he gets something in return. And what about the Vaughns—did they fight a duel over you?"

"Yes—but—"

"And did you agree to marry the Duke of Remington if you lost a card game?"

"Yes, but I thought you were—"

"Shut up! Did you marry Keith Montgomery?" His voice reached a thundering crescendo.

"Yes," she gasped almost totally destroyed by his accusations.

"I notice there were no buts about that one." Scott grabbed her by the hair and jerked her to her knees, his face snarling just inches from hers. "If I weren't in this predicament, if I weren't a convict bound to Mrs. Carew for another ten years, I would leave this colony where you are so fast it would make your head spin. Why did you follow me? It was almost bearable with you half a world away but this whole country is not big enough to contain the two of us! I hate you!"

"You can't hate me," she cried painfully. "I love you—only you! There was never anyone else for me. Please, just let me explain. Let's talk like rational human beings and straighten out our differences. I know you still love me!"

"Love! It's just a word dreamed up by poets. I don't love you now and I never loved you!"

"But—but—what about what just happened. . . ."

"Lust, Angela. I wanted you when you threw that bewitching body of yours against me in the street today. So I took what you were offering and paid dearly for my pleasure. But that's the last time. You caught me off guard today but never again! Hard as you may find this to believe you are not irresistible. I've known you were here since the day you began looking for me and managed to keep away from you. I saw you last night entering Government House and felt nothing for you but contempt."

"Liar!"

"I will admit," he said shaking her again to keep her still, "that I enjoyed laying you today. But that's the only thing you are fit for. You are worse than the lowest prostitute and how could any man love a harlot?"

"I'm not a harlot! I'm your wife. I'm the mother of your children!"

"Worse luck for me! Soon you won't be my wife, and if I ever get the chance I will take my children from you and you will never see them again!"

"No!" Angela slapped him across the face as hard as she could and his lip curled in disgust as he sent her sprawling onto the bed amidst the tumbled splendor of glittering jewels.

"You are dirt, Angela, and always will be! You deserve to be walked on and nothing more. Get out of here. Go home and destroy someone else's life, like you are so very good at doing." Scott walked to the door and turned staring at her coldly. "The divorce will take time but in a year or two we will both be free. In the meantime just remember—I hate you and I never want to see you again!"

Scott slammed out of the house and Angela gave way to an agony of weeping. She clutched Jack's emerald in her hand and even its warmth could not comfort her. The whole day had been a series of sharp contrasts, from elation to abject misery and she felt like a child's ball tossed high into the air, finally crashing to the ground.

Clyde stood dumbfounded on the veranda watching Scott Harrington gallop away. The man had brushed past him almost knocking him down, and Clyde didn't even think Scott had seen him. So Angela had found her husband at last and from the looks of him things were not going well at all.

Then Clyde heard her crying, the sound loud even from where he stood outside the front door. He remembered very well from his last meeting with the duke, his horrendous temper and he rushed into the house without even bothering to knock. If Harrington had touched even a hair of Angela's head he would have him flogged to death—for a gentleman did not call out a convicted felon.

The door to her room was open and he paused before

the darkened room. The heartrending sobs made him feel sick with anger at her husband. Just last night she had been so happy and carefree, dancing like a butterfly, glittering beneath crystal chandeliers.

"Angela?"

She didn't even hear him and Clyde entered the room. Curled on the bed surrounded by scattered jewels she shook like a small earthquake. A green velvet robe barely covered her and he could see one long leg bare to the thigh and a white shoulder marred with a scar.

He went to her, gathering her into his arms, pulling the robe back over her and rocking her gently. He didn't even think she knew he was there but he stroked her disordered hair and whispered soft crooning words.

Slowly Clyde became aware of the state the room was in: the rumpled bed, her torn dress and underclothes lying scattered on the floor. It was obvious they had made love violently in this bed not long ago and Clyde felt a hopelessness descend on him. Angela loved and wanted her husband no matter what he did to her, and he wondered how this could be so. He stiffened—had Scott raped her? He was capable of it, and Clyde vowed to kill him with his own hands if that was so.

Angela slowly became aware that someone was holding her, gently trying to help her overcome her grief. Through swollen eyes she saw the scarlet of his coat and knew it could only be Clyde. But still she couldn't gain control of herself and went on drenching his uniform with a flood of tears. She had been so shocked by the confrontation with Scott, by the unexpectedness of the attack, that she hadn't even fought back. And now he was gone thinking the very worst about her.

Divorce! The word brought on a fresh wave of weeping that she was helpless to stem. He was suing her for divorce on the grounds of adultery and bigamy! The irony of it. The damage begun by Keith was tearing them apart.

She could still see Scott's face in the myriad moods of this long afternoon: love, hate, disgust, lust, and studied unconcern. But through it all there had been an underlying rage so furious that he had been unable to conceal it, even when he had feigned indifference. He still felt something for her. Somehow, some way she had to find his one weakness, use whatever means she could to make him listen to the truth and effect a reconciliation.

Unwittingly Scott had given away that one chink in his otherwise solid armor, carefully put on against her. His sensual nature overrode even his hate for her and she knew that was what she would use in her battle to reclaim him. She would use her wits and her body, every seductive trick she had learned since the night he had first raped her. He had taught her well and now she would turn all that knowledge into a plan that would ensnare him for all time. She would force Scott to acknowledge that in spite of everything, nothing could ever kill the love they felt for each other.

Resolved in her mind as to what she would do, Angela's tears gradually subsided. She became aware of Clyde, that she was half lying in his arms in a state of shocking dishabille, but she felt so weak that she just stayed where she was and let him comfort her. He was a true friend in her times of distress and this wasn't the first time he had tried to help her. Good, sweet, uncomplicated Clyde with whom she didn't have to pretend, but could just be herself and be assured of his adoring love no matter what.

Scott galloped through the countryside surrounding Sydney until he and his horse were on the point of exhaustion. His hands shook as he held the reins and he couldn't help thinking of Angela. Why couldn't he keep that witch out of his mind? When he had learned she was in the colony seeking him, he had made the decision not to see her. It had been the hardest struggle of his life. He found himself starting for Sydney a dozen times a day to see her. But each time he controlled himself, turned his horse back to Thornhill and made violent love to Celeste.

Seeing her outside Government House last night had

been almost the last straw. He had recognized her even in the dark, her voice, her laugh, as she sat in an open carriage with a shadowy officer. Leave it to Angela to find another lover right away—the temptress! She could charm a corpse to life with just a smile.

But today, to suddenly find her in his arms with absolutely no warning; that was more than a cold marble statue could stand and he had done the most natural thing in the world—made love to her.

She was more beautiful than ever, with a maturity that enchanted him. But at the same time, and in spite of her almost twenty-five years she retained a youthful innocence that never ceased to amaze him. How could such a worldly-wise slut still look like a girl of eighteen? Why could she still affect him to the point of madness, the same way she had the first time he saw her? His blood boiled just thinking of her and when he touched her he dissolved into a seething fit of passion so strong and mindless only one thing could happen.

Scott closed his eyes with a groan. He could still see her: those wild, sad aqua eyes claiming him as her own; the full pink lips, ripe and made only for his kisses; the perfection of her body, that made him forget her past and his hate; her black hair, long and shining, as soft as mist, twining around his neck, binding him, strangling him until he was utterly helpless to resist.

And there were so many things about her that he didn't know. How had she gotten that scar on her shoulder that looked like a gunshot wound? Had she been so desperately unhappy that she tried at one time to slit her wrists? That was the other scar, thin and white slashing across one delicate wrist. And above all why was she here when she had proved beyond the shadow of a doubt that she didn't need or want him in the intervening years? Why wasn't she in England living with Montgomery who had finally gotten his wish and married her?

He wanted to go back and comfort her, wipe away the tears that still had the power to devastate him. And yet, at the same time, he felt like whipping her within an inch of her life. He wanted to see his children and didn't even know whether their third one was a boy or girl. Scott wished he had never heard the gossip, never learned about her indiscretions, and thinking back to their time together in Scotland he almost couldn't believe what she had done during the last four years. But she had always been volatile and passionate, too easily ruled by her own body. Hadn't she loved him violently even when she hated him?

He had to put distance between them, and since he wasn't free to leave, the only way was to make her go. Even London wasn't far enough away to please him. If the moon was between them that would be too close. If they were a universe away from each other he would still yearn for the unattainable!

six

"Don't go, Angela!" Clyde pleaded, pacing restlessly in front of the stable. "Let the divorce go through and you will be free of the monster! He hurts you all the time. He doesn't love you! The whole colony knows about his affair with Mrs. Carew. You are a laughingstock!"

"I don't care!" she cried, sitting astride her bay gelding anxious to be wherever Scott was. "I love him, I always will, and nothing will change that! I don't give a damn what people are saying about us, and never, never will I give him a divorce!" Her voice rose and the horse pricked up his ears at her irritation.

"There are things between us so binding that neither of us will ever be free. I fight for what I want, and I want Scott! I want him for my husband and lover. I want him to be the father to my children again. I want him no matter what he has done—and he wants me!"

"Well then he has a strange way of showing it! He hasn't been seeking you out, has he? In the past week even the servants at Thornhill have been outraged by their behavior, and they have known about it all along!"

"Scott is angry, he's furious at what he thinks I have done. And what better way to show me than by flaunting another woman beneath my nose? Well I won't stand for it a day longer! I have a temper too and when I get through with that woman she will wish she was dead! I'm going to get him back and I don't care what I have to do!"

Clyde looked up at her, hope sinking in his heart. She was as wild as the Highlands and as wayward as a spoiled child. Did she really think that just because she willed it her husband would see things her way? And when he saw her so angry that her eyes almost incinerated him with a glance, he knew that he would do anything to have her.

"Are you coming or shall I go alone?" She dug her heels into the horse's flanks and sprang off leaving Clyde to hurriedly mount up and start after her.

It was a long, hard, hot ride and Angela rode most of the day wrapped in silence with Clyde wondering what she was plotting. It took the whole day to reach the Hawkesbury even though they had left early in the morning and they would have to spend the night somewhere along the river. That was no problem because hospitality to strangers was an important commodity and anyone turning people away from the door was marked by his neighbors.

Angela knew where she was going to spend the night—in Scott's bed, once she got past his stubbornness. She eyed the lowering clouds apprehensively and hoped the weather would hold until they arrived. But an hour later stinging drops lashed down, growing into a downpour that in minutes left both of them soaked to the skin.

Her blouse was plastered against her and they stopped beneath a large tree to wait until the worst was over. But instead of letting up it seemed to rain harder and after noticing the way Clyde kept glancing at her out of the corner of his eye she got a short jacket out of her saddlebags and struggled into it even though it was too hot.

Rain dripped off her nose and sweat trickled down her shoulder blades and the storm went on and on. "I don't think it's ever going to stop," she observed miserably. "Why don't we just go on?"

So they began again with the road churning to mud beneath the horses' hooves. She swore beneath her breath at the untimely rain. How was she ever going to attract Scott when she appeared out of a wall of water looking like a mud-spattered, drowned rat? He would take one look at her and retire to Mrs. Carew's bed. She thought of turning back but night was almost upon them and the road was quickly becoming impassible. The horses were having a rough time of it and kept slipping in the mire.

Thornhill sat on the crest of a hill, high above the Hawkesbury River. The rain beat steadily on the roof only adding to the cozy atmosphere of the two that sat at the dining room table. They were halfway through the meal when a knock sounded at the front door and silent convict feet went to answer it swiftly. Celeste looked up at the interruption wondering who could be calling on such a bad night. A frown marred her smooth brow. She wanted no interruptions tonight, not with the mood Scott was in and had been in for the last week. It had given her a scare when he informed her of his wife's arrival, but he had more than made up for the bad news by his insatiable physical demands ever since.

The frown dissolved. Just thinking of their frenzied week brought color to her cheeks and a smile to her lips. And she was immensely pleased about another matter too—Scott had asked her to marry him when he was free of the shrew that was his wife. Celeste had been hoping for that ever since he had told her of the divorce suit the year before. There would be difficulties in marrying a convict, but on the day of their wedding the governor would hand over a pardon and all their problems would be over.

She loved him so obsessively that the thought of ever being parted was unbearable. But he didn't know that. No, it wouldn't do for him to know how much he meant to her, for then he would have the power to hurt her and he already had too much authority over her as it was. So Celeste played the game coolly and now it was paying off, for he was a man who didn't like being crowded.

"Who is it?" asked Celeste as the nervous convict girl tentatively interrupted the meal.

"A Captain Macdonald and a lady. They wished to see you, Mrs. Carew."

"Very well, show them in."

"But—but," squeaked the girl in despair, "they are dripping wet and would ruin the carpets. I left them standing in the foyer."

"I wonder what they want—"

"Go see," suggested Scott, more interested in his goblet of wine than the untimely visitors.

"I suppose I'll have to."

Angela stood dejectedly, aware of the sight she must present, and exchanged a mournful look with Clyde. Their clothing dripped onto the parquet floor as steadily as the rain outside. She didn't blame the servant for making them wait by the door for they must both look like thoroughly disreputable characters.

A tall, elegantly gowned woman emerged from one of the doors leading off the foyer and Angela fell back a step in surprise. It was her! The hated woman of the governor's ball. No wonder she had felt such instant dislike—this was Scott's mistress! She must be in a terrible state because Mrs. Carew didn't even recognize her but concentrated her attention fully on Clyde.

"Captain Macdonald, what may I do for you? Have you come on official business?"

"Yes, and no," hedged Clyde. "Actually we wanted to see your overseer. Governor Macquarie assigned me the task of finding him."

"Surely he hasn't done anything wrong—"

"No, Mrs. Carew. It's purely a personal matter that requires his attention."

Celeste breathed a silent sigh of relief. For a moment she had thought Scott was in trouble and that usually meant the dreaded Van Diemen's Land. "Please forgive my rudeness. You and your companion must stay the night. I will have rooms prepared immediately. Terrible weather, isn't it?"

She was instructing the hovering servant to prepare rooms when Scott ventured in. "Scott, Captain

Macdonald has come all the way from Sydney to see you."

Angela felt like hiding behind Clyde, anything but face the disdainful look of her estranged husband. But instead, as his insolent stare took her in from plastered hair to muddy boots she lifted her chin in the defiant way he knew only too well and stared right back at him.

He began laughing. She looked like a street urchin, and the fact that she had come seeking him out only to get caught in a cloudburst became more amusing by the second. Scott knew exactly why she was here; she had come to seduce him into dropping the divorce. And now she looked anything but tempting and knew it and her eyes blazed angrily at him. That only made him laugh harder because of the irony of her situation.

"Shut up!" Angela snapped, knowing she was starting out on the wrong foot and cursing her bad luck. She could have stood anything but his amusement.

Celeste looked at her aghast, this time studying her carefully. Those aqua eyes—she had seen them before. A wave of revulsion shuddered through her. The ball! The haughty, too beautiful creature who had stared her down. The celebrated duchess on a wild goose chase, and the search it seemed was ending here. She glanced in confusion at Scott. No, it couldn't be!

"Celeste, my dear," he said drawing her arm through his, barely conquering the laughter that threatened to erupt again. "Have you invited these people to spend the night?"

"Of course," she answered, wanting only to show them the door.

"Then let me introduce them to you. This," he said disparagingly, with a gesture toward Angela, "is the Duchess of Brightling, my wayward wife. And this is Clyde Macdonald, whom I last met upon the occasion of his elopement with Angela. A pity the incident didn't succeed. It would have saved me a lot of trouble.

"Angela," Scott pulled Celeste closer to his side smiling insolently, "let me introduce Celeste Carew, my fiancée!"

She flinched beneath his attack but drew herself up immediately. Now it was her turn to laugh and she did so derisively. "You are in no position to have a fiancée. Have you told her about the children?"

"Children?" repeated Celeste.

"Don't bring them into this, Angela!" Scott warned. "I won't have them involved in this sordid mess!"

"You see," Angela explained sweetly to Celeste, "how protective he is of our children. They mean a great deal to Scott."

"Angela, I think we should go." Clyde stepped in no longer able to bear the sparring between them, wanting only to be quit of the whole scene.

"No!" Scott challenged, looking at Clyde as if he was some insignificant species of insect life. "The rooms are ready. You will spend the night."

Angela lay in a comfortable bed staring at the ceiling. The room was dark and in spite of the hot bath and the degree of tiredness she felt, she couldn't sleep. Everything had gone wrong from the moment it had started raining. And Scott knew exactly why she had come, she had seen it in his eyes. What could she do now?

She turned over and punched her pillow in frustration. Where was he now? Probably in Celeste Carew's bed just as she had imagined on the long ride here. The thought made her squirm like a butterfly impaled on a pin and she buried her hot face in the pillow. Things never went smoothly for her. Why couldn't she be one of those people that skimmed placidly through life in a perpetual haze of happiness? Certainly she deserved some peace soon.

Just as she was dozing off a sound caught her attention and Angela's eyes flickered open in surprise. It couldn't be—yet she heard it again! Celeste's room was right across the hall from hers and the unmistakable sounds of violent lovemaking crept through her closed door.

"No—no!" she cried putting her hands over her ears

to block out the noise. Scott couldn't be so cruel! Shouldn't she have realized from past experience what extremes he could go to when enraged? It wasn't enough that he had flaunted Celeste as his fiancée beneath her nose, he must drive home the point by his obvious betrayal.

He was proving his disdain for her, purposely trying to drive her away, out of his life forever. What better way to prove his hate than let her hear their noisy combat, while she his rightful wife lay helpless and alone writhing in the dark?

A few more minutes and she could stand it no longer. What did he expect—that she would just stand calmly by and let them humble her into fleeing? Scott should know better! With her temper threatening to explode from the confines of her room Angela whipped back the covers and sprang out of bed.

The gall of Scott! She would show him and that hussy a thing or two. Fumbling in her saddlebag her fingers touched what she sought, cold hard metal hidden in the recesses of her bag. With no thought for anything else she dashed across the hall dressed in the filmy, beribboned silk nightgown designed only to distract and entrance a man.

Angela stood just outside the door pressing her forehead against the wood with a shaking hand upon the doorknob. She could hear Celeste's moans and Scott laughing, cajoling her into new acts of rashness. The fact that this show was put on expressly for her benefit only incensed Angela further. She had told Clyde that she would make Celeste wish she was dead and her fingers itched to scratch her eyes out and ruin her looks for good.

The door was locked! She was stupid to have thought otherwise, so in a frantic attempt to stem the sounds of passion she began pounding on the door with her fist, not stopping even when the sounds ceased.

"Who the hell is it?" But Scott's voice sent her speechless and she grasped the now warm metal in one hand, continuing to pound with the other.

The door jerked open and he stood there as magnificently naked as a bronze statue barring her way with one hand upon the door jamb.

"Well?" he taunted raking her scanty costume with knowing, amused eyes. "Did you come to join the orgy?"

Angela suddenly found herself in the room with the door firmly closed. Celeste looked at her with glazed, unbelieving eyes from the big bed recently vacated by her lover.

"What do you say, Celeste? Wouldn't a brief *ménage a trois* be a diversion?"

"Get her out of here!" The covers slipped down to her waist, baring voluptuous breasts heaving with resentment. "Now!"

"She is your guest. You throw her out!" Scott stood back vastly entertained and leaned against the wall, his arms crossed over his chest.

Celeste slid off the bed and stormed across the room entirely put out by the whole series of events that had occurred since Angela's arrival. Scott wasn't helping matters at all, in fact he was baiting her for his own reasons, which she didn't have the time to fathom at the moment. Getting the slut out of her bedroom was of paramount importance right now.

But as she neared Angela, the duchess pulled a knife on her and Celeste jumped back just in time to avoid the slicing arc of the blade. "Scott!" she cried backing away from the vicious little gypsy who seemed to know exactly what she was doing. "Scott, she's going to kill me!" But he just watched through suddenly narrowed eyes.

He had never seen two ladies fight before, and that they were fighting over him like a couple of cats interested him. She was as unpredictable as ever, more so, because she actually looked as if she could kill Celeste. And in a vivid flash Scott thought, she really does love me, and he wondered how far he would allow the battle to go.

"Yes," shouted Angela advancing menacingly on

Celeste. "I am going to kill you, you lily-livered bitch! But before I do I'm going to mark you up good! Do you think I'll let you take my husband away from me without a fight? If you want him, Celeste, you had better fight, because I'm willing to die for what I want!"

Angela slashed again at the retreating woman. Soon she would be backed into a corner and would be at her mercy. Celeste hurled a footstool at her and although she moved quickly it caught her painfully in the shin causing her to pause, tears starting in her eyes.

"Whore!" Celeste threw the wrong word at Angela and she closed in for the kill.

Scott couldn't believe his eyes. It was an uneven battle. Angela was much shorter and Celeste out-weighed her considerably but Angela had the knife—and the daring. He watched as his wife kicked Celeste in the stomach and when she doubled over Angela punched her in the nose with her left hand.

The blow glanced off but left his mistress with a bloody nose and Angela grasped the taller woman's hair throwing her to the floor. Then the two of them were wrestling on the floor, Angela straddling the stunned redhead. She twisted her fingers in her hair banging her rival's head savagely against the floor.

Celeste caught Angela's wrist as the knife flashed close to her eyes and held her off with her greater strength. But with black hair flying she bore down banging Celeste's head against the leg of a chair and scoring her cheek with long sharp nails. The red drops of blood sent Angela wild and lowering her head she bit through the skin of Celeste's wrist until her fingers unclenched and she let out a loud scream.

Scott started across the room but before he could put an end to the combat Angela sliced a long oozing trail of blood between Celeste's breasts all the way down over her cringing stomach. She shrieked like a madwoman even though the cut was only superficial for the knife was lowering to her cheek.

Angela was hauled unceremoniously off her

opponent and Scott held her firmly with one arm about her waist and the other squeezing all the feeling out of her wrist. She cursed at him, kicking back at him with bare feet but the knife fell to the carpet with a dull thud and Scott kicked it out of reach.

The fight, the untamed, bloodthirsty tigress Angela had turned into and most of all her unrestrained wiggling attempts to free herself incited Scott's lust beyond the point of control. He threw her to the floor not six feet away from a stunned Celeste, who lay very still as if she was in shock.

As Angela tried to crawl away from him he caught her around the waist, kneeling behind her, lifting the diaphanous whisper of material that separated his burning flesh from hers.

"No, Scott! Don't!" she cried as he bared her flesh, sliding one hot hand up her thigh. She struggled and pleaded and cursed him all to no avail.

He mounted her like a mare brought to stud and with as little consideration. As he pulled her hard against him she hung her head in shame, her long curls screening her flaming face from the incredulous, astounded gaze of Celeste. Angela was powerless before the frenzy of his attack and she cried out each time he jolted his body against her buttocks, ravaging her femininity in an excess of passion.

Scott bent over her cupping one breast and playing with it with brutal fingers. He whispered obscene things in her ear all the while with his arm clamped like an iron band around her waist, preventing escape.

"Angel, Angel, you drive me beyond the point of human endurance! Am I hurting you? I can tell I am, and you deserve it you little wildcat! You tear me to pieces with words, make me reckless with a glance, send me to heaven with your body."

She was crying with hurt and humiliation and he bit her shoulder, shuddering under the spell of this enchantress. "You make me want to die laying you; you confuse and contradict yourself. Even after the children and your leagues of lovers you're as tight as a virgin but as hot as a bitch in heat! Come, my little whore, don't fight it, give in! Let me make you feel the ecstasy you give me."

His hand brushed against her belly, grazed the satin flesh between her thighs and sent an unwelcome thrill through her. And in spite of her mortification, the discomfort, and the subjugation of the posture he forced a response from her.

"You bastard!" she screamed unable to stop crying, beyond stemming the tide of ardor that was buffeting her toward completion. "I hate you! I hate you!"

And then her debasement was accomplished as he vanquished her completely. She convulsed like a wanton, taking Scott with her to total forgetfulness.

Freeing herself, Angela sprang to her feet pushing her nightgown back down over her nakedness, covering the breast Scott had revealed. She was shaking with the ignominy of the act, horrified that her body had disgraced her. As she started for the door a gleam of candlelight glancing off the discarded knife caught her eye and she scooped it up from the carpet.

She wasn't thinking rationally, she wasn't thinking at all! Scott had degraded her before his mistress, proved once and for all that she really was a whore, to his satisfaction and hers.

As he stumbled to his feet Celeste's scream alerted Scott and he turned as Angela struck out at him and the blade sliced flesh and muscle. He took the full force in the back and he staggered as a pain seared across his shoulder blade. The knife fell from Angela's numb fingers and she stared at it stupidly.

He looked at her in amazement, at the bloodied knife on the floor and began laughing. "I should have known better than to turn my back on you!"

Celeste got up and then toppled over in a dead faint as she saw the blood covering his whole back, dripping down his arm and leg.

Once Angela had watched his pain with pleasure, taunted him as he lay half bleeding to death and reveled in it, but not now. "Scott! Oh, what have I done?"

cried Angela her face as white as his was rapidly becoming.

His left arm hung limply, dripping scarlet but the other shot out, grabbed her wrist and pulled her up against him. Scott held her tightly against his chest and she could feel his heart pounding against her cheek. His blood, warm and sticky drenched them both and he tangled his fingers in her hair wrenching her head back till he could look into her eyes.

"Savage!" he said before his lips crushed hers, reclaiming the territory he had just staked out.

Clyde chose that moment to investigate the unusual sounds that had wakened him from a deep sleep. The room was utter chaos, a gruesome scene from a horror story, and Clyde dashed his hand over his eyes wondering if he was sleepwalking. Scott and Angela stained with blood embraced in the middle of the room, and he didn't know which one of them was injured. Celeste looked like a naked corpse and a knife lay on the floor.

In a panic, thinking that Scott had murdered Celeste and fatally wounded Angela, Clyde strode to the bellpull and jerked it wildly. Angela and Scott looked at him as if they were awakening from a dream and before any of them knew what had happened half a dozen servants were swarming into the room.

Angela sat on the floor beside Scott's bed and he lay on his stomach, his face turned toward her. His hand clutched hers as it rested in her lap and in his brown eyes was pain but not from the wound she had inflicted on him. They were alone in his cabin, a small one room place she had not known existed until last night.

She and Clyde had tended the long ugly gash on his shoulder. At his insistence he spent the night in his own bed with Angela hovering anxiously. Now she could hardly believe that the events of last night had occurred. They were both subdued as her voice hesitated and he urged her on.

He was dragging the whole ugly story from her, all the horrid things that had happened during her long separation. Angela explained about Keith's cruel plot and deception, the deaths of their unborn child and her parents and the episodes with the Vaughns. Her lips trembled as she spoke almost incoherently of his bogus death and her marriage to Keith.

She told him how she found out the truth and burst out, "I challenged Keith to a duel and I killed him the next morning!"

"Oh, love! My poor lost Angel."

"I'm not that! I'm a murderess—he wouldn't even defend himself! I shot him down in cold blood because of what he did to us!"

"Shh! It's not your fault. He deserved it." Scott pulled her closer. "Come here, Angel, I want to kiss you."

"No! I almost killed you last night in a blind rage."

"And I deserved that!" Scott lifted his head with a grimace and pulled her to him but she pushed away and jumped to her feet. "Look, Angela, we have both done things we regret. I treated you abominably and you retaliated. Let's forget it. Let's wipe the slate clean and start over again. Come here," he coaxed. "Sit beside me again, or else I will get out of bed and come to you!"

She went swiftly to his side pressing him back down and he caught her hand and kissed each finger and then the palm. Angela brushed the hair from his eyes and he kissed her wrist with the scar.

"And this?" he asked. "There is more. And the scar on your shoulder?"

"Oh," she laughed tremulously, "only an encounter with the Maroons, who were intent on making me the sacrifice of a voodoo ceremony. Only a small slave revolt with Rosemont burned to the ground and Annee Wallace flayed alive."

So she told him about that, all the details he wanted. But somehow she couldn't bring herself to tell him about the pirate attack, the scuttling of the *Dark Lady*, or Molly, Angus, and Captain Darnell. She couldn't bear to utter Gaston Laporte's name or tell of her captivity, subjection, and rape. And Clare—how could she speak of her illegitimate daughter?

"Angel, there's something else." He looked at her bowed head, her lowered lashes and the guilty pink flush at his words. "Look at me, love—tell me!" He put a finger beneath her chin and forcibly lifted her face.

"I can't," she pleaded struggling to keep back the tears. "Please don't make me! I can't bear even to think of it!"

"That bad? Worse than everything else that happened?"

"Yes—much worse, a thousand times worse!" Her nostrils flared and her bottom lip trembled treacherously so she caught it between her teeth.

Scott watched her, aching to know the rest, wanting to hold and comfort her. She looked so pathetically brave trying to keep from crying but with her big eyes threatening to overflow.

"Come, come," he said trying to let her know that nothing could be that bad but those were the words Laporte had repeated so often and she shied away from him, pulling free and running from the cabin.

Then Scott got out of bed very stiffly and pulled on a pair of trousers and his boots. It took longer than he expected and when he emerged from the cabin Angela was gone. But he circled the cabin and found her out back crying silently against the trunk of a peach tree.

She spun around with her face streaming and shouted, "It has nothing to do with us or our love. Don't torture me! I can't tell you yet! I can't! I can't!" There was a hysterical edge to her voice.

"Shh, sweetheart," Scott soothed taking her into his arms. "You don't have to tell me anything. I love you just the way you are."

He kissed her wet cheeks, her quivering eyelids and her hair. "I love you, Angel! Don't cry. Everything is all right now. You're safe with me and I will protect you from ever being hurt again."

Scott's lips closed over hers tenderly, without passion, gentling her until he felt a response start and her arms went around his waist.

"I think you should get back in bed," she finally said with a smile breaking through her tears.

"I agree, but only if you join me!"

Celeste lay in her darkened room where she had spent the last week, ever since that disastrous night. She couldn't stop thinking about it and even dreamed about it when she slept. So she slept badly and there were dark circles under her eyes. She touched her wrist where Angela's teeth marks were fading and then thought of the ugly long line that marred her body.

Scott had come to see her once, tried to explain that he and his wife were back together again. He had apologized for everything, and the whole time she had felt like dying. He was in love with that she-devil even after she had tried to murder him. He admired her spirit and Celeste gritted her teeth so she wouldn't say the things she wanted to. She felt like screaming and throwing a tantrum, crying and having him comfort her. But instead she had kept silent and plotted Angela's downfall.

Their lives had been perfect before his wife had arrived and Celeste wanted it that way again. If Scott could believe the worst about his wife once, he could again—but this time let him have solid proof. If he saw some damning evidence against her with his own eyes, actually saw her cuckolding him, he would have to believe it.

So Celeste planned and plotted sure that Clyde Macdonald could be put to use in her idea. After all he mooned over her like a lovesick calf. They both had much to gain by separating Scott and Angela.

Celeste smiled. Separate them she would even if she had to tear them apart with her bare hands. Then she would have Scott again and Clyde could take Angela home to England far from temptation's path.

A knock on the door interrupted her web-weaving for the moment and her maid came into the room bringing her lunch and the latest gossip.

Everyone, from the governor to the chain gang

convicts, knew of the events at Thornhill. How the duchess had routed her husband and his mistress right in her house. The fight was embellished and rumor had it that she had knifed her husband in the back as she caught him in the act. The gossips had Scott at death's door but once more madly in love with the virago that disguised herself as a lady.

They were having a field day telling and retelling the story of her arrival and search for her mysterious husband. That Scott had turned out to be the errant duke surprised no one. Hadn't he proved his accomplishments beyond a shadow of a doubt, his virtues and his vices? They waited with baited breath for the outcome. Who would make the next move? Mrs. Carew wouldn't give up easily but she had to contend with a woman said to be the devil's daughter—or his wife! The duke was in between and on the shadow fringes Captain Macdonald also fit into the picture. Fans fluttered and calls were paid with unusual frequency during the hot summer days.

"I have a surprise for you, when you come to Sydney," Angela teased, snuggling next to him in bed.

"Tell me now!" Scott demanded.

"No, you must wait. I want you to see it with your own eyes, read every word yourself. Then you can really believe it's true. We must have a celebration!"

"I've had my celebration, having you all to myself for a whole week. I don't ever want it to end, Angel."

"It never will." And she buried her face against his neck laughing at her own delightful secret.

Scott stroked her hair, never tiring of the silky warmth of her tresses. The past days had been an idyll of joyous renewal and he was beginning to understand Angela's moods and caprices. He had found he couldn't blame her for the events she had revealed to him but in the back of his mind he still wondered about that blank portion of her life that she wouldn't share with him.

Each day brought further healing, not only of his back but of the wounds caused by time, separation, and suspicion. They were lazy and they laughed a lot, spending far too much time in bed. They hadn't seen another person in days and didn't need to because their present world encompassed only themselves. They basked in the warmth of their love and held it selfishly to themselves.

Angela cooked their simple meals and cleaned the small almost monastic cabin. And they talked and made plans for the future and she tried to paint a vivid picture with words of Robert and Lorna and the years he had missed of their growing up. He could never hear enough about the children and wanted every detail of every day she could remember.

They packed a picnic lunch and went out to the orchard and ate beneath the peach trees. The wine, the hot sun, and the smell of the fragrant summer made them drowsy so they lay watching the sky through a latticework of green branches. Her hand curled warmly into his and they were content to remain silent, barely touching.

The peace they had both so badly needed spread over them like a golden haze, a wonderful fantasy from which they need never awaken. The past and all its problems had disappeared and there was only the present. The sun was hot but beneath the shade of the trees a cool breeze played and birds hopped about tending their nests, calling to one another. The future was distant and nothing could disturb this interlude.

Except Clyde Macdonald. He strode across the grass toward them looking uncomfortably hot in his uniform and presented Angela with an envelope. "It's from Ezra," he told her as she opened it. "I saw him yesterday and the children are sick."

She read the brief note and knew where her duty was. The measles—why did they have to get it now? But they needed her and Scott needed her and she was torn with frustration.

"It's nothing, darling," she told Scott trying to hide her disappointment. "Just a childhood disease, usually not very serious as long as they are kept quiet and in a dark room."

"I'll go with you!"

"No! You will open your shoulder and your arrival would only excite them too much. Wait till they are better." She tried to smile. "Then I will come back and we can both ride to Sydney together."

"I will be glad to escort Angela back to town," Clyde volunteered and Scott glared at him thinking, I'll just bet you would!

Angela looked at her husband, at the unmistakable jealousy glinting in his eyes and felt warm with the realization that he really did care for her.

"We can't leave before morning anyway," she observed, smoothing over the awkward situation.

Scott made her forget all about her disappointment in leaving that night. He alone had the power to make her drink from the waters of Lethe.

seven

It was a long wearying ride in the full heat of summer and Angela was tired to begin with. Clyde kept glancing at her covertly, at the shadows beneath her eyes and the kiss-bruised lips that he longed to claim for his own.

Why couldn't she realize that she would never be happy with her husband? In a few days or a few weeks they would quarrel again and there would be something else to separate them. They fought like two gladiators, hacking away viciously at each other until they were both half dead, then barely waiting for the wounds to heal before they were at it again. If he was her husband their lives would be well ordered, peaceful, and serene, the way she seemed to want her life to be. But that man always got in the way.

He had seen Celeste the night before and found himself pouring out his thoughts to her in a way he would have deemed impossible. But she was such a good listener and she had agreed with him thoroughly, urging him to think of a plan. She felt the same way about Scott as Clyde did about Angela and proposed they pool their resources to find a way to break up the marriage. It shouldn't be difficult at all. The foundation was shaky enough already.

With Angela wrapped in a cocoon of silence they made the journey back to Sydney. Even she noticed the way people craned their necks to get a better view of them as they rode into town in the early evening. She frowned and glanced at Clyde to see if he had noticed.

"Gossip," he said. "They know everything."

"So it's starting again. I can't leave my notorious past behind anywhere."

"It's not that so much as what happened at Thornhill."

"But surely they don't know everything about that!" Her fair skin turned fiery and Clyde wondered what else had happened in Celeste's bedroom.

As they reached the house overlooking Cockle Bay Ezra greeted them at the door. He looked tired from caring for the children but brightened at the sight of Angela.

"How are they, Ezra?" Angela asked leaving the horses to Clyde and climbing the stairs to the front veranda.

"Monsters!" He smiled rolling his eyes. "But really, they are pretty sick. Lorna got it first, not long after you left. I thought it was just a cold at first, until the rash appeared."

"Has the doctor seen them?"

"Yes."

They talked while she washed some of the dust from her hands and face and then she went into the sickroom where they all lay with various stages of the sickness.

Clare was asleep, her golden curls tousled and the rash just begining on her face. Maggie smiled as she came in, a look of relief flooding her face as she sponged Lorna's brow with cool water. Poor Lorna was feverish and covered all over with red blotches. Her face was puffy and her eyes bloodshot and she moved restlessly on her bed.

"Mama!" She brightened as Angela gave her a quick kiss and smoothed her hair away from her face. "I don't feel good."

"Of course you don't, baby. But I'm back now and everything will be all right. And when you are well I have a wonderful surprise for all of you."

"What?" Robert bounced from his bed and threw his arms around her neck.

"Now you must be good and stay very still or I won't tell you."

"But I itch and feel all wiggily!" protested Robert.

"I know—but the better you behave the sooner you will be well and then. . . ." She dangled the surprise tantalizingly before them and laughed as he scrambled back into bed.

"I'm good Mama! See how good I am?"

He was so exactly like Scott that she felt like crying but instead she went to change. What was the matter with her?

The next days did nothing to alleviate the way she felt as their sickness took its toll on her too. Ezra and the two Murrays helped but it was their mother that the children wanted and that left her drained. She slept too little and her appetite all but disappeared as the summer proceeded with a hot blast. Sometimes the air was so still and breathless she could hardly breathe.

Silent Maggie was irreplaceable in her care of the children. She was so patient and loving with them, a calming influence at times when Angela felt like pulling out her hair. Often it was only the convict girl that could put Clare to sleep and a special bond seemed to grow visibly between them.

On a moonless night of black intensity Angela strolled slowly through the garden. She could barely see the plants and flowers but their sweet scent was soothing and there was a breeze off the bay. It stirred tendrils of hair across her cheeks and she leaned wearily against the wattle tree gazing into the dark void that was the sea.

Here and there lights bobbed upon the waves, ship's lanterns like skipping stars. The panorama of southern skies, different but now familiar to her eyes, was a hazy white veil against night's dark mantle. The sounds of the waves were hypnotic, the smell of the sea intoxicating, and she closed her eyes with a weariness she had not believed could possess her.

Lorna was much worse, worse than the doctor had indicated a healthy child should be. She had a dry hacking cough and no appetite, fading away into a translucent shadow of her former self. She had difficulty breathing at night unless propped up on several pillows into a half-sitting position, so after her brief walk Angela would return and spend the night by her side listening to the labored breathing.

Tears prickled at her closed eyelids as hot and sharp as needles. She could think only of her mother, the weakness of her lungs and the constant battle for breath. Could something like that be passed down from one generation to another? Could Lorna, such an active vital child till now, have inherited that predisposition?

Angela wanted Scott here, now, to help her shoulder the burden of her own worries. He could make everything right again. He would laugh and remind her of her overactive imagination and blow the cobwebs from the corners of her mind.

Footsteps sounded on the veranda and Angela opened her eyes to see a man silhouetted against the light from the house.

"Scott! Scott!" She ran straight to his arms.

He picked her up and swung her around crushing her against him. They kissed frantically and then she burst into tears, pressing her cheek against his chest so he wouldn't see her face. Scott stroked her hair, one arm around her too fragile waist.

"Aren't you glad to see me?"

"Oh, darling, how can you ask!" she burst out. "But it has been so long."

"Only two weeks," he said tilting her wet face up and wiping her cheeks with tender fingers. "An eternity!"

His mouth claimed hers in a deep soul-satisfying kiss that left them hungering for more and then he held her away appraising her with critical eyes. Both hands spanned her waist easily and in the light spilling from the doorway he thought how tired she looked.

"Angel, you haven't been taking care of yourself. You are far too thin—everywhere except here—" And his hand cupped her breast, hot through the cotton of her dress.

His eyes glowed down at her and Scott heard the

slight catch in her breath, felt her nipple spring up beneath his touch. The tears dissolved into a smile and her lips parted as her hands slid up and down the front of his shirt. She needed him and wanted him more than she needed sleep and Scott swung her up into his arms and carried her to the bedroom, her soft throaty laugh close to his ear.

She was a wild vixen in her demands on him and Scott could hardly contain himself after his abstinence of the past few weeks. For after their interlude together Celeste had retreated like a shadow and he was full of thoughts of Angela and no one else. How could he want another woman when perfection was his? His woman, his wife, his love! She was everything and more and his senses reeled as the softness of her breasts pressed against his face.

She was an innocent wanton, an enchantress, filling his eyes with her beauty, his nostrils with the dizzying woman-scent peculiarly her own, his head with bizarre fantasies that became reality when she was in his arms. Her soft moans and love words were urgent in his ears, her taut body accepted him with a sigh of pure pleasure. And then they ceased to be individuals, but were one in thought, movement, and purpose as they raced toward the ultimate goal and found it together in the whirlwind of their love.

In the aftermath Angela was all soft and warm, curled against him like a contented kitten.

"Angel, love, you drive me insane until madness is sanity and the only reality is you!" Scott brushed gentle kisses against her cheek and her fingers curled into the thick hair at the back of his neck. Her eyes closed heavily and he breathed against her ear, "You send me on a trip to the stars—so high, so fast—I never want to come back to earth!"

Angela stretched and turned over burrowing luxuriously into the bed. She felt warm and glowing and a smile twitched at the corners of her lips. Her hand reached out and found emptiness and her eyes flew open to a new day.

The sun was high spilling through the slightly parted

curtains with a curious intensity. The pillow beside her still held the indentation of Scott's head. How considerate he was letting her sleep late, knowing she had been in a state close to exhaustion last night. He was probably with the children.

"Children!" Angela sat bolt upright fully awake and petrified with fear. "Clare!"

She hadn't even told him about Clare! She had meant to after the children had fully recovered, was going to tell him when she met him at Thornhill before they returned together to Sydney. But he had come unexpectedly in answer to her unuttered plea and the sight of him had driven every thought of other matters from her mind. She still tingled from last night's interchange of passion.

Scrambling from the bed she shoved her arms into the sleeves of a robe and belted it around her waist. Quaking with dreaded anticipation of his reaction she searched for her other slipper and could find it nowhere so she ran barefooted down the hall and paused to catch her breath outside the children's door. Maybe he hadn't seen them yet, maybe he had gone for a ride, was eating breakfast, or walking in the garden.

She opened the door quietly and saw him sitting beside Lorna's bed holding her hand with Robert on his knee. There was loving adoration written all over his face as he spoke softly to them, a smile of rediscovery. Then he turned his head and saw her and the look was gone. Hard angry eyes reproached her, drove the breath from her body and the secret mask of studied indifference closed over his face.

Angela opened the door wider, saw Maggie sitting in the rocking chair on the other side of the room with Clare on her lap. The baby smiled and reached out her arms for her and uttered, "Mama, Mama." Her gaze wandered back to Scott and saw the way his lips clamped into a tight white line.

He said with a voice of winter ice, "Who is she?"

And Angela couldn't speak. She was numb with terror, her hold on the doorknob the only thing keeping her erect. She saw their lives cracking apart again and all because of her own foolishness. Why hadn't she told him sooner? To spring a surprise like this upon him was cruel on her part. If only he hadn't come—not yet—not before she had told him!

"But I told you, Papa," Lorna reminded in a thin voice. "She's Clare, my sister."

And from across the room Clare looked straight at Scott and repeated over and over, "Papa, Papa, Papa—"

Scott looked at Angela standing like a marble statue, only her huge frightened eyes alive in her face. The white silk of the robe over her bosom didn't even move with a breath and the only color about her was her black hair hanging to her hips and aqua eyes, too brilliant in the dimness of the room. Even at the height of this lying treachery she was desirable and in amazement he tried to sort out his careening emotions.

"She has the look of a Montgomery," he observed putting Robert down and rising to a frightening height over her.

"Not here," Angela managed to get out in a voice hoarse with pain. "Not in front of the children."

His hand closed around her wrist propelling her from the room, dragging her to their room and she stumbled docilely after him. She was as terrified as the time he had caught her leaving Seafield Castle with Clyde, as mesmerized as a doe cornered by a panther.

The crash of the door brought her to her senses and Scott was leaning against it barring any escape, with his face looking as dangerous as an attacking pirate and his arms crossed firmly across his chest.

"Why, Angela? Why?" Scott controlled himself with difficulty. "Why didn't you tell me about her? Why did you keep me in the dark? Why do you lie and conceal the most important parts of your life from me? Why didn't you trust me? Am I an ogre to be placated with half truths for fear I'll kill you? I forgave you everything else, why not this? If only you had told me! Why did you hide this from me, Angela?"

She swallowed hard, moistening her dry lips with the tip of her tongue. Her knees shook and he stared silently at her, waiting with golden flames of anger leaping from his eyes. "I—I didn't want to spoil our time together. I meant to tell you before you came to Sydney, but you showed up unexpectedly. Last night was ours and this morning you were gone before I woke."

"Whose is she?"

"Mine! Clare is my daughter."

"And who fathered her, Angela?" He grasped her shoulders and shook her. "Was it Keith? Was it him?" A snarl like that of a ferocious animal twisted his dark face.

"No, No!"

"You little liar! You said you had no other lover but him—your fake husband! Who else was there? Hell how many others have enjoyed your lovely little body?" His hand closed around her throat and he shook her again. Answer me, Duchess, before I do something I will regret!"

She was helpless in his grasp, her face as pale as alabaster, streaming with tears. Pressing her trembling lips together she shook her head until her hair flew, half covering her face. She could never tell him. It would be better to be dead at his hands than to tell him the truth—her black past of sordid degradation that she tried never to think about for fear she would go mad.

"Who are you protecting? Is she Clyde's? Ezra's? The prince's? Stop looking at me as if you were a martyr being tortured!"

"No! I will never tell you—never! I had no lovers, no lovers!"

"Then how did you get her—by Immaculate Conception?"

Scott threw her on the bed. "Our marriage is a sham! The only time we don't fight is in bed but we can't live our whole lives there, Angela! There are so many cracks and missing pieces our marriage can't stand the full light of day without falling completely apart.

"I just can't take it anymore—the constant battles

and bickering, the lies and deceptions! One minute I think you are an angel straight from heaven, the next I know you are a whore! I regret the day I first laid eyes on you. I regret everything that has taken place since then. It's just not worth the effort. You can consider the marriage over, Angela."

"Where—where are you going?"

"Straight to hell by the most direct route! I don't know. Back to Thornhill, to Celeste. Does it really matter?"

As he slammed the door she screamed something after him in a high, hysterical tone that was drowned out by the banging of wood on wood.

The closest proximity to hell in Sydney was the ragged area below Fort Phillip called The Rocks. Near the slaughter house it reeked from refuse and was the haunt of ravenous birds and escaped convicts. It was a lawless, unpatrolled area, and because of its unsavory reputation even watchmen and constables refused to enter it.

But Scott entered it unafraid. He could hold his own with anyone—anyone but Angela. He felt as if he had been punched repeatedly in the stomach with ironclad fists. Why did she have the power to defeat him utterly? Why did he let her? Once she had told him that he confused her with a thousand whys—but she presented him with the same quandary. Except with Angela it was ten thousand whys, a million whys, and all of them unanswerable.

Garbage, entrails, and dead fish sucked at his boots in the undrained streets. Even in the bright sunlight rats stared boldly from shadowy corners and there was an incessant scream of gulls fighting over scraps of food. Scott threaded his way down zigzag streets, past huts built at crazy angles, reached by flights of ramshackle steps. A chamber pot was emptied from a window without warning, spattering a drunk unconscious in the slimy quagmire. He sidestepped him without really seeing, swishing away a cloud of black flies that were everywhere.

A child of about two sat in the mud crying with flies

crusting his face while two dogs mated a few feet away. Scott turned up a lane with huts leaning together above the path so that the sun was almost blocked out and the air was still and stagnant with decay. He mounted steps that bucked and swayed beneath his weight, threatening to collapse, and pushed open a door.

The atmosphere inside was fetid and dirty but he took a chair and tilted it back against a wall. A big man wearing a filthy apron, overhung by a huge belly approached and Scott flipped him a coin. He caught it deftly, squinting at it in the darkness, testing it between his teeth.

"Rum!" Scott ordered. "Two bottles—and a clean glass."

A sailor off one of the ships in the cove eyed the promising newcomer, wondering if he could cadge a drink. But one vicious look from Scott squelched that idea permanently.

The day grew hotter and hotter until the tavern was an oven. But Scott didn't notice. He gulped down drink after drink and cursed women in general and Angela in particular. She was a lying, cheating slut fit only to be a whore in a place like The Rocks. He could just see her here mauled by criminals and sailors, crawling with flies, that should be her fate—not the comfort of the house on the hill or Brightling Castle or the London house on St. James's Square.

He was filthy, roaring drunk as he had never been before. Even after he had found Keith and Angela together he hadn't been this bad off. There was murder in his heart as he staggered from the tavern under cover of darkness and when a group of tattered criminals jumped him he fought like an enraged bull.

A long knife disappeared into the muck at his kick and the man ran howling into the night with a broken arm. Several fists made contact with his face but he felt it less than the flies. He grabbed two men and cracked their heads together, turned and kneed another in the groin. Moans and screams sounded in the Stygian darkness and the others fled before his counterattack.

With his head reeling from blows and spirits he could hear Angela shrieking at him again as he left her room. The words echoed in his rum-fogged brain becoming clearer and clearer.

"He raped me," he heard her yell in the recesses of his benumbed mind. "That devil raped me, and Clare is his daughter!"

What devil? If some man had hurt her he would kill him with pleasure. Scott's bruised fists clenched, ready once again to attack. Who had raped her? Who was Clare's father?

It was close to midnight and the air hung still and heavy, full of the cloying perfume of English flowers transplanted to foreign soil. A pale sliver of a moon hung suspended in an unmoving heaven and not one sound broke the silence of the night. Angela leaned against a pillar on the back veranda and even the wood was warm against her cheek.

She felt empty and feverish as if she had been sick for a long, long time and had just awakened in a strange place surrounded by strangers. Her body felt heavy as if it belonged to someone else but still there was an odd little ache in her bosom. It jabbed her every time she breathed as if to remind her of its presence. Her eyes were dry and scratchy and her throat was raw with crying. There wasn't a tear left in her, they all resided in a sodden pillow that just lately had cushioned Scott's head.

Angela felt almost as she had when under Laporte's spell, without a will of her own, vacant, controlled by outside forces. And the fact that she couldn't remember the part of the day after Scott had left filled her with panic. Laporte and Jules were with her on the veranda, along with Scott's angry eyes, and they laughed tauntingly—witnesses to their final revenge.

A soft, clear song filled the silent night. Hauntingly wistful, the words were in a strange melodious tongue Angela had never heard. Jules, Laporte, and Scott vanished and she stood very quietly drinking in the beauty of that voice. It was so lovely that accompanying music could not have added anything to the song.

She followed the sweet notes that lingered on the air, her bare feet a soft whisper against the smooth wood. Outside the children's room Angela crouched down resting her elbows on the low windowsill and her chin on her hands. By the flickering illumination of the night light she saw Maggie rocking Clare in the rocking chair and the baby's rapt attention was focused on her.

It was a lullaby coming from Maggie's lips! The silent girl who never spoke but made her presence felt in so many other ways. Angela stared unbelievingly, yet fascinated, as Maggie's face glowed from within with love for the child cradled against her breast. The unknown words were as smooth and comforting to Angela as they seemed to be to Clare.

A loud crash out front put an abrupt end to the enchanting moment. Angela stood up with her hand over her pounding heart, which only made the pain worse. What if it was an escaped convict trying to gain entry? They could all be murdered in their beds before anyone came to investigate.

Hurrying into the house she shot the bolt on the back door and stood with her back to it straining her ears for another telltale sound. A bang on the door and a scratching sound, slurred shouted words jarred her eardrums. She almost couldn't recognize his voice or her name which he called over and over again.

She flew to the front door and unlocked it, throwing it wide but there was no one.

"Angela!" He was lying on the floor and as she bent over him she caught the sour smell of alcohol and sweat.

"You're drunk!" As she straightened up he grabbed for her and instead caught her nightgown, ripping open the whole front.

"Gonna kill tha' devil!" Scott told her but the slurred words were so garbled that she thought he meant to kill her.

Backing away from him she started to scream, piercing the air even to where Ezra slept in the loft above the stable. "Ezra! Ezra! Help me!" He had his hand around her ankle but she struggled to get free. "Ezra! Kate!"

But Maggie was there first with the night light in one hand and a long kitchen knife clutched in the other. Angela kicked free of Scott's hand and when Ezra got there they were huddled in the doorway clinging to each other with Scott unconscious at their feet.

"What the hell is going on, Angela?"

She almost laughed. That was the first time Ezra had called her anything but my lady.

"He's drunk."

"And well he should be after the way he treated you today! What do you want me to do with him?"

"Bring him in the house."

"He belongs in a gutter! Are you all right?" Ezra saw the way she clutched her torn nightgown together with both hands.

"Fine," she reassured him taking Maggie into the house and instructing Kate to get the children back to sleep.

"Maggie," Angela said taking the knife from her hand and laying it on the kitchen table, "you were wonderful and so brave! Thank you." Then she kissed her thin cheek and smiled, noticing the way her face lit up at the small offering of affection. "You have been working so hard lately, go to bed and get a good night's sleep."

The girl left, as quiet as ever and Angela didn't mention her night song.

Ezra heaved Scott into the house. "Where do you want him?" Angela stood looking at Scott dangling over his shoulder, undecided. "Damn, he's heavy! Hurry up!"

"I don't know."

He dumped him on the kitchen floor and Angela gasped at the blood on his face, leaning closer with a candle to inspect the damage.

"Looks like he's been in a fight. Shouldn't you put something on?"

Angela flushed pulling the material back over her

breasts, trying to close the gap at her hips. He had seen her naked before, but only in times of absolute distress. She hurried to her room and changed and by the time she got back Ezra had Scott stripped of his filthy clothes and was washing off the dirt and blood.

One of Scott's eyes was swollen, turning different shades of blue, green, and black; he had a bloody nose and a cut high on one cheek. The only other injuries were the bruised knuckles.

"He's dead drunk," Ezra observed. "He will have some hangover tomorrow. It serves him right for the way he has treated you."

"No, Ezra, it was all my fault. I never told him about Clare. How would you feel if you found out your wife had an illegitimate child?"

"I don't have a wife, and I hope I never do!"

"Yes, I haven't set a very good example. But this is my doing and I'm a fool not to have told him. To have it sprung on him as a surprise—"

"Does he know everything now?"

"No." Angela's voice quavered as she sat back on her heels. "I couldn't! I just couldn't bring myself to tell that nightmare! I feel sick and shaky just thinking about it. I can't even speak that monster's name!"

"It's all right, don't get upset. Do you want me to tell him?"

"No, I don't know! Oh, Ezra! I don't know anything anymore. I'm so confused."

"Just wait and see what tomorrow brings."

"I'm afraid of that. I never know what Scott will do. If I had told him about the pardon on the first day he would have taken it and the *Cygnet* and left me immediately. I was going to give it to him this morning and then this! I'm afraid that if he is free we will have another fight and he will be off and I'll never see him again."

"Don't tell him. Wait until your lives settle down and you are both sure of yourselves and your marriage. If he thinks he is still bound here, he can't leave. . . ."

"But he is bound to Celeste Carew!"

"From what I've heard, she is easier to fight than your own husband's stubbornness!"

"Yes. Maybe you are right."

"At least he will still be in New South Wales. You will know where to find him. If he leaves," Ezra shrugged his wide shoulders expressively, "who knows if you would ever find him again."

Red-hot pincers were prying the top of his head off and inside a blacksmith was pounding with his hammer. A cannon ball was perched on his stomach and his eyes were blazing balls of fire. Scott groaned and put both hands to his head, trying to hold it together. Birds shrilled loudly outside the window and he licked his dry lips with a tongue swollen and foul tasting.

A cold wet cloth caressed his face and came to rest on his forehead and when he opened his eyes the darkened room blinded him. When his vision cleared he saw a disembodied face hovering over him.

"Angel!" His voice was a hoarse, cracked whisper and he reached out a hand to touch her but she moved away.

He was a mess! One eye was black and swollen shut, the other so bloodshot she could see no white. His lower lip was swelling and a dark stubble covered his jaw. In short he looked as if he was in acute misery. Holding the back of Scott's head she helped him drink some water and he sank back onto the pillows exhausted.

A frown knit his brow as he watched her. Something was wrong and for the life of him he couldn't remember. His brain refused to function, too engrossed in its own agony. Angela tended him as if he was a stranger she was nursing in a hospital and there was absolutely no expression on her face or in her usually naked eyes.

"Angel, what happened? What's the matter?" Speaking was a supreme effort.

But she looked at him dispassionately, with those sensuous lips pressed firmly together and said nothing. Had he done something wrong? He would think about it later.

All during the day he was aware of her moving quietly in the background. When the cloths on his head grew warm they were swiftly replaced with a cool one, when he felt sick she held his head while he vomited into a basin. She made him drink water and a thin broth but when he opened his eyes he always closed them quickly at the look on her face. Or was it that there was no expression on her face that bothered him? In between feeling like he was going to die and wishing he was already dead he slept and in his dreams Angela was smiling or angry but never impassive.

When he awoke in the night his head was much clearer but he was alone in the dark room. Scott stretched out his arm but encountered only a vast empty bed where Angela should be. Clare! In his rage over the child he had driven her away and he couldn't blame her for not being by his side. Someone had raped her, he remembered, and he knew now that her fright had not been caused totally by him. She was afraid to relive a terrible period of her own past and he had tried to force her to remember.

Getting stiffly from the bed he lit a candle and washed his face. He caught a glimpse of himself in a shadowy mirror and grimaced. The Rocks! His clothes, cleaned and neatly folded, were on the chair and he put on the trousers and went to search for Angela.

She was sleeping, curled in the rocking chair in the children's room. She looked like a child herself, a lost, very tired child dressed in her mother's nightclothes. What a brute he could be when angry! And after his ill-treatment she had nursed him faithfully through the day and night.

Scott picked her up and she stirred but didn't wake up. She must be exhausted. Soft and warm and light as a feather he cuddled her in his arms on the way back to her room. Putting her beneath the covers he doused the light and removed his clothes. And when he joined her she curled against him as if she belonged nowhere else and he held her, awake for a long time, setting himself impossible goals.

She stirred, the palm of her hand moving upward through the crisp hair on Scott's chest, her body molded warmly against his. Even through her nightgown he could feel the softness of her breasts against his side and then the rising hardness of their peaks rubbing against him. Her long hard thighs were naked against his leg, her nightclothes bunched up around her hips, and in her sleep she looked just like Lorna.

Angela was half-awake, half-dreaming. She was on a tropical island with a phantom-lover and he was everything that she had dreamed a lover should be. Kind and considerate, wooing her with flowers and poetry and then his body. He was the kindest, most considerate of men, never hurting her and they were surrounded by the peaceful tranquility of distilled happiness. He was holding her so gently, whispering words of love and she smiled opening her eyes.

"Oh!" She thudded back to reality as Scott's battered face filled her startled eyes. What was she doing in bed with him? His hand was on her shoulder and his thumb rested against the hollow of her throat. Frantically she jerked it away, sure he was meaning to strangle her and he frowned at the panic in her eyes.

"Let me go!" Angela began struggling away from him but he grasped her firmly with a puzzled look on his face.

"Love, what's wrong?" He turned toward her and she cringed, her breathing rapid and shallow.

"Don't—don't hurt me!"

"Hurt you?" he said with a confused half laugh. "I don't want to hurt you."

"Then let go of me."

"All right," he said releasing her, watching her scramble quickly off the bed.

Without a backward glance she ran from the room and he sat up looking at the door. "What the hell has gotten into her?" he wondered. She was still angry about the argument—what other reason could there be?

Angela was slicing a loaf of bread in the empty kitchen with hurried jerky movements. She had to do something to get her mind off her own problems. The last thing she remembered of last night was being in the children's room and then she had awakened with him. He could have murdered her while she slept and wondered why he hadn't. He probably wanted to rape her first and she snorted with disgust at the idea.

"Angela."

With a start she cut her finger, spinning around with the knife in her hand.

"I won't turn my back on you this time," Scott reminded her, giving her that crooked boyish smile that never failed to make her heart dance.

She looked from him to her injured finger and back again as if he had personally cut her, and her full bottom lip trembled. It was only a small cut, not worth crying over but her nerves were so jangled she couldn't seem to control herself.

Scott pulled a clean handkerchief from his pocket and wrapped it around her finger kissing it as he would have done for a child. She still clutched the knife between them sniffing back the tears.

"It's all right, sweetheart," Scott reassured her, reaching out to touch that irresistible cloud of dark hair but she backed skittishly away from him pointing the knife at his chest. "Do you want to finish the job you started at Thornhill?"

"No. Just keep away!"

"What are you afraid of?"

"You! You tried to kill me the other night when you were drunk."

"I can't believe that!"

"It's true! You ripped the clothes off me and grabbed me—you were talking about killing. Scott! Don't come any closer!"

"Go ahead," he told her moving until the point touched his chest. "If I frighten you that much, why don't you get it over with? Then I'll never bother you again."

The knife clattered to the stone floor. "I don't want to kill you. I would rather have you murder me than have another death on my conscience. There are too many already."

"How many?"

"Keith and Thurston Vaughn—and. . . ."

"You didn't kill Vaughn."

"He killed himself because he couldn't have me."

"And—" Scott prompted, "there are others?"

"I've lost count."

"What happened after you left Jamaica, Angela?" Somehow he was positive the key to the mystery lay in that direction. "Who raped you, Angela? Who is Clare's father?"

"The devil!"

"What was his name?"

"I can't remember." Her eyes were very large and horrified as if she was staring into an abyss containing every imaginary monster conceived by man to frighten others.

"It's all right, love. You don't have to remember." Scott pulled her into his arms and she was stiff and cold, shaking uncontrollably. She had given him a scare. "We won't talk about it now."

"Never!"

"Yes, we will never talk about it. Shh. Let's go back to our room and get you warm."

She was like a little girl awakening from a nightmare as he led her to the bedroom and although he burned to ask her more questions he didn't dare. Was what had happened that bad? If her reaction to even remembering it was any indication it must have been unbearable.

Scott took Angela back to bed and held her shivering body against his. After some time had passed she relaxed a little but when his hand brushed against her breast she stiffened.

"Don't," she gasped and he removed his hand as if he had touched a hot stove. "I don't want you to do that. I don't want you to hurt me."

"I'm not going to do anything to harm you, Angel. I love you." But although she allowed him to hold her she wouldn't let him do anything else.

When Angela woke up it was afternoon and Scott was

still beside her. She frowned in concentration. Hadn't it just been morning? She had been frightened, slicing bread.

"What worries are consuming you now?" Scott asked, relieved that she seemed herself again.

"Why are you here? I thought the marriage was over—you were going back to Celeste."

"I changed my mind. I'm sorry about our fight."

"You mean you've forgiven me?" Her voice quavered in amazement.

"There was nothing to forgive, love."

"I didn't tell you about Clare."

"Yes, you should have told me. I was extremely shocked to say the least and behaved abominably as usual. But will you forgive me for behaving like a beast?"

Angela gave him an incredulous look. Scott—begging her pardon? Impossible! She was dreaming!

"Well?" He smiled at her bewilderment. "Are you going to leave me in suspense? Do you want to torment me to make up for all the pain I've caused you?"

"No! I just want us to be happy. Call me that again!"

"What?"

"Love, as if you really mean it."

"Love, love, love. I really do mean it! My adorable little sweetheart—Angel—enchantress. I love you with all my heart and nothing you do or I do can change it. It's a fact of life, an indisputable law. We were meant for each other. Star-crossed lovers for all eternity."

His mouth claimed hers with swift desire, tongues flickering and pressing with an insatiable hunger. After their quarrel making up was unbelievably sweet. Her lips moved enticingly but when his hand smoothed the long supple curve of her hip, moving her close so she could feel his reaction, she froze. Jerking her mouth free she tried ineffectually to push Scott away.

"What's wrong now?" he asked in exasperation which she mistook for anger.

"No, no! Don't do that—don't touch me like that. You hurt me!"

"I did not! I was being very gentle. I just—" He

demonstrated again but the pressure of his heated loins sent her into an alarming panic. She hit his chest with small clenched fists and then fell back with her eyes wide and staring.

"Angela, stop it!" She was growing cold and trembling again. "Oh, hell! Snap out of it. I won't touch you again."

eight

"Ezra! Ezra!" Scott called out in the musty dimness of the stable. The sun was barely up and long shadows played in the dawn spilling in the open doorway.

He had left Angela sleeping, not wanting her to find out about the conversation he was determined to have with Ezra. For the last three days she had been as elusive as the mist and just as untouchable and Scott meant to get to the bottom of it once and for all.

There was a stirring in the loft and a shower of bits of straw descended, golden in the early light. Scott waited impatiently. He was at the end of his rope, not knowing what to do with his wife. Angela was fine as long as he made no advances, but then it was always the same—that withdrawn coldness that she couldn't seem to help. She was like two different people: herself and some pitiful creature afraid of every shadow.

Ezra came down the ladder and they went into the garden. The *Cygnet* was a black swan dancing on the dappled waters. The bush stretched gray all the way to the mountains which were a smoky-blue. They paused beneath a tree, far from the house and faced each other.

"Ezra, I need the answers to some questions, for Angela's sake as well as my own. You were with her in Jamaica and have been ever since. What happened?"

"I don't think I can tell you unless she gives me leave to."

"No! I don't want you to ask her and stir things up again. Every time I bring up the subject she goes silent, almost blank. Since I found out about Clare she has drifted farther and farther away from me."

"What do you know?" Ezra inquired, not at all sure he even liked the man that was Angela's husband.

"Nothing—only that Clare's father raped Angela and she's terrified to even think about it."

"What she told you was the truth."

"I know. I believe that, but I must know more. How can I convince you? Look, I love her. I know you think I'm a liar, a brute that mistreats her and you are partially right. Our relationship has always been stormy but my feelings for Angela remain steadfast. I love her and want to help her past this barrier.

"She hasn't let me touch her in days. She looks at me as if I'm a monster when I even try to make love to her. Angela wasn't like that before, she has changed subtly and I think it's because of my trying to force her to recall a painful incident she wants only to forget."

"Then why don't you let her forget it? Be patient and gentle and in a few days or weeks she will be herself again."

"I don't think it's that simple. Whatever happened scarred her emotionally. If only I knew, perhaps I could help her. At least I would understand." Changing his tactics he asked casually, "When you set sail from Jamaica on the *Cygnet* were you headed to Sydney?"

"Yes, but on the *Dark Lady*!" The correction popped from Ezra's lips before he had a chance to think about it.

"The *Dark Lady*! My ship! Then where is she? The *Cygnet* is down there in the bay. You don't change ships in mid-ocean. Where did you stop? What happened to the *Dark Lady*?"

"I've said too much already," Ezra said, turning and starting back toward the stable before he gave away anything else.

"The *Dark Lady* is the key to this whole mystery!" Scott said to himself with soft surprise. "But where is she?"

Had she been damaged in a storm, sunk? Where had they changed ships? That had to be the dangerous interval when Clare was conceived. Somewhere in some ocean lay the answer, but he was no closer to finding out what had happened than before. But at least he had something to think about.

Scott walked back to the house very slowly mulling it over in his mind. If he could get Ezra to unwittingly reveal more pieces of what had happened, he might be able to fit them together into a hazy outline.

Angela was up already and dressed, starting coffee in the kitchen. "Darling," she smiled going to Scott as he came in, "you're up early. I didn't even hear you go." She brushed a quick fleeting kiss against his lips and then pulled away. "Would you like breakfast now? I'm starving and I couldn't wait for Maggie."

He couldn't help smiling back, encouraged by her bright look and her returned appetite. Could Ezra be right—just let things settle gradually back to normal? She seemed fine today.

They ate a huge breakfast of an omelet, ham, fresh muffins, and coffee. And while they lingered over it Angela reached across the table grasping Scott's hand tightly in hers. Their eyes caressed each other and hers were beseeching.

"I don't know what's gotten into me lately, darling," she said softly. "Please, don't stop loving me. I couldn't bear that. To think that we have just found each other after such a long time is a miracle in itself. But there are adjustments to make. Please be patient. I love you too much to lose you again."

"Come here, Angel," Scott ordered, his voice husky with emotion and she did, much to his surprise. He pulled her down on his knee and her arms naturally went around his neck. "I have waited four years, love; you would think that would have taught me patience. But I'm an impatient man, especially where you are concerned. I will try, though. We will work things out. But know this; never will I stop loving you. You must resign yourself to the fact."

"Oh, yes!" She traced his perfectly formed mouth with her fingers, those liquid aquamarine eyes so close the brilliance of them blinded him. And then her lips took the place of her fingers, soft as a whisper, moving ever so slowly. Her little tongue traced his mouth and then she gently bit his lower lip, lying against his well-muscled chest, catching her breath in a half-moan as he kissed her back in earnest.

To say he was shocked was an understatement but he proceeded with infinite caution, one hand caught in her loose curls, the other at her waist. Very slowly he moved his hand to cup the fullness of her breast and she put her hand over his pressing it closer, feeling alive for the first time in days. She loved him with such intensity that she ached inside and today her behavior was finally beginning to make sense, even to her.

"Oh! Sorry!" Kate stood in the doorway, her face as red as her flaming hair.

"That's all right, Kate," said Scott. "We were just finishing breakfast. Don't go. We are going to see the children." He put Angela on her feet and winked at her wickedly.

She stifled her amusement until they were out of the kitchen and then gave way to laughter. "Did you see her face? Poor girl—we shocked her."

"I would like to do something much more shocking to you than that. But not now. Let's see if the children are awake. I've been worried about Lorna."

"So have I," Angela said hugging his arm against her side. "She isn't bouncing back the way Robert and Clare have."

Things slowly went back to normal and then Scott left for Thornhill. Angela almost put the pardon right in his hands on the morning he left but instead she quashed the impulse, kissing him good-bye and promising to join him there as soon as she could. Ezra was right, Scott's own unpredictable personality was more of a threat to their marriage than Celeste Carew could ever be.

Scott had asked no further questions about Clare, and the baby had enchanted him just as she did everyone else. She took her first steps for him and the doll he gave her was her prized possession. He didn't even flinch anymore when she called him papa. Things were going along smoothly, almost too smoothly, thought Angela, hoping against all odds that this time their happiness would last. After all what else could happen? The Bratach Sith was only a distant memory. They had all weathered the worst and clear skies had to be ahead.

One morning while Maggie was in the garden watching the children Angela called Kate into the sitting room. When Angela told her to be seated she perched on the very edge of the chair opposite her and clasped her hands nervously in her lap.

"Is somethin' wrong, milady?"

"No," Angela smiled reassuringly. "There's no need to be upset. This is a personal matter.

"I have come to depend on you and Maggie a great deal. Both of you have been completely devoted to me and my family and I wanted to thank you. I care what happens to you because I think you are fine, very brave girls. That's why I wanted to ask you about your sister. I hope you won't think I'm prying."

"Oh, milady. Ye have every right to ask anything. We're bound to you for seven years."

"Kate, I'm your friend not just your mistress." Angela plunged right in. "Has Maggie ever spoken?"

"Yes, milady. Before we were sent to prison."

"But never since, not even to you?"

Kate shook her red head vigorously.

"One night, not long ago, I heard her singing—a lullaby to Clare."

"Are ye sure? Maggie?"

"Positive. I was on the veranda and she was singing in a foreign language. I looked in the window. There is no doubt."

"Singin' in Gaelic was she? Is that a good sign? Do you think she may start talkin'?"

"It's a very good sign. But if we could only find out

what happened to make her so silent—''

Kate hung her head but Angela could see the fierce color rising on her face. ''It was a babe she had—on the ship comin' out. We are good girls, milady! But one of the turnkeys took a fancy to Maggie, forcin' himself on her, but she loved that babe. It came too soon—a pitiful wee girl. It was so close between decks we were faintin' and some died. It only lived three days. It never had a chance.

''I was thinkin' Maggie would die with grief for her poor unbaptized babe. Not even a proper grave to mark her bones, just tossed in the sea!''

Tears spattered the twisted hands and Angela blinked rapidly to keep from crying too. ''Poor Maggie,'' she murmured. ''If only I could help her in some way.'' And she couldn't help thinking of herself and the strange similarity between them. Except she had never wanted Clare and Maggie had wanted her baby and lost it. And now Maggie didn't speak, and Angela harbored a dark secret and in her own way she couldn't speak of it either.

After her conversation with Kate, Angela began giving Maggie more duties with the children and even though she didn't speak they behaved amazingly well for her. And Maggie was never so happy as when she was with them.

As Lorna slowly recovered under the tender care of the whole household every dark cloud vanished and Angela laughed at herself for worrying needlessly. She just wasn't used to the children being sick, for they were unusually healthy by any standards. But now they were back to normal, tearing the house apart and back to their pranks. It was wonderful to live in such well-ordered chaos. She had sorely missed it during their illness.

But now that her worries were over she began longing to see Scott again. It had been three weeks and although she had received a letter that could never be the same as his presence.Their being apart began to tell and she found herself needlessly snapping at Kate or Ezra for nothing. At night her room and bed were so empty that she imagined other terrible obstacles that could separate them for good. Celeste was always uppermost in her musings. She didn't trust her in the least and when Clyde invaded the house one morning, she ran to greet him with an overeager welcome.

Angela gave him a quick hug and for an instant Clyde's arms closed possessively around her delicate body. He felt deprived at the fleeting nature of the embrace, more like the affection between a brother and sister or old friends. As she laughingly ordered coffee and biscuits he marveled at the bloom in her cheeks and the vitality leaping from her eyes.

She positively glowed, a startling contrast to the last time he had seen her, exhausted with tending the children. Her glossy black hair was braided into a heavy coronet on the back of her head and though she wore a simple muslin gown there was the magnificent emerald shining against her bodice.

As they talked and drank their coffee from translucent bone china cups he noticed the way her fingers occasionally caressed the green stone, as if it was something alive—or a lover. It almost seemed to offer her some comfort. Clyde was more in love with her than ever and though he tried to keep away he couldn't. Just knowing she was in Sydney drove him to distraction and he had finally broken down and beat a path to her door. But seeing her and knowing she would never be his was worse than not seeing her and he knew he had been mistaken in coming.

But still he lingered, watching her laugh over some inane statement of his. The way her lips curved revealing white pearly teeth, the dimples deepening beneath her high exotic cheekbones, the fantastically unbelievable color of her eyes were all a conspiracy against him enticing him to defeat. Her slim smooth fingers touched his as she handed him another cup of coffee and he almost dropped it, thinking of those hands on his body rousing him to as yet unattainable ecstasy.

She was unique, Angela—that fierce, sweet mixing of cool English blood and wild Scottish blood that made her half angel, half devil, and totally mysterious. Celeste was right, such a fragile, ethereal, passionate, temptress could never belong in this land or with the hard, savage man she was married to. They were so completely different that one or both of them would be destroyed by their union. So as Angela gazed at Clyde, her green-blue eyes mixed with sorrow and joy, just as they were with two colors, he vowed to have her for his own wife—no matter how long he had to wait, no matter what he had to do.

"The Hawkesbury!" Angela clapped her hands in delight. "Let me go with you. I'm dying to see Scott!"

"But I'm leaving straight away. . . ."

"I'll be ready in fifteen minutes—less! Please, Clyde," her eyes melted his resistance, "say yes."

"Very well." At least she would be alone with him all day before he turned her over to her husband.

She fairly danced from the room calling, "Kate, Maggie, Ezra!" And Clyde sat staring into his coffee, hating the thought of her in Scott's arms tonight.

He would talk to Celeste! Between them they could surely come up with a plan to separate the Harringtons. She had been very encouraging and sure of success at their last meeting. This was it! He would dally no longer. Before the week was over Angela would belong to him and Scott to Celeste.

True to her word Angela was ready in fifteen minutes, dressed in her very disturbing riding costume. They left the house in a flurry of kisses and good-byes with a worried Ezra looking speculatively after Clyde.

"This time it won't rain," Angela told Clyde as they trotted side by side down the dusty street. "I dare it to rain! I challenge the heavens!"

He couldn't help but laugh at her carefree good spirits, the vivacious eagerness to put the city behind her and plunge pell-mell into the uncrowded reaches of the colony.

"I even have a picnic lunch for us to eat on the way,"

she said. "My Murrays are quck and efficient aren't they, Clyde? Did you ever think on that day in the garden that those two scarecrows would turn into Irish wonders?"

"You spoil them, Angela."

"Spoil them for what? They are perfect for me, and besides people sometimes need to be spoiled. It makes up for so much."

The summer was over already and a tinge of cool air reminded the riders that fall was fast approaching. As they covered the miles between Sydney and the Hawkesbury Angela longed with an intensity to be back in England for the autumn. Here there was hardly any change but at home the change of seasons was one of nature's splendors. But right now it was barely spring in England. Why the daffodils wouldn't even be venturing forth at Seafield Castle yet.

Soon—soon now, she would hand over the pardon to Scott and they could set sail in the *Cygnet* for home. Why if they left now, this very day, they might be home for the last of summer. Angela was tired of the tropics, tired of strange primitive lands where the seasons practically stood still. She longed to feel the snow stinging her face, to see the lochs glazed with ice and the mountains like crystal castles.

She talked to Clyde of home because he understood, but even though he longed to visit Scotland and make a whirl through London something about Australia had captivated him. He was more interested in the Blue Mountains than his own bare bleak Cuillins on the Isle of Skye. There was a challenge here, unexplored primitive land for the asking, and the bravest and those there first would reap the rewards.

"Sheep," Clyde told Angela, "will be the gold of this new continent. Someday they will stretch as far as the eye can see. I'm breeding merinos in Parramatta and as soon as my farm in the Hawkesbury is producing, I will transfer half of them there.

"They say there are vast, lush grasslands on the other side of the mountains. Once we aren't confined by that barrier to this area on the coast the whole country will open up. Hundreds, thousands, why millions of acres could make up just one vast estate! There's room to spread and grow here—room for everyone."

"But you can't be sure. No one has crossed the mountains yet. Those grasslands might not exist. There could be more mountains, a desert, anything—if they are ever crossed."

"Well I mean to find out! I would give anything," he glanced at her, "well almost anything to be the first across. Someday I will have a million-acre sheeprun on the other side."

Angela laughed at his enthusiasm and shook her head. "You can have your sheep and your million acres and your Blue Mountains! All I want is my family—Scott and the children and an ancient castle on an island. . . ."

"Good lord, Angela! If I could have you I'd never look at another sheep. I'd live in a dungeon—"

"Oh, Clyde," she reprimanded with a toss of her raven head. "You had better stick to unexplored territory. Your dreams will make you happier than I ever could!"

They stopped to eat at mid-afternoon and the mountains that enamored Clyde were huge and close, misty in the shifting sunlight. They faced them as they ate and she saw his eyes return again and again to the peaks and ridges, almost as often as he glanced at her face. She smiled secretly. Clyde was torn between her and his mountains, each with their own attraction for his divided attention. She hoped the peaks would win.

As Clyde went to help her mount he took her in his arms, kissing her startled parted lips. He groaned as his tongue found hers and he tasted the honeyed mouth that had tempted him from the first. Surprisingly, for half an instant, she lay pliant against him, her soft breasts molded tightly to his chest. Their heat through the thin blouse made his head reel.

Angela jerked away from him a moment later and pushed him firmly away. He was very good at kissing and she couldn't deny that caught off guard she had yielded at first. Before he could react she mounted her horse and stared unsmilingly down at him.

"If you ever do that again you will have Scott to answer to! He was gentle with you the last time; this time, he would kill you!"

"That convict?" spat out Clyde.

"He is not all he seems," she replied enigmatically touching her heels to the horse's flanks.

There was no pleasant conversation the rest of the way. Their silence deepened even as the shadows of the Blue Mountains enveloped them in twilight.

It was dark when they reached Thornhill and Angela rode straight to Scott's cabin. At the sound of hoofbeats the door flew open staining the earth with yellow light. He rushed to her side and as she slipped from her horse she fell straight into his strong arms.

"Scott, darling!"

"Angel, love!"

Clyde watched them embrace and kiss, straining toward each other in the pooled candlelight. Scott's arms were hard and brown around her and Clyde shuddered at the ferocity with which he almost devoured her. Didn't her husband realize what a fragile flower Angela was? If he wasn't careful he would crush or bruise her. He would never treat her in such a harsh savage way; she was a lady and needed delicate handling.

That was only one more log added to the fire of his determination to separate them. A moan from Angela added another, as he silently cursed the man's cruelty. With firm resolution he turned his horse and headed for the house, and Celeste.

Clyde rode over to the cabin to say good-bye to Angela and found her hanging dripping clothes on a line stretched between two trees. She paused and waved as he approached and the fury in him blazed that she, a duchess, should be toiling like a drudge for her good-for-nothing husband.

"I'm going to Parramatta for a few days and then I'll be back in this area. Is there anything you need?"

"No, thank you, Clyde. I'm so grateful to you for bringing me here." He looked at her swollen lips, the bruise on her neck and the slightly shadowed eyes, and realized that Scott had wiped every thought of his kiss from her mind and body. How could she stand for that—the casual way in which Scott used her and then betrayed her with other women?

It would be soon now, this plan he and Celeste had spent half the night devising. He had only to go to Parramatta and return and the time would be ripe. He would have in his possession the means to sever Angela from Scott forever.

Clyde rode off so preoccupied that he didn't even glance back at Angela. He held the reins tightly in his hands guiding the horse as firmly as he was controlling his own destiny. Their plan was deceitful and compromising but it would work. It was the only scheme that would work and it all revolved around Scott's bad temper and perfect timing.

Angela was making a cherry pie when Scott came back to the cabin early. Her eyes lit up with pleasure as he opened the door and his bold presence filled the room with vitality. How empty it was when he was gone and even though she had been busy all day she had missed him immensely.

Scott caught her in an embrace as she crimped the crust and placed a scalding kiss on the bowed nape of her neck. Wisps of ebony hair tickled his lips and he let his hands search out the full curves of her breasts, squeezing gently.

"You devil! You'll make me ruin my pie!"

"I remember another day and another time but you were making apple pies." Scott nuzzled her shoulder watching her quick movements. "You ruined my coat and sent me packing that time. You will not get off so easily today."

"Scott," she said laughing huskily as she helplessly felt one of his searching hands trail down over her flat belly. She couldn't help wriggling against him.

"What?" Very gently he nibbled the lobe of her ear.

"I don't think I want to make pies today."

"Let's make a baby instead," he suggested and she whirled around throwing her arms about his neck.

"Would you really like another one?" Angela's eyes were huge with disbelief. "You're only teasing me!"

"I don't care if we have any more or not—but I am partial to the process involved in trying to make one."

He smiled wickedly, hugging her tightly as she planted a moist kiss on the cleft in his chin. "You missed the target," Scott scolded lowering his mouth to hers but she pulled away, wiping her hands on her apron, sliding from his grasp with a coquettish glance over her shoulder.

With a laugh he darted after, chasing her around the room, overturning a chair in the process. By the time he caught Angela she had slipped all the pins from her hair letting the heavy mass spill over her shoulders and breasts. As he pressed her against his chest Scott felt the row of undone buttons on her blouse and slid his hand inside the gaping material.

Her head fell back against his arm as his fingers found the smoothness of her flesh and sent rivers of sparks exploding through her blood. He watched her eyelashes flicker closed and felt the hot arch of her supple body against his. Very slowly he lowered his head to hers rubbing the softness of her cheek against his lean brown one, losing control as her hands clutched his thick wavy hair and pulled his lips to hers.

There was an inevitable ending to this encounter but one that never failed to delight them both. Only when they lay panting with pleasure and exertion, tangled on the bed in a chaos of seething emotions did they fulfill the total oneness that was bringing them closer together day by day.

And when they could speak again Angela whispered breathlessly into Scott's ear, "This is much better than baking pies. I think I will create another little boy that looks just like you!"

"Angel, Angel—all I want is you!"

"And to be free? To go home to Scotland?"

She heard his indrawn breath. Freedom was in his blood as fiercely as she was but he wouldn't admit it. "You are enough, my love. With you I hold the world in my arms."

But, she corrected him silently, you would do anything to be free. And she vowed to give him the pardon as soon as they reached Sydney.

"Don't go." Angela twined her arms around Scott's neck and wouldn't release him.

"You are insatiable," he laughed, the corners of his sherry-brown eyes crinkling in a way that made her think of new ways to make him linger. Kissing her nose he loosened her clinging arms and slapped her playfully on the bottom. "Be good, now. You know I have to go. The meeting is important. It's only held twice a year and everyone at Thornhill attends. Everyone's grievances get aired and new ways of increasing productivity are discussed. I'll probably be very late."

"Very well," Angela pouted, then looked at her handsome bronzed husband with a mischievous teasing look. "Then don't be surprised if I have dinner with Clyde. He got back from Parramatta today."

She saw the jealousy flame in his eyes and laughed. Scott relaxed and grinned back at her. "Tease! You drive me to distraction. I will make excuses and get out early. I'll tell them my hot little wife demands my services and I am at her mercy."

"Don't you dare!"

"And," he threatened with a twinkle in his eyes, his hands circling her throat, "if you dare to even look at that puppy I'll throttle you!"

"Yes, my lord duke," Angela mocked as he started for the door. She swept him a deep curtsy and impudently stuck her tongue out at him.

"When I return you will pay for your insolence. I will have to think up a new torture."

"Make it a good one!"

"I will! Believe me, I will!"

Angela hugged herself and spun around, ecstatically happy in spite of Scott's absence. She felt secure now in their love that was slowly unfurling like the petals of a long dormant flower. A few more weeks together and it would be in full bloom for all to see and admire, for Angela to cherish for the rest of her life. After all their trials and tribulations the curse was finally dead, laid to rest beneath the flourishing plant of their love, nourishment that only strengthened them and brought them closer.

Going outside, Angela lingered in the orchard not far from the cabin. The trees were heavy with fragrant fruit and she reached out and plucked a ripe peach. Walking slowly through the rows of trees she watched the sun slip to its rest beneath the rim of the mountains. The peach was soft with fuzz against her lips and she bit into it savoring the sweet juiciness, watching the ever-changing panorama between the laden branches and gnarled trunks.

The sky was a sapphire blue at the mountains, shading gradually to indigo and black, and the high wisps of clouds tinted a delicate shell pink couldn't obscure the sprinkling of stars. They appeared, growing brighter as darkness descended, shimmering though the clouds like the bright eyes of a flirtatious Spanish lady through a lace mantilla.

Candles blazed in the big house, light pouring from every window and horses of every description were tied up out front. Scott was in there, with the other hardy outdoorsmen that ran Thornhill. The others would doubtless be ill at ease among the elegance of the house but Scott would move with an easy grace, accustomed to riches, but not a stranger to deprivation. He could make even a bare one-room cabin a palace with his presence, and Angela smiled in the dusk, knowing that she would prefer living in a tent with him than the most sumptuous edifice with any other man.

She threw the peach pit down and licked her sticky fingers clean, at peace with the world. Much later the meeting would be over and she would wait up for her husband. He would leave Celeste Carew's elegantly gowned, perfumed and coiffured presence and rush to be with her. And she would greet him with her hair floating loose, the way he liked it and ungowned so that no barriers would halt the quick progress of their desire.

With Scott she needed no artifice or tricks to win him. Just her presence and her lissome body would banish all thoughts of beautiful ladies, sparkling with jewels, tempting him from every side; because he was hers. A soft sigh escaped her, she was his—heart, body, soul, and mind—possessed of him, obsessed by him, bedeviled and bewitched.

The mellifluous tones of chirping birds, crickets, the breeze sighing softly through the trees, and her own breathing blended subtly, lulling Angela into a tranquil mood. She placed her hand on the tautness of her abdomen. Even now the seed of Scott's love for her might be sprouting and growing deep within her. She hoped it was for she would cherish it and carry it beneath her overflowing heart. And such a love-child couldn't help but fulfill their heart's desire.

The breeze turned cooler and she went back to the cabin sheltered and secluded in the embrace of the night. A light had been lit and she ran the last distance. So Scott had extracted himself from the dull meeting unable to endure their parting any more than she could! Angela flung the door open and the smile died on her lips, for there, building a fire on her own hearth, was Clyde.

Struggling to conceal her disappointment Angela managed a different smile for him as he rose to his feet brushing his hands off.

"Well," she said brightly, "how was your trip?"

"Fruitful," Clyde said, squelching further comment by his tone. "I've brought you a peace offering, Angela. I hope you will accept it."

It was then that she noticed the package wrapped in tissue paper and blue ribbon on the well-scrubbed table. Beside it was a bottle of expensive French wine and her eyebrows raised inquiringly. What could Clyde be up to now? She was alert.

"Peace offering?"

"Yes," Clyde said picking up the package. "For not believing you when you told me that you and your husband were reconciled. For trying to talk you into accepting the divorce when you didn't want to. For pressing my suit against your will. Will you forgive me, Angela? Can we go back to being good friends again?"

The sincerity of his face, the hesitant way he held out the gift, the slight catch of regret and shame in his voice, all worked to convince her that his plea was earnest. Poor Clyde, with his honest slightly ingenuous apology and his need to placate her and his conscience. She took the proffered parcel and saw his eyes flood with relief.

"I thought," he said eagerly, indicating the wine, "that we could drink to your continued happiness and to a long marriage for you and Scott. Let bygones be bygones and all that. But where is he? I did want us all to have a toast together and become friends."

"I'm afraid he's at a meeting and won't be back till later." Angela saw disappointment swiftly cross his face, and countered, "But we could have a toast and tomorrow I will tell Scott that we are all reconciled."

"Could we?"

"Of course, but let me open this." And her fingers untied the ribbon and loosed the paper to reveal a small rosewood box exquisitely inlaid with other precious woods and ivory. It gleamed with the delicate tracery of scrollwork surrounding a perfect white ivory thistle.

"Open it," urged Clyde and she lifted the lid and a Scottish air tinkled delicately, the movement of the mechanism visible through the glass bottom.

"Why it's beautiful, Clyde. Thank you! You remembered my longing for Seafield Castle didn't you? How thoughtful!" She went to him and kissed him fleetingly on the cheek. "We were always friends, Clyde, and I hope we always will be."

"Then I'll pour the wine while you put the music box away." He watched her go to the mantel, standing with her back to him and her head cocked deciding where to put it.

Swiftly, with rehearsed ease he took a small paper

from his pocket and emptied a powder into one of the glasses. Pouring the wine into each one he watched it dissolve instantly, invisible in the ruby liquor. As he picked up the glasses he swirled the wine around gently in one and when Angela turned back to him with a trusting smile he handed her the doctored wine.

"To you and Scott—may all your dreams be fulfilled." Clyde raised the glass to his lips and drank freely.

Angela sipped it and sat down on one of the chairs before the fire. "Won't you join me for a few minutes, Clyde? The wine is delicious."

He sat in the other chair, watching her drink again, feeling a shiver of excitement go down his spine. They chatted lightheartedly and the liquid in her glass slowly disappeared. A pink flush suffused her cheeks and he saw her eyes flutter.

Angela moved her chair back from the fire. It was making her all warm and drowsy, and there was a brilliant edge of light around Clyde. She refused when he offered her more wine. It was unaccountably potent and her head began to spin. Before her eyelids drooped irretrievably shut she saw him smile at her very charmingly.

He waited long agonizing minutes until Angela's breathing was heavy and even and then allowed the feeling of brilliant accomplishment to take over. The hardest part was over, the rest would occur as easily as falling off a horse.

She was his! In less than an hour Scott and Celeste would stroll to the cabin after an unusually short meeting and everything would fall into place. A jealous husband encountering his sleepy, unfaithful wife, caught in the act with her lover. There could be only one outcome.

Clyde picked up the unconscious woman of his dreams and laid her on the bed. With infinite care he began undressing her, pausing to touch each newly revealed treasure. Panting with passion, shaking with desire he stripped himself and rumpled the bed convincingly. His eyes swept the room; it was a perfectly set stage. The empty wine glasses caught the firelight beside the bottle on the table, the tissue paper and ribbons were discarded on a chair, their clothes were scattered across the room and the bed was revealed just enough to make the play of shadow and light dramatic.

He had spent longer than he had expected during the process of rendering Angela naked and glanced uneasily at the door. They would arrive soon—did he dare take the chance of taking her now, quickly? No, he'd better wait until it was over, for to be caught off guard could be dangerous to him if Scott went mad and attacked. So for a few minutes Clyde rested beside Angela, stroking her breasts, feeling the soft flesh quiver and spring to life beneath his touch.

She moved restlessly in her unnatural state, murmuring incoherent words, reaching out for Scott. Settling against the warm masculine flesh she was still again, secure in a fantasy world where only two existed.

Clyde heard the high, clear laughter of Celeste and he shook Angela violently until her eyelids flickered open and she looked at him without recognition. Rearranging her limbs he rolled on top of her pulling her arms around his body. She wriggled beneath him whispering Scott's name and Clyde cut off the sounds with his open mouth.

"Angela, we have a visitor!" Scott called from the door.

He entered just in time to see a shocked Clyde raise his head from Angela's. Their naked bodies were entwined on the bed and the languor of her movements made it evident that they had made love more than once during his absence. Angela's passion-flushed face turned slowly and her huge green-blue eyes registered surprise as they met his. As he crossed the room toward them with Celeste dragging on his arm she looked in bewilderment from her advancing husband to the man atop her.

Something snapped in Scott and enraged he snatched Clyde from the bed as easily as he would have picked up a blanket. In slow motion he saw his fists make contact with Clyde's face without letup and heard the sickening contact of flesh and bones. There was a hindrance tugging him back but he shook it off and blood spattered everywhere before his ineffectual opponent slipped to the floor.

Then he turned to Angela. She was still sprawled indecently on the bed her eyes blinking in bemusement. He struck her across the face with the back of his hand and her eyes didn't blink any more. As his fingers fastened around her limp white throat a sound penetrated his brain. With his wife still firmly in his grasp Scott turned his head and saw Celeste terrified and angry shouting at him.

"You fool—stop it! You will kill her and then where will you be? They will hang you or send you to Van Diemen's Land and for what? For a lying whore that takes to her bed any available man! Don't throw your life away on the likes of her! Think, Scott! Stop!"

Celeste pried his fingers from Angela's throat, shaking with fear. This wasn't supposed to happen. She was supposed to have stopped any violence before it happened but this part of their trick had backfired. Clyde lay battered on the floor unconscious and Angela had fainted from the effects of the drug and the blow dealt her.

Almost in a stupor Scott let himself be led back to the big house by Celeste. His dreams were shattered along with his love. Angela! Angela! How could she do this to him? She had lied all along, laughing at him behind his back, playing free and easy with lovers while convincing him of her undying fidelity. The perfidy of her act could never be erased from his memory.

He could still see Clyde lying on her perfect body, reveling in her soft surrender, performing obscenities upon the altar of his love. Angela! His mind shrank from that picture, cringing inward upon itself, lost in a dull throb that would soon give way to the excruciating pain of a severed love.

But Celeste was with him quietly pressing a glass of brandy into his hand, and another as quickly as that one was empty till the scene faded like a painting exposed too long to bright sunlight. Then the blessed relief of unrelieved darkness, an unthinking, unknowing void where time was suspended and nothingness existed.

A long shuddering gasp escaped from Celeste. Scott was slumped in the chair half laying on the table. She had had no choice but to slip him some of the drug Clyde had given Angela. She was still shaking uncontrollably from the scare he had given her and the night wasn't over yet. Taking a gulp of the brandy herself she steeled herself to go back to the cabin and assess the damages. She prayed that Clyde was still alive.

He was stirring when she knelt beside him and with a wet cloth she wiped the blood from Clyde's swollen, cut face. He would survive and Scott would remain at Thornhill, finally getting his divorce and marrying her. The stratagem was a success, with a few minor mishaps along the way, but the end justified the means. Clyde would have his adored duchess and she would have the only man in the wide world she had ever loved.

"Clyde, Clyde!" She shook him gently and he moaned. She owed him everything for together they had plotted and spun this web fit to catch a lady and her husband. Without his cooperation the ruse would have been an impossibility. But he owed her too. They had both been winners in the bargain they had struck and the losers would never, never know the truth.

Clyde's eyes opened and his hand went to his jaw tenderly exploring. With his tongue he felt a loose tooth, stinging cuts and smashed bloodied lips. Celeste helped him drink some wine and he recoiled in pain as the alcohol burned into his mouth and down his throat. Slightly revived she helped him up and he staggered over to the bed where Angela slept.

The cheek turned to him was swollen and a long bruise marred her face. A trickle of dried blood was at the corner of her mouth and there were darkening finger marks at her throat.

"Angela!" Clyde sat down suddenly turning her face to the light.

"She's all right—in better shape than you are."

"What happened?" He shook his fogged head to clear it.

"Scott went on a rampage. I couldn't stop him—I don't even think he knew I was here. You're very lucky you didn't get killed."

"You were supposed to stop him, Celeste! We agreed!"

"I tried to, but a whole army couldn't have held him back. I just managed to keep Scott from strangling her!"

"Is it really over?"

"Yes—and we won!" Celeste's voice was triumphant with victory. "They will never in a million years get back together again! She is yours, Clyde, all yours. Take her far away—you promised!"

"Yes," he said wearily. "I'll take her back to Scotland. After tonight she will be devastated, and I will be here for her to turn to."

"I have to go, if you are sure you'll be all right."

"Go, Celeste. We will leave for Sydney in the morning."

With exteme care Clyde stretched out beside Angela and drew the covers over them both. He should be reaping the reward of his subterfuge now, enjoying Angela's body while she was unaware; but the effort of just walking to the bed had left him exhausted. He closed his eyes quelling a sick feeling in the pit of his stomach.

Tomorrow he would feel better and then he could set about winning Angela's love in earnest. It would take time, perhaps years, but eventually his love for her would be consummated and he could wait since they had a whole lifetime ahead of them.

nine

Angela turned over, her body so heavy she could barely move. Her head pounded with a throbbing headache and she was slightly sick to her stomach. There was a dull ache along the side of her face and she rubbed her fingers against it but the effort was too much. Letting her hand fall it came in contact with warm-muscled flesh. Scott. Drawn to the secure comfort of his body she snuggled against him, feeling better immediately.

Her fingers moved automatically over his chest, but she stopped, frowning. This wasn't the lightly furred chest of her husband; this chest was as smooth and hairless as her own. Forcing her eyes open a crack she could only look in complete confusion at the stranger sharing her bed. It took several minutes for her drug-fogged brain to recognize Clyde Macdonald. Even then she didn't move but lay like a statue trying to puzzle out how they could be lying stark-naked in Scott's cabin with the morning light already in evidence.

With an effort born of desperation she got out of bed and hid her body in a robe. In a habitual move she put the coffee pot over the dying fire and stirred it up, then sank onto a nearby chair and shut her eyes. She couldn't even begin to think. When the aroma of coffe tantalized her nose she poured herself a cup and sat sipping it with her eyes still closed against reality. It wasn't until she finished the whole pot that Angela began to function.

She opened her eyes and forced herself to remember. Wine glasses on the table—yes! And there was the music box on the mantel. They had drunk a toast sitting before the fire and she had been so sleepy. That was all she could recall, except for some strangely muddled dreams that made no sense. And now Clyde slept in her bed with his face in sad shape. Where was Scott? Maybe Clyde knew.

"Clyde!" She sat on the edge of the bed calling him, shaking him and he thrust her hand away but she persisted. "Please, Clyde, wake up! Damn you, open your eyes!" Her headache was fleeing under the all-important desperation to know the truth.

"Angela?" His eyes opened, just barely; green slits in his swollen face.

"What are you doing here, Clyde? What has happened?"

"Don't you remember?"

"Would I be asking you if I remembered? Tell me what's going on right now!"

"What do you remember?"

"Our toast, talking in front of the fire, that's all!" There was a sharp edge to her voice that sliced through his own misery.

"After that I left and I was just getting ready to go to bed when one of the servants brought your note. I was overjoyed, Angela; I couldn't believe my eyes and—"

"What note?"

"The one you sent me begging me to come back."

"I sent no note!"

"But—but—you wrote you had a quarrel with Scott and needed someone to talk to. So I came and you were upset, crying and carrying on. We finished the wine and then we kissed and you wanted me to make love to you—"

"I don't believe it! Liar!" but as she looked at his puzzled innocence she wavered. Then a thought stung her like an arrow loosed from a bow. "Celeste!"

"Huh? What's she got to do with this?"

"Finish," Angela told him.

"Where was I? Oh, we made love. Sweetheart, you were wonderful—"

"Go on, Clyde!"

"And—and then we did it again and Scott and Celeste came in and saw us. He went crazy, trying to choke you and I dragged him off and we fought. I think he knocked me out because I don't remember anything else, I don't even remember getting back in bed."

"Scott! Oh no! Celeste! It's all her doing!" She shook like a ship caught in a storm, torn apart by swelling emotions. "The wine, where did you get it?"

"Why, from Celeste."

"And the note, where is it?"

"You said to burn it and I did."

Covering her face with her hands Angela sat very still dazed by her discovery. When she looked at Clyde's concerned face again her eyes were hard and cold with concentrated hate, but not for him.

"Celeste put something in that wine. She sent you the note. She cleverly arranged this whole scheme in order to get back at me."

Now her dreams started making sense: Scott's angry shocked eyes boring into her while he made love to her, but at the same time he was standing at the door with Celeste, and her lover turned into Clyde.

"What must he think of me?" she cried, her heart tearing in her breast. "He will never believe I didn't do this on purpose! He saw you making love to me! Never will Scott forgive me—never!"

Angela collapsed in a heap, frenzied sobs of anguish torn from her bruised throat. Everything had been perfect until that interfering, vindictive bitch had decided to tamper with their lives. What could she do or say to convince Scott that she was an innocent pawn in Celeste's game of revenge? Nothing! Not when he had seen her committing adultery with his own eyes. This was the end . . . . at last.

"Please don't cry," Clyde pleaded stroking her

quivering shoulders. "He will believe you. I'll go to Scott myself and tell him what happened. . . ."

"No! No! Get out, Clyde! Go now—I have to be alone!"

So he dressed quickly, leaving Angela to her distress and she didn't see his pained smile of accomplishment because her eyes were blinded with tears.

When she returned to her senses again, hours later, Angela was determined not to knuckle under to Celeste. She would tell Scott the truth whether he wanted to hear it or not, whether he believed it or not. At least she must try because she was no quitter and now she was fighting mad.

Several more hours were spent bathing and applying cold compresses to her eyes and jaw. Then Angela dressed in her riding costume and examined herself in the small mirror. Passable, but the bruises were unmistakable even though the swelling had gone down. She tied a silk scarf around her neck and it concealed the marks from Scott's fingers. Taking a deep steadying breath she marched out the door, her back straight with determination.

It took over an hour of riding over the estate questioning farmhands before Angela found him. When she did he was surrounded by people and sheep and his eyes registered an instant loathing.

"I have to talk to you," she told him, "now!"

"I'm busy, and we have nothing to say to one another." His voice was without emotion, almost as if it had all been drained out of him at the scene last night.

"I will speak here—right in front of everyone if you wish," Angela told him stubbornly and he saw the defiant tilt of her chin.

He touched his heels to his horse and it sprang off with her following closely. They rode some distance until they were completely alone and he stopped, staying mounted as if he was anxious to have a troublesome interview over with. Scott was unmoved by the mark on her face and the loving torment in her eyes. If she was suffering, she deserved it and he hoped she felt the same agony that was gnawing away his insides.

"Well," he prompted impatiently. "We are alone now. Say what you must and then get out of my sight."

"What happened last night was none of my doing. It was all Celeste's fault, a plot to separate us." Angela swallowed the lump in her throat. He wasn't even helping by asking questions. "Clyde came to make peace with us and brought a bottle of wine—her wine—with him. Of course you weren't there, so we drank one toast to our long marriage.

"Celeste drugged the wine! Clyde left but she sent him a note signed with my name, asking him to return. He did and I don't remember what happened but he said we—we made love and then you came and saw us.

"Scott, you must believe me! I remember nothing—nothing! Only waking up in the morning with Clyde. I never sent that note; Celeste did. Clyde is not my lover. You are!"

Scott hadn't moved an inch. His gold-sprinkled eyes stared at her unconvinced, his expression unchanged. "Are you finished?"

"No! I love you, only you! Please believe me. Celeste dreamed up this whole evil scheme to avenge herself on me. She wants you—don't you see? She would do anything to have you, anything, even going so far as to destroy our marriage. Because unless she does you can never be hers." Angela's impassioned plea didn't even affect him.

"I don't believe you."

"But you must, you can't fall right into her trap! Would you believe Celeste over your own wife?"

"I take no one's word on the matter. I saw it with my own eyes." Scott's voice was dripping with icicles. "Have you finished now?"

Angela nodded miserably, scalding tears prickling behind her eyes, a mute request for understanding and mercy in their aquamarine depths.

"Then I suggest you leave here now and for good."

"What about the children? Don't you care what happens to them?"

"There are always the children to fall back upon, isn't that so, Angela? I care very much but since I'm a convict I have no rights. If I was free I would fight you in every court in the land for Lorna and Robert, and I would win. So take them, take everything that has ever meant anything to me and go. I don't ever want to see you or hear of you again. If I do I don't think I could be held responsible for the consequences."

He wheeled suddenly and left her choking in a cloud of dust and she bent over clutching the pommel, dropping hot tears of defeat on the horse's thick mane.

The music box tinkled pleasantly on Lorna's bedside table bringing a smile to her pale face. The sound only reminded Angela of disaster, but if it made her daughter happy she could stand anything.

Lorna had had a relapse not long after her return to Sydney and that on top of everything else pressed so heavily on Angela that her heart felt like dead weight. She had Ezra move the small bed into her own room so she could be alert for any change during the night and when the coughing spells occurred she held Lorna with a desperation born of fear and the abject terror of losing her.

Angela was only half alive, so preoccupied with her personal sorrows that the rest of the world was forgotten. Clyde visited every day watching both mother and daughter become pale shadows of their former selves. He spent a lot of time with the children bringing them special treats, knowing that the way to his beloved's heart lay in that direction.

Several different doctors were called up to the house overlooking Cockle Bay and each prescribed different things that did absolutely no good. The Murrays scurried around crossing themselves constantly and Maggie's fingers were always busy at the highly prized rosary beads Angela had given her. Kate took to muttering under her breath and Ezra wondered if it was papist prayers she was reciting as she went about her work.

They all worked tirelessly to make Lorna comfortable

and to try and provide a normal atmosphere for Robert and Clare to live in. But as the weeks passed the tension increased until Clyde thought something must happen or Angela would snap.

"Mama, could you wind it again?" asked Lorna and Angela cheerfully complied, never letting her oldest daughter detect the worry she felt all the time.

She smiled and smoothed the warm flushed cheeks, holding the precious dark head against her breast. Lorna was her first-born child, herself as a little girl but with a dash of Scott added for spice. She could hardly believe that her baby was almost nine years old, so grown up. She could remember her crying lustily, a tiny scrap of humanity, still wet from her womb. And now she was like a faded rose and Angela wondered with a catch in her throat if she would ever survive long enough to grow up.

Weak lungs, the doctor said, brought on by her illness but inherited from her grandmother. Angela could picture her mother, an invalid for half her life with the same flushed face and those too-brilliant eyes. It had always been a struggle for her father and a burden on the whole family. Hadn't she sold herself to Percy Harrington so her mother could have special care and a warm climate? Her life was coming full circle and she would have bargained with the devil himself to save Lorna.

Maggie came in to relieve her and Angela affectionately tousled Lorna's black curls before leaving her to the convict girl's gentle care. Clyde was in the garden with Robert and Clare so she didn't want to go out there. Wandering around the house like a lost soul she finally came to rest in the sitting room and gazed vacantly out at the bay.

If only Scott was here. Should she send for him? No, he wouldn't come. He would probably think it was a trick to get him back. You always fall back on the children, he had told her. No, that wouldn't bring him to Sydney. She would send Ezra first thing in the morning. Ezra could convince him and if he couldn't he could always abduct Scott. That brought a brief smile to her lips. Why hadn't she thought of that before? He had abducted her at one time when he was losing her to another man—why not turn the tables on him? Have Ezra carry him off out of Celeste's clutches and keep Scott a prisoner in some remote spot, better yet set sail with him. It would be a long voyage with no landfall for months.

The idea excited her making her blood race and her hopes rise for the first time since leaving Thornhill. Angela laughed out loud at Celeste's imagined chagrin when she found her lover gone.

"You're in a better mood today," observed Ezra entering the room and sitting opposite her. "Is the princess better?"

"No, but I think we may all go on a nice long sea voyage for our health."

"You would leave here without the man you came for?"

"Oh no!" Angela sprang to her feet, barely able to keep still. "You are going to shanghai Scott! He will be at my mercy!"

"Hey, that's a good one! When am I going to spirit him away, and how?"

"As soon as we are fit to sail—and I think I will drug him, since everyone else finds that method so satisfactory."

"I almost believe you would do it," said Ezra shaking his head in amazement.

"Just watch me!" Angela promised, elation taking over completely. She would get Scott back yet!

The whole day was suddenly rosy and Clyde couldn't believe that the revitalized creature running to greet him in the garden was the same Angela he had seen yesterday. There was a secret sparkle in her eyes and as they talked her dimples came and went for no reason at all that he could discern. He almost asked her if she had news from Scott but decided not to rock the boat. If she was happy today, for whatever reason, it was enough just to bask in the warmth of her smile.

When Captain Macdonald left that evening, after having been invited to dinner and reveling in the simple familylike gathering, his step was jaunty and he whistled cheerfully. Angela was at long last forgetting her past and settling her affections on him. There was no doubt in his light heart that this was so. Her behavior had undergone a critical change and all because of his devoted perseverance in the face of overwhelming adversity—and his steadfast loyalty in her times of trouble.

"I don't trust him," Ezra admitted to Angela as they sat on the veranda watching Clyde leave. "He had as much to gain as Celeste did."

"What do you mean, Ezra?" She was only half listening, still absorbed in her fancy of abducting Scott.

"Clyde is in love with you. You are aware of that, aren't you? His story is too pat. I think he and Celeste cooked up that whole scheme so each of them could have their heart's desire. She wanted Scott, he wanted you."

Angela leaned forward suddenly interested in his train of thought. "Go on—what else?"

"I think it was a joint venture. I have no proof, just a feeling. You have always believed in feelings." Ezra tilted his chair back on two legs, pondering the night sky. "Why did one glass of wine affect you and not him? If his was drugged it should have knocked him senseless too. Yet he went back to the house and later returned to the cabin, supposedly sharing the rest of the wine with you.

"By that time I don't think he could have fallen out of bed, never mind make love to you twice. Don't you see, it was a trap all set and ready to spring. Their timing was perfect. You remember part of what happened—he woke you up!"

"Oh, Ezra! I think you are right!" Angela cried. "What a terrible thing to do to a friend! I'll kill him! No, first I'll make him confess it to Scott and then kill him!"

She buried her face in her hands. "Why?" Her voice

was very small and lost. "Why is it that I bring out the worst in people? The ones I really trust, turn on me—Keith and now Clyde."

"They loved too much, and excesses are never good. Each one of them in his own way, wanted you and had to make sure he got you—by whatever means. They forgot the first rule of loving, caring only that the one you love is happy. Love cannot be bought or stolen or commanded—it just is!"

The unveiling of Clyde's deceit left Angela sad and angry but at the same time hopeful of settling the breach between herself and Scott. Maybe she wouldn't have to shanghai him after all but just reveal the truth. Celeste would probably never admit it but Angela knew that she could force Clyde to break down.

They sat talking long into the night, losing all track of time when Maggie appeared gesturing wildly. Both of them ran after her into the bedroom.

Lorna lay propped up on four pillows with her black hair plaited into two thick braids. Angela touched her forehead and found her burning with fever. The little girl's eyes opened and she smiled at her mother, feeling secure with her presence.

"Mama." Her labored breathing barely allowed her to speak. "Don't leave me."

"Shh! I'll stay right here, baby. Close your eyes and sleep—yes, that's right. I will be here all night."

Maggie laid a cool cloth on her forehead and Angela turned luminous eyes filled with dread toward Ezra. He squeezed her hand comfortingly and she wouldn't let it go. An hour later he went for the doctor.

Angela kept a silent vigil by Lorna's bedside bathing the thin, wasted body in cool water. She was worse, delirious and incoherent though she seemed to recognize her mother. And when she was seized with the violence of a racking cough there were specks of blood on her pillows.

Heart-stopping terror took hold of Angela as she held her daughter in her arms staring at the blood. No—no!

This couldn't happen to Lorna! Not her! The attack ceased and she was quiet again, breathing very fast against Angela's bosom. She stroked the small head as Maggie changed the pillowcases and time did not exist outside the small dimly lit room.

Ezra returned with no doctor. "He is gone to Toongabbei and his wife doesn't know when he will be back!"

"I should never have brought them here," whispered Angela blaming herself. "This would not have happened at home with good doctors. . ."

"Don't, Angela—we can't foresee the future. It might have happened anyway, anywhere." Ezra got himself a chair and placed it close by, not daring to leave the room.

The candles flickered and Angela heard Kate just outside the door murmuring to herself, Maggie's beads clicking between her fingers. Ezra wrung out another cloth, just to have something to do, and handed it to Angela. She and Maggie continued bathing Lorna's burning body.

The ragged breathing slowed and her fever broke. Her eyes flickered open and she smiled wearily at Angela. "Mama."

Angela smiled back. "You're all right now, baby. Soon you will be well and playing with Clare and Robert. We're going back to England again on the *Cygnet*—I know how you love ships, Lorna. And your father will come with us. We will all be so happy!"

"Angela." The tone of Ezra's voice was so strange she almost didn't recognize it.

She looked at him, back to the peacefully sleeping face of her daughter and then at him again. A stifled sob came from Maggie and her hand was over her mouth, only her brimming eyes visible.

"Lorna!" Angela gathered the limp child into her arms, rocking her with her cheek pressed against the soft hair.

And because Ezra was now beyond speech, Maggie

said, "She's gone, milady, gone to join the angels."

"Why, Maggie," said Angela in amazement, "you spoke, you actually talked!"

"Angela," Ezra found his voice. "Let me take her. She's dead."

"No—you are wrong. The fever broke." She clutched her tightly, a dull blank mist enshrouding her from the others in the room.

Why were they all crying? Ezra, Kate, Maggie. The Murrays were both kneeling by the side of the bed with their red and brown heads bowed, shoulders shaking and hands clasped. The shimmering fog lifted and the room was suddenly cold and lifeless.

Dawn was never so bleak. It was a glory of purple and gold but Angela's eyes didn't see it stretching over the bay. The small coffin was lowered into the ground beneath the spreading branches of the wattle tree and the only sounds were awakening birds and the soft crying of the Murrays.

Angela stared at the hole in the ground dry eyed and didn't even hear the words spoken by the minister. Ezra's arm was about her waist holding her up. She felt nothing, an empty void residing within her. This wasn't real. Lorna was not in that box that would soon be buried beneath earth and grass.

But when she returned to her room there was no small bed, no trace of her daughter, as if every tangible evidence of her had been obliterated. Only the music box on the table, the gift of a traitor, remained. She lifted the lid and the melody tinkled delicately reminding her of Lorna and Clyde. With one finger she slammed it closed, then picked it up and hurled it through the window.

Crashing glass and a Scottish air that ended abruptly brought Ezra to the room. She was all right! He wasn't sure what he had expected, but not the calm white face she turned on him.

"I'm going to Thornhill. Scott must be told."

"I'll go, Angela. Write a note if you want but—"

"No, Ezra. Do you think I could let a stranger deliver a note? I must go, I have to be with him."

They rode hard and fast all day, approaching the Hawkesbury by mid-afternoon. They hadn't stopped to eat or rest, only to water the horses. There was a chill in the air and lowering clouds threatened rain later in the evening but Angela didn't notice it.

How odd, she thought, that when her beloved, first-born child was dead she felt nothing. No tears, no out-burst of grief—just nothingness. Everything was the same: the sky and sea, Sydney, the people around her, with exception of one. How in the world could she tell Scott?

When they reached the estate Ezra asked one of the foremen where Scott could be found and they set out in that direction. He was inspecting part of a gum tree forest, with the prospect of clearing the land in mind. It was a long way off in the deserted seclusion of unreclaimed acreage.

It took another hour to find him and as he saw Angela and Ezra approach, Scott sat stock-still on his big chestnut stallion. He was dwarfed by the tall shim-mering eucalyptus trees, their trunks a silvery-white in the afternoon sun.

"Ezra." Angela hesitated, unsure of her course of ac-tion. "I will meet you back at the big house. We have to be alone."

"Are you sure you will be all right? I don't trust him when he's angry and surely, even after all this time, he still is."

"We have other things to talk about besides ourselves. But how will I find the words to tell him? No matter—I must! I will see you later."

Ezra watched her close the distance between the hill where they had stopped and the fringes of the forest. He was uneasy but respected Angela's decision. The knowledge that this was going to be one of the most dif-ficult things she had ever done made him turn and retrace the way back.

His face was grim and Scott said nothing as Angela

approached him. She wanted to take him in her arms and smooth the burnished hair that ruffled slightly in the breeze. But his eyes were so harsh and distant as they coolly appraised her that she stopped some feet away, just looking at him beseechingly.

She looked fatigued, drained, as if all her lust for life had gone out of her suddenly—like a candle extinguished, only the glowing wick and spiraling smoke evidence of the once bright flame. She deserves to suffer, he thought heartlessly, looking at her white face. Even her lips were pale and her huge, shadowed eyes were lackluster, haunted by sadness. She was painfully thin, as if she hadn't eaten since their last meeting and the only reminder of the old Angela was her shining crown of glossy black hair.

"I told you never to come back. No, don't speak, I know why you are here. You have come to seduce me back into your life." He laughed sardonically. "As if you could. You are as skinny as a skeleton, Angela, you look like death warmed over."

She winced almost imperceptibly at his choice of words, his misunderstanding of why she had sought him out. Wearily she said, "You are wrong, Scott, as usual. I haven't come to seduce you or even to speak of us and what we once had. I want to talk about," she choked slightly, "Lorna."

"The children! It's always that bond you use to try and entrap me. You heartless bitch, you unfit mother! I told you before that I wouldn't be responsible for what might happen if I saw your face again!"

With no warning he jumped from the saddle, grasping her around the waist and dragging her forcibly from her mount. He was surprised that she didn't even attempt to fight him off as he crushed the flesh of her shoulders under punishing fingers. Angela even seemed to welcome the pain, a trace of color returning to her face.

"Now that you have proved your superior strength and your capacity for cruelty, it is your turn to listen." Things were not going well, certainly not as she had foreseen. If only he would let go of her. She squirmed against the iron bite of his hands, pushing feebly at his chest. "Let go. What I have to say is important—it affects us both!"

Scott struck her across the face and her mind reeled. "I will not listen to any more falsehoods from you! I'm sick and tired of your unimaginative stories, weary of your lies!" His voice was harsher than the slap he had dealt her.

"You, my dear wife, are a slut, you have been one from the beginning! I despise you and everything you stand for!"

His fingers pulled at the fastenings of her skirt, quickly loosening it, pushing it and her undergarments down over her hips.

"Wh—what are you doing?" she stammered trying to tug the material back up.

"I'm going to prove once and for all just what I think of you!" She kicked him but he didn't seem to feel it. "You are a whore opening your legs for any man that has the equipment to do the job! Well I, Duchess, am amply equipped and when I've finished with you, you will wish you had never come here today!"

"Stop it, you can't! Not today, not after what happened!"

He stopped her words with his mouth crushing her lips against her teeth until they bled, ripping her skirt off. Jerking her hair free of its pins he hurled her to the ground, watching her eyes widen in frightened disbelief as he unbuckled his belt.

Angela tried to escape, she screamed, beating at his face and body with clenched fists but she was weak from the sleepless nights, the hard ride and most of all grief.

The air was cold against her bare legs and hips; he hadn't even bothered taking off her blouse. Scott's weight held her still and then he released her for just a moment and flipped her deftly onto her stomach. Sharp dry leaves cut into her face, belly and thighs and still he pushed her down until she thought she would disappear into the ground the way that small coffin had just this morning.

"I'm going to lay you in the only way a well-used

whore should be taken! Maybe you will understand how much I hate you then, maybe you will give up and stop sniffing around me like a little bitch!"

She screamed, a muffled sound in the quiet forest, as his fingers spread her firm buttocks and she realized what he was going to do.

"Whore!" Scott growled as he impaled her shrinking flesh and a searing pain knifed into her body.

That he, her beloved husband, should commit such an atrocity upon her, hurt more than the rending of her flesh. A kookaburra laughed uproariously at her from high above and the laughter was Laporte's. He had subdued and vanquished Angela by the same cruel method, taking his pleasure from her suffering.

"Whore!" he said it loudly in her ear, punctuating each savage thrust with the word. "Whore! Whore! Whore! Whore!"

Time stood still, flowed swiftly backwards. It wasn't Scott's voice she heard, but a French accented one, humiliating her, tearing her apart. "Whore!" Gaston whispered hoarsely, foreign obscenities bursting from his lips. "Tell me what you are, *chérie.*"

The attack was lasting forever. Angela's gloved fingers dug into the grass, clawing deep scars into the earth—the badly healed ones of her own mind and spirit ripping apart. A black velvet void encompassed her, silver embroidery threads twined around her throat and limbs, as strong and entrapping as a huge web.

Scott finished with her but the fury was still in his heart. Quickly he pulled on his pants looking at her limp, unmoving body sprawled among the fallen leaves. The perversion of the act disgusted him and he hoped it had revolted her just as much. Maybe now she would know better than to accost him.

It surprised him that there had been only a token struggle at the beginning. He had expected a spitting, clawing wildcat screeching in humiliation, but instead she had given in almost too easily. Scowling he walked over to her touching her side with the tip of his boot, shaking her slightly. Had she fainted? If she had, he couldn't leave her in the forest alone.

Squatting down Scott turned her over, brushing the hair from her face. He had thought her pale when they had first met but now there was absolutely no color to her face and slightly parted lips. Her eyes were wide open, staring at nothing, the pupils so dilated that only a thin rim of aqua edged them.

So he had shocked her! At least she was conscious and probably playacting to get his sympathy. He picked up her skirt and threw it over her nakedness, frowning at the huge green stone wrenched from the concealment of her blouse. Why would she wear something that extravagant with riding clothes, and why with the gold locket he had given her a lifetime ago?

She moved, her fingers fastening on the emerald, eyes unblinking in the bright afternoon sun. With a curse he got up and went to his horse. What an actress! She should have played in tragedies. Without a backward glance he rode away.

Where he went, he couldn't say, but long after sundown Scott rode the exhausted horse up to the house. Wearily he walked into the foyer and Celeste burst from the sitting room hurling herself into his arms.

"Oh, my poor, poor Scott!"

"You are ruining your clothes, I'm filthy." A loud crack of thunder boomed and the sky opened in a cloudburst.

"It's terrible, just awful!" Celeste said. "Let me get you a drink."

"Dear, we will have children of our own, one day. I want to give you dozens, as soon as we're married."

"It might take a little longer, unless you plan on delivering litters," Scott said scowlingly. "What's gotten into you, Celeste?"

"We can talk about it later, after you have had a nice hot bath and dinner. You must be very upset. Where is she?"

"Who?"

"Why—your wife, dearest. A person by the name of Ezra is waiting for her in the library. He is most disturbing, I wasn't sure where to put him."

"Ezra is still here?" Scott went over to the library door and flung it open. The big mulatto got slowly to his feet, face ravaged with grief.

"If we could borrow your cabin for the night," Ezra said, "we will leave first thing in the morning. I don't think Angela is up to an all-night ride in the rain in her condition."

"In what condition? Everyone is talking in circles," said Scott, exasperated. "Yes, by all means stay at the cabin, she's probably there now. But keep her out of my sight!"

Ezra glared at the unfeeling brute who was so unaffected by the death of his own daughter. Couldn't he have at least a little compassion for what Angela was going through?

"You bastard! Would you rather have heard it from a stranger? Angela was so concerned about you that she rode all the way here, right after the funeral. She hasn't slept in two days! Yet her first thought was you, always you! She pushed her own feelings aside in deference to yours. She had to tell you herself—had to be with you!"

"I don't know what you are talking about. Who's dead?" Scott's question left Ezra genuinely puzzled.

"Lorna!" Ezra burst out, tears clouding his eyes.

"Lorna?" Scott repeated the name as if he had never heard it before.

"Your daughter, you fool! Lorna Harrington died last night. She was buried at dawn. Didn't Angela tell you?"

"Lorna?" His tone was incredulous.

Very slowly, as if all of the bones in his body had suddenly disintegrated, Scott sank into a chair. Lorna, his little girl, dead? Angela had come to tell him what? His thought processes seemed to have stopped. He was having difficulty assimilating the disjointed words that chased each other through his mind.

He saw Lorna, two and a half years old at their first meeting. Her hands had been full of cookies and she had offered him one. His daughter with her quick smile and quicker temper, learning how to ride a pony in the Highlands, sailing a toy boat on the lake. Trusting little arms clinging around his neck as he put her to bed, guileless eyes looking solemnly at him—just like Angela's.

Angela! He had raped her! She had been devastated and he had—no—he couldn't even put it into words. It didn't matter that she was a slut and he hated her, that he had caught her with Clyde; Lorna was her daughter too. And if he felt like this what had she been feeling when he had attacked her without provocation?

"I didn't know," Scott whispered, the words leaving his lips like a moan.

"She didn't tell you?" Celeste asked.

"No, I—I— Ezra?" Scott's deeply shocked eyes searched his face. "I wouldn't listen, I was angry."

"What happened?" Ezra wasn't sure he wanted to hear the answer.

"I think we had better find her!"

They went into the stormy night that lashed at them like a wild creature. It only took a few minutes to reach the darkened cabin. As they dismounted Scott felt dread enter into his heart. She wasn't there! They stood dripping cold rainwater onto the floor, staring at each other like antagonists.

"What did you do to her, that she couldn't tell you about Lorna?"

Scott stared into those compelling amber eyes and knew he couldn't tell him what had happened. "I hurt her. Let's just leave it at that."

"Son of a bitch!" A powerful fist knocked Scott right off his feet and sent him sprawling onto the floor. Pain and dancing lights exploded in his head. "I'll kill you!"

They wrestled silently together on the floor until Ezra got his hands around his opponent's throat. His powerful fingers began squeezing but suddenly he stopped. "I'll kill you after we find Angela. Now let's get going!" He hauled Scott to his feet and dragged him back into the rain.

It took two hours to find the forest in the dark and

the rain was slicing down harder, churning the ground to mud, dousing the lanterns they carried. They were both bone tired, freezing in the torrent that went on without ceasing.

"She's not here!" Scott looked at the place where he had violated his wife. The storm had washed every trace of the encounter from the earth.

The branches of the gum trees whipped over their heads, slashing the low clouds. They had to shout to be heard over the tempest. Well after midnight Scott and Ezra dragged back to the cabin after a partial search of the woods. It was no use, hardly able to see a foot ahead they would have had to trip over Angela to find her.

In silence, they dried off in front of the fire, brown and amber eyes clashing in a wordless duel. But until she was found they must join forces and work together. Afterwards there would be time for fighting.

A week later the massive effort of searching the bush for a lost duchess was abandoned. Virtually every man in the district had joined in and small parties had combed every inch of the explored territory and not a little of the unexplored. They were tired and dejected. Because of the intermittent rain not one clue as to her whereabouts had been found. It was as if she had vanished right off the face of the earth.

"But everyone has given up!" screamed Celeste. "She's dead—dead! You can't go off all on your own to search for a ghost!"

"I can do what I damn well please!" Scott turned on his heel and went for the door.

"You are bound to me, Scott Harrington, and I order you to stay here!" Her voice changed, wheedling, "Please, my love, stay with me. Your wife is dead and you are free at last. Go get your son in Sydney and bring him back. We can get married now. I will be a good mother to him and an even better wife to you."

"I'm going to Sydney," Scott declared. "Now Ezra will have to tell me her dark secret. I must see Robert."

"Yes, yes! But return soon. I will be waiting, dearest, waiting to make a home for you—and Robert!"

ten

Unseen eyes watched the woman from the safety of the bush. She was alone riding atop a strange beast and they had followed her progress for days. Her skin was a fiery red and her hair was the color of their own but her eyes had amazed them most. They were large, the color of the sky at dawn or the shade of the sea where it was very shallow over the coral formations.

Only once before had they seen such people, the two that lived right beneath the Blue Mountains, but they rarely went near there. Bad spirits lived in the mountains and they kept clear.

The beast stumbled and the woman swayed perilously but righted herself. The sun sparkled on a stone hanging about her neck. It was big, the color of certain leaves and plants. They had never seen anything like it before. There was a fire inside it and they wondered if a spirit was trapped within. These strangers were as colorful as the birds in the trees and her clothes were the color of high clouds and wild berries.

Abruptly the beast stopped and the woman flew through the air, head over heels, landing with a crash in the bush. The beast collapsed to the ground twitching and thrashing, then silent. They watched and she didn't move. Finally the bravest of the men darted over to where she lay, ready to run if danger threatened. He held his spear in readiness and looked down at the sprawled body as small and thin as his own. Her eyes were closed.

Very slowly the shy band of men, women, and children emerged in a thin trickle from behind trees and bushes. Was she dead? The beast seemed to be. Would it be good for food? The woman moved and made a sound and they fell back, afraid.

They had heard that there were many strangers in the land beside the sea where the sun was born. Like the white sands of the shore, it was said. But they never went there anymore, only the ancient ones could remember that land from which they had been driven. Huge white birds with many wings had floated them across the waters and they had brought sticks that smoked and boomed, putting round deadly holes in brown bodies.

The woman had no such stick, not even a pointed spear and she trembled in her sleep. Could she be afraid of them? They were many and she was just one, but the stone was alive and they were apprehensive. One of the little girls touched it and her mother snatched her away carefully examining the child's hand for burns. There were none.

Her eyes opened and they were so stunned by their brilliance they forgot to run. They sparkled like the stone around her neck but without the fire. She tried to sit up but fell down again. Could she be hurt? Crystal drops stole down her red cheeks, but they were not magic—they were tears. The spirits did not cry. Could she be flesh and blood just as they were?

One of the very old women went forward and helped her drink some water. Not too much because her lips were dry and cracked and she would get sick. She said something which they couldn't understand and then someone else offered her food. Her nose wrinkled and she shook her head pushing the offering of the choicest grubs away.

They butchered the beast and moved on to a safe spot taking the woman with them. She moved like one asleep and her fingers touched and rubbed the stone. Night descended and they built a fire and shelters. The aroma of the cooking flesh was good and this time the woman ate, slowly at first, then hungrily. She hadn't eaten in a long time.

For three days and nights the stranger was in their midst. At night while she slept she talked and cried but her eyes were closed. Was she sick, or hurt? One night she sat up screaming, scaring them all into the bush. It was a disruptive influence on them. She couldn't stay. So they approached the shadow of the mountains. It took over a week.

"Will! Willie Mudd, come here this instant!"

He dropped the hoe and went. Hazel never called like that unless something was wrong.

The garden was behind the house and as he rounded the corner he saw a group of dark-skinned aborigines. That was odd in itself because they usually didn't come so close to this place. He had only seen them two or three times and then always watching from the shelter of the trees. But right in among them was a white woman!

"She must be lost, Will," Hazel said her fat body quivering all over like jelly.

"I don't think she came to pay a call, old girl!"

She gave him a push. "Go find out!"

Cautiously Will approached the little group and they melted away into the forest. "Are you lost, girlie?"

She looked at him, frowning and then turned to find her friends gone. She hadn't even tried to thank them and now they had disappeared.

"Are you lost, dearie?" The fat woman echoed her husband, waddling over to the woman.

"Why—I don't know."

She had a lovely voice and under the dirt Hazel could tell she must be quite pretty. A bit on the skinny side though, but what eyes!

"She got to be lost, Hazel, otherwise what would she be doing with that band?"

She ignored him. "What's your name?"

Again that puzzled concentration. "I don't know."

"Don't know your own name, don't know if you're lost? Where did you come from?"

She shrugged her delicate shoulders. "I only remember being with them," she said pointing at the trees into which her companions had dispersed. "But I'm not one them, am I? I couldn't understand them and they ate my horse. Well I did have a little myself. I was hungry."

"Ate your horse! Damn, I could of used a good horse." Will slapped his hand against his thigh. "The one we got now is a bag of bones."

"I think it was dead already."

"Poor child, must be hungry now with only old horses to eat. Come into the house and rest up a bit. Maybe after some decent food and a good night's sleep you'll remember something." Hazel took her hand and led her toward the house. "You talk like a real swell, dearie. Like a lady from back home. Though heaven knows it's been long enough since I last saw London."

"London? Is that a place? London—it sounds nice."

"Well parts is and parts isn't; depends on where you live."

"It's nice here—yes, I think I like it here. There's nobody shouting at me."

"Did they yell a lot at wherever you came from?" Hazel's black eyes were round with curiosity.

"I'm not sure, but they must have if I said it."

The house was a small square one-room building containing the bare essentials. There was a fireplace, a table and four chairs, a bed and one rocking chair. The floor was raw wood, well scrubbed but with knot holes and gaps. The windows had animal skins stretched tightly over swinging frames and were open. Rough shelves lined one wall and on them were jars of preserves, dishes, kitchen utensils, and staples. An oval rag rug was the only touch of color.

"Sit yourself right down—take my chair." Hazel pushed her into the rocking chair and went to stir a black pot hanging over the fire.

A delicious aroma came from the thick bubbling stew, and the woman leaned her head wearily against the back of the chair closing her eyes. The motion of the chair should have been soothing but instead it was disturbing. Her arms ached to hold something, she didn't know what and a hard lump rose in her throat. She wanted to cry without knowing why but she forced back the feeling.

"Oh!" Her green-blue eyes flew open as an animal sprang onto her lap. An orange striped cat inspected her and curled up, and her fingers stroked the soft warm fur. It began to purr, a low rumble in its throat, and she felt a little better. But a cat was not a child and she knew then that her arms longed to cuddle and rock a child. Her child?

"What is your cat's name?"

"Marmalade. Don't she look just the color of orange marmalade?"

"Yes, she does." The woman scratched the cat beneath the chin.

"Still can't remember yours, dearie?" inquired Hazel pulling up a chair and looking curiously at her. "I should call you something, can't keep calling you dearie all the time. Any name in particular you'd like?"

"I can't think of any. Why don't you name me—until I remember. I don't know if I want to."

"Yes," Hazel sighed, her frizzed blond hair jouncing as she nodded vigorously, "there's lots I wouldn't like remembering too. Maybe you been blessed, maybe you run off from what you didn't like."

"Now let's see—a name. Always told my Will if I ever had a girl child I'd name her Rose. You like that? Seeing as how I'm too old to be having any babes you might use that name."

"That's fine, any name is fine. If you like that one then call me Rose."

"Well, Rose, would you like to wash before Will comes in for supper? You're quite a sight."

"Am I? Why I don't even know what I look like!" She ran her fingertips over her face and through her tangled hair.

"Soft hands, like a lady," commented Hazel patting one. "Guess you're no escaped convict, Rose. But if you're a lady there's probably folks looking for you. Maybe Will should ride into Sydney and have word—"

"No! No!" Rose stood up dumping the cat to the floor, her eyes wild. "Not Sydney! No one wants me, no one is looking for me."

"Settle down, dearie! Will only goes once a year—not for a few more months anyhow. Stocks up on things for the winter."

"Could you let me stay, for just a little while?" Rose begged. "I don't have any money but I could work and clean and do whatever you want."

"Of course you'll stay, Rose. Do you think Will and me would turn you out in the bush? Too bad you can't remember, both of us could do with some news of London. Been here for twenty years now!"

"Thank you. I'll work hard and I'll try and remember. Do you think I've ever been to London?"

"You're a lady and all ladies and gentlemen go to London. The tales I could tell you! Used to be a cook in a grand townhouse and Will was a groom." Hazel smiled nostalgically, a faraway look in her bright black eyes. "Enough talking! Let's get you cleaned up."

So she had a bath and washed her hair behind a blanket used as a curtain. Hazel talked the whole time exclaiming over the two necklaces Rose had been wearing. And when she was clean and dressed in a gown of Hazel's that hung like a sack on her thin body, the excited little woman thrust the gold locket into her hands.

"Look! Just look! I knew I had to open it when I saw it. Lockets can hold so many interesting things." She thrust it into Rose's hand and watched her eyes inspect the miniatures. "The little girl is the spit of you and the boy looks like the man on the other side. Look at them eyes! Don't they make you melt? Bet he's broken a few hearts and bedded a score of swooning women."

"I don't like him," Rose said covering his face with her thumb and looking at the vibrant faces of the two children.

"Don't like him! He's got to be your husband, dearie! Why just look at the resemblance—"

"The children are very pretty." She smiled at the painted faces with a distant look on her face. "But how could I forget my own children, if they are mine and. . ."

"And how could you forget a man like that!" Hazel moved Rose's thumb and gazed with rapt attention at the bold, handsome man. "You're a real puzzle, Rose, a mystery. Can't ever say I've met anyone before who forgot who they was. And if he was my husband I'd never forget the likes of him—or let him forget me!"

Rose shivered as she looked again at the man. In some way even the painting upset her. How much more would the real man? There was a sense of power emanating from those dark eyes, something that held her like a frightened rabbit about to be pounced upon. The chiseled lips moved before her startled eyes: "Whore!"

She dropped the locket on the floor with a cry that sent Marmalade flashing out the open door.

"What is it, Rose? Did you remember something?"

"I hate him! I don't want to look at him again. You keep the locket, Hazel, I don't want it!"

"I'll put it away. You might be wanting it later."

Before supper Rose examined her face carefully in the small hand mirror that Hazel handed her. The little girl did look like her and a stabbing pain jolted through her. She was beginning to get a headache from trying so hard to remember.

"Well, do you like what you see? Be pretty with some more flesh on you."

"I don't like my eyes," Rose said critically, staring at herself.

"Nice color, unusual. Too sad though. But we'll cheer you up, dearie! Will and me have a good time even if we do live a hundred miles from nowhere!"

After a supper of kangaroo stew and thick slabs of

bread dripping with butter, the night came down with a slam. Farmers were abed early and Hazel and Will retired to their bed in the curtained alcove. Rose soon heard him snoring and the sound was oddly comforting.

It was cold outside but she was warm and drowsy, snuggling deeply into the fur rug before the fire. Another patchwork of fur covered her. Kangaroos supplied them with fresh meat and the luxury of their pelts to ward off the night air. Without realizing what she was doing Rose slipped off Hazel's nightgown and rolled herself in the deliciously tickling, caressing fur. She stretched languorously with a little sigh. As she fell asleep she dreamed there were gentle hands on her breasts and warm lips against hers.

"Angel, love," a voice murmured and she reached out to him but he wasn't there.

He stared down at the small mound beneath the wattle tree. The sun was shining brightly and birds sang but Scott's heart was dark and heavy. Part of him lay beneath that earth, created by a miraculous fusion with Angela. A childhood disease and inflammation of the lungs were just words but the reality was being parted forever from his laughing black-haired daughter.

And now Angela was gone. He had driven her away—to her death, Ezra said and everyone else agreed. The differences between them had been too monumental to surmount but he could at least have curbed his rage and treated her with some understanding. If only he had known. But it was too late now for regrets—or was it?

"I can't believe she's dead no matter what they say."

The search had produced nothing. If Angela was dead they would have found her body, or at least her remains if the dingos had gotten to her. The thought of wild dogs tearing at her flesh was a torment that had left him sleeplessly tossing half the night. Angela! Angela! She haunted him. She troubled him more dead than she ever had in life.

Not dead, he told himself, never that! Tomorrow he would begin the search again, by himself if need be, with Ezra if he could convince him. He didn't care that Celeste had ordered him back to Thornhill, didn't care if he was branded as a runaway and hunted down. If Angela was alive he would find her and then . . . then what? He would send her home to the safety of England with the immense relief of knowing she was alive. There would be no more nightmares and no more regrets lying heavy on his conscience.

He went into the house. It was quiet with Robert and Clare on an outing in Hyde Park with the Irish girls. What would he do with Clare if Angela was never found? She was her daughter, not his. He had no responsibilities toward her. Could he send her to Jane? She would probably accept Angela's child eagerly, especially since she had been the source of her husband's title and riches.

Who was Clare's father? It always came back to that and Scott went in search of Ezra. The man hated him but he must convince him to talk. With Angela gone why shouldn't he?

Ezra was in the sitting room with papers spread on the table before him. As Scott came in he hastily gathered them up and turned them face down.

"I wanted to talk to you," Ezra said and Scott raised a surprised eyebrow. "I have been debating whether to tell you or not for two days. You don't deserve it after what you have done but there is no way I cannot tell you."

"About what?"

"Angela made me promise her once that I would bring you your children and these papers if she didn't survive."

"She thought she was going to die? Was she sick?" Scott's interest was captivated.

"It's a long story but you have been wanting to know. She wasn't sick. She thought that she might be murdered. . . ."

"Murdered! Who would dare?"

"Gaston Laporte!" Ezra spewed out the revolting name like a curse.

"The pirate?"

"None other. When we set sail from Jamaica he captured the *Dark Lady* and scuttled her."

So that's what had happened to his ship! The *Dark Lady* was residing beneath the blue waters of the Caribbean. Damn, but he would like to get his hands on that Frenchman! But how had he survived those vicious wounds he had dealt him at their first meeting?

"I didn't see the battle to capture Angela but I heard about it later. With two pistols she held them off in her cabin for half an hour. She hid the children and when they tried to break in she killed four of them. Even after she was shot and the pistols were discharged she still fought them like a fury."

"The wound on her shoulder," Scott gasped in astonishment, "that was from the pirates?"

"Yes. Even those cutthroats were impressed with her courage. Laporte took her, the children, and Molly hostage and it was only after seeing Captain Darnell hanged and Angus thrown to the sharks that she passed out."

"Angus!" Scott's face was grim with shock. "She never told me."

"There is a lot she never told you. All hands were killed and I only escaped by pretending to be an idiot. We were taken to Laporte's island in the Bahamas as his prisoners and kept in his house while ransom was demanded for our safe release.

"Life there was not pleasant. We were guarded, although as an idiot I had much more freedom than Angela. I began building a raft in secret, not even she knew about it. Laporte was polite and distant until he moved in for the kill."

"I crippled him," Scott said, "and I wish I had killed the bastard! So he wanted revenge."

"And he got it! It seems he was carrying on an affair with Jules but he had a taste for women as well as boys. He ordered Angela to his room and planned on making her his mistress."

"Because of what I did to him," Scott said with cold

rage eating into him like acid. "It was all my fault!"

"She didn't go even though he predicted dire consequences. Then Molly disappeared. Laporte requested her presence again, and again she refused. He took Angela to his ship and her maid was there. He tied her to the railing and made her watch as his crew raped Molly to death. That was Angela's punishment for rejecting him."

Scott's face had paled beneath his tan and there were harsh lines on his face. His lips were pressed tightly together and two deep grooves etched from his nose to his mouth. "That monster," he managed to say. "He didn't turn Angela over to them?"

"No. He wanted her himself. Angela blamed herself for Molly's death, if she had given in she would still be alive. But it was too late.

"Laporte played with her like a cat with a mouse. He had saved his winning hand for the last. He threatened the children!"

"Damn!" Scott sprang to his feet knocking over the chair in which he had been sitting. "I'll kill him! When I'm free I will seek out that—that—"

"He's dead," Ezra said, watching him control himself with difficulty, "but before he died he got his revenge.

"Laporte didn't mean to kill Robert or Lorna, just introduce them to the perverse delights of which he and Jules were so fond. Angela gave in. What else could she do?"

Scott sank deflated into another chair, his eyes accusing. "She saved your life, Ezra! Why didn't you kill him before that?"

"Because I didn't know. I didn't find out until much later exactly what had happened between them and then it was too late. She feared for her life and her sanity, and it was then she made me promise to get the children to you. I think Angela would have killed herself if it hadn't been for the children.

"Laporte was perverse and sadistic and he used her like a whore. He almost destroyed Angela! I thought at times that if he didn't kill her she would surely go insane.

"Then one night he and Jules got drunk. They took turns raping her. I never heard a complaint from her before but that night—" Ezra shuddered like a huge tree being felled. "Sometimes I still hear her screams echoing down the hall in my dreams. I thought they had killed her but they hadn't—only raped and sodomized her so brutally that she could hardly walk."

Scott's face took on a gray hue and his fists clamped onto the arms of the chair until the knuckles were white. A muscle twitched in his tight jaw and his eyes looked sick.

"It was then that Angela found out that they meant to torment the children anyway and then kill them and her. She went mad and while they were dead drunk she smashed Jules' head in and slit Laporte's throat.

"We escaped on the raft and drifted for days before being picked up by a wrecker. They took us to Key West and it was there Angela found out she was pregnant with Laporte's child."

"Clare! No wonder she couldn't tell me! But you should have, Ezra. I've made a complete fool of myself and wrecked our lives!"

"That's not everything," Ezra declared, "these papers are yours—a full pardon. You are free now to do what you want."

As Scott sat just staring in stunned silence Ezra related the rest: Jack and Amy, the attempted suicide and abortions, the Old Woman and finally the deception of Celeste and Clyde. He left Scott sitting with both hands covering his face.

His shoulders shook with silent sobs that wrenched his heart and soul. Angela! His abused, mistreated wife, and he had only compounded the brutality of the others. She was guilty only of loving their children better than herself. She had fought and when that wasn't enough had surrendered herself in their place.

But worst of all was the crime he had performed upon her at their last meeting. Scott could hardly breathe, seeing once again those wide shocked eyes staring at nothing, unblinking in their terror. Once again she had come to him even after his disbelief and rejection, to comfort him. He in turn had been his usual blind, stubborn self and ravaged her in an unspeakable way.

A knife twisted in Scott's insides and pierced through his beating heart, but still he lived. He wanted to die! He didn't deserve to be alive after what he had done to her.

"Angela! You're not dead! I won't let you be," Scott groaned, writhing with the agony of full knowledge. I swear I will find you!"

Much later, Scott was himself again—and went in search of Ezra.

"You said once that you would kill me for what I did to Angela," Scott told Ezra as they faced each other on the veranda. "Well, do it now. I won't lift a finger to stop you!"

Ezra looked at the complete devastation of the man standing before him. He looked as if someone had beaten him. "Why should I put you out of your misery? Alive, you will have to live with what you have done for the rest of your life. Besides, I couldn't orphan Robert. He has already lost a mother."

"Do you really believe that? I haven't given up. I will continue searching until I find Angela or have proof positive she is dead."

"And if she's alive, what then?" Ezra's look was skeptical.

"I will take her back to England and love her as I never have before. Ezra, will you help me?" There was a silent plea in his voice.

"When are you leaving?"

"First thing in the morning."

"I'll be ready." Ezra held out his hand. "It may be a long hard journey—we may as well start as friends."

They shook hands and Scott couldn't help but admire the big man who had saved his wife and children from destruction.

The day was almost done and the sun was impaled on

a peak of the mountains. This was the time of solitude that Rose devoted to herself and she wandered between the gnarled trunks of trees on the edge of the forest. She never ventured very far for fear of getting lost and even worse the fear of being seen by anyone besides the Mudds. For Hazel had convinced her that someone would be looking for her, but Rose had no desire to be found. Especially not by the man in the locket.

Hazel's never ending delight was making up plausible stories of why she was lost, why she couldn't remember, and who the people inside the golden heart were. But Rose didn't want to know, well maybe the children, but they weren't likely to be wandering around in the bush looking for her. No, if anyone came it would be that man with the dangerous eyes, that made her feel sick and weak when she studied his portrait. So she was careful on her solitary walks and alert for any danger.

She stretched putting a hand to the small of her back where a persistent ache resided from scrubbing the floor. Hazel had insisted that she was a guest but Rose stubbornly overruled her, needing to contribute to the work involved. Besides it was good to have something to do to occupy her hands and mind, since there was nothing to think about except her forgotten past.

She was suspended in time with no past and no future, only the present. There were three people in the wide world she could trust: Will and Hazel Mudd and herself. They had been wonderful, treating her like the daughter they had never had. Living at the foot of the Blue Mountains was simple and undemanding with only the basic need to survive from day to day.

Sometimes Will let her ride his old horse and Rose felt strangely upset because it wouldn't move past a walk and had no pep. When she sat astride she closed her eyes and could feel all the vigor of a powerful mount surging between her knees. She was galloping with the wind, taking high jumps and almost dashing over the edge of a cliff straight into the sea. But when her eyes opened again it was not a young stallion she was mounted on but the sad old hack.

And Hazel would nod her head sagely. "You're a lady," she would say, "all ladies ride to the hounds in England. English women have horsemanship in their blood!"

They spent happy hours together cleaning and cooking and doing chores around the farm and Hazel taught her how to serve kangaroo in at least fifty different ways. She would reminisce fondly about the grand dinner parties she had cooked, the wonderful compliments she got. Once a duchess had actually tried to steal her away from the people she had worked for, because everyone knew a good cook was hard to find. But Hazel had stayed where she was, perfectly content. After all who knew what it would be like working for a duchess?

"A duchess," Rose repeated as she walked along. "Duchess." And the word had a familiar ring to it. She could almost hear in her mind a laughing masculine voice saying that word. But it didn't upset her as so many whispers from her past did. Instead she felt warm and very safe and her fingers rubbed the emerald that she always wore around her neck.

A koala bear with a baby clinging to its back looked down at her with round curious eyes. Rose smiled up at it. They were so cuddly looking but Will had warned her against touching them. They were wild creatures, unused to man and for all their innocent looks had sharp claws which could tear open flesh.

That reminded her of her dreams, such confusing swirling pictures troubling her sleep. They started out so nicely with a faceless man gently but thoroughly making love to her. But then right in the middle of it she saw his face and it was the man in the locket with his face twisted with hate. He hurt her, taking pleasure in doing vile things which she could never escape. He shouted at her, horrible words, until her eardrums shattered and she woke up screaming in the night.

There were other dreams too and she was drowning in a sea of red wine and crimson blood. A ship with white sails was sinking too and on it was the monster with a leering scarred face who had thrown her in. *"Chérie!"* he shouted pointing at the scarlet waves and she looked to see a fin hurtling toward her.

Every night she had those nightmares mixed up with a jumble of faces and places. It was a relief when the dawn approached and she could get up and start the fire, beginning preparations for breakfast.

Darkness was descending like a slowly falling curtain and Rose hurried through the shadowy forest toward the warmth of home. The closed windows glowed from within with a subdued light. The tightly stretched and oiled skins didn't let much light in or out. They should have glass inserted but it was too precious and Rose saw tiny diamond panes glittering in the light. She blinked and they were gone.

It happened all the time—brief split-second glimpses into her past. Inconsequential things like a yellow flower, a white horse, a glowing fire in a huge stone fireplace, a torn faded flag waving from the top of a tower. They made no sense, only served to remind her that her memory had been wiped clean—almost. But it didn't bother Rose that she couldn't remember, it was the flashes of the past that upset her. If not for them she could have been very happy in her new surroundings.

As Rose opened the door she smiled. It was always the same familiar thing each time she returned at dusk. Fragrant aromas greeted her and Hazel was at work, in her glory, basting the wild ducks that Will had shot this morning. This was a rare treat for them and the evening had the festive atmosphere of a gala party.

"It smells divine!"

"I always did have a way with ducks," Hazel said. "What I wouldn't do for a real stove! We would eat like kings."

"But we do already," complimented Rose sitting in the chair before the fire and taking up her sewing.

She was making over one of Hazel's dresses to fit herself. They were much the same height but there was enough material to make three dresses for her own slender figure. It was plain brown cotton, far less expensive than the clothes she had arrived in but that didn't matter. Hazel had very few clothes and the fact that she was willing to share freely with her was only another facet of her generous personality.

Marmalade curled up on the rug not far from Rose and she laughed as the cat sniffed the air and eyed the birds on the spit.

"You greedy thing," she cooed leaning down to scratch Marmalade's chin. "You already gorged yourself on the giblets. For shame, you ate long before we did."

Will came in and his eyes lit up at the domestic scene that spread before him. Rose was a charmer and had brought a bit of sunshine into their routine lives. He wished now that they had been able to have children. What a comfort and help it was to have a young one about the house. Even her nightmares didn't disturb him because she gave so much of herself that she made up for any commotion she caused.

They dined on the tender ducks stuffed with rice, and vegetables fresh from the garden, washed down with homemade wine. Excitedly they went over the plans for his trip to Sydney for he would be leaving in just a few days. Hazel wouldn't accompany him this year, although in the past she had looked forward to it with barely suppressed jubilation, because Rose refused to go. Nothing would induce her to go near the city and seeing how upset just the mention of it made her they let it drop.

So his journey would be a solitary one and he would miss them dreadfully. Will was becoming very fond of Rose and the thought of her absence made him wish the trip could be put off.

"You won't tell anyone I am here, Will?" Rose asked rising and beginning to clear the table.

"No, I promise. Couldn't stand having you leave us just when we're becoming a nice settled family. My lips are sealed."

"And if you see—that man—you must not even speak to him or look at him," Rose murmured apprehensively. "I couldn't stand to see him. The very thought makes me ill!"

"You can depend on me, Rosie!" Will patted her hand as she stood beside him. "Don't want no stranger coming here upsetting you. You'll be safe here, girl. Never have no visitors, except for a party of fools trying to climb them blasted mountains. Nothing on the other side but a desert!"

Rose froze and then said slowly, "I've heard there is supposed to be rich grasslands for sheep—"

"Them fools think so but not me. Break their long necks trying to cross them. Tried before, even had a fancy soldier with them."

"A soldier? With a red uniform and gold braid?"

"That's right, real fancy duds for roaming the bush and climbing mountains. . . ."

"They won't come again, Will?" Rose clutched the edge of the table with one hand and put the other over her eyes.

"You all right, Rose?" Hazel put her arm around the swaying woman's waist.

"Yes, yes. It's just that—I don't like soldiers in red uniforms."

"Don't fret, no soldiers and no handsome brown-eyed strangers will get into my house!" Hazel laughed cheerfully. "I'll crack them on the head with my big castiron frying pan, addle their brains so they can't remember their own names either!"

"Oh, Hazel!" Rose threw her arms around the stout shoulders and clung like a frightened child. "You are so good to me—you and Will—and I do love you both!"

eleven

Rose stood very still in the forest with Will's rifle in her hands. There was a rustle in a bush and she raised the gun in a smooth silent motion and looked down the sight. He had been gone for a week now and she was determined to put fresh meat on the table. A tiny bird streaked skyward and she lowered the rifle. It wasn't even big enough for one mouthful.

She continued on in the early morning chill. The cold weather was invigorating and for a moment she paused closing her eyes. And she felt the sting of snow against her cheeks, smelled peat smoke ascending in wild wisps driven before the wind. Glittering ice mountains indented by blue fingers of water spun by in a glimpse, as if she was riding very fast on a horse.

The fragrant scent of the smoke lingered even when she opened her eyes and a desperate longing to be in that bare enchanting scene overwhelmed her. Where was it and what had it meant to her? Instinctively Rose knew she had been happy there, even more contented than she was here. Should she close her eyes and go back again? No, there was food to find and besides she never knew if she would visit the same scene again in her mind.

Cautiously she crept up on a small glade and was rewarded with a glimpse of a gang of fleeing kangaroos. With quick precision she raised the rifle and fired. One of the largest of the animals fell and she ran into the clearing to inspect her kill. Pulling a knife from her waistband she squatted down to slice open the throat and bleed it when her hand froze.

She couldn't do it! With each blink of her startled eyes pictures flashed through her brain like lightning. It wasn't an animal's throat being cut but a man's and her hands were doing the deed!

"Don't be stupid!" Rose shouted at herself. "It's only an animal! You've eaten kangaroo dozens of times before. Stop it!" And before she could run she slit the animal's throat and threw the bloody knife down.

Now there were other images: a knife slicing through a muscled shoulder and the man turning, shocked—and it was he! She started running, leaving the kangaroo, knife, and rifle all behind, not knowing where she fled, just wanting to be rid of those brown eyes shot with gold.

Rose tripped and fell sprawling full length on the soft ground. She couldn't get up or control the weeping that shook her like an angry storm. When she came to her senses again it was hours later and she passed a hand over her blurred eyes, forcing herself to get up. She must retrieve the rifle and knife and take the kangaroo back to the house.

With jerky movements she brushed off her white shirt and the divided skirt of burgundy velvet. She shivered; it was growing cooler and a blast of cold air made her hurry back to the glade. She had just picked up the gun when crashing sounds made her whirl around.

Through the trees, some distance away, were two men mounted on magnificent horses. For one second she stood very still just looking and then she bounded into a clump of bushes and crouched low, frightened out of her wits. They came closer, always closer, and Rose put her hand over her thumping heart lest they hear it.

It was he! She almost fainted with the shock of seeing him in the flesh. He attracted and repelled her at the same time, and when they stopped in the glade he jumped from his horse with the ease of a great jungle cat.

Another man was with him, huge and dark-skinned. Not an aborigine, Rose thought, they were small people. He was different, but she wasn't afraid of him the way she was of the other one. They inspected the dead kangaroo and the forgotten knife. His gold-dusted eyes swept the forest pausing where she was hidden and she pressed her fingers against her lips to still any sound, even her breathing.

If he found her, Rose was sure he would attack her just like in her dreams. She almost screamed at the thought. The eyes moved on and the men talked but she was too upset to pay any attention to the words.

She must escape at all costs. But first she had to remain undetected, then she would run home as fast as she could and bolt the door. Hazel would protect her, she had promised, and they had the rifle. If it was loaded she might have shot him he called up such violent emotions within her.

No sound alerted him but suddenly the brown-eyed man turned and stared straight at her. Rose knew he couldn't see her even though she could see him through tightly laced foliage. It was as if some instinct told him she was there. He stood very still listening, so close she could feel the heat from those hot golden points of light in his eyes.

Her knees began to shake as he moved toward her hiding place and by the time he reached her she was quaking all over, unable to move. His hard brown hand parted the bushes and those eyes looked down at her with incredulous joy.

"Angel!"

Yes, it was the man of her dreams, of her worst nightmares. His surprised voice fell gently on her ears calling up some forgotten response, but before long he would want to hurt her as he always did. Cringing, Rose tried to back away from him but his arm flashed toward her and hauled her to her feet.

She screamed, trying to break his grip on her wrist and he looked at her in confusion pulling her closer. In a panic she swung at him with her other hand and the butt of the rifle cracked against the side of his head. Pain and surprise registered on his face before those troublesome eyes closed and he fell to the ground.

Rose was running, fleeing her nightmare come to life. "Angela! Angela, come back!" But she didn't heed the other man's words or even slow down. She crashed through the bushes and trees breathless with fear and the exertion of running. Branches whipped at her, tearing her clothes and tugging at her hair but her terror kept her going. Finally she saw the house between the thinning trees and with a last spurt of energy sprinted out of the forest, across the open ground and burst into the house.

With a slam the door closed behind her and she banged down the heavy bar that would keep her safe from him. Hazel looked at her distraught countenance and waddled over as quickly as her bulk would allow.

"What is it, dearie? Are you all right?"

Rose was incoherent and she ran to shut an open window then collapsed on the rag rug in front of the fire. She huddled there, a small inwardly curled ball of shaking velvet and black hair. Her face was buried against her knees, arms tightly clasped around her legs as she cried for the second time today.

Gradually Rose became aware of comforting arms around her as Hazel rocked her like a child, cooing softly, "There, there, Rose. Shh, everything will be all right. Come, tell old Hazel what happened. There's nothing to be frightened of, dearie. Did you remember something?"

"He's here," she said her voice muffled against the vast softness of Hazel's bosom.

"What!"

"The man in the locket. He—he grabbed me in the woods and I hit him with the rifle. He fell on the ground and the other man—"

"There's two of them?"

"Yes. I'm afraid, Hazel—so scared. What if I killed him? What if he comes and takes me away?"

"Well if you killed him how could he take you

away?'' she asked practically.

"Then I hope I did—only he looked so surprised, as if he couldn't quite believe what I did. I'm so confused. Oh, Hazel, don't let them take me!"

"If he's your husband, how could I stop him? Good grief! Do you really think you killed him? Wonder if someone so good looking could be as wicked as you make him out? Could just be the dreams."

"He frightens me. I thought I would die when he touched me." Tear-bright aqua eyes looked beseechingly at Hazel and Rose's delicate nostrils flared in panic. "If he is my husband he would have every right over me. He would own me. I couldn't bear that."

His touching her wrist had been bad enough but what if he didn't stop there? Suppose he wanted to have her the way he did in her dream? She shuddered as if he was forcing her already and Rose knew she couldn't let those nightmares become a reality—no matter who the man was.

A shout sounded outside and both of the women started. "I'll get rid of them, dearie. Won't let on you're even here. Just stay put."

Hazel went to the window and opened it cautiously. A huge man with dark brown skin stood near the door, the reins of the two horses in his hand. Across the saddle of one horse was the body of the man whose face she had memorized.

"What do you want?" she asked uneasily, aware of the fact that Will wasn't there to protect them.

There was a sound behind her and she glanced back to see Rose reloading the rifle with a stubborn slant to her chin. The child was terrified out of her wits and Hazel had no doubt that she would use the weapon if she was forced to.

"My friend here is hurt and needs help," Ezra told the suspicious woman. "We would pay if you could let us stay the night."

"No! I don't know who you are—could be a couple of escaped convicts or bushrangers."

"Please, he's hurt bad. Is there a woman staying with

you by the name of Angela Harrington? We have been searching for her. She disappeared over three months ago."

"Go away!" Hazel slammed the window shut.

"There's a reward for her safe return," he persisted, shouting outside. "Five thousand pounds! Her husband, the Duke of Brightling wants her found."

The window opened again. "Who's the man?" Hazel jerked her head toward the body.

"Scott Harrington, the missing woman's husband."

"The duke?" Her black eyes were round with astonishment. "Wait.

"Rose," Hazel said with a perplexed frown wrinkling her face. "If he's your husband, he could cause a lot of trouble being so powerful. A duke! They know you're here. Would only be a matter of time before they come again with soldiers and make you go back to him. Gentry's funny—when they get an idea stuck in their minds, nothing shakes it loose.

"Look, I'll leave it up to you, dearie. But if we turn them out I guarantee big trouble—oh, not for you but for Will and me."

"Let them in," Rose said wearily. "But I'm keeping this gun loaded and ready to use. I will not let myself be mistreated."

"And who's going to mistreat you? The duke's knocked out cold and even if he wasn't, would a man willing to pay out five thousand pounds for you damage the goods?"

Hazel went to the door and lifted the bar. "You can come in, but don't try no funny business. Got a rifle pointed right at you so just don't try nothing."

Ezra came through the doorway stooped with Scott over his shoulder. She was here! Angela stood defiantly with the rifle pointed right at him and absolutely no recognition in her angry eyes. What was going on? The fat woman hastily spread an animal skin before the fire and he dumped his burden on it.

"Do you have any weapons?" Rose asked and the man nodded. "Then hand them over—all of them. You can't stay unless you do."

"What in the world has come over you, Angela?"
"My name is Rose!"
"She don't remember nothing," Hazel piped up, "not her name, nothing. Aborigines found her and brought her here. You sure she's the one you're looking for?"
"Positive! I have known Angela for years and we are old friends."
But with the gun pointed at him he complied with her wishes and handed over pistols, rifles, and knives. Then he set about tending Scott while Angela watched from across the room. Hazel helped him but Angela wouldn't go near him.
Angela, Angel—that's what he had called her in her dreams: Angel, love—then whore. So her name was really Angela, yes, it seemed to fit her better than Rose. Her alert eyes watched every move the man called Ezra made. His big fingers were tender as he cleaned the ugly gash that slanted high across Scott's cheek and temple. It was gaping wide and wouldn't stop bleeding.
"Can you sew?" The question startled her. "Do you remember your embroidery, Angela?"
"Yes."
"Then get needle and thread because this wound has to be stitched up." Ezra's amber eyes commanded obedience.
"I won't touch him!" She stamped her foot, angry at being ordered around.
He laughed. "Well you didn't forget your temper, Duchess!" Ezra's tone turned more serious. "You will do as I say. It's your fault that Scott is hurt and you will kindly help me tend him. He's your husband. Surely you must feel something for him."
"I hate him!"
"And how can you hate a man you can't remember? You must have recalled something."
"She has dreams," interrupted Hazel going for her sewing basket, "not pleasant either. The duke's always hurting her and she wakes up screaming."
Ezra pulled a flask from his pocket and soaked the needle and thread. "Come on, Angela."

She washed her hands and then he made her rub them in the liquor. Kneeling down beside the stranger that was her husband she looked at his defenselessness. In his state of unconsciousness he looked young and boyish, not frightening at all. Taking a deep breath she touched his cheek lightly with one finger assuring herself that contact with him wouldn't destroy her.

When Angela was finished the cut was neatly closed with minute stitches that wouldn't show once they were removed in a few days. His skin was pale beneath the tan and sweat beaded his brow. He moaned and she jumped. Outrageously long eyelashes curled against his lean cheeks and all at once he reminded her strongly of the little boy in the locket.

Scott's slightly parted lips moved and Angela knew how they would feel on her own; tender, then hard and bruising. It was a strong face belonging to a man of determination and vigor, bronzed by the sun, all lean lines and angles. His eyes flickered open and looked straight into hers. The golden specks dazzled her, held her there against her will and then he smiled, lighting up the whole house.

Never in her dreams had he laughed or smiled, and his teeth flashing white behind that lopsided grin made her legs weak so that she couldn't get up. With hesitation he reached out a hand and touched her wild mane of black hair that was all undone from her dash to the house. Reverently his fingers curled in the silky mass as if she would at any moment waver and vanish into mist.

"My love, is it really you?" His voice was husky and low the way it always was at the delicious beginning of her dream. "Thank goodness I've found you! I can't believe you're alive and unhurt. Angel, love. . . ."

He was pulling her head dangerously close to his. In a moment those parted lips would claim hers and it would begin. Angela struck his hand away and jumped to her feet glaring down at him with anger and distrust. A fleeting look of pain passed across his face.

"So you haven't forgiven me for being a blundering, selfish fool. I'm so sorry, Angel. I would do anything if

I could undo the deed—anything!" He was convincing in his dazed apology. "I love you more than anything in this world, or any other. Please believe me. I suppose you hate me now?"

She didn't even answer him but turned and flounced across the room taking the rifle with her. He upset her, this man of contradictions. She could have sworn he had meant to do her violence when he had caught her in the forest and now he was tender, spouting endearments and love talk. But Hazel was right about one thing—those eyes could make a woman melt. She could feel their warmth all the way across the room.

Angela writhed on the bed. His hands were removing her nightgown and she was helpless to aid or stop him. Every sound she tried to make caught in her throat, unable to reach her lips and then his mouth came closer.

"Angel, love," Scott whispered before his lips burned against and into hers. His tongue probed the recesses of her mouth, tasting of champagne, intoxicating her until she was dizzy with delight.

She struggled against the feeling, knowing what would follow. But it was useless, laid out in a predetermined pattern that couldn't be stopped. Those mobile lips seared the tender hollow of her throat where the pulse leaped at their touch and she grasped his thick bronzed hair in both hands moving his head lower, arching in delirious shock at the wet fire burning into her breast.

Angela moaned thrusting her nipple deeper into his mouth, hardening against the expert machinations of his slippery tongue. Scott pressed his face against the quivering tautness of her belly with little nibbling bites and she cried out as the glowing coals deep inside her burst into an inferno. His lips caught hers, smothering the sounds and it was then that he changed.

The insistent demand became an overwhelming struggle as his mouth viciously assaulted hers. His passion was on a rampage, unstoppable, and she was helpless beneath the brutal caresses that left a trail of bruises over her shrinking body. With one swift movement he turned her over, his hands stroking down her twisting spine, fingers tracing the deep cleft between her rounded buttocks.

She began screaming, shrieks intended to wake the dead and the curtain around the bed she shared with Hazel was jerked back with violence. Her wide staring eyes, catlike in the dark, fastened on her tormentor with the devilish wound slashing his face. She continued screaming while Hazel shook her gently.

"Shh, dearie, you're awake now. It's only that same old dream." Then to Scott, "For heaven's sake, Duke, close the curtain and get away from her or she'll screech all night."

Scott obeyed and Hazel rocked the distraught Angela until her sobs ceased. "Go back to sleep, Rose. Won't have that nightmare no more tonight. That's right, child, lie back and close your eyes—it's almost morning."

Angela pulled the blankets over her shivering body. In spite of the fact that her nightgown was drenched with sweat, she was freezing and her teeth chattered with fright. Her hands clenched into tight fists that made her fingernails cut into the soft flesh of her palms, and she stared wide-eyed at the ceiling until the blessed light of dawn crept through the windows.

Then silently she got up and dressed, slipping like a wraith through the house and out into the foggy morning. The cleansing chill dispelled the last vestiges of her bad dream and she breathed deeply of the misty air. Everything was pale gray and white and the line of trees wavered in and out of sight. The bulk of the mountains was right behind her and though she couldn't see them she could feel their presence.

Oh, to be able to take wing and fly over them far away from all her troubles and every living person. On the other side her husband could never reach her and the painful tug of war of emotions wouldn't be struggling within her heart, turning it into a battlefield.

"Angela."

She whirled and Scott looomed out of the gray tendrils of fog like the devil appearing in a puff of smoke. His face was drawn as if he hadn't slept well and the bandage was gone revealing the stitched cut. Reaching one hand toward her he smiled appealingly but stopped short at her words.

"If you touch me, I'll scream!" She became aware of her vulnerability and that she had left without the rifle, leaving herself open to attack.

"All right," Scott said, holding both hands up in resignation to her mood. "I won't lay a finger on you. I won't do anything you don't want me to."

"What do you want?" Angela was suspicious, taking a step backward.

"Just to talk—nothing else. Is it true that you don't remember anything?"

"I remember some things," she replied, never thinking of not telling the truth. "There are times when scenes and faces flash through my mind, but so quickly it's hard to make any sense of it."

"You remember me?"

"There is a locket with your portrait in it. It seemed familiar but you are a stranger to me. I don't know anything about you or our lives together. Are you really my husband—are we truly marrried?"

"Yes, I swear we are, my word of honor." Scott hesitated, very much aware that she was like a small frightened animal, alert for danger and ready to bolt at the least provocation. "Will you come home with me?"

"No! I want to stay here with Hazel and Will."

"Why?"

"You frighten me. If I go to Sydney with you what will happen? You are my husband and we will have to live together."

"Does that seem so unpleasant? You are my wife, Angel, and I love you. Never would I hurt you. You will have whatever you want. We can go home to England or Scotland or stay here. I have a lot to make up to you and will do everything within my power to make you happy!"

His impassioned plea fell upon deaf ears for she shook her head vehemently. "No! I could not be your wife again—not in the way you would want. . . ."

"How do you know what I want, love? Is there something else you haven't told me?"

Angela's lashes veiled her eyes and the color mounted furiously in her cheeks. Scott smiled.

"You do remember other things! My kisses perhaps, or the way we made love? Even when you knew me I could take you past remembering to a place of oblivion that only we two could find together.

"I know your body as well as my own. There is a scar on your wrist and one on your left shoulder. And on your charming little bottom—"

"Stop it!" Angela put her hands over her ears. "I won't be insulted!"

"But I'm not insulting you. You are beautiful and everything about your face and form is captivating. I'm complimenting you and what better praise could a wife have from her husband than the fact that no other woman can compare to her?"

"I will not go with you."

"What about the children?"

He had caught her attention. The hands came away from her ears and she said with a touch of yearning in her voice, "The little girl and boy in the painting? They are ours? They are in Sydney?"

Scott's hesitation was only brief. "Yes, they are in Sydney. Your children need you desperately. They cry for you and ask me where you have gone. And because of my search for you I too have had to leave them alone." Scott drew a breath and said sincerely, "You may deny me all you want, but I can see from the look on your face that the bond between you and the children is undeniable."

He read the indecision in her eyes, the fright of him and the need for her children. She was wavering. Scott pressed home the advantage.

"Don't your arms ache to hold them and doesn't your heart clamor for their love? They are growing up separated from you at the time when they need you the most. Don't let fear of the unknown steal their most precious years from you.

"I know that you're terrified of me. We have had our clashes and differences in the past but that is over. I have hurt you deeply but I promise never to again."

With a dramatic gesture Scott ripped his shirt off baring his bronzed chest. Angela gave a little cry but his eyes held her still.

"Every mark on my body was put there by you. So you see, you have hurt me also. I don't hold any of these against you." He touched the round scar on his left shoulder. "You shot me once, not long after we met and I won't deny that I didn't deserve it. This," his fingers traced the streak on his side curving around his ribs, "was the result of a duel—over you of course. I was at fault there too."

He turned his back to Angela revealing a new scar still pink. "You stabbed me in the back, love, but what went before was worth it!" Scott faced her again. "But the blow you dealt me yesterday was decidedly unfair. I won't take the blame for my newest scar, I lay it at your feet.

"My scars are highly visible but the ones I've left on you are etched into your soul. Maybe they go deeper than mine and still pain you at times, but if I'm willing to forget, can't you forgive?"

She was crying, tears sparkling like dew drops on her hot cheeks, lower lip trembling like a child's. Closing the short distance between them he touched the tips of his fingers ever so gently against the tears, then put his wet fingers to his lips. She swayed; it was almost as if he had kissed her.

"We have fought and loved and separated but have always come back together again. Sixteen thousand miles couldn't keep us apart, deceptions and the plots of others couldn't, pirates and brigands couldn't, even our own differences couldn't. We belong to each other, and nothing and no one can change that." Scott's voice was a low husky whisper, enticing, urging—and those eyes drew her into them. "Now, I won't let this final hurdle separate us. Without you, love, I'm only half a man. I need you, the children need you, and hard as you may find this to believe, you need me. Say yes, Angel—come with me and be my wife again, be my love. I can't live without you; I don't want to! Come home. Oh, love, say yes!"

Her mind searched frantically back into the mists of time. Hadn't this happened before? Hadn't she been helpless to resist Scott then too? Angela tried to deny him, but his will was overpowering, bending hers to his. His golden-brown eyes begged her more eloquently than all of his words and she could see in their gleaming, mysterious depths that he truly did love her.

She was lost, and in spite of the dreams and the terror that they would become a reality she sighed, "Yes—yes—yes!"

"Oh, love!" Scott was weak with relief and he looked at her closed, quivering eyelids so fragile in their distress.

He wanted to sweep her into his arms, cover her with kisses, carry her off into the woods and make love to her—but that was impossible. He must go slowly, gradually winning her love and respect all over again. To Angela he was a stranger and if he didn't want to lose the foothold he had gained this morning he must be scrupulously patient.

She caught her breath as he took her hand and pressed a kiss on the back. Her eyes flew open, alarmed at what would happen next. Alone and helpless he could do anything to her he wanted. But Scott smiled in that disturbingly disarming way and turned her hand over pressing a searing kiss onto her soft palm. Angela gasped at the implied intimacy of what he was doing, at the tingling sensation spreading through her fingers and up her arm, dispersing warmly into her body.

She knew then that he was an impatient man, but for her he would wait forever. And she couldn't breathe as he kissed her palm again, eyes glowing with suppressed passion—and she wondered what it would be like when the waiting was over.

Throwing her arms around Hazel's neck she sobbed helplessly, leaving the only home she could remember. Angela was setting out for parts unknown with virtual strangers and what would happen next she didn't know. Safety and security were being left behind.

"Shh, dearie, don't cry. You'll write to old Hazel and tell her how you're faring, won't you?"

Angela nodded, sniffing, and parted unwillingly from the comfortable embrace. Reaching around her neck she undid the necklace and smiling through her tears put the emerald around Hazel's thick one.

"I want you to have this—to remember me. Wear it always."

"It's too grand for the likes of me!" Hazel said touching it lovingly. "And I'm no flighty duchess, needing a reminder of the past!"

"But you will keep it," Angela said, "because I want you to. I will miss you and Will so! Tell him—thank you for everything. I love you both!"

"You were a daughter to us, Rose, and parting is hard." Hazel leaned forward and whispered in her ear, "But look at that man who's your husband! Could a woman ask for more? He loves you, I can tell. If you only give him a chance I know you will be happy."

"Good-bye, Hazel," Angela said, dashing the tears from her eyes.

"Good-bye, dearie!" Hazel kissed her again on the cheek and smiled, touching Angela's hair in a motherly caress. Then her black eyes sparkled wickedly. "Don't his eyes just melt you?"

Angela burst out laughing and nodded her head. "Oh Hazel—they do indeed!"

She went over to where Ezra and Scott were waiting, far enough away so that the leave-taking had been private, and Scott handed her his handkerchief. After wiping her face and blowing her nose he lifted her onto the saddle of his horse and mounted behind her. Angela stiffened as his body touched hers and his arms went around her waist grasping the reins in front of her.

"Sorry, love," he said, his lips far too close to her ear. "I did bring a horse for you to ride but it went lame weeks ago. We'll have to ride double until I can find another one. But you're as light as down, the horse won't even know he has a second passenger."

Angela waved at Hazel's rotund figure as it quickly receded and was obscured by the trees. The bush closed in around them like a vast, mysterious sea of gray-green and the three of them were alone. Uncomfortably aware of his hard thighs against hers she tried to shift her weight so that there would be no contact. It was impossible and Angela sat rigidly so her back wouldn't touch his chest. But his loins were still tight against her buttocks, reminding her of her dream.

Miles passed in silence and Scott did nothing more alarming than touch her waist briefly. The half-remembered motion of a good horse and the fact that Ezra was with them lulled her into a sense of security. She felt she could trust Ezra in a way she could never depend upon her husband and gradually she relaxed.

His broad chest supported her back and the long length of his thighs no longer bothered her. There was a familiarity about his masculine body, as well there should be—after all they were husband and wife and had done much more than just touch in the past.

"Feeling better, Angel?" Scott inquired, well aware of her inner turmoil.

"Yes, a little," admitted Angela. "Scott!"

"Yes, sweetheart?"

"Are we rich?"

He smiled behind her back. "Filthy!"

"You—you—said that I could have anything I wanted," she reminded him hesitantly.

"Anything your little heart desires!" He wondered what she wanted—clothes, houses, or perhaps another emerald to replace the one she had given Hazel.

"I would like a stove."

"A stove?" He couldn't be sure he had heard her correctly.

"Yes, small but very modern, with lots of cooking utensils. . . ."

"What in the world for? You already have one or more in every house we own."

"For Hazel, not me. She would like that more than anything. Do you think we could find someone to bring it all the way out here?"

"Hell! I'll pay someone enough to bring out a dozen stoves if you want."

"One will do nicely," she said primly and Scott burst into laughter startling her upright again.

"You're priceless, Angel," he laughed squeezing her waist. Then he said soberly, "I'm so glad I have you back again and you came of your own free will. Because otherwise I think I would have had to carry you off like Helen of Troy. You would be worth fighting ten wars over!"

At dusk they stopped and Ezra and Scott soon had a roaring fire built. Angela sat wearily on a blanket and held her cold hands out to the warmth, rubbing them together. They ate the food that Hazel had packed for them and she watched apprehensively as Scott began spreading out two bedrolls. Surely he wouldn't expect anything from her with Ezra just on the opposite side of the fire.

She delayed as long as possible, until her head was nodding and her eyes fluttered in a desperate effort to keep awake. It was fully dark with the leaping orange and gold flames crackling and the Southern Cross hazy through high wisps of clouds. Angela jumped as two strong arms lifted her and laid her down on the blanket so near the one that was Scott's.

He pulled off her boots and she started to protest but he quickly covered her with a blanket tucking it in around her neck. Her eyes closed with exhaustion, the warmth of the fire playing over her and she heard Scott settle down beside her. He touched her hair in a fleeting caress.

"Good night, my love," Scott whispered, his voice as warm as the fire.

And then it was morning.

Every day was the same and at night Scott slept protectively near her but made no overtures. There were no nightmares either, which surprised Angela. It was because she was so tired at night and slept soundly, she reasoned. By the time they got to Sydney she had almost forgotten them.

How busy the city was and how the people stared as the three of them rode bedraggled and dusty through the streets. Angela had her own horse now, purchased in the Hawkesbury. It was a great relief not to have to ride with Scott in that enforced intimacy but her mind raced ahead to tonight. What would happen when they were alone at last? Would Scott demand his marriage rights—force her to play the unwilling wife? Her heart pounded in panic at the thought.

Then they were stopping before a small house on the outskirts of town with a breathtaking view of the bay. As Scott helped her down she clung for a moment to his coat and whispered, "What are their names? The children's I mean."

"Robert and Clare," he replied, raising a mocking eyebrow at her.

"Milady! You're found!"

"Mama! Mama!"

He spun her around and she saw the children running across the grass toward her, two thin girls clinging together and crying on the veranda. But the little girl had golden hair and wasn't the one in the locket; she was much younger.

Angela tilted a perplexed face up to Scott. "Is she ours too?"

His eyes looked straight into hers and he said simply, "Yes!"

She ran and met them halfway and knelt on the grass gathering them both into her arms at the same time. Angela's mind didn't recall but her mother's heart remembered and when they went into the house her cheeks were streaked with tears but she smiled.

An hour later she was bathed, perfumed and dressed and stood near the bedroom window examining the locket. Where was her black-haired daughter? No one had said anything at all about her and although she was elated at the rediscovery of Clare and Robert she wanted to know where the other one was. Could she be in school in England? Yes, that must be it.

Angela sought Scott out and found him sitting at the kitchen table joking with the Murrays, sending them into paroxysms of laughter. There was a cup of tea in his hand and a half-eaten piece of cake on the plate in front of him. He looked up at her hesitant entrance and she went to him handing him the open locket.

"Where is she?" Angela asked and she saw a shadow of intense pain wipe the smile off his face.

Scott stood up abruptly and took her hand, leading her through the house and out into the garden. She clung to him upset at the silence and suffering, wanting to comfort him but not sure how.

"Scott, wait."

Stopping he swung around to face her, dropping her hand and Angela thought she saw carefully concealed tears glittering in the depths of his eyes. Drawn to him she touched his cheek, tracing the scar that gave him a rakish, rather reckless look. Could his firm lips be trembling? Somehow she couldn't stand that and going up on tiptoe, her arms circling his neck, Angela pressed her warm, full lips against his.

He stood immobile, not touching her as her mouth moved gently against his. Then she felt him shudder and his arms enveloped her, one hand moving in her hair, the other clasping her waist. Scott's lips opened hers and her head fell back as he tasted the sweetness of her mouth.

It was the very beginning of her dream, heady with sensuality, and the hot desire of his lips and hands and lean body incited a total response from her. Angela's breasts molded against his chest and she wanted the hardness of his thighs against hers. Even the way his hair felt between her fingers was hauntingly familiar and her body shook.

Scott drew back slowly, looking down into her heavy lidded aquamarine eyes. She was so bewitching with that look of abandonment on her face, lips reddened and moist from his kisses. And she had made the first move! His heart leaped with joy and great tenderness, and he bent to kiss her cheek.

Go slowly, he warned himself, for it would be much too easy to sweep her off her feet and carry her into the bedroom. This reciprocation from Angela was one more step in the right direction and he didn't want to spoil their tenuous relationship and have to start all over again.

"I love you, Angel," he whispered breathing in the delicious scent she exuded. "Your kisses are so sweet, like honey-wine. I could get quite drunk on just one."

She smiled at him shyly and Scott couldn't resist kissing each dimple. As they walked farther into the garden he kept his arm around her slender waist, wishing he didn't have to show her what she had asked about. They stopped beneath a spreading tree and she frowned, looking at the grass covered mound in the deep shadows. Taking a few more steps toward the tree she saw a small black marble stone and sank to her knees tracing the sharply cut letters with her fingers.

LORNA HARRINGTON
BORN—ENGLAND 1803
DIED—NEW SOUTH WALES 1812
DAUGHTER OF
SCOTT AND ANGELA HARRINGTON
DUKE AND DUCHESS OF BRIGHTLING

A pain like a sharp hot knife sliced into her breast and Angela collapsed, her face against the cool grass and her fingers touching the cold marble. A paroxysm of weeping seized her and shook her prone body violently. The sweetly smiling face in the locket wavered beneath her tightly closed eyelids and all the grief of the past swept over her like a great tidal wave.

Scott leaned down and picked her up holding her limp, shaking form in his arms. Angela pressed her wet face against his neck and her sobs were loud in his ear. Swiftly he carried her away from the place where their daughter rested into the haven of their room.

PART THREE

Secret Fire

England

1813

Dear, if you change, I'll never choose again;
  Sweet, if you shrink, I'll never think of love;
Fair, if you fail, I'll judge all beauty vain;
  Wise, if too weak, more wits I'll never prove.
Dear, sweet, fair, wise, change, shrink, nor be not weak;
And on my faith, my faith shall never break.

—Anonymous

Go—and if that word hath not quite killed thee,
  Ease me with death by bidding me go too.

—John Donne

twelve

A crystal shower of snow flew beneath the horse's hooves. Angela's silvery laughter drifted over her shoulder to the man pursuing her on the chestnut stallion and the sound enticed him on. She looked like a snow queen in white velvet and silver fox, bending low over her mount's neck. Damn but she can ride, thought Scott, urging his horse on, following her into the frozen woods.

The trees clattered, branches silvered with needles of frost and ice. The early morning sun shone through a blue haze, sparkling on the dazzling white expanse. She broke a trail through the virgin snowfall, her quickened breath misting the air as she lost herself in the forest.

Quickly, before he caught up to her, Angela jumped down sinking into a drift, laughing as she floundered and righted herself. Scooping up a handful of the powdery Arctic snow, she flung it just as he broke through the trees.

Scott swore dashing the cold snow from his eyes and face. "Damn! You've led me a merry chase and is this my reward? No! I claim a better one."

She screamed as he flung himself at her and ran only to fall face down in an even deeper drift. Then he was beside her turning her over as she laughed helplessly, his own booming laugh echoing through the naked forest.

Angela's hat came off spilling coal-black tresses into

the blinding white snow. Tiny stars beaded her lashes and Scott wiped the flakes off her rosy cheeks. Her lips were cold but they parted warmly beneath the pressure of his and her tongue was a hot arrow darting into his mouth. Their breathing mingled and she withdrew her lips only to nibble and tease and drive him mad.

The fur around her throat tickled his face as he kissed her deepening dimples, her defiant chin and the icy tip of her nose. She pulled off one glove so she could run her fingers through his thick bronze hair. In spite of the cold morning she was warm, glowing inside from the exercise, but mostly from her husband's kisses. There was no danger here in the woods of anything more frightening than a few kisses and caresses so she was relaxed, without the usual fear of driving him past the point of no return.

Not that he had ever reached that point with her. Angela wondered briefly if he had a mistress tucked away somewhere near town. Surprisingly the thought was unpleasant and she concentrated instead on the way his strong teeth were nipping at her earlobe. She touched the white scar on his cheekbone with her finger tips and then with her lips and he raised his head to look down at her.

She was the most fascinating, beautiful woman in the world. As fragile and perfect as the snowflakes glittering like mica on her dark lashes and in her outflung hair—deep and mysterious beyond comprehension even though he knew most of her multifaceted past. What was she thinking of behind those pale, brilliant aquamarine eyes? Was she beginning to thaw at last? Could she be falling in love with him, even a little?

That was his fondest desire, the goal he tirelessly pursued every day. But the closer he thought he came to possessing her the more remote she became. There had been the separate cabins on their voyage home on the *Cygnet* and now separate rooms at Brightling Castle. And though he believed they were now friends and Angela seemed to trust him, there was a barrier he could not get past.

Scott had wooed her long and hard with gifts, compliments, love words, and kisses but there was always a certain point where she stopped him. Angela wasn't adverse to a little love play like now—in fact she liked the innocent tussling, that he knew. But whenever he tried to press the issue she froze. So although she was his wife it was in name only and Scott wondered if it could ever be more.

He could have taken her a hundred times if he had wanted to use force but what good would that do? It would only alienate her further, wipe out all his careful cultivation of this fragile exotic flower. She wasn't disinclined to a frolic in the snow, but he wanted her in his bed.

There had been no other women either. Not because they hadn't been wiiling, in fact many had thrown themselves at him, but because he simply wanted no one but Angela. On some nights he thought he would go insane with wanting her, the way he had in Scotland during his self-enforced abstinence.

Scott kissed her again, liking the way her fingers raked through his hair pulling him closer. He dared to cup one breast lost beneath layers of clothes, wishing it was her bare satiny skin instead of velvet and fur. Angela strained against him and he covered her body with his pressing her deep into the drift.

She stiffened beneath him, no longer laughing and he knew that he had gone too far—again. Not that she ever told him no or even fought him. She would just lie there with her eyes tightly closed and the color draining from her cheeks, shaking as if he were a rutting animal about to rend her frail body. Yes, it was starting again, her long dark lashes trembled against white cheeks and she went limp, a look of panic on her face. The hands that had been clasped around his neck slid down pushing gently against his shoulders.

She was not his Angela anymore, but a frightened little snow-bird trying to escape from him. Time and circumstance had changed her; yes, that and a French pirate and his own selfish cruelty. Lack of understanding, plots, and counterplots and had all brought this new frightened creature into existence. Her wings beat frantically, uselessly against him but escape was impossible. Scott would never let her go—not while he lived—not while she breathed.

He rolled off her and helped her to her feet, retrieving her hat and glove. Angela brushed the snow from her clothes and glanced shyly at him beneath her lashes. No longer was Scott her laughing companion. His face was smooth and impassive, that of a stranger, as it always was when their play ended in this way. She wanted him back the way he had been a few minutes ago, bold and slightly wicked, but not at the price of surrender. She wanted to let him love her but she just couldn't. Something inside her always stopped the passion before it really began.

"I'm sorry," she whispered accepting her hat and tucking her hair into it. Looking into his dark, inscrutable face she almost wished he would get angry, shout at her, vent the rage and frustration he must be feeling—but he never did. She couldn't recall his ever raising his voice to her and never had he touched her with anything but gentleness. Still she was afraid, thinking of her infrequent nightmares, knowing that at one time he had treated her worse than a whore.

"No matter," Scott said lightly, but she knew differently. "I wasn't going to do anything."

"I know, it's just that—" She stopped unsure of herself. Now the rest of the day would be spoiled and she had been so happy.

Scott walked over to the horses and she followed him catching his sleeve and he half turned, his sherry-brown eyes cold. She looked up at him appealingly and those brown eyes that could melt ice softened. She smiled tentatively, wanting to offer him an explanation, wanting to trust him.

"Forget it, Angel. I will."

"No, you won't," she said so softly he had to bend his head closer to hear her. Grasping the front of his coat as if he meant to leave her there Angela whispered,

"I . . . . I wish I could be a proper wife to you. I like it when you kiss me. I feel all warm inside, but when you go too fast it scares me. All I can think of is my dream."

Scott gazed at her with one raised eyebrow. He knew she had nightmares sometimes, he heard her scream in the night and heard, through the adjoining door, her maid come to her aid. But he didn't know before this minute that her nightmare was the cause of her coldness and she had never volunteered any information about it before.

"What happens in your dream, love?" He put his hands over her small fists clinging to his clothing.

Angela looked down at the snow, but not before he saw the telltale blush staining her face. Now all he could see was the silvery fur crowning her head.

"You make love to me!" she burst out suddenly trying to pull away. But he wouldn't let her go.

"That is nothing to be ashamed of—we are married you know."

"But—but—"

"Don't you like what happens in the dream?"

"At first," Angela admitted. She hadn't talked about this to anyone, even Hazel. All she had told the woman was that he hurt her.

"Do I kiss you and caress you?"

"Yes."

"Are we naked in bed?"

Only a jerky nod.

"And you like that?"

"I'm on fire for you!" Angela said, startling him and herself with her stark honesty.

"Then what's wrong? Why do you scream?" Scott inquired gently.

"You change—you hurt me. 'Whore' you shout in my ear. You turn me over and press me into the bed. You—you—"

"Shh!" Scott said taking her into his arms, holding her heaving body close against him. There was no need for her to finish because he knew the conclusion. Angela dreamed about what he had done to her in the gum tree forest at Thornhill. His sins were coming back to haunt him.

"I would never hurt you again—you know that don't you, sweetheart?"

"Yes, but I can't help the way I feel. Did you do that to me? I can't believe you would!"

"Yes, I did. In a fit of blind rage I ruined our whole relationship. You will never know how sorry I am for that mistake—not because I want you physically and can't have you, but because of how deeply I hurt you! You are the only one that matters, Angel. It's you I care about—you I love!"

They rode home in silence. What more could either of them say? He was being denied what he wanted most because of his stupidity in the past. If he tried to make love to her again it would probably be worse than before because now it wasn't just a nightmare, now she knew it had really happened. What must Angela think of him?

As soon as they reached home Angela fled, disappearing without a glance at him and Scott dejectedly led the horses to the stable.

"Your Grace," the butler said as she rushed into the house. "The Duchess of Remington is in the morning room."

"Oh!" Angela had never felt less like a duchess herself, still flustered from Scott's confession. "I will be down shortly."

Hurriedly she changed wishing Jane had not chosen this particular morning to call. Although Angela couldn't remember their friendship from the past they had built a new one and were again fast friends. She and Owen were at Bentwood for the winter and they often visited bringing their two boys. But right now her mind was in a whirl and she didn't feel like making pleasant conversation.

When she joined Jane she found, much to her relief, that she could remain relatively silent while her friend chatted on about everything. Angela found herself relaxing in spite of herself and the blazing fire and a cup of tea warmed her so that she slumped drowsily in the chair.

Jane was a blond English beauty and being round with her third child only added to the bloom in her cheeks and her radiance. Angela watched her enviously. She had a perfect marriage to a charming, devoted husband, two healthy sons and another baby on the way.

Impulsively Angela leaned forward blurting out her secret yearning: "How I envy you, Jane. I would give anything to have another baby—a black-haired daughter like . . . . Lorna."

Jane stared at her shocked into silence for a moment. "Obviously not anything, Angela. You need a man to get a baby."

"Oh!" She turned scarlet with mortification at the implication of those words. Had Scott told her? They were fast friends.

"Servants do talk. Everyone knows that you have separate rooms and haven't slept together since you ran away in New South Wales."

Angela stood up ready to flee but Jane's next words stopped her.

"Sit down, Angela. Since we're on the subject you need a good talking to—and since no one else seems to want the task I guess it falls to me. Your own husband won't even talk about it!"

She sat down abruptly, glad the chair was there, otherwise she would have collapsed on the floor.

"We have been friends for a long time, eleven years to be exact and we haven't always seen eye to eye."

"I don't want to talk about it," Angela protested finding her voice.

"You will! Many times in the past your own outspokenness has been directed at me and I didn't like it at the time. Only later did I realize it was for my own good. Now it's your turn to listen—and listen you will!"

Jane paused for a breath looking quite stormy and Angela stared at her with her mouth open as she continued. "What are you trying to prove, holding out on Scott? He's a man with hot blood in his veins and this monkish existence of his can't last forever. Ten months is a long time, Angela—especially for a man like him. Do you want to drive him into another woman's arms? Do you want to wreck your marriage? Because that's exactly what you will do if you don't put a stop to this foolishness.

"Oh, right now he's punishing himself for his cruelty to you, like a fanatic wearing a hair shirt or flagellating himself for past sins. But that won't continue indefinitely. Sooner or later he will need a woman, and if it isn't you then it will be someone else!

"Are you playing with him to see how long he can last? It's been almost a year now—do you think he can manage two? Stop torturing him! You are his wife; you owe him that much. He has every right over you under law. A husband cannot rape his wife because if he takes by force what is his, there is no crime. In the past he wouldn't have hesitated, but he's changed.

"Scott has been kind and patient and considerate in a way I have never seen before. He has changed, Angela; his love for you has worked a miracle! He wouldn't hurt you for the world and if it means giving up what he covets above all else to please you, then he will. But things will not remain the same and if they change you have only yourself to blame!"

Jane looked long and hard at Angela. She had seen anger and shock chased by embarrassment cross her face and now she sat very still with her hands clasped tightly in her lap, her eyes downcast like a scolded child. She wanted to shake her.

"Go to him, Angela! Be his wife in the full sense of the word—be his lover! Only when you give yourself completely, asking no reward in turn, will you know the total meaning of love."

"I'm afraid," she said in a very small voice.

"Then conquer your fear. Force yourself to do it even if it gives you no pleasure. Believe me, it will get better as time passes and you get used to it. He has given you so much, not just material things but himself. Can't you do this one small thing—make this one sacrifice? Stop thinking only of yourself. Scott needs your love as he never has before. You will never regret it."

"I—I've tried to let him love me, but I go all cold inside."

"Think about something else, anything. Look, everyone has told you how much Scott loves you and so has he. But somehow I don't think you believe it. You think he just wants you physically or because you're the mother of his children. Do you really want to know how much he cares for you?"

Jane's sapphire eyes challenged Angela to say no, commanded her to listen. Leaning forward she said very softly, "Clare is not his daughter! She is your illegitimate child, fathered by a pirate that got you pregnant as revenge on Scott."

"No! You're lying. I won't listen to this!"

"It's the truth! He loves you enough to accept his enemy's child as his own—because she is yours. And he has never reproached you for it, knowing how it would hurt you."

"Scott said Clare was ours," sobbed Angela.

"Because you couldn't remember and he wouldn't have you upset needlessly. That's how much he loves you. Can you deny him now?"

Angela ran from the room near hysterics and Scott looked after her and then at Jane who came out of the morning room.

"What happened?" he asked, upset because Angela was.

"I just got something off my chest and Angela didn't like it one bit; but maybe she will think about it." Jane smiled sadly. "For your sake—and hers—I hope she does."

Angela stared at the sensual creature in the mirror unable to believe it was her. She glowed pink from a hot bath and her hair hung to her hips like a shimmering mantle. Maggie had just finished brushing it for over half an hour. The nightgown she wore was a cobweb of silk, the same color as her eyes and the only thing holding it on her were thin silver straps. It fell straight to the floor in a myriad of tiny pleats. No, not straight, she corrected herself, for her breasts thrust the material out in front and when she turned the firm curve of her hips and bottom was clearly visible.

Nervously she looked at the door separating her apartments from Scotts, wondering what her reception would be. Surprise, surely—and after that? Would he be gentle or would all the pent-up passion rush out in a fury, hurting her in his frenzy to possess her?

Force yourself, Jane had said, and that was exactly what Angela did, for each step toward the door was harder than the last one. She didn't even knock for fear she wouldn't go through with it.

Scott was standing by the bathtub, naked but for a white towel around his hips. As he looked up shock registered in his glowing eyes at his recalcitrant wife entering his room for the first time, and dressed in only a whisper of a nightgown!

"Is something wrong, my love?"

But she said nothing, her eyes riveted on him. And he feasted his eyes on the glimpse of paradise long denied him. The light from her room cast a golden glow around her, outlining every curve through the sheer material. Rosy-tipped breasts rose and fell quickly and her hair was a glory of silky curls. The long supple line of thigh, hip, and waist made him shake with frustration.

She found his man's body no less beautiful in symmetry and looked at him curiously. The long, hard legs that had so disturbed her on the ride to Sydney were bared almost to his narrow hips, strong columns supporting his body. He gleamed like bronze in the candlelight and even the scars on him didn't detract, but rather added to his masculinity. Curly hair covered his chest which looked as unyielding and hard as carved stone. The firelight threw the corded muscles of his arms into sharp relief. He was a lean virile animal and he was her husband.

But his face had lost the harsh expression she had seen earlier, and even though the white scar on his cheek made him look like a dashing barbarian, his eyes were as full of love as they were of golden sparks.

"Don't they just melt you?" Hazel's words echoed through her and Angela smiled walking toward him.

She knew then that he would be gentle and she only hoped that she wouldn't disappoint him and disgrace herself. Stopping just inches from Scott she raised her hands and undid the silver cords. The silk slithered to the floor with a sigh and pooled around her feet like a Jamaican lagoon.

She heard his gasp of surprise as she stood naked before him and then with a shaking hand Angela reached out and touched his chest lightly with her fingers. They trailed down through the light fur and still he made no move to touch her. Reaching the towel she pulled it free and it too fell on the carpet.

Angela couldn't look down, she was too scared—of what she would see and of her own boldness. But when his arms slowly pulled her against him, molding their bodies together, she felt the wild surge of his desire and slid her arms around his neck.

Scott's hair curled damply beneath her moving fingers and he gazed deeply into her huge eyes, shining like aquamarines. Had today's confession, on both their parts, finally laid to rest the ghosts between them? He could think of no other explanation and with infinite care not to startle her he lowered his head to hers, grazing her velvet cheeks with light kisses. She shook in his embrace and he realized what an effort her coming to him had taken.

"Sweetheart," he whispered huskily in her ear. "It was worth the wait, and you are a brave little temptress. I am completely in your power. You have woven your spell well, my love, let me take you to Cythera."

Scott's mouth found hers, rediscovering the nectar of her yielding lips. Slowly, the heat from his kiss spread through Angela's veins like golden, melting honey. Those strong brown arms lifted her and he carried her to the bed, placing her in the middle and lying by her side.

A soft moan escaped her as Scott leaned over her, his face dark with desire. His hands moved, one in her outflung hair the other cupping a breast, fingers making it tauten and quiver.

"Angel, love!"

Her dream had begun.

Fire turned to ice, as cold as the winter landscape outside their window. She shivered under his hot ardent kisses and caresses, stiffening involuntarily at his boldness.

The tide of his passion, so long pent up burst the barriers he had built and in spite of the way that Angela lay, cold and rigid, he couldn't stop himself. With a groan of defeat and frustration that she was no longer his wild Angela of the past, Scott took her.

She thrashed beneath him, half fainting with fear. So this was the way it was between a man and a woman—the awful invasion of her body, an animalistic ritual where the man became the victor forcing submission. It wasn't happening exactly as her nightmare went but the panic was the same.

Scott had changed from the gentleman he always was into a beast with no control over himself. His powerful body heaved against hers and Angela cried out against the attack, struggling to free herself from the hardness searing her insides. Her protesting muscles tried to forcibly eject him but he only lunged at her faster, hurting her, until he collapsed in a shuddering convulsion that burst with sharp agony deep in her belly.

She screamed once, tears gushing from her eyes and into her hair. Then they were still. They were both drenched with his sweat and her tears and Angela shook beneath him with silent weeping.

Scott looked down at her tightly closed eyes, tears squeezing out of the corners and swore silently at himself. She had offered herself so willingly at first, how could he have known it would end like this? He should have stopped himself at her first adverse reaction. It wouldn't happen again.

"Oh, my love! I'm so sorry!" he whispered, kissing her cheek but she turned her face away. "Please, Angel, say you forgive me!"

"Let me go!"

As soon as Scott released her she sprang from the bed and raced for her room.

"Angel, I love you!" Scott called after her.

The door slammed and he half rose wondering if he should go after Angela. He could hear her crying, the sounds muffled in her pillows. Falling back on the bed Scott punched his own pillow with all the violence he felt for himself. Swearing he put his hands over his ears so he couldn't hear her sobs.

He would give anything for just one hour alone with the old Angela. She had been a tempestuous wildcat, a little wanton no matter what he did to her. Even when violence crept into their lovemaking, as it often had, her body had responded, many times against her will, giving him exquisite memories with which to torture himself.

Angela, angry; Angela, melting with submission to his outrageous demands; Angela, shooting him, stabbing him; Angela, meeting and exceeding his own passions, her body sweetly demanding—but never a cold Angela. Even her first defeat when he had claimed her virginity had been a fiery battle and the times when she had feigned indifference he had known the coals were glowing, just beneath the surface, ready to burst into flames with the right handling. She had been passion personified, now she was a frigid ice maiden.

Scott had to break through the barrier she was encased in, but how? Would his true love ever return to taunt and tempt him beyond thinking? Somehow he had to hope she would or else everything was in vain.

She woke screaming in the night and Scott heard Maggie go to her. The soft-spoken Irish girl was the only one that could calm her down. He had had a devil of a time convincing Governor Macquarie to pardon the Murrays and had finally won their freedom by endowing the governor's newest pet project—a hospital. Any amount would have been worth it and Scott never regretted his decision. The sobs quieted and he heard only hushed movements from the other side of the door.

"Where is your nightgown, milady?" Maggie inquired, drawing the covers over Angela's shivering shoulders.

It had been real! Her humiliation came back to Angela in a flash and she wanted only to be alone.

"I want a hot bath!"

"But—but it's the middle of the night," Maggie said, confused.

"Now!"

The sleepy girl left the room to do as she ordered. If the duchess wanted a bath at three in the morning, who was she to gainsay her?

Angela lay in the hot scented water before the fireplace and let herself relax. Warmth crept slowly into her shivering limbs and the crackle of the flames soothed her into a state of drowsiness. She had disgraced herself, just as she had known she would. There was no way she could blame her husband for taking what she had so enticingly offered. He was only a man and she realized now that he had been very gentle and considerate. It was only her own fears and the fact that she had been tense and unreceptive that had made Scott hurt her. But then why, understanding the situation as she did, couldn't she relax and let herself respond? Had too much happened between them to ever make that possible?

Behind closed eyelids images flashed of herself and Scott in different situations. Had they happened in her dark past or were they merely wild imaginings? Had she ever loved him and wanted him in the way he had wanted her tonight? She thought she had and that made her irrational behavior even harder to understand. If only she could reciprocate, match the passion that she ignited in him.

She had to try! Surely nothing could be as bad as the scene a few hours ago. Jane had said it would get better and she must know. Her friend had a happy marriage and doting husband, was there some secret? Angela steeled herself, determined to try again. What did it matter if Scott hurt her for a few minutes as long as it drew him closer to her? She could endure it for his sake, and because she wanted another baby. She would be a proper wife yet!

Not able to sleep Angela was dressed warmly and striding toward the stables just before dawn. A pale light lit the eastern sky and big floppy snowflakes swirled down gently to the ground. She saddled Apollo herself, gentling the big white Arabian that Scott had given her on their return to England. He blew gently through his nostrils as she rubbed his soft nose with her fingers and whispered to him in the semi-darkness.

As she rode out into the freezing dawn not a servant or groom was stirring and Angela was glad to go alone. Riding, more than any other activity, soothed her nerves and she was badly in need of that. She headed toward the ocean and pulled up just short of the cliff. Hadn't she done that before? The overcast clouds glowed pale pink over the sea, turning the sand below the same color. But the waves tossed heavy and gray making her shiver.

Across that endless sea was a golden tree where it was now summer and beneath that tree was a grass-covered mound with a black marble stone. She could see it even with her eyes open and as the tears froze on her cheeks some of the ice melted in her heart. Pressing on her stomach with both hands she willed Scott's seed to take root, to make her another daughter.

Suddenly last night lost its terror. She would go and beg Scott's pardon for being such a failure. He would understand—he must! And then she would ask him to love her again and she would try harder this time.

Wheeling Apollo around she dashed through the snow giving the horse his head. They raced on and on through a morning that turned to a dull gray. But to Angela the day was still as rosy as the dawn had been and at the stable she jumped down and threw the reins to a sleepy, surprised stable boy.

She walked through the long curving colonnade

though she wanted to run. After all the boy's eyes were still on her and she must behave. But as soon as she was out of sight she broke into a run, arriving breathless in the house. As Angela darted up the stairs the frozen tears melted and impatiently she wiped the moisture away. This was a new day and she would make a new beginning—a new life.

Very quietly she opened the door to Scott's room only to find it empty. Her heart plunged to the tips of her boots. So he had gone already, unable to face her after the way she had disappointed him. Suppose he had gone to another woman because she had failed so miserably? She stamped her foot in a rage at the thought. She would scratch his eyes out if he even looked at someone else.

The bed was rumpled and across it was her nightgown. Snatching it up Angela went into her own room and threw it angrily on a chair. Why wasn't he there when she wanted to talk to him? Where was he? She hadn't passed him on her way home.

Scott was gone all day and the snow came down harder, blanketing everything, thudding softly against the windows until it was impossible to see out. Angela made a mess of her needlework and threw it down disgusted. She couldn't concentrate on any book in the library. Even the children didn't want to be with their short-tempered mother.

She dined with Ezra and her eyes flashed a dangerous warning every time he tried to hide his secret amusement. "What's so damn funny?" Angela asked annoyed and totally put out over his attitude.

"Now you sound more like yourself when you shout and your eyes sparkle like that! I remember a time when the boldest pirate in the Caribbean would have cringed before your anger. No wonder your husband has absented himself from the house today. That veneer of being a gentleman would surely crack if he saw you like this!"

Her cheeks flushed bright red and Ezra laughed uproariously, ducking as she threw her buttered roll at his head. It missed the mark and only incensed her further, sending the big man into gales of fresh laughter.

"What are you so angry about today, Duchess?" Ezra's amber eyes danced with merriment as she flounced from the room.

She wasn't sure why she was angry, only that she felt hot and jittery inside, as skittish as a horse with a new owner. Instead of going to her room she wandered through the huge castle, unable to keep still. It was so big and elegant and Angela felt that it was totally alien. She didn't like Brightling Castle, with all its modern accouterments and every luxury. She longed for some place smaller, more lived in but couldn't think of where that place could be.

It wasn't New South Wales, and that was the only other place she could remember, so it must be a place she had forgotten. All at once it was of the upmost importance to think of that place where she had been happy. If she could find it Angela was sure she could recapture that former contentedness and perhaps her memory.

Closing her eyes she tried to conjure up an image but saw only white driving flakes like those blasting against the windows. Why couldn't she remember? Why couldn't things be different?

Going to her room Angela collapsed on the bed, staring at the ceiling, lost in a turmoil of confusion. Emotions she couldn't even recognize rioted in her trying to break free. If only she could talk to Scott he might understand—explain away the tumultuous feelings battling within her. But he was gone and suddenly she felt abandoned and utterly desolate.

"Scott, Scott!" she murmured not even knowing why she needed him. "Where are you? Please don't leave me! I can't bear to be alone!"

It was pitch black in her room, only a ribbon of yellow showing under the door from Scott's room. Angela sat up abruptly aware of the silence in the rest of the house. It must be very late.

She was still wearing her clothes and they were all

wrinkled from being slept in. Getting up Angela quickly started unbuttoning her dress and when it went too slow for her liking she ripped at the bodice, hearing the soft thuds of buttons on the carpet. Her fingers shook with impatience as she lit a candle and hastily chose a nightgown from the closet.

He was back! Thank goodness! She couldn't have stood it if he had gone away. Quickly she washed her face, donned the nightgown and ran a brush over her loose hair. Then with unseemly haste Angela rushed to the door on silent bare feet.

Scott was sprawled limply in a big chair before the fire drinking brandy. His back was to her and he didn't hear or see her until she hesitantly touched his shoulder. Slowly his head turned and his brown eyes darkened as he saw Angela in a clinging nightgown of virgin white.

His clothes were rumpled and his shirt was parted to his waist. Dark hair and gleaming browned skin were revealed and she shivered, thinking of that hard chest pressing her down into the bed.

"Wh—what do you want?" Scott slurred his words together and only then did she realize that he was drunk.

"I—I wanted to apologize—for last night," she whispered, her eyes on the Oriental carpet beneath her feet. "I'm sorry, Scott."

"For what? I'm the one that should apologize, I was wrong! I am always the one at fault, always!"

"No!" Angela knelt in the deep pile beside him. She touched his hand but he jerked it away. "It was my fault. I disappointed you, I led you to believe I was willing to give something of myself that is beyond my power to give."

She hesitated, looking at his flushed face, the way his eyes roamed over her body leaving a trail of warmth over her tightening breasts. "I want to be your wife, Scott! Please, can't we try again? I can't make any promises that this time will be different or the time after that. But we must at least make the effort."

"Why?" Scott's angry eyes were piercing to her very soul. "Do you love me?"

"I'm your wife!"

"So you don't love me. Do you hate me?"

"No!"

"Not even that!" he shouted throwing the glass into the fireplace.

The crystal shattered and blue flame erupted into the chimney. Angela sat back on her heels startled. He had never lost his temper before, perhaps she should have waited until tomorrow. But it was too late. Scott grabbed her wrist and wouldn't let her go.

"You loathed what happened between us last night! Don't you think I knew? You didn't even try to pretend, Angela!" His eyes closed with momentary pain, then he shook her angrily. "Don't worry, Duchess, it will never happen again!"

"But—but—don't you want more children?" She was baffled by his anger and hurt that he didn't seem to want her.

"So that's it," Scott said in a dangerously understated tone. "You want me to be at stud to sire another baby. Then what happens when you're pregnant? Will I have to wait a few more years until you want another one?"

"Stop it! It isn't that way at all! Why do you twist everything I'm saying?" Angela struggled to get away, needing the safety of her room but his grip tightened.

She shook with trepidation. What would happen next? His face was hard and dark, very close to hers and she wanted to close her eyes against the flames leaping in his eyes, but couldn't. She should have known better than to try and talk to him in such a mood, but she hadn't noticed it until it was too late.

"Do you think I want you? You!" Scott stood up abruptly and released her so that she tumbled onto the floor.

She could see her round eyes reflected in his black polished boots and looked up at him towering over her with a scowl on his face. Angela's heart slammed frantically against her ribs, he looked as if he could kill her and enjoy it!

"You," he said with a mocking laugh, "are a poor

imitation of the woman I love. You're a changeling, an imposter! Oh, you have her face and body, you talk like her and even have the same name, but it's only an illusion.

"Angela was a woman with blood in her veins. She could make me want her with a glance, a smile. You have ice-water inside you, freezing a man until he is never the same again. I don't want you and never have! It took last night to prove it to me."

"No!" she cried. "I am Angela; I am your wife!"

"You are another person masquerading in Angela's body, an insipid, unlovable iceberg. You don't even know what you want. She knew what she wanted and went after it! She wanted money, she married my father; Angela felt mad enough to shoot me, so she did it; she wanted me to make love to her, she threw my mistress out and made me forget there was anyone else in the world!

"Angela was my wife, not you! She was everything to me—friend, enemy, bitch, lover. But no matter how much we loved or hated or hurt each other, both of us knew there could never be anyone else. She could send me to heaven and hell in the space of one minute but she was never indifferent. And in spite of everything, I always wanted her!"

She stood unsteadily before him, her eyes blurred with unshed tears so that when she brushed past him to run to her room the ribbons caught on his buttons. It was a tangled mess and in a frenzy Angela jerked away, hearing the thin material tear, feeling the cool air upon her breasts. Two steps away from Scott brought her up short for his boot was planted firmly on the hem of her nightgown and she tried to free herself.

His mind reeled from the brandy and his anger. In the flickering golden light he saw the pink crests of her breasts peeking through her fingers as she tried to shield her nakedness; those huge, sad, mysterious eyes; the trembling of her full lips; the slow flush of embarrassment on her cheeks. Reaching out he twined his fingers in that silken hair that was hers and Angela's, and the two women wavered, merged.

"Let go of me, beast!"

Scott laughed as she struck him. This was Angela—his little spitfire!

"I told you once that I would give you anything within my power, so if it's a child you want I will give you that!"

He raped her on the carpet without even removing his boots.

Angela locked herself in her room all day before she learned that Scott had left for London. Maggie gave her a note with the dinner tray and with shaking hands she opened it:

Angela, I'm sorry. Scott.

Nothing else—and it was then that the tears gushed from her eyes. He had hurt her more by leaving her than he had during last night's rape.

She couldn't eat and angrily threw the crumpled note in the fire watching it blacken and disintegrate in flames. Now she knew better than to try and reason with a drunken man. But he had revealed a part of himself always carefully hidden away before and his bitter words still echoed, cutting into her heart.

Why did she care so much? Why did he have the power to wound her unless. . . . No! It was impossible.

It was gray and snowy the whole time Scott was gone. For three weeks Angela dragged around the house alternating between damning him and praying he would come back. She was bored, completely at loose ends, just drifting toward she knew not what.

Then one dark frozen night she woke from a sound sleep. A candle flickered in her room and the bed moved beneath a heavier weight than her own.

"Angela." Scott was leaning over her dressed only in a black velvet robe and she reached out to touch him and he was real. He shivered as if her fingers trailing across his chest were icicles. "Are you pregnant, Angela?"

"No."

He pressed her into the bed, his lips silencing hers, swiftly joining his body to hers. It was over before she was even awake and then she was all alone. The only reminder that he had been there was the ache between her legs and a single candle on the mantel.

She couldn't believe that he had done it, like a distasteful duty to be finished quickly so he could go on to more important matters. Angela lay there stunned. She would rather be raped again than have him perform like it was a mechanical necessity, as if they were strangers. At least the act of violence had been tinged with passion. But this—this had left him as cold and unmoved as he always accused her of being. She couldn't even cry.

The situation went from bad to worse. At least before they had been friends and companions, if not lovers. Now there was only the brief, dispassionate nightly mating. They saw each other at meals and made polite conversation. They were strangers drifting further and further apart, together only when he came to her room for the few minutes of required closeness. Scott had promised her a child and meant to fulfill that obligation.

He never told her he loved her anymore, never called her sweetheart or Angel or anything else that she longed to hear. Why was it that when she desperately wanted to hear those words he retreated in silence? Why were his eyes cold and distant when she wanted them flaming with desire? Could she only appreciate him now that he was irrevocably lost to her?

Angela laughed bitterly. She was in love with her own husband and he was in love with the ghost of her past. Her rival was herself—the way she had been long ago, and she couldn't compete, couldn't even begin to win Scott back from her passionate competitor.

Jealousy ate into her and she continued laughing at

the paradox, tears of frustration slipping down her cheeks. He didn't want her the way she was today, but as she had been yesterday. And she wanted him in every way but the one way he desired her. If only she could remember! The old Angela could regain his love in an instant; the new one was helpless.

thirteen

"I'm leaving you."

He had her full attention now and her eyes were large jewels in the morning sunlight overflowing the room. She didn't speak and Scott repeated the statement without emotion.

"When?"

She seemed serene and unruffled as if she had been expecting it and the only indication of surprise was the breathless little catch at the end of that one word. He admired Angela's control for he had been sure there would be a scene. And perhaps if she had gotten angry or protested, like the woman he had known long ago surely would have, things would have ended differently.

"Today. I'm all packed. I just remained to tell you."

"How thoughtful of you. You could have left a note."

Her words were cold and clipped, not in the least sarcastic, but there was no mistaking the dangerous tilt of her firm chin and he quelled the impulse to reach out and touch her. Instead Scott went on calmly, as if they were discussing the weather, with his heart as heavy as a piece of granite in his chest.

"I won't be back, Angela. It's over."

She was dying inside, very slowly, with each indifferent word he uttered. And he didn't even know it, couldn't sense the shock and destruction each of his carefully detonated bombs wrought as they exploded, leaving her stiff and outwardly unchanged, bleeding and raw inside.

"I won't take the children. I think they need you more than they do me. But I will visit them occasionally and will have Robert up to Seafield for a few months in the summer. . . ."

There was no help for it, no way to stop him for he had made up his mind and he had made it clear in the past few months that he didn't want her anymore. Angela had tried to talk to him and explain her feelings but he refused to listen—worse, he didn't believe her.

Once she had told him the truth, when she was all drowsy from being wakened in the middle of the night, and his body was hot and hard and naked against hers in the darkness. She had gasped out her love for him unable to stop the spontaneous outburst but he only put his fingers over her moving lips, silencing her. "Don't lie, Angela," he had said. "If nothing else, let's at least have honesty between us."

So they had lived in a total silence. They were married strangers, reluctant lovers, nonexistent friends. Angela never saw him drunk again and hardly ever saw him smile. Only the children were worthy of his affection and she blamed herself for the entire state of affairs—and Jane. If she hadn't interfered this would not be happening. Things wouldn't have been perfect but at least Scott would have stayed. His guilt would have forced him to remain.

"You are very adept at breaking promises." The slight but furious flare of her nostrils gave her secret away.

"Promises?"

"Yes, you are free with your promises, but then I suppose all men are."

"All right, Angela," he said wearily. "Say what you have to and get it over with so I can go."

"Once," she whispered with the unshed tears running through her like a river, "you promised to love me forever, you said you would never leave me. To get me back you vowed to give me anything within your power, you bribed me with love and tenderness and understanding. Once, you swore you would never hurt me again."

Scott closed his eyes for just an instant and let the strident pain of the past sear his soul, course through every part of him. The torture was exquisite and he had become quite addicted to it, to the bitter regrets over his transgressions, to the guilt that could never be blotted out. The blame lay with him but he was tired to death of punishing himself for the past. It was over and done with and he could never go back and undo the damage. But he could and would go forward, and somehow, if he was lucky, he would overcome his ingrained habit.

So he went on resolutely, knowing exactly how she felt and what he was doing to her, because each word he uttered severing their relationship was a blade turned inward upon himself. "You are right. I have broken every promise I ever made to you and I'm sorry. But the fact remains, we are not happy together.

"If I stay I will hurt you and if I go I'll hurt you. So I've decided to do what is best for me for a change. Make a clean break of it and try to pick up the pieces of my life and make it whole again.

"You will never lack for anything—except my presence—and you will be free to do whatever you want. You may divorce me or not, it's up to you. But I will give you ample grounds for it—"

"With a hundred beautiful whores?" Angela's smile was grim; pale, sparkling aquamarine eyes eclipsing her face as she suppressed an impulse to slap him. Instead she tore the splendid heart-shaped diamond from her finger and threw it on the floor at his feet. It winked at her like a conspirator and she couldn't stop herself from continuing.

"Have all the women you want—glory in them, drown yourself in them. Acquire willing harems that will cater to your every sensual need; not one of them will matter because they won't be me. Every time you touch or kiss or lie with a woman you will compare her with me, and find her lacking.

"You can leave me but it won't matter. I will be in your bed and your house. I will follow you to Scotland and back. I will go horseback riding and sailing with you. I will eat with you and get drunk with you. I will cry and laugh with you. I will be with you always. You know it's true. I'm in your heart and your mind and your soul, and you will never be free."

She turned then and left the room and the air trembled with her quiet truths. He had expected a tempest, cloudbursts of recriminations, but there had been no thunder and lightning and the storm had passed from the scene without condescending to shed one raindrop.

He clenched her ring in his fist trying to control himself, to keep from going after her. Everything she had said was true and they both knew it. He felt as if he had been keelhauled.

"Oh, Angel, I love you more than life! I can't live with you or without you! I might as well be dead—but then I still wouldn't be free, for you would follow me to the gates of hell!"

She rode and rode and rode but riding Apollo into the ground and herself into exhaustion could not exorcise the hurt or the need to strike out at someone. Angela had resisted the urge with Scott but now the reality of his desertion was becoming clearer with each passing moment.

"It's over—over! I hate you, Scott Harrington, hate you for doing this to me!"

And why, when her vision cleared, did she have to find herself at Bentwood, sitting her trembling horse while the half-timbered house wavered between the trees? She had lived there once with Keith in dark ages past, Jane's beautiful golden-haired brother, who was dead. They had told her about it and she believed them, had looked upon his portrait in a shut-up room, but didn't remember. And they never spoke of him—his life or his death—as if there was a terrible secret connected with both.

But now Jane and Owen lived there. Jane, whose advice had precipitated this awful day. Jane and Owen who were ecstatically happy while she—

The white stallion moved reluctantly through knee-high bluebells, the nimbus of the sun brilliantly outlining the interlacing branches, each tiny furled bud, every new leaf, the outstretched wings of a bird. Winter was over but not in her soul.

She moved in a dream, the quick, sweet song of a willow-warbler barely brushing the fringes of her mind, her tiredness and despair no impediment to the inevitable outcome of finding herself in this spot. Delicate yellow splotches blurred against green. Why did daffodils always make her cry?

The scene hadn't changed, instinctively Angela knew that, but everything else had. Bentwood was the magnet drawing her on; apple-green vines climbing and cascading over mellow old brick, yellow and white ducks on a tiny, blue-mirrored pond, diamond panes of crystal and stained glass blinding in the morning light. Could it still be morning?

Apollo drank thirstily from a trough and she dropped the reins unheeded into the water, crunched along a gravel path and opened the front door without knocking and without closing it. Jane was alone in her sitting room eating a late breakfast from a tiny table placed close to a new fire.

"Angela!" Her smile faded but her surprise did not. "What's wrong?"

"He left me!" she screamed, her inner agony bursting forth in a torrent of words and a blind panic that obliterated every tie between them. "Scott left me and he's never coming back!"

"No!" Jane rose and started toward her.

"Yes, and it's all your fault! Friend—you call yourself my friend but you have ruined my marriage, my whole life! You forced your opinions and advice on me, you said it would work. Oh God, why did I listen to you? Everything was fine between us before you opened your mouth and interfered. It would still be the same, he would have stayed. But now I'm alone—because of you."

"Stop it, Angela, you will make yourself sick. I'm sorry Scott has left you and I'm sorry you think I'm at fault."

"Sorry, sorry!" Her outrage echoed down the halls and out the open door. "My life is over and you say you're sorry!"

The slap was a sharp retort in the suddenly silent room.

Owen saw it all from the doorway. Jane, delicate and eight months gone with his child, with one hand on her cheek and the other on her swollen belly; Angela, a fury, bent on revenge, a friend turned enemy attacking his wife. He was across the room in an instant roughly shoving Angela aside, gathering a stunned Jane into his arms. And because all his concern was for his white-faced wife he didn't see Angela fall heavily against the sharply pointed edge of the desk and crouch stunned and speechless with pain before lurching unsteadily from the room.

"I'm quite all right, Owen, but Angela—you must go after her!"

"She can take care of herself. Why in heaven's name did—"

"Scott has left her. Perhaps it is partly my fault, but what does that matter now? She is upset and hurt, and I'm afraid of what she might do in such a state. Please, dear, go find her."

"Hell, no!"

"Owen!" Jane admonished pushing him away and transfixing him with a determined sapphire stare. "I am fine but she is not. Do you remember what happened when Keith gave her that letter from Captain Carew? She wanted to die then, and this must be much worse because he has left of his own free will. Besides, she fell when you pushed her—here against the desk."

Her fingers came away wet and sticky and Jane went even whiter as she held them out to Owen. He turned without a word and left the room.

Apollo's mane was stiff beneath her cheek and each movement or breath sent a sharp pain through her. The reins had slipped from her fingers and the horse picked his way slowly and delicately through the trees, hesitating now and then as the light inert burden slid sideways, then righted itself.

"Angela! Angela, where are you?"

She opened her eyes in response to the faint call of her name but the effort was too much. Even the effort of clinging to the horse was too draining and Angela released her grip and slid to the ground. The purple-blue haze embraced and hid her, cool and damp and mossy. Little glints of light darted over her like dragonflies playing through an eyelet canopy. The Arabian nuzzled her shoulder with an inquisitive velvet nose.

Owen found her an hour later in a bed of ferns and wildflowers blinking dazed and bewildered at the sky.

"Oh, Angela! My poor lost girl."

Kneeling beside her he brushed the tangled hair from her face and began unbuttoning her blouse. Her fingers stopped him and her lovely, tear-bright eyes focused on his face.

"Don't, Owen."

"But you're hurt and it's my fault. I'm so sorry, Angela." He touched her cheek and she started crying. "Come now, be a good girl. Let me see what has happened and then I'll take you home."

"Just leave me here—I don't want to go home—ever! Scott is gone and nothing will ever matter again!"

"Of course it will. You are just upset right now—"

Wild, hopeless sobs drowned the words in her grief and Owen stopped trying to reason with her and peeled the bloody blouse away from her ribs. Her side was bruised and the skin torn and bleeding. Touching it lightly he heard Angela gasp with pain and wondered if any ribs were broken.

"Shh, sweetheart, pull yourself together," Owen said placing the clean white square of his handkerchief over her wound. "Having the vapors now will only make it worse."

"I don't care!" Prostrate and forlorn, between hard, hurtful sobs she gasped out, "I wish I was dead! Dead!"

"No you don't!"

But as she lay there shaking like a broken, dying bird brought suddenly from a free blue sky to a hard treacherous earth, he thought, perhaps she did.

"Angela, Angela—what am I going to do with you?"

A brown ruffled head blocked out the braiding and unbraiding boughs, hard lips closed on her sobs forcing the hysteria within. His tongue found and played with hers, salt-wet and hot as if with a fever. And then Owen's capable fingers found her unconcealed breast, his other hand holding her frenzied head still while he kissed and caressed her like a lover whose passion is just discovered.

Sorrow still engulfed and convulsed Angela as she tried to elude Owen's shocking demands. Jane's husband—her friend! Good lord, what was he doing to her?

But he wouldn't stop, as if some desire hidden deep within had suddenly burst its bounds like a dam giving way, sweeping everything from its path. His attentions did nothing to Angela but make her angry and in a furious explosion she jerked her mouth free of his and slapped him back to his senses.

She paid for it with an agony in her side that left her limp and hazily fighting for consciousness, while at the same time she was aware of the ashamed chagrin on Owen's face, and an expression that was quite unfathomable in the sea-green depths of his eyes. Passing his hands dazedly over his face he took control of himself once again and proceeded to button her blouse back up over the exquisite flesh that had elicited this unthinkable dilemma.

"You won't tell Jane?" Owen burst out desperately.

"Please, Angela, she must never find out about this!"

Quiet at last, with fragile eyelids closed in her ashen face, she refused to answer him. With a sigh of regret he picked her up trying not to hurt her but she gave herself away with a tight arm around his neck that almost strangled him. And in order to avoid the jolting a horseback ride would cause Owen walked the mile to Bentwood with Angela limp and silent in his arms.

"Send for the doctor," he told the housekeeper at the door.

"But he's already here!" she cried as Owen swept up the stairs with his burden.

She raced after him, passed him in the hall, flung open the door of the best guest room and proceeded to whip back the covers an instant before Owen laid Angela down. A muffled moan jerked his gaze from the bed to the doorway and opened Angela's weary eyes with surprise.

"It's milady. She's having the baby."

"A month too soon!"

"It is all my fault!" cried Angela aghast at the implications of her actions. She struggled up holding herself tightly but Owen's voice stopped her cold.

"Lie down. You have done enough damage for one day. I will send the doctor to you when he can be spared."

And she collapsed, suddenly boneless with remorse, to listen to Jane's moans for the rest of the day.

Tightly strapped, hardly able to breathe, sleepless with the screams in the hallway, Angela stared wide-eyed into the darkness. The candle had burned down, spluttered and gone out long ago, and she was so tired she couldn't even reach out for the china bell on the nearby table to summon Maggie, who had hastily settled herself at Bentwood.

The excesses of the day had burned themselves out also and she was emptied of all spirit and hope. Owen had made himself conspicuously absent but she had learned from the servants that the birth of his third child was not going very well. It was her fault that Scott was gone; her fault that Jane and the baby might not survive till dawn; her fault that Owen had undergone a metamorphosis from steadfast friend to frustrated lover.

It seemed as if an unnamed curse overshadowed all her undertakings, as if she was doomed to failure and misery all her life. And the essence of this malison wafted from her person, touching and destroying the people she loved; her friends and those who moved within her predetermined orbit. She could agonize about it and her unpredictable actions within the depths of her soul, as she was doing now, but when the strange circumstances were happening she was helpless to halt them. Only afterwards could she see the havoc and destruction she wrought.

Drifting in a half-awake, half-sleeping limbo, Angela prayed that Jane would live and the baby escape its prison unscathed. A spatter of raindrops, the rising wind, and a banging shutter drowned the noises inside the centuries old house and finally she slept.

Gasping in sheer panic Angela woke, struggling to draw another breath into the tortured lungs beneath her cracked ribs. A weight as heavy as her burden of guilt pressed steadily and firmly against her mouth, nostrils, eyes; shutting out the room and every sound.

The woman that only this morning had wanted to die now fought like a loosed demon to stay alive. Flawlessly embroidered linen and down crushed against her face and her flailing hands struck broad shoulders, glancing off ineffectually. Her movements slowed and an excruciating, unwanted void smothered her, lit by bright incongruous sunbursts that flared briefly and died away to nothingness.

To awaken, with the pearl-gray, watery light of day trickling into the room, was a jolt when she had not expected to wake at all. The white pillows were properly beneath her head and the bed undisturbed—as if nothing had happened! Angela ached all over and the quick breath of amazement she took reminded her sharply of everything that had happened yesterday. It couldn't have been a dream. It was so real—that feeling of not being able to breathe, that was somehow terribly familiar, as if it had happened before.

But it must have been a nightmare for who would want to kill her? She was surrounded by friends and people that cared about her, and besides, with Jane having her baby the house had been bustling with activity. No one could have surreptitiously slipped into her room to smother her.

Jane! She struggled upright with difficulty immediately aware of the silence in the house. But what did that silence mean? Had the baby finally come or—No! She couldn't even think that!

Angela's fingernail snagged a thread on the quilt and she looked with dawning horror at the two nails broken off to the quick. She had fought so desperately against last night's attack. But maybe it had happened in the woods with Owen, her common sense told her, as she opened her clenched fist and looked with complete disbelief at what it contained.

She knew positively that that hadn't been in her hand all day and night. The silver button embossed with the Remington coat of arms had a small three-cornered scrap of dark-blue cloth attached to it and it could only be from the coat Owen had worn yesterday.

"Owen! He just couldn't!"

Angela sagged, suddenly deflated, against the treacherous pillows, a thousand jumbled, tumultuous thoughts vying for her attention. And to make matters worse a sharp knock sounded on the door and when she found herself unable to answer, it opened.

Owen filled the doorway, rumpled, unshaven, his face lined and shadowed with fatigue. He stepped menacingly into the room, closing the door, with surprise evident in his eyes.

"When you didn't answer I thought you were asleep."

Angela choked on her heart which had leaped distressingly into her throat and shoved her hand hastily beneath the covers hiding the damning evidence of the nightmare that was no nightmare but reality. Why? Why? She couldn't think! Had he expected to find her dead? Was he here to finish the job?

"Angela, are you all right?" He bent over her and took the hand she thrust out to ward him off, holding it tightly in his warm grasp. There was a small tear in his cuff, a three-cornered tear where a button should have been, and her fingers convulsed under his.

"Ja—Jane—" she stammered casting desperately for something to distract him, to buy herself more time.

Owen smiled and sat beside the bed, her hand still captive in his. "She's going to be all right. The baby was born a few hours ago. It's a girl."

"Alive?" Angela eyed the bell on the other side of the bed. If only he would let go of her she could reach it and summon help.

"Yes, tiny but perfect and healthy. We have named her Regina, Gina for short. She is just like Jane . . . ."

How could he go on and on so enthusiastically about the baby when all the time he meant to do her harm—and why? That was what she couldn't begin to fathom. They were friends and had been since before she could remember. The only thing she could think of was that he had been overwrought and angry about her treatment of Jane, the premature birth and the idea that his wife and child were in dire danger of dying because of her. Had Owen done it in an unthinking rage, in the depths of despair when everything seemed at its worst?

He was acting so natural now as if nothing out of the ordinary had occurred and they were back on their old footing. Was he regretting last night's actions or had he already forgotten about them, as something unpleasant to be pushed from his thoughts? If it wasn't for the button she couldn't have believed it herself.

"Yesterday was a horrible day for all of us," Owen said with a jaunty smile. "Why don't we forget it ever happened? Soon you and Jane will be better and we will all be friends again. We need one another and must not ever let anything come between the three of us. Scott would want us to look after you."

Angela closed her eyes with relief. Whatever had happened was over as quickly as it had begun. But she would never forget it. Even the most loyal of friends and the most steadfast lover could turn on you if the situation warranted it. And both had happened to her on the same day. It was a lesson she would remember and the nagging familiarity of it all having happened before in another life cemented the feeling that there were very few she could allow herself to trust.

"You don't look well, Angela. Shall I send Maggie to you?"

"Oh, yes, please! And, Owen—I'm glad everything is back to normal again and that you don't hate me for what I did."

"Silly girl," Owen teased kissing the tips of her cold fingers. "I could never hate you!"

Somehow those bright, cheerful words chilled her through and through, and she couldn't cast off the events that had changed her safe world. Every long day that she spent at Bentwood until the doctor allowed her to go home was tinged with an evil quality that nothing could dispel.

With his tutor's hand heavy on his shoulder Robert watched the open carriage sweep up the drive and come to a smooth halt before the door. It was two weeks since the disastrous day his father had left, and just as long since he had seen his mother, and no man could have restrained Robert Harrington. With the easy grace that belonged to Scott he shrugged from Louis Garamond's tightening grip and escaped down the steps.

He stopped short as Angela gingerly withdrew her hand from Owen's grasp, remembering Kate's specific orders not to embrace his mother for she was recovering from an accident. Robert hung there for a moment, unsure of himself and aware of the fast approaching Mr. Garamond behind him, when Angela turned her full attention on him and smiled.

"Oh, Robert, my baby! How I have missed you!"

And she embraced him, ruffling his light brown

hair, pressing his head to her breast, and for once he didn't want to squirm from her maternal arms. He clung to her choking back unmanly tears and not even caring that she had called him a baby, because with his mother back the world was right again. The scent of her, the feel of her and her soft voice whispering words only to him helped dissolve the tension and fright of the past weeks, the fear that she wouldn't return.

He was used to his father's absences but not Angela's and both of them leaving on the same day had upset him more than he had let anyone know. Yes, that, and the strange man-to-man talk Scott had had with him before leaving; Ezra's extended holiday in Paris, and a new and demanding tutor, had made a shambles of his life.

But even Angela's presence could not obliterate a small, nagging voice inside him, something that Robert could barely sense but would not be gotten rid of this easily. The innate knowledge that something was terribly wrong and threatening the very fabric of his life. He remembered, dimly, feeling like that once before; imprisoned on an island by a pirate who in some way had made Angela withdraw unexplainably from him, though physically she had been there.

She kissed him on both cheeks but though she was smiling and as beautiful as ever there was a secret pain in her eyes, so sharp and unconcealable, that Robert felt it too. "Mama—" he began but Uncle Owen took his hand, pulling him from Angela's side, and escorted her into the house.

"Well, young man," said Mr. Garamond grasping his errant change by the scruff of the neck. "You have disobeyed orders—as usual. We will just have to see what punishment Kate will mete out. Probably too light as always. In the meantime you can spend the rest of the day at your lessons instead of with your mother."

With narrowed brown eyes and a scowl on his face Robert looked up at the blond head towering over him. Discipline never sat well on his shoulders and with a quick twist he kicked Mr. Garamond soundly in the shin and was free.

"Damn you to hell, you bloody Frenchy!" Robert taunted just beyond the reach of his doubled over tutor who was clutching his shin with murder in his darkened eyes. "My mother needs me and no one will keep me from her!"

"She will spank you when I tell her of your despicable behavior and foul mouth!"

The threat and the consequences of his actions were soon left far behind as Robert charged up the stairs and into the round drawing room. Clare was on Angela's lap, as she sat on a sofa opposite Owen, with an elegantly spread tea table between them. But his sister was no threat because his mother looked up at his entrance and stretched out her hand for him with that special, loving look on her face that was for him alone.

So he sat beside her, squirming impatiently, as Uncle Owen drank gallons of tea and Angela distractedly glanced out the tall windows at the garden, caressed Clare's hair, pretended to drink her tea and answered Owen in monosyllables. And he wished they were alone so he could talk to his mother about his troubles and have her explain them away. Also he must confess his transgressions before his tutor appeared and disclosed them himself.

There was something wrong between his mother and Uncle Owen. He saw, with the unworldly, uncluttered perception of a child, what the adults couldn't and what even Owen missed. On the surface everything was as still as a becalmed sea but beneath, in the depths where it mattered, was an abstract undercurrent that replaced all the worries so recently dissipated with Angela's homecoming.

Kate came for Clare and soon after that Owen took his leave. "Now, my son," said Angela, holding both his hands in hers and gazing deeply into golden-brown eyes that were so exactly like Scott's it pained her. "Tell me what's wrong."

But how could he explain what he hardly understood himself? Instead Robert said, "I missed you, Mama, and I don't like Mr. Garamond!"

"He seems a very nice young man. What is it that you dislike?"

"He's a Frenchy!"

Angela hid a smile. "Is that all?"

"All Frenchies are pirates and I hate pirates!"

"Oh, Robert, you're wrong. Not all Frenchmen are pirates any more than all Englishmen are scoundrels. You can't dislike someone just because of where they were born or the way they talk. Mr. Garamond can't help it—"

"Mama! Don't you remember the pirates?" asked Robert desperately. But from the frown between her brows and the puzzled concentration in her eyes he knew she didn't.

His father had explained it all very carefully to him, about her lapses of memory and the past she couldn't remember, but sometimes it was beyond his comprehension. But this flaw in his mother made her dearer still and brought out a protective feeling that he must shield her from the unpleasantness of the past. He was now the man in the family since Scott was gone; his father had told him that straightaway during that disconcerting talk. So to spare Angela, Robert, who would not be seven till the end of December, changed the subject.

"When will Papa be back?" He had no way of knowing that this new subject was one even more distressing than Angela's lost memory. But he found out quickly enough.

"I don't know," Angela choked out looking as if she was trying not to cry. Than she composed herself instantly for she had known the question would be asked eventually and she could not lie. "Your father is not coming back to live here again."

"Never?"

How could she explain to this incredulous little boy, who in some ways was too old for his age, what had occurred between her and Scott? "Never. You will understand better when you are older; that sometimes adults find it impossible to live together no matter how hard they try."

"But you are married, and husbands and wives live together!"

"Not in this case, Robert. Most definitely not in my case!"

"Don't you love him anymore?"

"Yes. Yes I love him but that's not enough—"

"Then he doesn't love you; he left you, he hurt you! I hate him!

"No!" Angela reached for her son, with the worry, pain, and misunderstanding marring his face, and held his head against her shoulder. Only she could set things right and reconcile him with Scott, even at the cost of losing his love.

"He still loves me but I was the one that drove him away. You are too young to understand it all but you must believe me," Angela explained very slowly and precisely. "Scott could not live with me any longer because I was the one hurting him. I would have destroyed him if he stayed. And if he hurt me by leaving it was something he couldn't help. Your father would never harm me on purpose. Believe me, Robert, for I'm telling you the truth."

She held his face between her hands, very close to hers, and watched the angry fire die in his eyes, confusion taking its place. "You must not hate your father because he was wise enough to know what was best for everyone. And in the long run this will be best. He loves you, Robert, and you will visit him often and he will come to see you. But our lives will never be the same as before, and we must help each other get used to it. You will help me won't you, son?"

"Yes, Mama, but I still don't understand—"

"No, and you may never understand. When you are a man you will come to know that the only consistent thing about a woman is her unpredictability. I am a woman and sometimes I can't even fathom my own actions, so how could you or Scott comprehend them?"

Robert looked at her with puzzled concentration. She had soothed his anger and left him bewildered with an unknown anxiety. She had driven his father away yet he couldn't hate her the way he was prepared to hate Scott at the drop of a hat. Angela seemed somehow helpless in the chaotic strands of a net that was tightening inexorably around her.

"I think you should send for Ezra right away!" he burst out sharply. "I don't know how to help you but he could."

"Nonsense. You help by loving me and trying to understand and just by being here. Besides, we don't want to spoil Ezra's holiday. He hasn't had one in such a long time. There is nothing for you to worry about, baby; everything will settle down now that we know the way it has to be.

"Now, give me a smile and a kiss so that I can go to my room and rest. And how would you like to stay up late and have dinner with me?"

Robert complied with her wishes and then left hastily. In the privacy of his own room he penned an incoherent misspelled letter to Ezra pleading with him to return immediately.

He had forgotten completely about Mr. Garamond's bruised shin.

After dinner with Robert and a hot bath, when the household had settled down and she remained sleepless, Angela went to the connecting door she had avoided looking at for hours. She opened it and the room was cold and dark and irresistible.

She had been in the room twice and once Scott had made love to her and once he had raped her. Candle flame leaped yellow from Angela's shaking fingers and she forced herself to stay calm and coax the golden glow into stability. Very slowly, holding the candle high, she walked around the room that was devoid of Scott's presence.

Strange that they had lived in this house together since their return from Australia and she had only come to this room willingly two times, and left both times in a panic. How cruel and how gentle he had been to her in this room, her enigmatic husband that she couldn't understand anymore than he could understand her. She touched the exquisite linenfold paneling; a brown leather armchair; the smooth, polished walnut desk; a painting of a storm at sea all angry and violent with motion; and another quite different and serene, a landscape of autumnal colors. The room was elegant but masculine, done in forest-green, with touches of burnt orange, brown, and yellow scattered about. She had never noticed any of those things before.

Beside the bed was a book upon a chest of drawers; the only sign of recent occupancy. She touched the grained leather and picked it up. Who would have expected a man like Scott to read poetry? With fingers trembling again Angela put down the candle and flipped quickly through the well-worn pages. Love poems. Her discovery was becoming even more disconcerting.

For the past weeks she had kept a tight rein on every emotion and even after the scene today with Robert she had refused to break down. And now she felt her control crumbling. She could not give way. So Angela threw the book on the bed intending to flee but it opened automatically to a place near the beginning; obviously a poem he had read and reread, pondering over it in the agonizing nights when she had been all too aware of a light burning in his room into the early hours of morning.

How could she resist picking it up and reading it, and discovering what words had filled his mind and disturbed his sleep? Turning the book away from the deep shadows and into the flickering light she smoothed the page that had been ripped halfway down, fitting the letters evenly together.

> Put your head, darling, darling, darling,
>   Your darling black head my heart above;
> Oh, mouth of honey, with the thyme for fragrance,
>   Who, with heart in breast, could deny you love?

The letters blurred and she couldn't finish. As her control shattered completely Angela ripped the page through and crumpled it in her fist. She wept for herself and the agony of Scott, who had waited in vain for only one true uncomplicated sign of her affection. It had been beyond her giving and was even now.

"Scott! Scott! You were right to leave me," she sobbed into her hands. "The way I am now, I could never make you happy. And I want you to be happy, more than I want you here, more than I want to remember! I want you to find peace more than I want your love!"

The candle went out after a long time and Angela lay crumpled, brittle, and sleepless on Scott's bed. She had to pull herself together but not tonight. Tonight she needed only oblivion so that the words would stop echoing in her mind, so that the pain would stop for at least a little while. Tomorrow she would be strong and cheerful and resolute; tomorrow she would let Scott go. He would have his divorce and be free. That was the only thing she could give him—his freedom.

Smoothing out the crumpled page Angela put it back in the book without looking at it and then put it in the top drawer of the chest. She straightened the rumpled velvet on the bed, picked up the candlestick and went back to her own room closing and locking the door behind her. With an economy of movement she washed her face, put on a robe and slippers, lit another candle, and went downstairs.

The huge, cold library had a well-stocked liquor cabinet and she chose several decanters of wine without hesitation or even caring what they contained. It didn't matter. In a dark corner Angela curled up small and lost in a big chair and began drinking her way to oblivion. Her vision blurred and her cramped legs became numb, and when she reached for the other decanter the empty one fell crashing on the floor. She found that quite amusing. When she went to get some more wine from the cabinet she found negotiating the short distance the height of hilarity. Lord! At least she had stopped crying and she couldn't even feel the ache in her side anymore.

The half-open door opened wider and another candle

advanced into the room. In the faint glow his hair was very bright, glistening gold.

"Mr. Garamond." Her soft laughter drew his attention farther into the library and then he stopped, realizing the state she was in.

"Excuse me, milady. I think, perhaps, I should go."

"Then why did you come, if only to go?"

"I heard a noise and came to investigate."

"And now your investigation is complete. *Bon soir,* Mr. Garamond." Angela raised her newly filled glass and said with red, curved lips, *"À votre santé!"*

"Goodnight, milady," he said with stern disapproval before he turned to go.

"Bravo! Very strict and tutorlike. Excellent English too. Why is it that I can't ever recall hearing you speak French? Do you do it only at lessons?"

"Perhaps," came the vitriolic reply, "milady had another memory lapse."

"Perhaps," she mimicked, "milady wishes for another memory lapse!"

"Le coeur a ses raisons, que la raison ne connaît pas."

Angela slammed down the goblet and wine sloshed over her fingers. "Don't speak to me of hearts," she screamed, "reasoning or otherwise! I have had my fill of hearts—broken and whole!"

He put down his candle and stood looking solemnly down at her, tall and young and magnificent. There was concern and a certain sadness in his large expressive eyes, and he looked very untutorlike at the moment with his hair falling over his forehead and dressed in his nightclothes. He did not apologize for upsetting her but watched silently as she gulped down the rest of the wine with her eyes closed and lashes still wet against her cheeks from crying.

"You need a friend," Louis Garamond finally stated. "And you are tipsy."

"Only tipsy?" Angela asked opening her eyes with a hollow laugh. "Then I must have another bottle, because I mean to get quite drunk."

"You are already quite drunk. I was only being kind."

"Kind and cruel—kind and cruel," she said in a singsong tone. "Another friend is the last thing I need. People who are kind to me always end by being cruel. Now, how will you be cruel? But you couldn't be, because I don't care a fig for you, and only people I care about can hurt me."

"Quite drunk," he repeated taking the empty goblet from her hand.

"I mean to get drunker still, till I can't think or move or hurt anymore. What do you think of that, Mr. Garamond?"

"I think you should go to bed."

"But I don't think I can walk to that door, never mind climb the stairs."

"I'll help you."

"And what else will you help me do? Help me into bed and help me out of my robe? I know men, Mr. Garamond. Yes, I know—"

"Ma foi! You may know men but you don't know me! I think you do need another bottle of wine. Shall I fetch it for you?"

"Yes, do. And have some yourself, Mr.—"

"Mon Dieu! Stop repeating my name over and over again."

"But I've made you angry, Monsieur Tutor. This is an interesting conversation. Too bad I won't remember it tomorrow."

He handed her a full glass and refrained from replying. Pulling another chair into the circle of light Louis Garamond sat down with a smile on his angelic face and mockingly lifted his glass toward her. "To you, milady. Drunk or not I think you are extraordinary. And your husband must be insane to leave you alone—and you must be also to let him go."

"And if I wasn't so dizzy I would slap your face!"

"I am only trying to be diverting and what harm will it do when you have told me yourself you won't remember this conversation in the morning? You are badly in need of diversion."

Angela's head was spinning and Louis Garamond was laughing with a pleased and somewhat endearing expression on his face. And she wasn't even sure if he was making advances to her or only teasing her. Whatever he was doing, gone was the prim and proper attitude of the past, replaced by a disarming and rather caustic individual that was much more interesting than his former counterpart.

"And how would you divert me?" she wondered aloud with her eyes half closed and her head flung back against the chair.

"You seem to think I have designs on you. Banish the thought, milady. I prefer young, uncomplicated diversions who are unpreoccupied with broken hearts, disloyal friends, precocious children and faithless husbands. Who do not have to get drunk alone to forget what little they can remember. Who are not slightly, but charmingly, deranged and who are not completely, and without a doubt—frigid!"

Angela's mouth dropped open but she was beyond speaking now. Louis Garamond laughed at her astonished look and continued.

"Entertaining? Wondering how I know so much in such a short time? Rumors, madame, rumors. But it seems I am right, *n'est-ce pas?*"

"You—you—"

"But I am only saying to your face what everyone else whispers behind your back. Shouldn't it all be out in the open if we are to be friends? Now, there are no secrets between us and you know for a certainty that I have no devious designs toward you.

"And now," Garamond continued with sparkling eyes and a guileless smile, "you will stop being angry with me for those rather intimate disclosures, because in spite of everything you must admit it was amusing and that I have thoroughly distracted you. *Oui*, you are beginning to smile again, and that is good. Finish your wine, for that is your last glass—"

"Don't tell me what to do!"

"No, I will not tell you." Taking the glass from her nerveless fingers he placed the candlestick in her hand

and picked her up easily. "You are dripping wax on your robe. Hold it straight or I will not make it upstairs. I charge extra for putting employers to bed and even more for dealing with drunken mothers—"

Angela laughed helplessly against his shoulder and gasped, "Oh, you are very amusing and I am quite drunk!"

"I thought we had already established both those facts. If you aren't quiet you will wake the whole house and then the servants will really have something to gossip about. And I shall pretend to be walking in my sleep—"

She giggled even harder spattering wax on both them and the floor, the stairs, and the banister.

"Voilà!" Louis Garamond whispered, depositing her quietly outside her bedroom. She swayed unsteadily and he opened the door and pushed her inside. "You also owe me a new dressing gown for you have ruined this one."

"Shh! The servants!"

He smiled indulgently for she was the one causing the disturbance with her muffled laughter. "You see, I have not put you to bed or removed your robe. So much for your knowledge of men. You should not try and make accurate characterizations of people while you are quite drunk."

The door closed firmly between them and somehow Angela found herself in bed, without her robe and with the dripping candle flickering on the table. He had been verbally brutal, totally honest, and vastly amusing; and had at least chased the resounding poetry from her weary head.

"But I don't want another friend!" she reminded herself emphatically.

A thin, sheer crimson curtain wavered, billowed and expanded in the draft from a slightly open window. It grew, crackling, edged with gold, and Angela tossed uncomfortably, coughed and flung a hand toward the edge of the bed. She woke instantly from a sound sleep dazed and gasping with pain. Clouds of black and gray smoke choked her scream and blinded her eyes as she threw herself to the opposite side of the bed to escape.

Heat like a blast from an oven sent her back to the center as the bed hangings flamed around her on all sides. Yellow, glowing sparks flew as thick as gnats, lighting on her nightgown and making tiny black-edged holes before going out. An army of flames charged up the counterpane licking and dancing in a wild frenzy, and she curled her feet beneath her, away from the advancing inferno.

"Oh lord!" she whispered, barely able to breathe from the smoke and the heat. "Maggie! Maggie!"

Her heart raced and stopped, jerked in panic and raced again as she cast desperately around for a way out. There was no way out except right through the flames. I'm going to die, she thought, just as the whole bed collapsed toward her.

But there were hands pulling the burning draperies away from her, blackened hands that ripped away one sheet of flame and dragged her from the conflagration by the hem of her nightgown. She clung blinded, coughing as someone lifted her and delivered her to safety, calling hoarsely for help.

She was shivering on the floor of the hallway lying across someone's lap. "She won't let go of me," he said and then convulsed with a fit of coughing.

"Mama! Mama!"

"Can't you carry her downstairs?"

"My hands are burned—someone else will have to—"

"Kate, take Robert and Clare away. Someone send for the doctor!"

"The fire is out and the doctor has been sent for."

The jumble of unidentified voices went on without ceasing making Angela's head pound. She opened her eyes and Louis Garamond gave her a jaunty, if somewhat pained smile. His face was scorched and his beautiful golden hair singed, the tips of his lashes were charred.

"You can let go of me now," he told her in his lightly accented English. "I charge exorbitantly for rescuing employers from infernos. And please, don't ever get drunk again."

fourteen

"That is no *billet-doux.*"

"Mind your own business!" Angela said putting down her pen and concealing her letter with a hastily drawn sheet of blank paper.

"I am finding it extremely difficult to mind my own business since I cannot even turn the pages of a book." Bandaged from fingertips to elbows Mr. Garamond gazed with serene, questioning eyes from beneath his delicately cocked singed eyebrows. His blistered nose, chin, and forehead were peeling and he had fared worse than Angela.

She had only been lightly toasted by the fire while Louis had been roasted rare. And while Angela was completely recovered with a few fast fading reminders of that most extraordinary night, he was wrapped as thickly as a mummy and was obviously becoming bored with inactivity.

Had it only been six days ago? In spite of her protestations that she would never remember their remarkable conversation it was firmly fixed in her consciousness. Perhaps the fire had seared it into her mind. Louis Garamond had saved her life at the risk of his own, and not a little pain, and then shrugged it off sardonically as a sensitive nose and an overdeveloped sense of chivalry from reading too many epic poems.

But she did not remember setting fire to her bed hangings or much of anything after her timely rescue. The doctor had come with his powders, his bag, salves, and bandages; pronounced her in shock, Louis badly burned but apt to recover, and had left very hastily when the tutor whispered to her between clenched teeth: *"Mon Dieu!* I should have put you to bed and blown out that damned candle!" Then she had laughed herself uproariously, hysterically to sleep and woke with a horrendous hangover.

But though she had resisted, groping through the chaos of her ruined rooms, her badly patched heart, her shattered pride, and her raw nerves, Louis had kept her intermittently laughing. She wasn't sure how he did it only that he became, in the midst of a bland conversation, wildly outrageous. He made her furious with his intimate probing and then turned the facts of her tragic life about face into a comedy of errors. When she was about to break into fits of weeping or a tempest of execrable anger, one word, a look, a peculiar gesture renewed her equilibrium.

"I don't want another friend," she told him tartly. "If you can't read then—then go practice your French!"

"My French is excellent, thank you, and not in need of any practice. If you want me to go, then dismiss me."

Angela said nothing, her lashes secretly veiling her eyes for a moment before she looked up. He was being difficult on purpose, but to what purpose she didn't know. Only when Louis Garamond was ready did he reveal his motives. She shivered slightly at a sudden hardening in his eyes—or had she imagined it?

"You see, madame, you do not want me to go. Diversion. We agreed that was what you needed. If you don't want me for a friend then I would make an excellent—"

Abruptly she stood up, her letter crumpling beneath her rigid fingers. She stared at his suggestive smile with enormous frightened eyes and a quick staccato leaping of her heart. Now, he was making his move after almost a week of lulling her into a false sense of security. Now, his true motive would be revealed. Her instincts weren't wrong, she knew men.

". . . enemy," he finished.

The air rushed into Angela's lungs like a shock and only then did she realize she had been holding her breath. Garamond was laughing at her! He had turned the tables on her again and she had fallen for it.

"You look like a fish out of water, milady. Don't you think you should close your mouth?"

"You—you—" she stammered angrily, with a smile quivering at the corners of her mouth.

"Are you disappointed? Or did I scare you silly?"

"Sir!" Violently Angela threw the object in her hand at Louis, but it was only a wad of paper and he caught it deftly against his chest with gauze-swathed fingers.

"The latter I think," he observed astutely. "Your cheeks are as red as a tropical sunset."

"Have you traveled in the tropics?"

"What have we here?" Garamond asked painstakingly undoing the paper. "Ah, your missive to your husband!"

"Give that back to me right now!"

"You have stopped smiling," he said with a mischievous sparkle in his eyes. "What can I do to cheer you up again?"

White with rage she flew at him trying to snatch it back but Louis held it beyond her reach.

"You have really gone too far this time!" she yelled. "You are fired!"

"Then I have nothing to lose by reading it. Shall I read it aloud? It might amuse you."

The fine control snapped and she went for his eyes with her fingernails. Very efficiently he fended her off and held both her wrists imprisoned in one big hand. The grip was brutal and must have been excruciating for him.

"I'll kill you!" A long string of expletives followed, but Louis only smiled and waved the letter enticingly beneath her nose.

"Will you challenge me to a duel and shoot me down

in cold blood the way you did your third husband?"

"Wh—what?"

"Sit down, you look like you might faint." Garamond tenderly lowered her into a chair and then stepped beyond her reach. "You don't remember? No one told you? Lady Vaughn's brother, Keith Montgomery. Why don't you ask her for the details, she was there; her husband was your second."

While Angela was helplessly frozen to her chair by the offhanded viciousness of his disclosure, Louis examined his bandages carefully, settled himself comfortably in another chair, gave her an innocent smile, and began reading her letter out loud.

" 'Scott. You are free. I release you from all your promises and your marriage vows. I am divorcing you.

" 'I hope you have acquired your seraglio because my solicitor informs me there will have to be blatant grounds if it is to be over quickly. You are right, a quick clean break is best.

" 'There is only one thing I ask of you: that you never see me again. Promise me that and forget the rest. Don't look for the reason why, don't look back with regrets, just accept the only gift I can give you—your freedom.

" 'Make yourself a new life with the peace you could never find with me. It is over. Be happy. Angela.' "

She was weeping silently and Louis watched her. He didn't offer her his handkerchief or touch her or try to comfort her as any other man would have.

Finally he said, "*Oui*, I have gone too far this time. I am sorry. I didn't think a love like that existed outside fantasy or books. You know, of course, that if he loves you he will be here two hours after reading that letter."

"I made it perfectly clear that—"

"It's what you didn't say that matters," Louis told her wisely. "He would have to be made of stone to resist you. *Mon Dieu!* Doesn't he realize what he has in you? You are *recherché*. Surely, he could overlook a few faults!"

"I will rewrite the letter," Angela whispered, very pale and subdued. "I will delete all my unsaid insinuations—"

"No! Send it exactly the way it is—wrinkled, smeared, with all its terrible, wonderful intimations. You will get him back."

"I don't want him back."

"Now you are lying," Louis said, proffering his handkerchief now that she had stopped crying.

"I am beginning to hate you, Mr. Garamond!"

"Ah! Your spirit is reviving. I think you hate yourself. Why else would you insist on moving into his room when there are dozens of others empty?"

Putting her hands over her face Angela sat very still. This was tomorrow. She had promised herself she would face reality. So she had moved into Scott's room, had read the poem all the way through; over and over again until she became numb from self-inflicted torture. She had opened her gold locket and put it on the desk in the bedroom so that Scott's eyes followed her everywhere, and perhaps this had brought on the recurrence of her terrifying, degrading nightmare where she could hate Scott instead of love him. If she could survive this regimen she could face the rest of her life without him.

"I am going to send this letter to your husband as it is," Louis told her firmly. "You owe it to yourself to see what will happen. Why, milady? Why do you insist on punishing yourself like this?"

"You are doing a very good job at that yourself!"

"I said I was sorry. Why?"

She looked up with wet transparent eyes and said with a bittersweet smile, "It will either kill me or cure me, I don't really care which."

It took Louis three days to coax the Duchess of Brightling into forgiving him. He bided his time cajoling her and drawing her out, and above all making her smile. For he was determined to be her friend. She was desperately in need of someone's protection and he was there to cosset her.

Because of a chance remark of his she had shakily and blindly sought some answers herself and forced Jane to tell her of Keith. Both women had been bundles of exposed snapping nerves when the encounter was over, with Angela dazedly repeating, "I can't believe I ever did that. I can't believe I killed your brother."

Bitterly Jane remonstrated, "I saw you murder Keith with my own eyes. Ask Owen, ask anyone from the village. Why—why did you have to dredge it all up again? It's only hurting us both!"

"I'm sorry."

"Let the past be, Angela," Jane finally said. "It is too unpleasant to exhume. In some ways your amnesia is a blessing. Maybe it is nature's way of protecting you from what might destroy you. Forget it—forget it! Keith deserved what happened. He drove you to it purposely because he knew he couldn't live without you."

Angela smiled tragically with tears standing like diamonds in her eyes. "To die at your lover's hand instead of your own. What unholy ecstasy!"

Was that her secret wish, her dark desire inadvertently stripped bare beneath the acid of Jane's disclosures? To think of it was to lose touch with reality. There were the children to live for. They needed her. Jane and Owen were withdrawing from Angela's realm and Louis Garamond was filling their place.

The very next day Owen called with an extravagant gift that momentarily tore her mind from forbidden longings. He was nervous and too attentive and Angela knew instantly that her last words to Jane had been repeated frantically in his ears. It was difficult to be natural with him, mostly because of the events of the last month. Their relationship would never be the same again.

What a vast relief it was when Louis intervened.

The three of them went to the stable where the new tack was tried on Apollo. It had been specially handmade to exact specifications; maroon leather expertly worked and gold-tooled. The saddle and reins were embossed with a tracery of stylized flowers and birds, intricately entwined with her initials. The stirrups and all metal pieces were gold-plated. The wine color on the white stallion was breathtaking.

"Will you ride now?" inquired Louis at Owen's

departure. "You are always better after a gallop."

"Later," said Angela, too wrought up to want anything but solitude.

But later did not come that day.

Instead she had a visitor.

The knock on her door when she had made it clear she did not want to be disturbed was irritating. "Who is it?" she asked shortly, her hands clenching on the arms of the chair where she had been sitting staring vacantly into space for several hours.

There was a brief pause during which she became as tense as an overwound clock.

"Scott."

No, her whole being silently protested. No! No! No!

Her door wasn't locked and she flew straight to it but the key was not in it. He had only to turn the knob. She pressed herself against the portal, hands flat, holding it closed. She couldn't bear to see him only to lose him again.

Louis was right; Scott loved her, he had come as soon as he received the letter. That awful, self-betraying letter. Why couldn't he leave her alone? Angela's breathing was harsh and ragged in her own ears. Surely he could hear it and feel her agony on the other side of the panel, just inches away.

Taking two deep breaths and swallowing hard she said with a calmness that amazed her, "I don't want to see you or talk to you. It was all in the letter."

"Angela, are you all right?"

She felt his hand touch the other side of the door, was enveloped in his concern and anxiety, and wondered if she could answer him and lie. She would never be all right again. Wheeling around with her back to the door Angela managed to keep herself erect with her hand frozen on the doorknob.

"Fine. Go away."

Her temples throbbed in time with her heart and she was sick with reaction and longing and the desire to open the door and die in his arms. To see his face once more before the *coup de grâce*.

"I had to be sure, Angela. Are you sure?"

It was evening already. The sky shone jade green banded with apricot through the thick panes of glass. Tree shadows were long and tessellated, moving silently on the floor. He would be spending the night. She had to be strong. He needed to be free.

The knob turned under Angela's fingers and he hesitated. If she wanted to stop him it had to be now. "I'm sure," she blurted out breathlessly. "Don't come in. Please Scott, please!" She clapped her hand over her mouth. The words sounded hysterical even to her. There was a gentle pressure on the door and she screamed, "If you come in I will kill myself! I swear I will do it right in front of you!"

The knob was released instantly.

"Angela! Angela!" Scott groaned and his fist thudded against the door making her jump. "Promise me you will do yourself no harm. Promise: Promise! On the lives of our children."

"If you go away," she managed to say hoarsely, "if you promise never to see me again—"

"Yes, yes! I swear I will never try to see you again." Then very softly, "Oh, Angela, what have I done to you?"

"Then you have my word. Good-bye."

"Good-bye . . . . Angel," came his last reply.

The sky fell in on her. She collapsed to her knees with her hands jammed against her mouth, fingers halfway down her throat to choke off her screams. Angel, Angel! He had called her Angel. She knew that if she started screaming she would never stop.

Within the next hour every object that could possibly be considered lethal was quickly removed from the room by Kate and Maggie under Angela's orders. Scisssors, a letter opener, hat pins, the powders that made her sleep; anything made of glass or china that when broken could cut. The shutters were closed over the windows and barred from the outside, the inside shutters closed over the window panes, and the curtains drawn. She didn't trust herself to keep her promise.

Scott stayed at Brightling Castle for two days during

which Angela didn't eat or sleep or allow another person into her locked room. He didn't try to see her again.

On the third day he left in the morning and in the afternoon Angela emerged. Gaunt, pale, eyes black-shadowed in her drawn face she walked through the house without speaking to anyone, directly to the stable. Apollo was waiting undemanding, safe, beautifully fitted out; and she mounted and rode away from Brightling Castle without a backward glance; astride like a man.

She had won her battles against all odds, surely now she deserved some peace.

The ride was furious and cleansing and she headed for the beach. It was going to rain. Gray boiling clouds streamed with her, swifter than her horse. The spinning landscape kaleidoscoped by; tender green, sienna, pale lilac, sky-blue. The speed increased, wonderful and free, and the first light misting of rain sprayed gently against her face.

They played their game, Angela and the stallion; slightly dangerous but that made it exciting. Both of them knew what to expect and her control of the animal was absolute. The grass was wet but they had done this in the rain before, a little more cautious and alert; the timing must be perfect.

Now, her blood was flowing faster and she laughed for the first time in days. Angela always did, that was part of the game. The void approached. Now! She pulled up. The reins snapped in her hands.

In an instantaneous decision she jerked her boots from the stirrups and launched herself into space. Hitting the wet grass she tumbled over and over before skidding to a stop to lie spread-eagled looking at the spinning sky. Then the screams began.

Not even checking to see if she was all right Angela got up and ran to the edge of the cliff falling down on her hands and knees. Apollo screamed and thrashed on the rocks and sand below, broken and bloodstained and in torment.

"No! No! Apollo!"

The screams of the anguished stallion that had been her true friend grew shriller and she had to stop it—but how? Sliding and falling she hurried down the path to the beach grabbing a huge rock as she went. He must be put out of his agony.

All of his legs were broken and his ribs caved in, bones poking hideously through his skin, gushing crimson—but still he tried to get up. Sobbing wildly Angela threw her scarf over his eyes, raised the rock and brought it smashing down on his head. She had to do it twice.

Then she crawled away and was violently sick, and huddled stunned on the wet sand while the waves lapped at her skirt. The rain washed her face clean and when she could begin thinking again, when she was dry inside from crying and soaked through and shivering with convulsive chills, she forced herself to get up. She made herself look at the red and white corpse steaming in the rain; made herself go and examine the brand new reins that Owen had given her three days ago.

It was obvious what had happened. One of the metal rings was not closed all the way and the leather had slowly worked itself through the gap, pulling free under the extreme tension. She couldn't stay there any longer, for in a moment she would begin to ask herself why and there were only two answers.

The climb back up the cliff path was slower and Angela found herself limping without being aware of a pain anywhere but in her heart. She started the long walk home with the rain beating black strands of hair across her face. And then the questions came.

Could she have saved Apollo if she had remained in the saddle? Or would she too be lying dead on the beach? She knew why it had happened—the reins—but that brought her round to the thing she didn't want to comtemplate. Had it been an accident or was it done deliberately?

The harness maker could have overlooked tightening the ring, but it wasn't likely. In a lucent flash she knew the truth. Someone was trying to kill her! Angela stopped and put her hands over her eyes. The attempted smothering, the fire, now this. Too many things had happened and two of them pointed the finger unerringly at—Owen! The silver button from his coat, the reins he had given her; the fire could have been an accident but also could easily have been started by him.

She was sick again. Owen, why Owen? He was her friend. Why would he want her dead?

"Oh no!" said Angela, sitting down abruptly on the soggy ground.

Because he wasn't her friend. Because he had wanted to be her lover and had almost taken her, hurt and lost and hysterical in the woods, while Jane was giving birth to his premature child. Owen had pleaded with her not to tell Jane and she had refused to answer. He thought Angela would tell her and that's why he wanted her out of the way.

He had to be mad! If it wasn't for her quick thinking and unconscious urge for survival it would have happened today. If it wasn't for Louis Garamond she would have died horribly in the fire. If it wasn't for Owen's own incompetence it would have been done the night Gina was born.

But she was still alive and Apollo, her homecoming gift from Scott, was dead. Slowly all the links between them were being severed. The only thing she had left that was theirs was Robert and he would be gone to Scotland soon.

Laughter bubbled uncontrolled from her raw throat. Who was she to defy death? She longed for it. The promise made to Scott would never be broken by her. Owen would do it for her.

She waited impatiently, and nothing else happened. Apollo was passed off as an accident and she had a new horse, a roan gelding, but it wasn't the same. Owen was biding his time; it must look accidental. Angela trusted herself to open a letter now without the fear of breaking her promise and putting the letter opener through her breast. It was only a matter of time.

The divorce would be final by the end of summer but what did that matter? Scott could be free any day now and she went to her solicitor's and made a will. When she and the children and Louis were invited on a picnic by Jane and Owen she accepted without hesitation. Pray it wouldn't happen in front of the children!

During the interval between the invitation and the picnic Angela spent most of her waking moments with Robert and Clare much to Louis's mystification. When she was gone Scott would care for them and love them, and they would forget her. And even though Clare was not his she knew he would treat the toddler like a daughter, because Clare was hers.

The day finally dawned and Angela hadn't spent any of the night sleeping. There were too many things to look back upon and regret. How much more cause for remorse would she have had if she could remember beyond the past year? But now she was happy for soon she would be free of a life that was a mere existence, to sleep undisturbed forever by sorrow and pain.

She bathed and had breakfast and gazed at the miniatures in her locket as Maggie laid out her clothes for the day. It was very warm and the maid had chosen a white muslin dress embroidered with daisies. Angela looked at it and shook her head. White would never do. She could still see Apollo brilliant with blood.

"I must have a red dress, Maggie. No other color will do," Angela said going to the wardrobe and beginning a quick search through dozens of garments.

Fifteen minutes later Maggie produced a simple cotton dress with a smile of triumph. It was a little out of style, extremely plain, rumpled, and bright cherry-red.

"A good pressin' and it'll look like new," the Irish girl promised. "Are ye sure you'll be wantin' this on? The other is so pretty and you've never even worn it yet. . . ."

"Positive!" Angela declared while the maid made a hasty exit.

A calmness settled on Angela as they made their way to the lake. There were hampers of food, rugs to spread beneath the trees, fishing poles, and tucked beneath Robert's arm a very battered toy ship. Louis carried Clare, and their golden heads were the same bright color. Angela couldn't help staring and he, of course, would notice.

"Our coloring is alike," Louis observed. "You could almost believe she was my daughter."

"Jane says Clare looks like my mother," Angela said quietly, "though I wouldn't know."

Robert gazed at her with a solemn intensity that made Angela uneasy. It was almost as if he knew who Clare's father was. "They sank the *Dark Lady*," Robert said abruptly, holding out the toy ship. "This is the only one left. It was Lorna's but now it's mine.

"There was blood on the deck and dead men, and sharks ate Angus. Molly went away and never came back. He killed her too."

"Stop it, Robert!" Louis commanded as the color slowly drained from Angela's face.

But he continued his tirade, face scarlet with remembered anger. "That Frenchy pirate wanted to kill all of us. He wanted to hurt Lorna but I kicked him and if I had a pistol I would have shot him dead!"

"He is dead now," Louis told him gently, "and will never hurt anyone again. Yes, Gaston Laporte is most definitely dead."

Robert stopped and Angela felt as if she were going to be sick. Laporte! Laporte! The name frightened her to death and shudders coursed down her spine in spite of the hot sun. Jane had once said that Clare's father was a pirate. Gaston Laporte was her daughter's father.

"How do you know that name?" Angela inquired. "I did not know it myself."

"Rumors," Louis said with a shrug. "Isn't that how I find out everything? I couldn't allow your son to continue. It was upsetting you both."

"Thank you," she said unable to even smile. She was more upset than he would ever know. The day was already a disaster and Angela knew it would only get worse.

But it was a lovely day to die; with a blue silk sky and

the chestnut trees in bloom. Honeysuckle drifted sweet upon the breeze and buttercups and moon-daisies etched the grass with color. Swans were on the lake with new offspring and Angela caught her breath because for a moment she thought she had seen two hats floating on the water. Why she had imagined that she couldn't begin to understand but a sudden longing for Scott melted through her. The feeling was so quick and intense that she closed her eyes with a tremulous sigh of half-remembered passion.

Scott, Scott, she thought, how I love you, my darling husband. But I am no good for you, and we both know it. It will be better this way and you will find someone else.

There were blessed distractions then to keep her thoughts from turning inward: the arrival of Jane and Owen and their two young sons; the flurry of activity and chatter as they prepared to make a day of it; the children shrieking with laughter as they ran off to play. At least Robert had forgotten his melancholy outburst, though Angela had not. She would have to do something about Lorna's boat lest Robert continue his unhealthy dwelling on the past. Maybe it would sink in the lake, be broken, or get lost in the woods.

In spite of what Angela suspected it became a joyful day. Jane and Owen were more at ease than she had seen them in many weeks; everyone relaxed, and Louis curbed his biting tongue. The children were wild and carefree, and the weather was superb. They went boating on the damascened lake, fished, ate, and the two youngest children, Clare and Darrell, had brief naps. Paul Vaughn fell into the lake and Louis, laughing, pulled him out of the reed-laced shallows, sopping wet but unhurt. Jane only shook her head with a fond smile for she knew her older son and had been prepared for every eventuality. She made him change into the dry clothes she had brought and told him to play near the woods.

It was Owen who suggested a game of hide-and-seek in the late afternoon and the children squealed with delight as Angela covertly scanned his face for a sign. But there was nothing there until his light green eyes met hers with a look of fond regret.

"I wouldn't have told," Angela said to him softly so that no one could overhear. A perplexed frown creased Owen's brow and he was about to reply when he was interrupted.

"You're It, Mama! You're It!" shouted Robert eager to begin. "Count to a hundred and don't peek!"

And the moment passed as everyone scattered, even Jane holding Darrell by the hand. With a laugh Owen swept Clare up, and Robert and Paul began running toward the woods, sure to change directions as soon as her back was turned. Louis stood looking at Angela for a minute and she said: "You must play too. Come on, get into the spirit of the game. You look so . . . . worried."

"Something is wrong," he stated abruptly. "I don't—"

Angela laughed. "What could be wrong on a day like this?" Then unable to stop herself: "Tell Scott I loved him." She whirled around and put her hands over her eyes. "Hurry, Louis! I'm starting to count now."

She counted aloud, slowly, unable to keep herself from thinking. Of course Owen wouldn't let the children witness it. What better way to scatter them and have them hidden from sight? Dear, dear Owen—considerate to the very end; thinking of everything.

She searched through the green-ferned woods scanning the trees where a small boy might be hiding. Circling back Angela peered into the boathouse unaware of two pairs of mischievous eyes watching from the lake's edge beneath an overturned rowboat. The scolding of a blue jay drowned muffled laughter as she passed close by a crumbling stone wall overgrown with ivy.

Eventually she wandered much farther than she supposed anyone would go. But it would be the perfect hiding place with its granite walls staggering crazily over the landscape and the dower house just visible between the trees. The ruin of the old castle was roofless but the structure had been built to last forever. Some walls of the old keep were twelve feet thick with stairs and passages like a rabbit warren.

A rusty iron gate creaked protestingly as she walked through an archway and a thundercloud of rooks flew from their high places with a rush of wings and raucous cries. It was empty but for the weeds struggling through the cracked, uneven stones paving the interior and a broken wine barrel. There was a spiral staircase going up and steps descending to a dungeon, a dried up well covered with a grate. There were dozens of openings like Swiss cheese in the towering walls. Angela didn't fancy exploring those walls that in some places reached six stories but a minute sound coming from her left enticed her to explore one opening.

"Angela, look out!"

She whirled around, to see Louis pop like a jack-in-the-box from the dungeon, but she didn't move from the spot. A slight rumble above made Angela look up and she closed her eyes quelling the instinctive urge to save herself. A hail of granite blocks, rubble, and masonry ended the matter.

Or would have, except for Louis cannoning into her and knocking her breathless to the stones; shielding her with his own body while half a wall all but interred them. And the thing that frightened Angela most was the utter silence afterwards and the dead weight of Louis lying over her as still as a corpse.

When she could breathe again the huge cloud of dust and debris made Angela cough and sneeze violently as she struggled from beneath Louis. His head lolled as she turned him over and blood dripped into his gray dusted hair from a wicked gash on his forehead that cut right down to the bone.

She swore angrily. "Why did you have to get yourself killed for me?" She caught her quivering bottom lip between her teeth to keep from crying, with the sudden realization that she cared. Because he had insisted on being her friend, Louis Garamond was dead.

Shaking, she just sat there staring at his unmoving face, aware that she should go for help, or do something, anything, but unable to move. "Oh, Louis," she whispered, "it should have been me. It should have been me!"

He stirred and a moan made her catch her breath with surprise and relief. Searching his pockets she found a handkerchief and pressed it to his wounded head. Thank goodness he was alive! But why did she have to be? Slowly Angela's senses returned and she put his head on her lap stroking his hair and calling his name. Her fingertips discovered an old scar completely hidden by his blond hair and when Louis opened his eyes she was frowning with her fingers still and laced through his hair.

They didn't speak for a long time but just looked into each other's eyes and his slowly focused and darkened till they were almost black. She could actually see what he was thinking as Louis read her mind and her face. The dawning realization, the rejection, the crystallization; anger, despair, concern.

"Mon Dieu!" he said sitting up abruptly with his hand to his head, looking sick and dizzy and apt to pass out again. Louis swore in French, so obscenely, Angela couldn't think of the English translation. "You knew!"

"Yes," she said without emotion, "I knew. But I didn't think there would be anyone else involved. I'm sorry you were hurt." Some emotion crept into Angela's voice as she continued. "Are you all right, Louis? I thought at first you were dead and it was my fault because I didn't heed your warning—"

"You little fool!" he shouted. "Why didn't you tell me? All these accidents—the fire, your horse, and this!" His eyes closed against a throbbing headache and she reached out and touched his hand comfortingly.

"You know why I didn't tell you, Louis. It didn't matter to me. But you have interfered twice now and I can't bear to see you hurt because of me."

Very slowly and wearily his eyes opened and he searched Angela's face and she couldn't look away. "It's because of him, but is your husband worth your life? Can't you live without him?" She shook her head with her mouth turned down distressingly in her dirty face. "I am not going to let you do this! I am not going to let you be—murdered!"

"Please," Angela pleaded, "don't interfere. Let me be. It will be easier this way. You won't lose anything, Louis. I have left you a legacy, for being my friend. You know I can't go on the way I am."

"I will lose you. You! To hell with legacies and death wishes! I will not let you go. I am going to find your enemy and put a stop to this."

"No!"

Louis gripped her hand tightly in his till she winced with the pain. Blood trickled down his cheek making paths in the dust that covered his face and he reached out with his other hand and brought Angela against him. He held her with her head in the crook of his arm and his face very close to hers and said, "I am not going to let your husband or this other person hurt you. I am not going to let you hurt yourself. You have been deserted by everyone, even your friends, and now you are mine. You are sad and lost and wounded almost to death, but I have found you. You need me, Angela, and I will make you whole if you just give me the chance.

"I don't want anything in return but that you should be happy again. And when I am finished you and Scott will be together once more. Believe me—I promise this will happen."

She stared at him, mesmerized, wide-eyed and with her lips slightly parted, while his blood spattered her bodice. And for the life of her she couldn't move or utter another protest or begin to understand how he meant to accomplish his purpose, or why. Then Angela was afraid, paralyzed with the fear of having hope instilled in her again. She had already given up on Scott, and love, and life, and if Louis brought her back to life only to fail her the end would be worse than anything she could begin to imagine.

"Louis, don't do this to me." But there was already a flicker of belief in her eyes and he saw it and smiled at her sweetly.

"Oui! I have already begun, my lost lady," he told her confidently, gathering her up and setting her on her feet. "I will not let Lady Vaughn get you into her clutches again. I will protect you with my own life—like today."

"Jane?" said Angela in bewilderment. "What has she to do with this?" One of the loose stones slipped beneath her feet and Louis caught her elbow, steering her away from the rubble and out of the keep. Her head was spinning and he set her against a low wall overspread with white dog roses.

"I thought you knew, or had guessed. She is your would-be murderer. Your so innocent best friend."

"Oh no." Angela gave a hollow laugh of disbelief. "You're mistaken. Not Jane! There is no reason."

"You killed her brother."

"But we talked about that," she protested shaking her head. "Jane forgave me. She said Keith deserved to die!"

"That is only what she said," Louis continued sagely with pity welling in his eyes. "He was her beloved brother, the only family she had left. And then there was the other matter. The matter of a lover."

"A lover?"

"Your lover—and her lover. First her fiancé and then your husband. Scott Harrington had you both at the same time but he chose you. And all the time she was passionately in love with your husband while pretending to be your friend."

"But Owen!"

"Ah yes, she married him when Scott was believed dead. They seem to be happy now but," Louis shrugged his shoulders, "who can tell? In any event Scott is now lost to her forever. Any idiot can see that he cares for no one but you. And Lord Vaughn—" He paused and looked at her piercingly. "He has noticed you too. He has more than a passing interest in you, doesn't he, Angela? Men find it very easy to fall in love with you and Vaughn is no exception."

"I can't believe—" she began.

"But you can!" Louis stated positively. "You didn't deny Vaughn's interest in you. Do you think Jane will let you steal her husband the way you stole her lover? Never! She has become a cunning, devious woman who will even resort to murder to rid herself of a rival.

"You are a threat to her happy family, her way of life, and her husband. And whomever she has hired to do her dirty work for her is very clever. But for me—"

"I would be dead," Angela finished. "But Jane! I thought it was Owen. I don't want to believe this." She pressed her hands against her eyes so she wouldn't see the way he was looking at her.

"You must believe what you wish but if you could remember you would know for a certainty that I speak the truth." Louis pulled her hands from her face. "Look at me. Why would I lie about it? This is hurting you but you must face it. Isn't it better to know she is your enemy, rather than to delude yourself into thinking she is your friend?

"Write to Scott and ask him if he was Jane's lover. Ask Jane herself or Owen. They will admit it was so. And I think you know the answer as to how Owen feels about you. *N'est-ce pas?"*

Angela was silent for long indecisive minutes with her thoughts fluctuating wildly. Everything Louis said made sense and it hurt to the quick to think of how she had been betrayed. Jane hated her, and perhaps, in a different, strange way Owen hated her, because she hadn't yielded to him. Could both of them, unknown to the other, be setting these death traps for her?

"Oh, Louis," she choked out, "I have been betrayed and abandoned by everyone. What use is it to fight it or try to go on? I feel so . . . . desolate inside and so alone."

"You are not alone," he told her firmly with the light of battles to come sparkling in his eyes. "You have me and I will not allow anything to happen to you. I am your friend, Angela. Your friend!"

Louis held out his bruised hand, still healing from the fire, and Angela took it and knew she was safe and protected.

fifteen

Given one week Louis had indeed worked miracles. He had brought Angela from the very edge of destruction and kindly and patiently led her a few steps away from the beckoning abyss. Unflagging in his devotion he had forcibly injected some of his spirit into her and almost had her believing in his fantastic promises.

Then Scott ruined everything.

Angela locked the door to her room, took the key from the lock, and threw it across the room. It hit the wall and thudded on the carpet and she clenched her fists around the bedpost. In another second she would either begin smashing every object in the room or burst into unceasing tears.

He was coming today to take Robert to Scotland. She had known it would happen but unknowingly he had chosen the worst possible time. There would be the sleepless torture of knowing he was in the same house with her for a whole night and then the separation from her son which would last for months. Angela's whole world was being very carefully torn to shreds and not even Louis could comfort her.

And while Angela fought her own lonely battle two horsemen approached Brightling Castle from different directions. One galloped furiously and the other progressed almost reluctantly, but steadily. There was a strange stirring on the sea and it boded no good for the horsemen, a black-haired woman, and her son.

"Angela!"

Her cheek jerked away from the polished wood of the bedpost but her nails dug in scarring the smooth surface. "Go away! I don't want to talk to you."

"Mon Dieu! Do you know what's happening outside your room? Disaster!"

"I don't care."

"Open this door immediately or I will have it broken down."

"Go to hell, Louis!"

He swore right back at her with a terrible desperation spilling over into his voice. "It's Robert! Robert!" He pounded on the door. "Angela, you lovesick little fool! Do you hear me? Your son is in danger!"

But she had heard and was frantically searching for the key on her hands and knees. Good lord, where was it? She couldn't even recall where she had thrown it but it had to be somewhere on the floor. After an eternity she found it but her hands were shaking so she could hardly fit it into the lock.

Louis charged into her room with his face pale and his riding clothes coated with dust. He smelled of horses, leather, and sweat, and he gripped her shoulders and shook her.

"Get hold of yourself and do exactly what I say," he ordered. "There is no time for explanations, no time for you to change. By the time we get to the stables your horse will be ready. We are going to the beach, and maybe, if we are in time, we can save Robert. I have pistols. Now come!"

Angela needed no urging to follow as they ran all the way and then hastily mounted. Her son was in danger—but how and from whom? On their wild, pounding ride Louis breathlessly tried to explain but she couldn't understand the snatches he spoke of a note and deceit. The skirt of her yellow silk dress was hiked up above her knees and the matching slippers were not meant for riding, but speed was essential and she ignored her discomfort.

Terrible thoughts of Robert abducted or hurt or dead swirled through Angela's head. How had Louis discovered it? Thank goodness he had! And Scott was coming today; he wouldn't let Robert be harmed. But time was of the essence and there was only Louis to depend on.

As they approached the cliffs Angela slowed nervously. Apollo had died there and she hadn't been there since. Now the cliffs terrified her and a premonition of disaster and death jerked her to a sudden stop.

Ignorant of her feelings Louis dragged her from the saddle and propelled her toward the edge of the cliff. The height made her sway dizzily and impatiently he clamped his arm about her waist.

"Where's Robert?" Angela asked breathlessly, obdurately resisting the pressure forcing her closer to the precipice. Her eyes were glued to the white-foamed rocks and she couldn't tear them free.

"Look," he said pointing at the blue-green swells and she looked and froze.

For there was a specter from her past: barely moving, almost invisible; a sight that drowned her in panic, despair, and humiliation. She felt herself being mentally and physically tortured by forgotten fiends.

Angela gasped for breath, there was suddenly nothing beneath her feet but air. Louis chuckled softly in her ear, put her back on solid ground, and the ghost ship that had been there a moment ago vanished. She shook like a flag in a gale as Louis spoke to her softly.

"Do not be afraid, *chérie*. Robert is safe and Scott will rescue him. We will wait for him here and I will keep my promise. I always keep my promises."

Angela broke away from him with wild frantic eyes; remembering smooth, self-assured words; trying to remember what she didn't want to. Louis smiled radiantly as if nothing was wrong.

"I must be losing my mind!" she said. "This is not

real. I thought there was a ship and now it's gone."

"The ship is there, with Robert on it," he assured her. "You can see it when the sun is right. But it's painted the color of the sea and sky and is very difficult to discern."

"Louis," Angela said in tentative bewilderment, "what's happening? I'm so afraid. Who has my son and why are we waiting here?"

"Chérie, chérie! You are so delightfully obtuse." Louis laughed shaking his head with his long-lashed violet eyes beautiful in the sunlight. "You have been summoned to a meeting with fate and I will give you what you desire most. Oblivion, death, and your precious husband. You and he will be together forever—side-by-side, inseparable. . . ."

She choked on pure, unadulterated fear and turned and ran to the horses. Blood was a quick torrent in her veins sounding a distant alarm. Hoarse words haunted her: *Chérie, chérie. . . nous verrons ceque nous verrons!* She put her foot in the stirrup and grasped the horse's mane. A hand caught her by the hair and flung her to the ground. Louis still smiled as he aimed a pistol at her breast.

"Not yet, Angela. The game has just begun. If you attempt to escape I will have Robert killed immediately."

"You!" Her thoughts careened and steadied, the insubstantial threats congealed into reality. Those deliberate words, that voice, the golden hair, and violet eyes; the charming smile and debonair manner—he was an enemy from the past. "Who are you?"

Louis put his pistol away, confident she wouldn't try to flee now. She was maternal to the end. "My name is Jules," he said clearly. "Jules!"

She stared at him blankly. The name meant nothing to her. What mattered was his treachery. Half an hour ago she would have entrusted him with her life, now—Now he was her *bête noire.* Terrified for Robert and Scott, she tried to suppress her turbulent emotions.

"You still don't remember?" Jules questioned

gleefully. "Then you don't even know why I mean to kill you. Let me refresh your memory."

Angela sat perfectly still on the ground, only her aquarmarine eyes moving, following his pacing. Maybe when he had told her, she could think of a way out of this but until she knew what and who she was up against she didn't stand a chance.

"I met you in the Bahamas," Jules reminisced with rage flaring in his eyes. He went on to describe her captivity and torment until Angela could stand no more and put her hands over her ears writhing at the dark dread encompassing her. *"Mon Dieu!* But it was a night of wild perversion. Gaston had you in every way, while I preferred my own method.

"Then," he gasped, eyes purple bruises in his face, "you killed Gaston! You slit his throat and left me for dead. I vowed to kill you for what you did to him!"

Angela gagged and put her hand over her mouth as he described everything in vivid detail. She shivered, astounded by the bizarre revelations that laid bare the corpse of her past. What Jane had said was true; it was better left forgotten. But if she had remembered in the first place Jules would never have wormed his way into her life and blasted it apart.

He laughed madly, raking his fingers through his gilt hair. "I wanted to hurt you and torment you, *chérie*—more painfully and slowly than death could. So I pretended to be your friend and gained your confidence. I planted suspicions in your mind that estranged you from your friends. That hurt, didn't it? Like a knife stabbing and twisting."

"Then the accidents were your fault!" Angela shouted. "To make me hate Jane and Owen."

"Yes, everything," Jules gloated, "anything to break you. I even brought about the separation with Scott!"

"No! You couldn't!" she cried with disbelief and a fury that brought her to her feet.

"But I did—with a subtle word dropped in his ear, a brief, compassionate conversation now and then, a commiseration on the pitfalls and agonies of unrequited love. Scott was already restless and at the end of his rope. I just gave him a little push and told him it would be best for both of you to be apart.

"That really killed you," Jules said. "But I wouldn't let you die yet. I played you out like a fish on a line and then hauled you in; then did it again and again."

"You sent my letter!" she said scathingly. "You knew he would come!"

"And made sure you would reject him—for his own good. That time," Jules said triumphantly, "I let you both torture each other while I watched from the wings. You will never know what a pleasure the whole charade was!"

Hate and vengeance pounded through Angela like a tidal wave, sweeping every vestige of feeling and friendship from her. "I hate you!" she shouted, crimson-cheeked. "You are mad, a raving lunatic! And I will stop you no matter what it takes!"

"And Robert?" Jules inquired calmly. "Try to leave or attack me and he's dead."

The fire was drenched with his intimidation. "Robert," she whispered going limp. "What are you going to do?"

"Now, now—that would be telling," Jules said smiling cherubically with a shake of his head. "Wouldn't you rather wait and see?"

What a fool she had been, completely duped by his innocence and friendliness. But others had succumbed too and they had all danced like puppets to his tune. All but Robert who had seen through the facade.

"But—but," Angela stammered, "why didn't Robert recognize you?"

"Ah, *chérie*, that's the beauty of it all. You see, we never met on Gaston's island. I saw your son and daughter from a distance, but you were protective and kept them out of my presence. Robert knew of me but never saw me. I had only to change my name.

"And what luck that Ezra was away! I had meant to kill you outright but his absence and your lost memory made possible this very amusing diversion."

There was nothing she could do—right now. Any action would cause Robert's death. It only remained for Scott to be drawn into the trap along with her and then—Angela put her hands over her face, trembling for her husband and son. Why couldn't Jules just kill her and be done with revenge? She was the one who had murdered his lover.

Jules grabbed her wrists and hauled her to him till his face was only inches away from hers and she shrank from the fanatical amusement twitching at his lips. "Oh, cold lady, that can't even suffer her husband's embraces, just think of what you did in the past!" He spoke softly and slowly, deliberately intensifying her distress.

Angela closed her eyes against those awful words but could not close her ears. "I know all of you," he taunted. "The taste of your mouth and the texture of your breasts, the firmness and softness of your thighs, the roundness of you derriére. . . ."

"Stop it!" she pleaded. "Stop!"

"No, my little pirate's whore. Why should I, when you prostituted your charms so prettily?" Her open eyes now glared into his, sparking in her anger and fright. "But now," he mocked, "just a hint of lechery sends you into an icy fit of indignation. So, you never recovered from what Gaston and I did to you.

"I wonder," Jules mused diabolically, "what else you would endure for your son—for your husband? Would it be so abominable with me? I would try and make it so!"

His terrible, lovely mouth grazed Angela's and she nipped at him with her teeth. Jules drew back startled and she began screaming and screaming, twisting and kicking, fighting in a frenzy of such unmitigated terror that he struck her as hard as he could with his open palm. She fell on a cushion of thrift very close to the cliff's edge with her ears ringing, still shrieking like a banshee. If he made one more advance she knew she would faint. And even if he promised to spare the lives of Robert and Scott for her favors Angela knew that never in a million years could she submit herself to him.

Nausea gripped her and there were tears on her cheeks from the blow. Jules stood over her gazing serenely at her sprawled, disheveled body and said: "If you don't cease at once I will give you good cause to continue screaming."

Angela closed her mouth so fast she bit her tongue and the tart taste of her own blood helped bring her to her senses. Blood and death were her shadows. Of all she knew, suspected, and half remembered of her past, disaster was her twin and never left her side.

Jules's attention was diverted from her and he gazed out at the ocean and then at his pocket watch and back. A boat was approaching the shore and he turned to Angela and said derisively, "I don't desire you, you know, I prefer—other forms of amusement. But I would have done it just to see your reaction and draw out our little game. It's too late now."

Disbelief was released from her like a sigh and then everything began happening. Robert was brought up the cliff path and thrown down next to her. Angela hugged him frantically, kissed him, and stroked his hair. "Oh, baby! Thank God you're all right!" Four armed sailors precluded any thought of escape.

"Don't be afraid, Mama," Robert whispered. "I will protect you. And they said my father's coming."

"Don't do anything rash, son, just do as Jules says and everything will be all right. He doesn't want to hurt you." They remained close and quiet while Jules and his cohorts waited impatiently.

The sun sank lower, growing huge and distorted, glowing orange. The distant trees, the horses, and the pirates were oddly dwarfed by its power; smooth black shadows drifting across its face. The sky was amber drenching the clouds in pale citrine and the ocean was a sheet of beaten gold. Angela could see the ship now, like the shadow of a bird on the water, and she shivered despite the heat. It was summer and would stay light for hours.

Robert, who had been playing with the top of his boot, glanced up. Angela closed her eyes and held him tight. She didn't need to look to know what was happening. Thudding hooves of a galloping horse filled her ears and reverberated through the ground making her heart throb and her insides churn. The pounding stopped.

Scott had pulled up and was silhouetted against the center of the sun as motionless as an equestrian statue. Then he came. Because of the strange angle of the light he didn't seem to be moving at all or growing any larger. Heat waves rippled and made him shimmer like a dream and the whole scene was of a beautifully golden nightmare suspended silently in time.

Until Jules grabbed her and she shuddered in his clutches as Robert was torn from her side. A large, unkempt pirate held Robert firmly in front of him and Angela twisted, then screamed as a knife was put to his throat.

"Don't," she gasped with tawny tears glittering on her face. "Jules, please! I will do anything!"

"Be still," said Jules against her ear. Putting his hand beneath her chin he forced it up and her head back against his shoulder and Angela felt sharp, cold steel sting her skin. To move would be to die and she felt something warm and wet trickle down her arched throat. Tears or blood?

Scott slowed to a walk. His wife and son were illuminated like a book of hours, every minute detail magnified and glowing with intricate color. And they were as still as a painted page as he approached slowly with his hands in plain view. He had never known such fear and fury but not a sign of it showed in his face or manner.

He was one man alone against five, unarmed, and with those he loved in dire peril. And he didn't even know the reason why. They obviously wanted something and he would give anything to see Robert and Angela safe. Reining in, Scott dismounted carefully, unable to miss the lurid grin on Louis Garamond's face.

"What do you want, Mr. Garamond, for their lives?" Scott asked, his voice as smooth and unemotional as honey.

"My name is Jules," he replied, not missing the tensing of Harrington's broad shoulders. That had disturbed his opponent but with the sun behind him he couldn't see Scott's face.

He moved, dragging Angela with him, but Scott outmaneuvered him and managed to keep the sun at his back. The question was repeated and Jules answered: "What I want is vengeance and you are going to be my tool."

"How?" Scott queried, assessing the position of every one of them. Three of the men stood to one side watching every move but with weapons undrawn. Only Jules and the man holding Robert had knives unsheathed, but pistols gleamed at Jules's waist.

"An eye for an eye, a tooth for a tooth, a life for a life. Isn't that the rule?" Jules's dulcet voice dripped poison. "Your wife killed the only person I ever loved—Gaston Laporte. Her life is forfeit to pay for his. But—" he paused letting Scott squirm. "But you have a choice. Your wife or your son. Angela or Robert. Which shall live? Which shall die? The decision is yours."

"Bastard!" The one word erupted from Scott's lips before he could choke it back but the wild look in Angela's glowing eyes stopped a further torrent of abuse. "I will not choose."

"Then they will both die."

"Robert," gasped Angela though the blade cut deeper into her throat. "Choose our son's life. Scott, you have to!"

"You have," Jules informed him with a fanatical look glazing his eyes, "to the count of three to decide."

"No," Scott objected. "I will give you anything you want, every penny I have. You will be rich, Jules, beyond your wildest imagination."

"One."

Scott's fists clenched in frustration. There was no getting through to that warped mind. "Kill me," he told him. "I will die for Laporte. Let my life be the one forfeit!"

"Two."

His goldstone eyes shifted quickly from Robert to

Angela. A thin river of red flowed down her white throat to her heaving bosom, spattering her yellow dress.

Robert was silent and straight and when Scott's eyes touched his they widened slightly and he managed a smile. Though curved, his mouth was grim, but it did not tremble. He was braver than a man.

"Darling!" Her plea captured Scott's attention completely. How could he choose? Between his son, his only living child, who was so young and had never lived, and Angela, his wife, the woman that he could not stop loving no matter how hard he tried. He was being torn in two.

Abruptly, Angela threw herself forward against the knife but Jules had been expecting it and was quicker. In less than a second he had her pinioned again, still alive but vastly shaken. Scott hadn't moved but she could feel the agony of his tempestuous thoughts.

"He chooses Robert," Angela said clearly. "My husband chooses his son's life. Kill me now, Jules, and let them go!"

"Oh, no. He must decide himself who will live."

"Scott, you have to choose Robert!" Angela told him angrily. "This is ridiculous. You must save our son—there's no other choice. I will never forgive you if you don't save Robert's life!"

"Oh, my God," Scott said wearily passing a hand over his eyes. It came away wet but they couldn't tell with the brilliant sun blinding them. "I'm sorry, Angel." He gathered his wits and strength for the inevitable. "I choose—Robert."

"Three!"

Angela drew one last breath, her eyes glued to Scott's. The knife tightened against her throat, flashed red with the dying sun, and Jules turned swiftly and tossed her over the cliff.

For a moment there was no sound but the surf and the seabirds as Scott stood rooted to the grass. Then he emitted a roar from the depths of his outraged soul, so horrible, so hideous, and heartrending, it froze the very marrow of the bones. No one moved but Scott who flung himself headlong at the edge of the cliff.

Nothingness spun out beneath her feet, sharp-toothed rocks waited hungrily for their victim. Her heart had stopped but still the fingers of one hand clenched a sturdy weed firmly embedded in the rock. There was no foothold and Angela swayed in the breeze as her torn fingers slipped. Scott's face blocked out the sky and her heart resumed pumping.

He reached for her from so far away and the tips of her unengaged fingers grazed his. Bracing himself Scott slid closer and his eyes glowed golden with every emotion spilling unhindered from their depths. Their hands met, clasped, and Angela managed a ragged breath. There was no world outside their ambience.

"Let go of the bush and give me your other hand."

But she couldn't, no matter how hard she willed it, let go of the bush that had saved her. "I—ca—can't."

"I have you, Angela, and I won't let go. I promise I won't drop you."

She believed him and somehow loosened her grip and swung wildly from Scott's grasp for an aeon before he caught her frantically clawing hand.

"You are safe now, love," he whispered as he began raising her painstakingly toward him.

Her blood-soaked hands slipped in his and they tightened till she clenched her teeth, sure all the bones were crushed. The steep rockface swung before her eyes and Angela looked up instead at Scott, at his strained, determined face, and the figure above him.

Her eyes were immense, the pupils wide with shock, as they had been that day in the gum tree forest at Thornhill. And reflected in their mirrored blackness Scott saw his own death. For Jules was standing over him with a glinting blade uplifted in his hands.

"No—no!" Angela screamed. "Let me go and save yourself!"

He ignored her words lifting her ever upward, closer and closer, ready for the attack. "I will never let you go," he said breathing heavily. "Never, beloved."

The sun-crimsoned blade struck and Scott didn't move or make a sound, only grasped her tighter. Angela began sobbing painfully and uncontrollably. His hot panting breath was against her mouth. The knife was still red but now it dripped.

"Put your arm around my neck, Angela." This time he gasped. "Now!"

The razor-sharp steel made its third descent and Scott jerked but held her to him. She couldn't let this continue, couldn't let him sacrifice his life for her.

"Darling, I love you," Angela wept. Her blood-slick fingers slid through his like wet silk; curved instinctively and held, tip to tip, for an endless moment, and were gone.

She fell.

Scott sprang to his feet and wrenched the knife from his back. There were now no restraints to rage or emotions. Even though Jules had a pistol pointed at his heart from only a few feet away, he would kill him.

The yellow-haired man laughed dementedly and his finger tightened on the trigger. But he had overlooked one detail.

Robert broke free from the suddenly distracted, lax embrace of his captor. He was crying. For though he was all Scott, his heart was all Angela's. Stooping he slid the dirk from his boot-top and let it fly.

If he'd had time to get positioned he would have killed Jules. As it was he hit his target exactly where he had aimed. The dirk quivered in his tutor's right shoulder, the pistol discharged, and screaming gulls and terns billowed and whirled with the smoke.

Thunder crashed in Scott's ears as he closed. The knife, drenched with his blood and Angela's, swept in low, jerked viciously upward and eviscerated Jules. He sat down on the topaz-hazed grass with an incredulous look in his violet eyes as his entrails spilled and slithered through his clutching fingers. He screamed in chorus with the birds and then Scott was upon him.

Scott's arm struck unceasingly like a machine out of control. Again and again and again till the twitching body stilled; until there was nothing left of Jules but blood and bones and ribbons of flesh strewn in a wide circle around him. He would have continued in a murderous frenzy but was hauled to his feet by bruised, gentle hands.

The knife fell to the blood-puddled grass and Ezra asked: "Where is Angela?" He had made short work of the remaining pirates.

Then Scott was running and skidding and falling down the cliff path in a shower of sand, tamarisk, rocks, and sea lavender.

She lay on the beach, on her back with arms outstretched, just inches from the rocks. Robert sat beside her, weeping, with a yellow silk slipper in his hand. Dark hair spread around her head like seaweed and one bare foot peeped beneath her skirt. But it wasn't loose hair surrounding Angela—it was blood. It flowed and soaked into the greedy sand like darkly spreading tentacles.

"No one could survive that fall. She is dying. It could take a few days. How can I tell? I'm not God!"

"If you are not God," Scott murmured without looking at the doctor, "then you can't say positively that she will die." Angela's hand was limp and unmoving in his and he had refused to leave her side.

Doctor Jarrold swore. "She had a broken arm, broken ribs, and a fractured skull! I can't even begin to imagine what the internal injuries are. Don't delude yourself, Lord Harrington—she is dying.

"And you should be in bed," he continued. "You are doing your wife no good by refusing to take care of yourself. If you continue like this, who knows? Maybe you will die first."

"I will never leave Angela," Scott told him adamantly. "Never!"

"You're crazy! Damn, I need a drink." Doctor Jarrold stalked from the room.

Scott sat stiffly in the chair; he couldn't lean back. The doctor had dressed and bandaged his wounds but they were deep, viciously placed, and still bleeding. Angela hadn't moved or uttered a sound since he had found her on the beach. Her breathing was shallow and sometimes stopped completely for a few seconds. There was a blood-soaked bandage around her shorn head and he couldn't tear his eyes from her pale face that was miraculously unmarked. If it hadn't been for her masses of thick hair braided into a chignon at the back of her head she would have died instantly.

"Angel, Angel," he said. "Open your eyes. Please, don't go."

Scott had brought her back from the dead once before in Scotland. Couldn't it happen again? He continued talking to her through the night calling her back from the dark place where she resided. At dawn Jane had another bed moved into the room and placed next to Angela's.

"You are going to rest," she told Scott with firm determination. "You will be right beside her and so will I. If Angela stirs or opens her eyes I will wake you immediately. Please, Scott," she said touching his arm. "I have never seen you look worse. Do this for Angela."

When he woke Jane was exactly where he had left her but with Gina sleeping in her arms. "No change," she uttered tersely.

It continued like that for days, for two weeks, and the amazed doctor just shook his head and said: "I never thought she would hold on so long. The broken bones are healing but I don't think she will ever regain consciousness. Lady Harrington will either starve or develop respiratory trouble. There are too many complications that can and will happen as time passes."

Scott never left the room and Jane too was in almost continual attendance. Sometimes, when they were exhausted, Ezra or Owen sat with her and the Murrays took care of their every physical need.

But the mental anguish could not be dealt with until something happened. Optimistic hope was followed a few minutes later by despair and Angela slowly wasted away before their eyes and they were helpless.

"She did it for me!" Scott flung at Jane with misery etching deep lines into his face. "What a fool I was not to have believed Angela when she said she loved me. I thought she had only grown dependent on me. But now I know and it's too late. She sacrificed her life so I could live and would have done the same for Robert."

"And she would do it again if she had to," Jane replied gently. "But don't dwell on it. Just be glad that you finally know how she feels."

He rubbed his knuckles into his eyes and was silent. The raging fever and infection he had fought had left him gaunt and exhausted, and during the whole time he had battled for Angela's life too. Jane went to him and stroked the hair out of his face. She felt like crying. She loved them both but could offer no comfort but her presence.

The rain stopped and yellow pools of sunlight spread thickly across the carpet. Though it was warm the windows were tightly shut for a draft could be disastrous in the sick room. Crisp shadows undulated across the carved paneling as the door opened and closed without a sound.

Owen went and stood beside Angela and smiled at the pair opposite him. They were both asleep, Scott with his head on Jane's shoulder and she with her blond head against his brown hair. Her face had the beauty and purity of an angel from a Renaissance fresco and he felt no jealousy at their closeness. Now they were only friends and all Jane's love was his.

Unfocused green-blue eyes opened for a moment, Angela's lips moved and then her lashes fluttered shut. Owen bent over her in astonishment and whispered her name. He touched her hand and her fingers curled weakly against his and then were still. Scott sat bolt upright, shot forward toward the bed and touched her cheek.

"She opened her eyes," Owen choked out. "She moved!"

Jane, in her drowsy, half-awakened state, finally started crying but she was laughing too. She repeated

Owen's words joyously over and over. "Angela's going to live!" she cried as her husband caught her in a bear hug. "Oh, thank God!"

For the next few days Angela became increasingly active but was totally unaware of her surroundings. When she finally spoke she called Robert's name continually in a frantic undertone. They sent for him and he stood by her bed for hours at a time but Angela didn't know he was there.

"The last thing she remembers is her son being in danger," Doctor Jarrold said. "It's only natural for her anxiety to continue until she becomes aware he is safe. This is truly a miracle! I never would have believed it possible. But we must watch her carefully for signs of complications."

A pounding headache made Angela clutch tightly at the hand in hers. But when she opened her eyes and the blurred brightness began to spin crazily, she closed them tightly again overcome with nausea.

"Scott!"

"I'm right here, Angel," he said putting the back of her hand against his cheek. "Shh, everything will be all right now. Robert is safe and so are you. No one will harm you again."

"I'm so sick," she whispered. "My head hurts."

"I know. But you are alive and are getting better every day. Just lie still and—"

"Stay—please!"

"Oh, yes! Yes, my love, always!" Scott told her. He brushed a whisper of a kiss against her cheek and she smiled.

As the weeks passed Angela had longer periods of awareness but the headache never ceased and she had difficulty keeping anything in her stomach. Everyone coaxed her to eat but it was an ordeal and she only did it to please Scott. Her vision was blurred and when she opened her eyes all she saw was whirling colors that made her so dizzy she thought she would spin right off the bed.

But there was always Scott: encouraging her, cajoling; taking care of her; rocking her in his arms in the long nights when the pain was so intense that she couldn't stop sobbing and even one candle hurt her closed eyes.

He snuffed out the candle with his fingers and cuddled Angela against his chest. She had been like this for three nights, like a helpless baby, and he caressed the back of her neck and continued rocking in the chair. The front of his robe was wet through already and her short black curls brushed softly against his cheek. Her face was flushed and hot with a fever.

But she was alive and even if this went on for months or years he would take care of her and never, never complain. She was so fragile and with her long hair cut off looked like a child, younger even than when they had first met.

It was long after dawn when she at last fell asleep and Scott was so afraid of waking her that he didn't dare put her to bed but let her stay on his lap. Then he too drifted off with his head against the back of the rocking chair.

The headache was gone. Angela stayed very still with her eyes shut just letting herself get used to feeling again without the overwhelming distraction of pain. She was warm, birds chirped outside, and Scott's arms were around her. Absolute contentment flowed through her.

And then, because the pain had finally vanished, she became aware of a subtle difference in herself. Memories, like fragile silken filaments, spun out, reaching and searching back into darkness. They sought, touched and joined with other thoughts and experiences, stringing them together like gleaming pearls. Shining, precious dreams glistened in the shadows of her mind and she remembered it all—the good and the bad, the anger and the passion.

When she opened her eyes she could at last see clearly and Scott's sleeping face filled her vision. Oh, how she loved him, more than ever before! They would be together again and it would be good between them, because nothing mattered but the present—now that she had her past back. And Scott was her future.

Angela touched his face tracing his parted lips, strong chin and lean brown cheeks. His dark lashes stirred as she ran her fingers through his tousled bronze hair. Even with the frosting of silver at his temples, that hadn't been there before her accident, Scott still looked boyish in repose.

Then his eyes opened. Those wonderful, devilish, tender brown eyes, glowing with golden sparks of love, that could incinerate her with a glance in a fire of desire that only Scott could ignite—and put out.

"My love, you're better!" he said smiling down at her.

Angela pressed a scalding kiss on his mouth hearing his gasp of surprise. Joy flooded her and she felt a resurgence of strength and vigor as she strained closer in his embrace. The pressure of his lips was so gentle and she opened hers kissing Scott back deeply and tenderly. His tongue moved against hers, exploring and rediscovering her mouth with the most delicious sensation. Little flickers of desire raced through her veins, so familiar, so long suppressed. She was reborn.

Wonder and a strange realization dawned in Scott. This woman that had once frozen him was now a flame, recalescing him, melting in his arms, trembling. But not with fear. The crippled Angela of the past year had never kissed him like this, never responded like now.

He kissed her dimples and deeply searched her beautiful eyes. "Angel, is it you? Is it really you?"

She didn't need to speak. Her radiant face told him more than words ever could. Love flowed in an invisible torrent between them.

"I adore you!" Scott whispered huskily in her ear. "Welcome home, my sweet Angel."

EPILOGUE

Forevermore

Even so we met; and after long pursuit
  Even so we joined; we both became entire;
No need for either to renew a suit,
  For I was flax and he was flames of fire:
    Our firm united souls did more than twine,
So I my Best-Beloved's am, so he is mine.

—Francis Quarles

The summer passed.

The flame of autumn was on the land. Birds, geese, ducks, and swans winged south, their incessant calls filling the days and their spread wings shadowing the skies. The weather turned crisp; leaves changed and dropped; berries and nuts appeared; animals scurried to the harvest. Heather was blooming in the Highlands.

And love bloomed too.

Angela was herself again, renascent and happier than ever before. Her recovery had been slow and she still suffered periodic migraines that could incapacitate her for days. But those spells were becoming less frequent and more time elapsed between each bout.

Scott cherished her like a fragile china doll that might break at any moment. Her delicacy was a barrier between them barring total oneness, but it was as insubstantial as a gossamer curtain. If only he would rip it aside!

But he delayed, afraid of losing her again, and Angela chafed against the restraints he enforced on their passion. She never realized how strong Scott was when it came to that and how much he cared for her alone until they had their first fight. How he laughed at what he called her "temper tantrum" but inadvertently he revealed a secret. That the women he had been seen with in London in order to get the divorce had never shared his bed. "I didn't want them," he explained simply, "only you."

Jane too shed light on an event that had troubled Angela, her *tete-à-tete* in the woods with Owen the day Scott had left her.

"Owen told me about it as soon as I recovered from Gina's birth," Jane explained, laughing at the perplexed look on Angela's face. "Why not? It was perfectly innocent on his part. Owen is always a gentleman—well almost always—and he preferred to shock you to your senses with a few kisses rather than a slap. He was too appalled at the injury he had already done you to risk another. It worked, didn't it?"

So Angela had her friends back that had been driven

from her by Jules's machinations. And she had her husband back and her memory. Perfection only awaited the time when Scott would make her completely his in body as well as spirit.

"I won't wait another day!" she said aloud and turned as Scott entered their room.

"What won't you wait for?" he asked.

Scott had been riding and was windblown and glowing with vitality. She couldn't resist him. Angela flew straight to him and threw her arms around his neck. "You," she said going up on tiptoe and covering his face with kisses. "Oh, darling—please? I'm not afraid. Love me! Oh, love me!"

Her dimples deepened, full lips curving into a seductive smile. Scott knew the power she held over him when she was like this. He couldn't refuse her now when she was so wildly passionate and meltingly sweet, when her eyes were sparkling with urgent desire and her delicate nostrils flared as they always did just before he did something to pleasure her.

"Temptress—you are incorrigible!" he murmured pulling her closer and running his fingers slowly through her silky ebony curls. Tilting Angela's head back he kissed her long and hard till they were both quivering with their need.

Then the floor tilted beneath her feet as Scott swept her up with a triumphant laugh and kicked the door shut. The barrier between them ripped as easily as the bodice of her dress and pearl buttons cascaded across the bed and carpet.

"Oh, love, I'm sorry—I just can't wait!" Scott uttered as he frantically tore at the rest of her clothes. Angela helped him, laughing, impatient, and then they were naked in each other's arms.

His lithe body against Angela's was a fevered delight. An unquenchable thrill coursed through her turning her into the savage wanton that only he could subdue. She writhed under his expert fingers and exploring tongue, kissing him back with hunger so fierce, so demanding, it drove him wild. .

"Sweetheart," Scott moaned burying his face against the soft curve of her breasts, losing himself in the sweet oblivion that only Angela could bring him to.

Time melted away, memories dissolved in the inferno of their rediscovered love. He alone had the power to make her remember—the power to make her forget.

"I love you, darling. Only you!" Angela cried out, gasping for breath in the melee that made them one.

They were two halves of a whole coming together in a perfect union, consubstantial, each essential to the other's existence.

The exquisite flow of ecstasy built and surged, towering, carrying them to the ultimate crest of feeling. Their hearts and souls merged, renewing the final bond that would bind them forever.

"Angel, love," Scott said, kissing away her tears of joy. "My heart is yours for the rest of eternity."

Scott had renewed her and brought her back to life and made her entire. Without him she was nothing. Beyond speaking, Angela wearily laid her head on his chest and closed her eyes as he caressed her dark hair. The thunder of his heart against her cheek lulled her to total contentment and she sighed softly, filled with a peace she had never known before.

She smiled as Scott whispered, " 'Who, with heart in breast, could deny you love?' "